praise

THE SHIMMERING STATE

SEPTEMBER 2021 BELLETRIST BOOK CLUB PICK

"A dreamy and dazzling first novel . . . As the story deepens, the timelines—past and present—grow closer, and Westgate skillfully tightens the tension so that readers turn pages quickly, needing to know what will happen next. . . . Its setting is fully realized—Westgate conjures a vivid Los Angeles full of aspiring dreamers and those who would take advantage of them. . . . *The Shimmering State* spins a compelling story about what a person will do in order to relieve pain—and what is lost in that release."

—*USA Today*

"In chapters alternating before and after the rehab stint, Westgate weaves a tight tale of relationships and loneliness in a city populated by people always on the hunt for the next big escape. [*The Shimmering State*] is a captivating story, one that leaves readers wondering if a life scrubbed of pain and real connection is a life at all."

—*Publishers Weekly*, starred review

"Who are we without our memories? Who might we be if we could relive someone else's? Meredith Westgate's captivating first novel wrestles with these existential questions without sacrificing her characters' distinctive and emotional essences. An impressive, unsettling, and surprisingly romantic debut."

—HELEN SCHULMAN,
author of *Come With Me*

"*The Shimmering State* is a slick, LA-set gel cap, easily digestible, where memories and trauma are wiped away, though their imprints remain. At a rejuvenation center, a photographer and a dancer let their old selves go—every last unwanted memory—while out in the world, strangers' memories are available for consumption in pill form. A classic tale of artists trying to make it in LA, flipped on its head."

—KATIE M. FLYNN,
author of *The Companions*

"Cinematic, dreamlike, at times brutal yet poignant. The premise of this new memory drug is tantalizing, and the storylines that unfold from the abuse of it are compelling."

—FRANCES CHA,
author of *If I Had Your Face*

"Contemplative and wonderfully evocative. Finishing *The Shimmering State* is like waking from a dream, where you reenter the world with fresh eyes and wonder at the frailty of your own memories."

—JESSICA CHIARELLA,
author of *And Again* and *The Lost Girls*

"Like an *Eternal Sunshine of the Spotless Mind* for the #MeToo era, *The Shimmering State* is a riveting, nuanced, and ultimately haunting meditation on the triangular relationship between sense, memory, and identity. There must be something in the California air because, like Joan Didion, Meredith Westgate has an extraordinary ear, not only for the stories we tell ourselves in order to live but for the ways that we endlessly revise them to suit the new selves we continue to construct."

—ADAM WILSON,
author of *Sensation Machines*

"Westgate's novel does what the absolute best books do—it makes you experience the world so differently. Who are we? Are we our memories? And if so, how do we know what memories are true and what might be manipulated? Moving, astounding, and totally unsettling. But also, as fascinating as memory itself."

—CAROLINE LEAVITT, *New York Times* bestselling
author of *Pictures of You* and *With or Without You*

"*The Shimmering State* gives readers what its title promises: a shimmering, dreamlike experience of multiple lives that collide and repel through fate and coincidence. In this hypnotic novel, Westgate offers her characters, and her readers, a beautifully dystopian shot at redemption, and shows the lengths people will go to remember and to forget."

—LYDIA KIESLING,
author of *The Golden State*

"Stirring, lush, and thought-provoking, *The Shimmering State* is an entrancing novel about the losses that bind us and the memories that define us."

—ELAN MASTAI,
author of *All Our Wrong Todays*

THE
SHIMMERING
STATE

THE
SHIMMERING
STATE

a novel

MEREDITH WESTGATE

ATRIA PAPERBACK

NEW YORK   LONDON   TORONTO   SYDNEY   NEW DELHI

ATRIA
PAPERBACK

An Imprint of Simon & Schuster, Inc.
1230 Avenue of the Americas
New York, NY 10020

This book is a work of fiction. Any references to historical events, real people, or real places are used fictitiously. Other names, characters, places, and events are products of the author's imagination, and any resemblance to actual events or places or persons, living or dead, is entirely coincidental.

Copyright © 2021 by Meredith Westgate

All rights reserved, including the right to reproduce this book or portions thereof in any form whatsoever. For information, address Atria Books Subsidiary Rights Department, 1230 Avenue of the Americas, New York, NY 10020.

First Atria Paperback edition August 2022

ATRIA PAPERBACK and colophon are trademarks of Simon & Schuster, Inc.

For information about special discounts for bulk purchases, please contact Simon & Schuster Special Sales at 1-866-506-1949 or business@simonandschuster.com.

The Simon & Schuster Speakers Bureau can bring authors to your live event. For more information or to book an event, contact the Simon & Schuster Speakers Bureau at 1-866-248-3049 or visit our website at www.simonspeakers.com.

Interior design by Kyoko Watanabe

1 3 5 7 9 10 8 6 4 2

Library of Congress Cataloging-in-Publication Data

Names: Westgate, Meredith, author.
Title: The shimmering state : a novel / Meredith Westgate.
Description: First Atria Books hardcover edition. | New York : Atria Books, 2021. |
Identifiers: LCCN 2021012852 (print) | LCCN 2021012853 (ebook) |
ISBN 9781982156718 (hardcover) | ISBN 9781982156732 (ebook)
Subjects: LCSH: Memory--Fiction. | GSAFD: Dystopias.
Classification: LCC PS3623.E84925 S55 2021 (print) |
LCC PS3623.E84925 (ebook) | DDC 813/.6--dc23
LC record available at https://lccn.loc.gov/2021012852
LC ebook record available at https://lccn.loc.gov/2021012853

ISBN 978-1-9821-5671-8
ISBN 978-1-9821-5672-5 (pbk)
ISBN 978-1-9821-5673-2 (ebook)

For Olive

The only true voyage, the only bath in the Fountain of Youth, would be not to visit strange lands but to possess other eyes, to see the universe through the eyes of another, of a hundred others, to see the hundred universes that each of them sees, that each of them is.

—Marcel Proust

Los Angeles is a microcosm of the United States. If LA falls, the country falls.

—Ice-T

PART ONE

ARI SHAPIRO, HOST: I'm Ari Shapiro, and this is *All Things Considered*. On today's episode we'll visit LinkTech, the Silicon Valley–based pioneer in the artificial intelligence workforce who suggests automated systems may be taking more jobs than you think. Namely, in the hospital. But first—cutting-edge treatments, revolutionary drugs—just how *do* we define safe practices where no precedent exists?

DR. ANGELICA SLOANE: The World Health Organization estimates that "one in four people in the world will be affected by mental or neurological disorders at some point in their lives." Of the 450 million experiencing mental illness, two-thirds of those people never receive treatment due to lack of accessibility or stigma. The goal of Memoroxin is one that I believe in: treating mental illness with our most essential tool, a patient's own memories. To spread the message that one is, in fact, *the solution* to their own disorder. My dream is to have facilities in local communities worldwide, where patients come in for regular maintenance toward mental health management. To move away from releasing Memoroxin in pill form.

SHAPIRO: That's Dr. Angelica Sloane, psychiatrist and chief practitioner at the Center in Malibu, which specializes in treating those who have illegally consumed Memoroxin, a new drug that targets and delivers patients' own memories for medical management of Alzheimer's, PTSD, depression, schizophrenia, and other mental disorders with direct links to memory.

Dr. Sloane, thank you for being here.

DR. SLOANE: Thank you for having me.

SHAPIRO: Your rehabilitation clinic, the Center, has come into the spotlight recently for treating victims of Memoroxin abuse, including many from the homeless population here in Venice, California—at no cost. Can you tell us a bit about how the Center came to be?

DR. SLOANE: First I should say there are no quick fixes. We are helping people, yes. As best as we can, we are helping, but we are also gaining
valuable insights into how the side effects of Memoroxin—caused only by
misuse—might be treated. I prescribe Memoroxin on a case-by-case basis
when treating patients at my private practice outside of the Center as well.
My work covers everything from depression and anxiety to post-traumatic
stress disorder—even low-dose couples therapy and increased empathy
trainings. Needless to say, I'm acutely aware of Memoroxin's potential
benefits, and what they could mean for the world. So far, California is the
first state to approve use of Memoroxin in a clinical setting. Naturally, that
makes it a hotbed for abuse, and an interesting case study for how to address this secondary risk moving forward.

SHAPIRO: Let's talk a bit more about that. Because benefits aside, and I
would like to discuss those later, Memoroxin does seem to cause intense
trauma to the psyche if consumed illegally.

DR. SLOANE: Memoroxin was never intended to be shared, or to complicate the fragility of one's consciousness. If taken appropriately, as prescribed, it is entirely safe and proven effective. Each pill is coated with just
enough benzodiazepine to ease a patient into a tranquil state of sleep so
there is no confusion, or disorientation. Of course, our safety measures are
null if pills are crushed, cut with other substances, or simply taken recre-
ationally. Clearly, better management for keeping it off the streets needs to
be implemented. In the meantime, at the Center we are learning so much
about what can be fixed—or I should say, neutralized—in the psyche once
Memoroxin has been illegally consumed. Along with, unfortunately, what
elusive second sense occasionally remains.

Chapter 1

TODAY

Their arrival is reflected like a head-on collision as Liv's car lurches across traffic and into the driveway of a glass structure along the Pacific Coast Highway. Lucien locks onto the details, trying to still his mind. Like where does all that glass come from? And how did they get it out to this frantic stretch of highway in one impossibly long piece? The frothing sea is mirrored around its sharp corners, and Lucien looks away, swallowing the salt-heavy breeze and the sourness of car exhaust. He concentrates on more questions. Like, how do the gulls miss it in their soaring arcs above the ocean, and goddammit why, surrounded by so much glass, is it still so hard to see?

Cars whiz behind him as Lucien stumbles toward the entrance. When did he get out of the car? His body is sore. Exhausted. The visions that coursed through him hours ago still rumble under his skin.

The building might otherwise be a getaway for some rock star or more relevant tech mogul, instead of a rehabilitation center for those who, like Lucien, have "lost themselves." This was the phrase used on the website he found during the hour-long drive over Mulholland and down the twisting roads of dirt-dry Topanga. He'd come back to consciousness when the car sickness set in, grounding him in his body and restoring his vision, albeit intermittently. Liv had to pull over twice on the no-shoulder roads for him to vomit sheer iridescence over their railings.

"For those who have lost themselves." The website hardly loaded, given the spotty service, but that phrase populated his screen immediately and resonated just as fast.

Shocks of fractured light and color interject with the sun overhead, and Lucien holds a hand over his eyes to find the steps. He feels Liv's gaze hot on his neck, but he cannot turn. Maybe he's ashamed. Maybe he just doesn't want to see her face.

A woman with a low ponytail meets him inside. Her hair sweeps her back as she walks, and over her shoulder Lucien notices the leaves of a fern pressed against the glass, like fingers feeling for contact. Or escape. The woman wears a beige jumpsuit that highlights the lack of color inside, where she shows him past a large fire pit in the common area, marked by its natural stones and sunken living area, then down a hallway to his room.

On top of a twin bed in the corner is a stack of towels and what appears to be a uniform. Beige. The woman pushes her lips into a tranquil smile as Lucien's eyes fall to where one might find a name tag. He stares at her breasts, his mind too slow to move on. She blinks.

"Thank you, sorry, I didn't catch your name," he says, the words sticking to his tongue.

Without answering, she hands him a slim folder, open to the first page. The rules here are like the glass, clear.

No phones.
No laptops.
No jewelry, watches, accessories.
No names.

"Your initial treatment will begin in one hour. Please be dressed and ready."

Once she shuts the door, Lucien pulls off his sweater and lets his pants fall to the floor. For a moment he feels self-conscious; he looks up to the corners of the ceiling, but they disappear into shadow. He pulls the linen jumpsuit up his body and hooks it behind his neck. Then he runs a hand through his hair, surprised for a moment to find it still there, still his. His fingers linger, remembering a curl.

What will they do to him? What intrinsic, untouched things still inside might this treatment redefine? He tries to imagine what those things are, where they lurk ether-like underneath his skin, or within the cage of his ribs, impossible to sense until they are gone.

In the quiet, his brain longs for variety—anything to ground him here. His finger twitches back and forth against his thigh, feeling for some imaginary shutter click, and he follows the shades of gray along the wall. When the shadows start to twist, he closes his eyes and feels a rush of her again.

Holding her baby, the curse of her joy. Lungs full of desert dust. The hum in the editing room; eyes on her back, her hips, waist. All the eyes that will never—

Lucien blinks hard until the room shifts into focus. Over and over, a fly buzzes into the closed window high in the corner, a shock of blue beyond it. One hour. How long is an hour?

His clothing sits slumped like a snakeskin, shed. The clothes look like him, like New York thrift; clothes that have spent months under layers, building up some impenetrable front to face the winter. Here they look defeated, futile. His sweater's navy and olive stripes have grown to look like one another. Holes for his thumbs.

He lifts it to his face and inhales. This is how it feels, then, to have nothing. To know it. He hopes he doesn't lose this, of all things. The knowledge of his failure.

Florence is gone; what does it matter now? There's no fixing this. Not for him. And who is worth fixing him for? No, that's not right— how is he who's worth fixing? How is he the only one left? Everyone, everyone, has finally left.

Next to the pristine white towels, his clothes appear to have given up, too. Another time he might have wanted to photograph the stark contrast of such loaded objects. The long clean shapes they cast. Another time, he might have had a camera.

He eyes the folder that was forgotten in his hands. He pinches his arm to stay focused and opens its cover to a welcome letter.

Congratulations!

You've taken the first step in joining us at the Center. After your initial treatment you will be matched with a therapist who can assist you with any questions or support, 24/7. Prior to your initial treatment, you will remain in isolation to respect other patients' space in the common area.

The treatment runs in three parts. Some steps may happen consecutively and some simultaneously depending on the severity of your contamination. Rest assured, we know opening yourself up to such a procedure can feel intimidating, even violating. That's why transparency is vital at the Center.

Phase 1: Diagnosis

You will be placed in sensory deprivation and sedated for several hours to detox from all present Memoroxin and external stimuli from prior to arriving at the Center. During this time, our patented machine will use noninvasive laser technology to mine and categorize your memories—both visual and sensory—for the memory map we will use to code them. Don't be nervous: this feels just like your standard eye exam!

In this phase, we will separate your core memories from all foreign ones, including any of your own that have been compromised. All memories since the first instance of Memoroxin abuse will be removed, given that they contain the corruption to your consciousness.

Phase 2: Cleanup**

Once your core memories have been mapped and triple-backed up, we administer a gentle drip that effectively cleans out the memory system. In this phase, all sensory and visual memories will be cleared. Consider this a form of helpful amnesia to reset your system. Given the gentle sedative in the drip, you won't have a moment to realize that your memories are missing before passing into the next phase.

Phase 3: The Return

In the final phase, we reintroduce your own memories using a custom mix of what we mapped in Phase 1. Keep in mind that any memory, no matter how arbitrary, effectively holds every one that came before, so the chance of a single memory slipping through is almost impossible. This drip feels like a smooth wash of feeling, lasting over several hours at a low-level stimulation to reinstate your baseline. Phase 3 is reinforced by steam infused with sensory notes pulled from your most pleasing memories, along with light projections to further activate your return.

"Okay, so now I'm cleaned up and back to myself . . . What's next? Can I leave?"

Not quite. It is vital that you stay in our sanctuary to allow the reinstated memories to settle and to take while you are protected from all excessive stimuli. We will supply your room with nutritious juices and meal shakes multiple times a day, to nourish your body without triggering an excess of cravings in your mind. It may require days or weeks for you to truly feel like yourself again. Breaking protocol too quickly after your treatment may cause side effects such as loss of memory, distortion, personality disorder, apathy, and, most important, relapse.

While in recovery, your therapist will provide you with a custom mix of supplements. These are a series of enzymes that activate precisely the same synapse the organic memory triggered in your brain, thereby re-creating the original memory, synthetically. While these memories have already been encoded in the initial drip, your supplements mimic the organic process of memory—an initial implantation, followed by a gradual reinforcing to solidify the memory.

Add-On: The Clean Slate We have the unique opportunity to remove any traumas you would rather not hold on to moving forward. Prior to Phase 1, any selections must be run past your counselor, who will guide you in crafting the best memory map to maintain a cohesive identity, even with your chosen omission.

We hope your time at the Center is grounding and regenerative. You found the Center, now let the Center find you.

Lucien's mind takes time to process. Being addressed with such assurance is calming, but also terrifying. To wipe him of everything that's come before? To trust that anyone could reinstate such things that feel so unalterably organic, so tied to who he is?

But who is he now?

He violated his grandmother, Florence, the moment he took her pill. And every time after, when he disappeared into her, or swallowed her into him. He shivers with the knowledge, the irreversible truth. He cannot hold on to something that was never his. And still, he wants to remember everything before it is gone.

The desert, a baby, her secret.

He should put it all down.

A triumph, never hers. Ashes in the kitchen sink.

He looks at his fingernails, the subtle shimmer around their edges. If he could only find something sharp, he could scratch it into the floorboards under his bed. A note to himself that he'd never remember, that won't be taken away. An arrow to guide him there. Something sharp, he thinks, scanning the room. Something sharp, when his mind feels so soft.

He could close his eyes. Just for a moment. He holds a cool fingertip against his eyelid and feels the flickering underneath. But there isn't time.

He examines the papers again, rereading the final option for this "Add-On." He thinks of his mother, the wave of her crashing against his ribs. Her slim, sick body between his arms, and the tickle of her wavy hair under his nose; her hand on his back, back when he was the small one; pulling the covers up, a kiss on the forehead. Everything in him, built on her.

The desert. Dust everywhere. Ashes in the kitchen sink.

He rests a moment on the imperfections he alone knows. Her vacant face staring at a canvas in her studio, the distant anger when his father called unexpectedly, always, always following a successful show. Her disdain for anything new, until disproven. Moreover, what she did in the end, alone. But only in one memory is his mother dead. Lucien still feels his grandmother's cresting on top of his own.

He knows he cannot hold on to both. But could he let go altogether? No, he cannot stand the thought of a future without his mother. Even if that future promised more happiness, less weight. Lucien unclips the dull pencil from the folder and writes his answer.

"I'd like to leave everything else as it were."

The words look overly formal and possibly in the wrong tense. But what is one to use when determining their own past in the future? This requires a new grammar; perhaps we have finally outreached the limit of ours, he thinks. Or perhaps tense as a construct will not survive, if at any moment one can alter their present by rearranging memories from the past.

He looks at the first page again. All those words. Words, when he needs to write. Letters, right there in front of him. He hears a low laughter, his own.

Lucien tears the paper, freeing its letters despite his clumsy fingers. *C* waits in the very first word. Beside it, *O*, and he can keep that, too. Even the *N* is there already—*CON*—but everything is always there, the past doesn't change because you learn it; knowing where to look, that was the thing. He holds the three tiny letters, the beginning of it all, and is tearing an *R* when a knock interrupts him.

"It's time," the voice says, and he hears the doorknob turn.

The same nurse stands at the door when he greets her. They match.

She nods to the bed, where his clothes are piled, belt coiled on top. Then she glances at the folder, open on the floor. The torn page. Lucien turns to the bed and hands off his clothing. Their weight—once gone— is heavy in his open palms.

The three tiny letters stick to his pointer finger, then flutter to the floor.

Chapter 2

BEFORE

Lucien squeezes acrylic onto the torn flap of his moving-box-turned-palette. *Safety Yellow*, that's what the color is called. He dips the paintbrush into water then acrylic and then water and finally turns back to the canvas. The color bleeds down and everywhere as he traces the overexposed photograph again.

He watches as young Lucien disappears under the yellow wash, like sepia after the fact. This photograph is one of the few things he brought with him to Los Angeles, the rest packed away in a storage facility advertised on billboards along Tenth Avenue. Those same advertisements that appear larger than life from the High Line. BECAUSE YOU LOVE TO SHOP . . . BUT AREN'T IN THE MARKET FOR A LARGER APARTMENT!—they say, and—YOU LOVE YOUR IN-LAWS, BUT NOT THE ANTIQUE CLOCK COLLECTION THEY GIFTED YOU!

None of the advertisements ever mention his scenario.

Lucien dips the same brush into red then orange then water again and flicks his wrist to splatter the canvas. His hand whips back and forth, until flecks spray his cheeks, his upper lip. He stops when the canvas is covered with a sort of fiery confetti—sparks as if burning from behind. As if the flames might finally break through, the entire canvas crumbling.

Lucien finds a wide, dry brush among the rest of his mother's tools and drags it across the canvas. The photograph now looks submerged in water from all the layers of paint and gloss. It reminds him of an image in its chemical bath, as if it might still develop, change. What is more hopeful than watching an image appear, dissolving into life? And yet—even then its fate has already been decided. What's happening is only the reveal. An illusion of discovery, of change.

Only his mother's smile still shines through. Hers is—or was—one of those smiles that's hard to look at without mirroring; you caught yourself smiling back, even when you didn't want to. In the photograph, only the tip of Lucien's chin perched on her shoulder shows from underneath the paint. Otherwise, he is gone.

He grabs his SLR off the bed and photographs the canvas close-up, so that there isn't any reflection off the once-glossy picture. He clicks over and over, moving and zooming, looking for anything that works. Any piece that's interesting. Then he steps back to look with both eyes.

He kicks the canvas across the room.

Lucien tosses the camera back onto the mattress and pulls a cigarette out of his pocket. He places it between his lips. He can't smoke it inside, his new lease says so in bold print, but something about it dangling there—caught by the dryness of his lips—helps him think.

He just needs something, anything, to send Natasha. Even if it's only the start of something new. He pushes both hands into his hair, letting his elbows fan out. Lucien isn't a painter. In the series featuring his mother, he used paint because all his photographs of her felt wrong. Photography was his way of processing, of seeing. Everything he shot of her then felt incomplete, and only something added could have changed that. In a way, the paint was an homage to her. But now Lucien's whole world is off, and nothing, no amount of paint, can fix it. He throws a sheet over the canvas and turns it gently to the wall.

He collapses onto the mattress, staring out the window at the many shapes and shadows of leaves so foreign to him that they should be intriguing. His new normal. It's only a matter of time before he hears from Natasha, his art dealer, again. Before she learns that he has nothing. Nothing to say, nothing to show. And maybe he never did.

Was it Bernini who said he didn't carve into marble, but rather revealed something already inside—or was that Michelangelo? Lucien always preferred Bernini, perhaps that's why his memory ascribes it to him. No, certainly it was Michelangelo. His pieces so often look only just released from the stone, with remnants still at the base or around the edges. Bernini's sculptures look as if they had never been stone at all.

This idea of trying to uncover what was already there, versus pulling something from yourself, has always been inspiring—or reassuring—to Lucien. It takes the pressure off the artist. They are only revealing something. And isn't that what photography is? Revealing something already there, for everyone else to see. Capturing it permanently. Showing how one sees, in a moment, an angle, a look, and freeing everyone else to do the same.

For the collages of his mother, Lucien used a palette knife to smudge and layer thick clouds surrounding her photographed in various stages of illness. Her treatment. Then remission. A feeling of hope for the two of them trapped inside. For his always active mother, bound to the bed or the couch, reclined with nowhere to look but up. His mother who told him she never realized how heavy ceilings were before, how they hovered. How claustrophobic they made her. What choice had he had then, really?

That series never felt like effort, or planned, but like expressing something he needed to see, that he wanted to make real. He wanted it for her. Now every time Lucien looks through his camera, there is a quaking inside him. And not an energy from within, but a warning. A foreshock he cannot ignore. Now the white-painted wood floors of Lucien's apartment are speckled red and orange. Why, with his mother gone, does he keep opening her paints?

His mother loved the freedom of painting; she lived for the possibility in every blank canvas. Lucien finds that freedom terrifying, not liberating. He likes the control of photography. The limit of a moment even if that is something to be played with—subverted, inverted, rotated, fractured, split, overlaid. Every piece of his started with the constraint of reality, his source material. His true medium.

Only now, reality is off.

Lucien needs constraints. Isn't sickness a constraint? Responsibility?

To be untethered feels unhinged. His newfound freedom is a void, not a chance.

His phone chirps, meaning his grandmother will be ready for visitors. Lucien gets up and wets a washcloth at the sink in his tiny bathroom. Then he wipes the cloth across his face, tasting where the bitter paint got on his lips.

Chapter 3

TODAY

Sophie lies in bed, holding her body to keep herself there, as if she could.

Alone in the dark, she misses touch with a fire burning under her skin. Each day at the Center, she both fears and longs for someone to inadvertently make contact. When they pull chairs into a circle for sessions with Dr. Sloane, she winces, ready to recoil if someone steps too close. But seated there, close together, she feels her skin pulling in spite of her. Begging for the thing she cannot have.

Her room is impossibly dark, devoid of much to catch moonlight. At this time each night, as she waits for sleep or something else, Sophie wonders if it is worse now being unable to remember, unable to place the thing that continues to torment her. Or is she spared, not knowing?

These phantom terrors should not linger. Dr. Sloane said so. And yet, night after night they return, an amorphous dread creeping up her chest, until all she can do is cry out.

Her throat is still sore from last night, when she cried so hard she had to be treated again, another drip in that misty bright room. Every time she swallows, she feels the pain of those screams. How strange, that something like sound can hurt.

That what we breathe can do such harm.

She remembers a time, not long ago, when she wanted so much. So much more than simply this, herself. So much more than feeling whole again. With that, her fingertips begin to turn foreign against her skin.

She releases her hands from her shoulders and rubs them together, using her knuckles to massage the other, then switching hands.

She takes a deep breath. *Sophie*, she whispers into the dark.

A bottle of pills sits on a ledge built off the bed frame. The custom bed in sleek, light wood is the only attention to design in the room. In another world, the ledge might have been perfect for a book. An alarm clock. A cell phone.

A small indent in the birch accommodates the pill bottle perfectly. This bottle is marked SLEEP. Another across the room beside her crumpled-up uniform is marked RETURN. Its contents offer a more subtle daytime supplement for use as needed. SLEEP is clinical strength with a mild sedative, plus magnesium and melatonin to encourage healthy sleep cycles. Dr. Sloane has made these special for her.

Sophie taps out a pill, pearlescent in the moonlight. The moon is one of the only things that changes, a variation they cannot control here, and Sophie notes its changing shape each night through her window with something like hunger.

She waits as the pill slides down her throat. The feeling starts in her back, warm fingertips kneading her into sleep. Then the day, like so many others, blooms inside of her.

Rehearsal, another lift, another throw.

Driving east from the studio, her leg so exhausted that it quivers over the pedal. She is light-headed with anticipation. Korean letters begin to appear along Olympic Boulevard, first under English signs on banks, then tea shops and beauty centers, bookstores and BBQs, until the English letters disappear entirely.

Inside the bright space is a ricochet of voices, and as the door chimes shut behind her its bell fills her with a Pavlovian calm. She waves to the two children who join their mother on weekends, reading picture books and chatting with other customers, and only then does Sophie remember it's not a weekend but a holiday.

Another lift, another throw.

Sophie limits these massages to her tip money, after subtracting the necessary allocations to groceries, gas, new practice socks and tights, lest she "ten more minutes" herself into debt. Plus, she likes to pay in cash.

Cash professions understand one another, she thinks, and this is one of her favorite places in all of Los Angeles, a place where she feels both at home and anonymous.

Another lift, another throw. Another order. Table 5 is waiting. Jonathan, bent over the bar. Her feet throbbing, her back no more than a standing ache.

Atop the table, the masseuse's fingers dance up Sophie's shoulders and across her back; she deftly plucks each knot, clenched and taut as a tightly strung harp. Gradually the movement deepens and Sophie's body relaxes under the pressure. Each push of the masseuse's fingertips, the tickling sting of their pressure, strokes nerves that make Sophie feel she might start sobbing, throw up, or both.

Another lift, another throw. Table 5 is still waiting.

Aside from dancing, these massages are the only moments Sophie loses track of time; when she wishes it would cease to pass. She lies suspended in the freedom of surrender, not waiting for the moment to be over, or wondering what comes next. When she dances, there is nothing then, too, only the music and the movements of her fellow dancers puzzle-pieced with her own. But even if her mind forgets the world outside her body and beyond the stage, afterward, she is still left with a body of denial.

Tension is a tool. Sophie depends on it; physically, where her muscles learn to hold tight for balance, but also emotionally, where the pressure solidifies inside her, pushes her further. Even the fastest, most passionate choreography in ballet has to be executed with precision, with perfection. Sometimes, the thought of this release is the only thing that gets her through the structured restrictions of her life.

Another lift, another throw.

Her time offstage is spent with caution. With control. Even these trips feel somewhat forbidden. The masseuse traces a tendon behind her heel. Is it not a risk for any ballerina to put her body, let alone her feet, in someone else's hands? Now the masseuse's thumb circles the skin below Sophie's inner ankle, then nearly folds her foot in half between her hands. The release ripples through Sophie's body. Perhaps the risk is part of the pleasure.

She hardly feels the pillow on her bed at the Center under her face anymore; her cotton sheets have turned to the vinyl of the massage table, tugging her skin with each sway as she presses farther into it. Then, just when Sophie feels the softness of the masseuse's body leaning over hers, the room loosens, its memory fleeting.

Her stomach twists.

The fingers stop and she is falling, fading into some unknowable darkness where her stomach isn't the only thing twisting, and what she feels is cold and wet and red.

Everywhere, red.

And then it is dark, until a sliver of light in the corner turns to more, and Sophie feels the needle in her arm before her own screams—the sharp breath returned, as if it never left.

Chapter 4

TODAY

Remember, remember, before you forget.

The night after Lucien's initial treatment is endless and amorphous. He touches his face, still his. He makes fists around the bedsheet, still there. He feels emptied, the vague sense of himself lingering as if only recently retold. A story he can almost remember. It may take time for the memories to settle, they said. The first night is the hardest.

In fits of sleep, he watches himself as if perched from the ceiling. Ashamed of the body below. Soon he drifts back into that place he cannot control, where parts of him insist themselves known, and others recede only to return in veiled fantasy. In dreams he is back in that blinding room with no walls. He feels around on hands and knees but finds only more light as he crawls toward some unknowable edge. To be trapped in a limitless space! Then he is back on the table, his body motionless as his mind claws forward, searching for edges because edges mean exits.

There are no doctors in lab coats anymore. A faint mist floats up from under him, charging his skin until he no longer feels the weight of his body. Only a tingling, as if floating in the cold bright air. When he breathes, with the mist comes a shock of familiarity. His chest tightens, like walking into the ocean, each wave breaking higher, pulling out more breath. Until finally, he lets go. The air settles everything he knows, a warm blanket laid under his skin.

He smells nothing.

He remembers it all.

He is on the way to freshman soccer tryouts on Randall's Island; identical buses from all the prep schools pass, kids he recognizes in each, their faces hovering then falling back or racing forward. Their curious, condescending grins. He mostly knows of them through new crushes and their crushes, this network of tallying that his new friends who went to Collegiate and Dalton introduce him to. Back at M.S. 51, Lucien fished oysters from the Gowanus Canal for science class, and he could walk home after school. Home. Musty fallen leaves on a damp autumn day. The dry, powdery scent of canvas being stretched.

Back on the bus he's carsick as his new friend Miles tells another classmate across the aisle that Lucien's mother has sex with women *and* men. Lucien watches it spread in whispers across the rows, zigzagging his pulse. He doesn't know his mother to have sex with anyone, but Miles says his parents read an interview and she said so herself. Lucien looks down to where the seat sticks to the backs of his legs. He peels them off, the pain sharp like a Band-Aid.

Street-cart meat in Washington Square; the fountain's sparkling mist. Warm air from a subway grate. Flickering fluorescent lights at the bodega, paying for a pack of Hi-Chew. Soaked socks from practice in the rain; mixing hot chocolate, licking the powder off his spoon before it dissolves. Standing alone in their tiny, dark kitchen. Waiting for his mother.

Is he still?

Lucien wakes to daylight outside the high window in his room, so sealed against the ocean breeze that even the waves below crash on mute. The tightly pressed pane gives him the impression of holding his breath, squirming to relieve the growing pressure. For just one gasp of fresh air. All this, after just one night.

On the small ledge attached to his bed, Lucien notices a pill bottle. Then voices, from outside the room. He shakes out a pill and slips it into his pocket.

His door is cracked open. He walks into the hallway and toward the sound of those voices until he reaches the living area. He passes what must be the front entrance, though he has no memory of it. This place, with its blankness—no context, no names, no triggers—is disorienting. He already feels it loosening the parts of himself that once felt tied to specific places and times. He is static. Ever present, but entirely indescribable.

Wiped clean, comes to mind.

And yet, what had felt fuzzy during the night is now clear. His memories are there. He can retrieve them like trivia he might hold in his hand. Where did I go to high school? Stuyvesant. What did it look like? Endless red brick, the new kind, rising. Looming. Heavy. What did it smell like? Candy and Axe bodywash. Dry-erase markers and computer stations. What did it feel like? Pressure. Opportunity. Nerves on fire. All these facts, yet there is something different. Something distant. Maybe this is what they mean when they say it takes time. Maybe this is what the pills will fix.

Lucien's fingers flicker, feeling for something. A cigarette. The body remembers, though the urgency is gone. He gravitates toward the open fire in the sunken heart of the room. Does he like fire? Loves it, in fact. Bonfires in Montauk. Lucien's braces got stuck in Stefanie Lewis's and they never spoke again. Still, he loves fire.

He sits on the stone perch along the fireplace and looks out. Men of all ages relax in comfortable chairs and sofas scattered throughout the space, as they might to watch television together. But there is nothing on, no television. They have the same sedated smiles. Virtual reality without the headsets.

Lucien pulls the tiny, opalescent pill from his pocket and observes it in the daylight. Its appearance changes with the slightest movement, containing every color and then none at all. How strange to be given the thing that got you caught in the first place. As if oysters could consume their pearls.

He could join these men, eyes glazed and checked-out, but right now it feels important to stay. His dreams last night held nothing remarkable; the memories were overwhelming if anything. Lucien places the pill back into his pocket. Sparks from the fireplace flicker into the air above, where an open atrium looks like a painted ceiling, so blue and cloudless that only a gliding seagull confirms its reality. Lucien leans in closer, holding his hands to the flames. He crosses his legs and notices the stiffness of the jumpsuit he had nearly forgotten. The space is so neutral that their clothes are like camouflage. His eyes rise. Strangers in matching disguise.

Beyond the glass walls, ocean stretches to the horizon. A cormorant nearly lands on its gleaming stillness, wings flapping as its talons cause a ripple in the water. Lucien pushes himself, abs tightening, trying to summon a recent memory. Or better, to remember the thing that got him here. All he turns up is the room where his treatments took place, its walls and floor so brightly lit as to defy perspective. He was left on a slim table for what seemed like hours as the drip hydrated him—and cleared his mind. He remembers a woman with a doctor's mask, no words. He remembers two shiny curtains of dark hair swinging past her face as she leaned over him; the closeness of her as she shined a light in his eyes. The orange glow under his lids.

Lucien is startled when he hears a voice across the room. The voice isn't what startles him—the hum of others is a comfort after the past hours of isolation.

What startles him is that he recognizes it.

Her.

Lucien scans the room, his entire body newly alive. He sees only more men—no one belonging to that voice. He catches sight of her just as she unwraps a tea bag by the coffee station. Her neck is long, her hands graceful, and her eyes stare off just past the mug, past the countertop, absent from her own delicate movements. She looks about Lucien's age, in her twenties, so this might be a recent memory—one of his own.

A piece of him reverberating up from the rubble.

Her movements are graceful but cautious, weary of pain. Before Lucien can approach her, her lips pursed and blowing on her tea, the space fills with other patients arranging seats in a circle around the fireplace. Within moments, a line of chairs separates him from her. As everyone finds a spot, she falls into arrangement directly facing Lucien, missing his attempts to catch her eye. As she turns to sit, Lucien notices on her cheekbone is a piece of gauze, and above her eye, a butterfly bandage hugs her brow. Even her forearm is wrapped. Then she crosses her legs, shifting so that only her profile faces him again.

A woman with a sleek black bob—the only person in the void of Lucien's memory from the past day, or weeks—takes the last open seat. She wears the same jumpsuit as everyone else, but by the way the room adjusts to her, Lucien guesses she must be the head doctor.

Lucien loops his fingertips under his thighs to stop them from fidgeting. A teen with crusty, sun-bleached blond hair and chapped lips sits to his side. A white residue cakes the cracks in his lips. He smiles and looks down to his own hands, also tucked, while his feet bounce to some invisible pulse. To Lucien's other side is an elderly man with short gray-flecked hair. He sits in a wheelchair, and the dark skin on his thin legs is loose under his rolled-up jumpsuit. Lucien wonders if what brought him here were memories from his own past, memories of movement—to run, to walk, to stand—or if he disappeared into another's for what he never had. Or harder still, what he lost. Who wouldn't let themselves slip away? The man winks at Lucien, and the doctor clears her throat.

"Wonderful to see so many new faces here today. Welcome. To those who have been here some time, I hope that you take solace in the repetition of today's session. It is only through repetition that we truly find clarity."

As she continues, Lucien is so lulled by the pace of her words that it becomes a sort of meditation, an affirmation, and he hangs on the pauses. She looks around the circle before she continues with a tight smile.

"Water, fire," she says with a new strength to her voice. "These are primal groundings. Look around. It's no coincidence that you find them here. Let them anchor you. Let all other sensations leave your body but these, and when you feel overwhelmed, come and sit. Look into the flames. Stare out at the sea. The first days are the hardest. You'll crave something, anything, to latch on to, but just wait. By day seven, what's left will be you, in your purest form, and that is when you can truly rebuild. Savor your new beginning. This simplicity won't last forever. You'll never get another fresh start like this. And as we learn from those who have departed too soon, if you try to rush, or become impatient—if you introduce that which we keep out—you risk the entire process."

She turns to a petite man with round glasses beside her. He speaks in a sort of recitation, looking eager to please her. "A drop of water on a dry paper towel will spread," he says, "until it has crept into every corner, every vein."

"Thank you," she says with a single nod. "A healthy reminder from our session last week, for those who were here. We find ourselves in this place because the human spirit is precious, delicate. No matter how strong you feel, consciousness is a fragile, sacred thing. The basis of who you are depends on consistency, coherency. Some of you have taken that for granted. Many of you have suffered unimaginable pain. You are here because of the generosity of others. Now what you have to ask yourselves, as the unraveling begins—as the work is done—is who do you want left once you're finished?

"I know you feel broken. Some of you feel empty. Tainted. Compromised."

Lucien notices her gazing at the girl, attempting to find her eyes.

"I assure you, where you are now—right here, together—is a privilege. Consider others who escape themselves, who lose themselves. Where do they end up? You are here. You've already found the Center. And we're here to help you find yours."

And you to yours, they say as a sort of amen.

"For those I have not yet met formally, I am Dr. Sloane."

Lucien had almost forgotten how good it feels to place a person. To hold them, static, by the name. *Dr. Sloane.* He sighs. The stability of a name.

Lucien senses her speaking directly to him, and he looks up just in time to meet her eyes. Then one by one her gaze moves across the circle, a nod introducing each person in the absence of their names.

"Here, you are all equal. Whether you are married, single, divorced. Unemployed, self-employed, partner, or the boss. Here, you are all patients."

The teen beside Lucien lets out a sharp cackle.

She tilts her head in his direction.

"We're all patience!" he says, delirious. "Been here so long, patience is all that's left!"

A slow rippling laughter breaks out across the circle. Lucien is unclear as to whether the teen sounds mad or absolutely revelatory, but maybe that is the point. The silence pulsing through the room makes him anxious, but when he looks down, his entire body is shaking, too.

Dr. Sloane sighs. Her disappointment stings.

Lucien feels in awe of her cohesion, how it sparkles when set against those she is tasked with fixing. He is, for the moment, ashamed to be among them. When she stands and walks toward the wall, gazing out across the ocean as the faintest ripple moves out to sea, Lucien wonders if their disruption crossed even the glass. She lingers with her back turned to them and the laughter dissipates. When at last she passes behind Lucien on her way back to her seat, he smells cigarettes, or at least the lingering staleness of a smoker. The air holds the scent for just a few seconds, his mind chasing it, until he finds himself second-guessing whether it was ever there.

"Where do you want to go from here?" Dr. Sloane says. "The only thing we can truly teach you is that you are the Center. And when you leave, that is all you can take. That's it. You. It's very simple what we do here. Now, go there. Go inside."

Lucien looks around, watching each set of eyes, with names he doesn't know and never will. They turn inward at her command. He can guess the ones who have been here for a while. They reemerge found, present, still.

Two seats down from Lucien, a middle-aged man with a buzz cut hits his forehead with the base of his palm. He whispers, in argument. Beside him is another man, in his early thirties, with freckles covering his face. He blinks long and hard, spending deliberate time behind his eyelids. When they open, his eyes are cloudy with tears.

Lucien looks back to the girl, her perfect posture and long neck. He watches as she swallows, focused, then tucks a strand of dark brown hair behind her ear.

He notices it then—the faintest outline of a tattoo on her knuckles. One by one, though he is supposed to be looking inward, he names the letters. There it is, upside down and backward. His call to action, or maybe hers.

L-O-O-K-U-P

And when he does, their eyes meet.

Chapter 5

BEFORE

A bar graph of cocktails in differing heights and widths sits atop the marble counter in the courtyard of the Chateau Marmont. Sophie scans the paper ticket, her eyes alternating between its water-stained ink and the lineup as Jonathan applies the finishing touches behind the bar. Sugared ginger on a bamboo toothpick. Thinly sliced jalapeño. A handful of torn mint. Jonathan rubs an orange rind around one rim, then lets its curled peel slide down the ice cube held in place by the diameter of its lowball glass.

"Two Pimm's Cups, Moscow Mule, Jalapeño Margarita, and one Negroni."

Sophie stabs the ticket onto a metal rod already piled high with the night's orders. Another server comes up close behind her, and Sophie knows not to move. This is the silent choreography one learns on their feet. Break a few glasses in your first week, and you store it in your bones. It's Eva, Sophie can tell by the perfume. Sandalwood and citrus. Or maybe that's the orange rind.

"I need a glass of Bourgogne Blanc and a Taittinger for table seven, and I need it, like, five minutes ago."

Eva is shorter than Sophie, and as she twists past her toward the bar, her petite frame and French bob make Sophie feel giant and plain. A blunt object next to a feather in the breeze. Eva's tray lands hard on the bar top, splattering old cocktail spills and condensation. A drop of something gets in Sophie's eye, and she lifts a finger to stream it out in a tear without drawing attention. As if even an injury—Eva's fault—would mark her as high maintenance. Rather than accepting that Eva might just not like her, Sophie has made it her mission to disprove her, regardless of whether the insults are fabrications of Sophie's mind turned on itself.

Jonathan uncorks the Bourgogne Blanc without looking away from Sophie.

"You okay?"

"Fine," she says.

"How about a drink when your shift's over?" Jonathan says. "My treat."

Her eye is on fire now, the bubble of champagne traveling her iris like hot oil on a skillet.

"Sure," she says, still hoping to blink it away. "You know what I take."

"Oh my god," Eva says, leaning toward her. "What's up with your eye?"

Sophie wipes away a tear and it's black with mascara. She grabs a napkin.

"Nothing, it's fine. Allergies or something."

"No, not a shift drink," Jonathan continues. "Somewhere else. Expand our horizons, what do you say?"

"Just the two of us?"

Sophie is still aware of Eva, her eyes perfectly lined and flicked up at the end, while wet mascara no doubt fans Sophie's cheek à la *Clockwork Orange*. Finally, the stinging passes and Sophie feels the tears subside. Eva hands her another bar napkin, with *Chateau Marmont* printed on it in a script so tall and stretched as to be almost illegible. Sophie has learned that glamour has to be a little bit strange, a little off. And that is why she will never be glamorous; she seeks perfection and it shows.

"Building castles in the sky," hums Jonathan, flirting either in spite of Eva's presence or because of it. How unfair, that what might make him cooler could make Sophie more disliked.

"Huh?"

Eva scoffs beside her, and Sophie hears her own voice come out squeaky clean. "I have rehearsals at eight a.m. tomorrow." She lowers her voice before continuing. "Besides, why would we complicate a perfectly good workplace flirtation with actually seeing each other outside of this den of iniquity?"

"What if I told you it was my last night?" he says. "Last-chance rodeo."

He's corking the Taittinger, winking at Eva, who rolls her eyes before darting away under the ivy trellis. Somehow she always gets her orders filled before Sophie.

"Well, then I'd congratulate you," Sophie says, freed from Eva's gaze. "Like I do every time you say that."

"I mean it this time. Take a good look, Sophie Marden, I'm gone after tonight."

"All right, then I'll take a Veuve, here, and remind you how fond I am of your wife."

Jonathan looks down, pretending to be surprised by his own wedding band, and then licks his finger, as though trying to pull it off.

"You forget that I liked Ellie before I ever liked you," Sophie says. "She's the reason we tolerate you."

"What else are you waiting on?" Jonathan asks.

"A taste of the skin-contact for table seven. I'll drop it on the way."

"We're out of the orange. How about the new Chablis? Bitches love it."

Sophie rolls her eyes and turns with the fresh tray of cocktails, when a woman in platform heels and a tight bandage dress sways drunkenly in her direction. Without hesitation Sophie rises to her toes and spins on one leg, the other lifted and turned out. She stretches the arm with the tray of drinks straight up to where the twinkle lights dangle. Then she comes down with a light pas de bourrée.

The young woman continues on her staggered path a few steps farther and then rests against a topiary, her hair tangling in its leaves. She pulls each strand back—one after another, a revelation, how plants work!—then begins poking at the tarp to the smoking area. A cloud of smoke sneaks out from behind the plastic sheet. The woman coughs, and a bare arm covered with diamond bracelets reaches out for her. She disappears.

Sophie lowers the tray. The margarita's salted rim went straight into one of the courtyard's low-strung lanterns and spilled all over. Before she looks back up, Jonathan is already shaking a fresh one. He mimics her aggression in furious movements, while she sets down the tray and removes the other glasses to mop up the spill.

"Quite the reaction on your part," he says. "Two thumbs up."

He taps the shaker on the side of the bar, then strains the concoction—a frothy sea foam flecked with jalapeño—into a new glass with a chipotle-salted rim. Sophie takes a moment to roll her neck out, letting her head circle, feeling its weight stretch every vertebra of her back.

"Rough rehearsals?"

"The usual," Sophie says, head still tilted back. "So, yes."

Jonathan dips a straw into the remade cocktail, pipes a taste to his lips, then tosses the plastic blindly to the trash. "Perfect."

"Excuse me," a throaty voice calls from behind the tarp. "Do y'all have, like, a lighter?"

Sophie grabs a pack of matches from the dish on the bar and tosses it in the direction of the tarp without looking. Then she turns once more with her tray.

"Fucking tourists."

The Chateau's courtyard is relatively quiet for a Thursday. Save the standard tables of regulars, tonight's crowd is mostly hotel guests doing their best to stave off jet lag with Moscow Mules in sweaty copper mugs and truffle fries overflowing from their paper cones. Hard to believe that this place has survived the stereotypes, the deaths, the clichés, the ever-changing scene, but then again people hate change. They want to live in the memory of some enchanted evening, especially if it isn't their own.

On a quiet night, Sophie is often struck by the magic in the air—the way twinkling lights and ivy can transform a patch of land off Sunset Boulevard into a French dream. In those moments, she catches herself—back in her bedroom in Minneapolis ten years ago, if she could see herself now—and laughs that she gets paid to stroll between tables of beautiful people on feet sore from ballet rehearsals led by Auguste

Demarchelier; that her day job's duties (though more often at night) involve assuring Sean Penn that his salade niçoise will not have tomato, or bringing Jennifer Lawrence soda water for a *jus stain* from particularly rare steak frites, and that Leonardo DiCaprio still "owes" her for his date's unfortunate incident involving a glass of Malbec and Sophie's lilac satin shoes. Once she helped Bella Kingston stop a nosebleed from a mountain of cocaine at two a.m. On a Monday.

Whenever she returns to visit her parents, friends at home ask about *celebrity sightings*, expecting to hear that she saw so-and-so at a coffee shop or pumping gas. Not only does Sophie wait their tables, take their orders, and make them feel safe, but she has spent late nights at their after-parties. She has been not only witness but confidante. How could she ever explain? Mostly, she doesn't really care anymore. The brain can only hold so many stories before it starts to prioritize sleep and waking up with a semblance of energy above all else. She gets paid to be out. To be on her feet. Would it not stand to reason that her free time should be spent alone and comfortable and preferably reclined?

"Hey, Soph," calls Jonathan before she's out of earshot.

He nods in the direction of table 5, just off the entrance from the hotel lobby. The table that implies prominence with just the right amount of privacy. The table they give as a subtle show of respect when someone powerful, or bankable, walks in. Also, Ray Delaney's table. Sophie can tell from Jonathan's expression that it's him. He must be asking for her.

A couple years ago during the mass-purging of men who used intimidation, sex, and coercion to reinforce their own power and subjugate the women around them, Sophie had looked for Ray Delaney's name in the headlines each day as she poured her coffee, rolling her ankles in the tiny kitchen of her apartment. She had checked for him among the tally of large, forceful bodies in *The Hollywood Reporter*, Deadline, the *LA Times*; she even set a Google Alert, just waiting for the results: "Thirty Women Come Forward Against Hollywood Producer Ray Delaney!" "Big Shot Producer Loses Overall Deal—Faces Damages!" But those headlines never came. Any results were populated instead by his most recent films, and what new projects he was developing with so-and-so.

Sophie cannot figure out what keeps him safe, what lets this man get away with that same pushiness pardoned by power or, worse still, what causes the unnerving lurch in her stomach. What happened to the so-called revolution?

Soon after starting at Chateau Marmont, Sophie learned what such spaces offer people like Ray Delaney. It is not the same fairy tale that intrigues tourists, or those who come hoping to see someone famous. The Chateau delivers on the fantasy of a world curated to your tastes, your enjoyment, your privacy. What could be more appealing to powerful men? The waitresses beautiful, the waiters respectful, no one inconvenienced—never the customers, at least. Most important, they find the privacy their success has taken away momentarily restored. For celebrities especially, this kind of protection is assured by the Chateau's seclusion, by the exclusive privilege of being let inside—but also by the vanity of its other customers, lest they admit their own insignificance by placing any importance on another's. The NO PHOTOGRAPHS rule is almost unnecessary. These people only take photos of themselves.

The presence of celebrity still alters the space; its power wafts behind the entrance of So-and-So, even more if she is with a new Mr. So-and-So. Such a presence leaves a room charged, electrified. Even the dullest tables of obligatory work breakfasts suddenly perk up, ignited to be in the presence of fame or beauty. People who never smile bare their teeth until their cheeks hurt. And the surrounding tables either go silent or cannot stop talking, even with absolutely nothing to say. Ah, the ambient noise of celebrity. The performance of pleasure that must follow them everywhere. Sophie recognizes it within seconds now—the hush—whispers traveling like wildfire across tables and in between them. The paralysis of proximity.

And yet, having spent her first several years at parties across Hollywood, in homes stilted into the hillside, caterers brought in for a handful of guests, Sophie has learned that in the industry's ranking, the actors often come last. In fact, the actors seem almost cheap, embarrassingly cheesy. Desperate. Those petite, polished men who rely on others to get them work. They are Hollywood fish food. Sure, writers call their own shots and can kick-start projects. But it is the producers and directors who really shift a room of industry people. Actors fawn over them; writers suck up to them. People drive across town for catered dinners at their homes, dip their toes in their pools, pet their dogs.

This hierarchy of Hollywood power, of course, is how Ray Delaney gets the same table at the Chateau every night and fills the seats at said table with a constant rotation of actors, actresses, models, and writers. This is why he gets to creepily rest his hand on your forearm uncomfortably long; to call you sweetheart; to ask you why you never smile. This is why you still are not meant to complain.

Sophie looks over toward table 5, immediately spotting Ray Delaney by the popped collar on his leather jacket, the salt-and-pepper of his close-cut hair. He keeps it tight on the sides but fluffed on top, masking his impending baldness. She wonders what ingenue would be at his table tonight. Judging by the ambient hush, and the fact that he has sat her in the most prominent seat, she must be someone big, or as he might say—on the verge.

Sophie passes a fiddle-leaf fig and hustles back to the private bungalows. The bungalows are curtained booths tucked into the most secluded nook of the courtyard, usually reserved for high-level meetings or illicit rendezvous. Tonight, she has three Russian oligarchs with much younger counterparts, all there on business. Their bungalow sounds unusually quiet now, where cheers had filled it earlier and many drinks had been ordered.

Inside the curtain, the three men sit at the table with their heads tilted back, a salute of Adam's apples, mouths agape. Two women—of questionable drinking age—teeter over one of them, giggling, and trying to light their cigarettes without falling over. Sophie looks around for the third, as one of the women fumbles her match and drops it into the man's lap, eliciting even more laughter.

Sophie sets the tray down and the sound must startle one of them because her stiletto catches on the cobblestone, and she falls, nearly overturning the man's chair with her. Upon landing, she crumples into a ball with laughter, which the other joins in, until they are heaving with such fury that someone stumbling upon them at that moment might call for help.

Once the laughter subsides, Sophie gestures back to the table. "I'm leaving the check here with your drinks. No rush, of course." She accidentally looks to the men, unconscious, and regrets the implication.

"You're very pretty," one of the women says in a thick Russian accent, looking up at her with the glazed eyes of too many drinks. "Like swan."

She lifts her arm, wrist limp, and presses her thumb together with her fingers, into a beak. The other looks up, then spits out another laugh and hits her with the back of her hand.

As Sophie ducks out from the curtain of the bungalow, another server, Ariel, nearly bumps into her with a tray carrying beet salad, tuna tartare, and pommes frites—the truffled smell nauseating to her since her second week. He stops her midstride.

"Delaney is asking for you," he says.

"I know."

He shifts his weight impatiently.

"Willow asked me to tell you. He's at five. Obviously."

Sophie takes a deep breath and walks through the center of the courtyard, around the exotic plants. She sees the girl seated next to Ray Delaney better now. A startling beauty even from afar, with olive skin, bright eyes, and—as Sophie gets closer—an Australian accent.

"Here she is!" says Ray Delaney.

He clasps his hands, then spreads his arms as though to introduce Sophie to the table. Instead he holds out a pudgy, tanned hand for her to kiss. She forces a smile and squeezes the ends of his fingers before returning her hand to the empty tray by her side. Ray Delaney chuckles.

"Another round of drinks?" she asks.

Ray Delaney's leather jacket crunches as he adjusts himself in his chair. He pulls his pants at the crotch. Under his jacket is a black V-neck, always revealing just a hint of groomed chest hair in the same salt-and-pepper. The young man beside him wears a buttoned-up oxford, thick-frame glasses, and a persistent frown, and the two to his side wear identical gray suits and seem to move in unison. This is a classic Hollywood meeting. The fresh young starlet, the slick producer, the thirsty writer. The suits.

"I'll take another bourbon," the hypothetical writer says, tilting his glass.

"Whiskey, neat," says one of the suits.

Ray Delaney waves a hand, beckoning Sophie closer to his side, which she obliges. Once close, he pulls at her forearm until she leans half her weight on the arm of his chair. He takes her hand in his, placing his other on top. His skin looks nearly orange in the candlelight, and it takes every effort for Sophie not to yank her hand away and spit in his face.

"You can sit with us for just a moment."

"I really can't," says Sophie. "I have other tables."

"We can just tell Willow it was my fault," Ray Delaney says with a smug smile. "Willow and I are tight."

Ray Delaney's face is blown up and laminated in the VIP binder Sophie committed to memory three years ago upon being hired by Willow first as a hostess. Deep down, Sophie senses that Willow likely despises him for all his crudeness and entitlement, but Ray Delaney had long ago secured his place with her and thus plays his hand freely inside the Chateau's storied walls. Sometimes it feels like he's testing them, like a child wanting to be scolded.

"Five minutes," he says. "Ruby here was just telling us about her mind-altering experiences."

The young actress smiles, a hand to her bare breastbone, her silk top glowing rose-gold in the candlelight. "Oh, no," she says, her Australian accent stretching the words, "I've never done Mem. I've just heard things."

"Never? And why's that?" Ray Delaney says, getting off on her shyness. "It's expensive, I know. But I'm sure you've been offered. In your circle? Please."

The starlet cups the candle from the tabletop with both hands, the votive cutouts flickering shadows across her face. "Well, I don't mean to be rude but I guess I figured I've already got a life. It's pretty good, yeah? Why would I want someone else's?"

Sophie feels a spark of triumph for her. Go Ruby.

"But only one," Ray Delaney counters. "And therein lies your problem, kid."

The two suits laugh.

The starlet turns her face toward her shoulder and gives a coy smile, punctuated by dimples. But Ray Delaney has now lost interest in her. He picks up a glass of rosé off the table and holds it out to Sophie.

"Whose is this?" she asks.

"Yours. It's—a table wine. That is, wine for the table."

Sophie laughs until she realizes he is not making a joke.

"It was mine," Ruby says. "But then it was way too sweet for my taste so he—"

"Blah blah blah, extremely interesting—look it doesn't matter how we have it. We do, and now it's yours."

"Sorry," says Ruby.

"Don't apologize, look at you—you should never drink anything you don't want. Not with that face." He turns back to Sophie. "Have a sip. Take the edge off."

"Thank you, but I can't," says Sophie, still processing the implication there. That she, unlike Ruby, should drink whatever and whenever she is offered. "I'm working."

"What are you, delivering babies or something?" he says.

Sophie is still leaning on the side of his chair, her thigh beginning to cramp. The skin on the back of her leg is turning sore from the wicker. She looks toward the bar, to Jonathan, but he is too busy mixing cocktails to notice her.

"It'll loosen you up," he says. "Make you even better at this very important job of yours."

With the rest of the table watching, Sophie takes the glass from him and takes a sip between clenched teeth. Before she puts it down, she twirls the glass, watching the reflections of the others at the table stretch and spin as they blabber on, examining their distorted faces in the rose-gold glow.

"So, you've never done Mem," Ray Delaney says to the starlet, back in his good graces again. "Tell us, then, what do you do for fun? All this talk of our film, we better know that you can act the part. Imagine, someone never having had a good time." He turns to wink at Sophie, like this is their inside joke—her the prude to his scoundrel.

"I don't know," Ruby says, accent thickening with every sip. She brushes the short blunt bangs from her forehead, presumably to think. "I like to hike with my friends, at Runyon or Topanga. Road trips to Joshua Tree, Big Sur. Oh, and I love a good massage."

Mass-age, Sophie thinks. It does sound more fun with an Australian accent.

"You adorable thing," says Ray Delaney. "Don't you love this girl? America is going to love this girl."

Ruby beams. Sophie feels bad for her, though she knows she should not. After all, Ruby is probably only a few years younger than her, and seems pleased with her place at that table. In another world Sophie might consider finding her later in the bathroom, telling her to go home, get out of there. Find some real friends her own age.

"Look, can I be blunt?" says Ray Delaney.

"Please," says Ruby.

"These activities—hiking, massages, drinking—they are ordinary things for ordinary people. But you, kid, you're anything but. Look around. We're lucky. We have the chance, and the means, to do the extraordinary."

Ray Delaney glances at Sophie with another wink that makes her jaw clench.

"If anyone knows about being lucky it's Ray here," snorts one of the suits.

"I'm serious—and not just because I think it would help Ruby get into character for the film, which it would, undoubtedly. But because she deserves a little life."

"Get into character?" says Ruby, curious now. "How do you mean, then?"

"All the big names are doing it. Daniel, Bradley, Margot. Hard to imagine how they ever acted without it now. It's practically the new school of method acting."

"Gosh, what would I do without you?"

"A lot more hiking?" says the other suit between crunches of ice from his drained Moscow Mule. Ray Delaney shoots him a look and he shuts up.

"These are just the things you pass along, to younger generations," says Ray Delaney. "I'm a mentor. It's what I do." Then he turns to Sophie, still perched against the arm of his rattan chair. She feels his breath on her shoulder. "And how about you?"

"I should get back to my tables," she says. Now drinks really are piling up beside Jonathan at the bar.

"We live in a fucked-up time," he says, ignoring her. "Everything is accessible at any hour—all you need is a Wi-Fi password and a pair of eyes. Do you know what that's like for someone in my generation? I'm an old fuck. My father was a real estate guy, raised four children. They did okay, but they weren't traveling or eating like we do today, like we expect. Maybe once a year they'd scrape together a few extra bucks to get away—to Cuba, or the pyramids. And do you know why?"

"For the romance?" The starlet blinks, wide-eyed.

"Because none of their fucking friends had been," Ray Delaney says. "They'd come back with photographs and blow minds. Kaboom. The pyramids—massive, towering structures—built when? Kaboom. French bread. Moroccan rugs. No one had ever seen these things in person. Life was all competition then, too, just a simpler one."

The suits nod along, and Sophie looks anxiously to the bar, wondering how long this speech will go on, and whether the punch line will be a warning to her, a threat of some sort. Or most important, when he'll loosen the sweaty grip on her wrist.

"They'd have a big party just to scroll through blurry photos on the projector, retell their stories, describe the fucking food. Do you know what people would say to that now?"

"Oh yeah, I've seen that online," says one of the suits.

"Check my fucking Instagram," adds the other, shaking his head.

This gets a laugh from everyone but the writer, swiping at something on his phone.

"Point being," says Ray Delaney. "We have the means to travel anywhere faster and cheaper, but so what? We've already seen it all. It's all waiting on the other side of this." He plucks the writer's phone from his hands and dangles it between his fingers.

"Fuck off," says the writer. "If I have to listen to another talk about connectivity—"

"You fuck off," says Ray Delaney. "Know your place."

Then Ray Delaney extends a finger to his temple and taps it there. "So really—what's left of luxury when there's no place left unseen? No destination exotic enough?"

"Space?" says the starlet.

"Why do people do drugs?" says Ray Delaney, exasperated. "To escape themselves. But you know what—they can never get away."

The writer pushes his chair out to get up, but Ray Delaney keeps talking.

"This smug shit over here will always be a smug shit, even after a bump of coke, which I'm sure he's off to do. Go on, go on," he says, and the writer scoffs before heading to the bathroom. "No, to truly leave yourself, the one place you can never escape, and to experience a moment as someone else. That is the ultimate luxury."

Just then, up the Chateau's courtyard wall, a window opens and two shaggy heads appear against the ivy-covered brick, yelling something about a party in room 204 before immediately retreating back inside. The window slams shut with such force that another waitress across the courtyard instinctively ducks under her tray.

Sophie sees her opportunity and pushes herself back up to standing, her heels uneasy on the mossy cobblestones.

"For example," Ray Delaney says, "I'd love to know what it's like to walk around on a pair of legs like these." He makes a show of looking Sophie's legs up and down, grinning.

"Oh relax," he says, her discomfort apparently evident. "I'm kidding, princess."

Sophie manages to smile, her heart racing, as she slips away. She keeps it up—big and forced—until safely facing the bar.

"Join us for a taste later," he calls after her, tapping his gold ring against the half-empty old-fashioned. "We've got business to take care of first, but I brought some top-shelf shit."

Jonathan is shaking a martini as Sophie leans against the bar.

"I can't do it," she says. "I can't go back over there. I hate everything about that man."

"Well, he's very hate-able," Jonathan says.

"You have no idea what it's like."

"Please, I work every waking hour I'm not here on a pilot no one will ever see, while that guy drinks twenty-five-dollar cocktails and makes shitty blockbusters. I'd love nothing more than to punch him in his little pug face."

Sophie laughs, and it feels good. "He actually makes some good movies, isn't that the worst part? If he didn't he wouldn't be here anymore."

"So help me god, Sophie Marden."

Sophie rests her weight against the bar to relieve her throbbing feet, then slips one foot out of her shoe. She rolls her ankle, undoing the damage from the morning's rehearsal and the pain of these heels that bring in better tips than wearing sneakers. The pain, and the pleasure of its release, travels all the way up her body.

Sophie hesitates to linger on the unwanted attention she gets while working there, at least not to Jonathan. She can sense how little he understands; how, like so many men, he still thinks such attention is a privilege that women simply don't know how to spin. How, in her position, he would do something with it. Nothing she could say would make Jonathan comprehend what it feels like to be seen by a man like Ray Delaney. To feel trapped in your own skin.

Sophie has no idea how Jonathan keeps writing. Ballet can be thankless—hard on her body, her nerves, her social life—and she also trains endlessly for delayed gratification, but at least her efforts are externally validated by her director, Auguste. Jonathan toils at scripts no one sees. That no one may ever see, on paper let alone the screen. Sophie knows he took this job to get proximity to the industry and that instead it is torture, watching other careers launch from up close while he serves them. Invisible.

Just a few weeks ago, Sophie had impressed someone, finally. After four years in the Los Angeles Ballet Company, Auguste announced Sophie would move from soloist to principal, and dance the title role in *La Sylphide*, one of the oldest ballets in existence. She would fill the role dancers like Natalia Osipova and Cynthia Gregory have all performed, a role aspiring ballerinas dream about from their very first pair of toe shoes. Now in just a few months it will be Sophie who is the envy on-stage. She still remembers the first time she watched the haunting, tragic ballet—the sylph, a spirit effervescent and charming enough to lure a betrothed away from his future wife, who is similarly destroyed in the process. Whoever plays the sylph must be tempting and magical—the highest challenge for a dancer, alluring one moment and fluttering the next. She must capture the audience and then captivate them as she dies. The greatest romance, perhaps, is that between the spirit and her crowd. Oh, to be a woman who inspires men to do the most craven things, to break the rules of society, to leave a true love without another choice. This is what little girls are taught, after all. To be a glimmering, precious thing. Delicate, and ultimately cursed.

Sophie's mother cried when she called home with the news. And Sophie cried back, hugging her phone as she sat fully clothed in a bathroom stall during her break.

"What's up with the group in the bungalow?" says Jonathan. "Think they'll need more drinks? I want to start tearing down."

"They're out cold, the men at least. Hard to tell whether they're super stingy with their Mem, or their dates are just smarter than them."

"Damn. How many is that tonight?"

"I lost count."

"Just because they're here they think they can do whatever they want."

"That band coming off their Troubadour show did a line on my check earlier," Sophie says. "I had to shake it off!"

"Maybe that was your tip?"

Ariel comes up behind Sophie and sets his tray down. "Did you ever make it to Delaney? He asked me about you again. Y'all should get him a fucking pager."

"I just went."

"In the past five minutes?"

"Oh, come on!" says Sophie, letting her head fall between her hands on the bar.

"Don't shoot the messenger," says Ariel. "Between us, my roommate was a PA on his last movie; lord, the things I've heard."

"Let's send the new girl," says Jonathan.

Their eyes travel down the bar to a younger waitress with side-swept bangs, sorting through drink tickets.

"Really nice."

"What?"

"Just give me their drinks," Sophie says. "I'm not going to make her do it."

Jonathan pulls a fry from under the bar and aims it at Sophie's mouth. She bites at it, but he pulls it away.

"Fuck you," she says.

"Isn't she lovely . . ."

Sophie ruffles Jonathan's combed-down hair until it stands on end, then plucks a fry with the other hand. The sound of yet another broken glass brings her attention back to table 5. She taps her tray until Jonathan pours the last bourbon on the rocks.

Only a few remaining candles flicker from table to table, lighting up the courtyard like fireflies. As Sophie approaches Ray Delaney's table with the young starlet and her collection of admirers, she sees the pointed silhouettes of five noses facing straight up. Sophie looks upward, expecting to see the same revelers making a commotion in the hotel room above, but it is dark and dead-quiet behind the closed windows. Only then does she notice the starlet's limp arms, both manicured hands grazing the ground below, where her broken glass mingles with the moss-covered brick patio, the tiny fractures twinkling like dewdrops.

Chapter 6

TODAY

.

Lucien sits alone with Dr. Sloane in another room that juts out over the coastline. Two walls of glass, with ocean on both sides. This room is smaller, more intimate. Dr. Sloane sits in a chair, while Lucien fidgets on a firm couch facing the water.

"I'd like to talk about your mother," says Dr. Sloane.

"My mother?"

"Part of your work here will be talking with me," she says. "Getting comfortable with that. With whatever might come up. That's true for our group sessions, too, but I like to start one-on-one, to make sure you're at ease."

"All right."

She waits, but Lucien doesn't know where to start.

"We can begin elsewhere. Why don't you tell me a bit about how you came here."

He wonders just how much was culled from the memories they collected to remake him. What she saw while he was blinded by the bright. Or had she simply read some mundane summary? A list of the things that make it hard to wake up. The abridged version.

"Maybe you could tell *me*," he says.

"Well, I know about your mother. That you chose to keep your memories of her in your treatment, as is. You chose to keep everything as is."

"I did."

"And why wouldn't you? You love her."

"I do."

"I also know that you blame yourself. I know that's why you came to Los Angeles."

Lucien shifts in his seat, but she doesn't look away.

"I came to Los Angeles to help my grandmother," Lucien says evenly.

Dr. Sloane's eyes shift.

"Tell me about your grandmother, then. What do you remember of her?"

"Oh god, not a lot," Lucien says. "I spent time with her maybe twice that I can remember, but I was so young that those memories are almost gone."

"Of course," says Dr. Sloane, studying his face. Then she writes something in her notebook for the first time. "A child's relationship to the past is often built on two people's memories; they rely on another's to plant the very seed that gets remembered as if it were their own. Like with photographs, too."

"Right, well, we didn't have those either."

"Tell me about those times, then."

"She came to New York once, before my dad left, when I was—"

Lucien remembers wetting the bed a few times, the disorienting dampness and the following shame. His father was either gone or smoldering, and his mother was falling apart. He hasn't thought of that period in years, but here it is crisp like a freshly developed photograph. Lucien watched his mother then, waiting to see if pieces might actually come undone; things he knew as constants—her smile, her smell—fell away. Even the floor felt unstable. Then one day his grandmother appeared—moreover, existed!—and packed him a bag.

"And how was it, when she came?"

"She took me away and things felt normal again, or like there was another world still working normally outside of ours, which was nice. It was nice, I guess. But yeah, like you said, afterwards I felt like maybe I imagined it because my mother hardly asked, hardly mentioned it. And I didn't hear from my grandmother again, not until we visited her in LA years later."

"Do you remember where she took you?"

"Disney World, if you can believe it."

"In California, it's Disneyland."

"She took me to Florida."

Dr. Sloane blinks, unmoved.

"I guess it's only funny if you knew my mom. I'm not convinced my grandmother hated it any less, but it was probably the nicest thing you could do for a kid. She gave me this Mickey Mouse stuffed animal from Animal Kingdom that I slept with every night until my mom found it and I think threw it away. One day it was just gone."

"That sounds hurtful, to lose something you cherished."

"You have to understand something about her, my mother; she kept out all these things, but there was so much in their place. Disney, she thought, was the commodification of childhood, a funneling of our collective values. So—there was no Disney in our house. But one rainy day, she papered the walls of our living room and then painted this underwater scene with fish and sharks and coral for me to play in. She left it up for months, we built a cardboard submarine. She was against some things because she could do them better. I had an incredible childhood."

"But you were also facing things like an adult might. The loss of your father."

The irony was that Lucien's father leaving gave his mother the success she'd been working toward for years. She buried herself in painting and never really stopped. She translated her pain into brilliance. Lucien never took it personally, that just the two of them translated to a loneliness she could only see out of if facing a canvas. He was proud of her; he felt like fuel to her fire. He chose to.

"I never felt like a kid, I guess. Even when I was little, I was encouraged to think. I hung out with her friends. I don't think that was a bad thing. If the alternative is being sat in front of cartoon movies with princesses whose only dream is to be saved."

"And yet you said that toy was your favorite."

"I'm sorry, do you get extra points for every time my mother is at fault? She did her best. What does it matter what some stupid stuffed toy meant to me as a kid? I also would've liked to eat Sour Patch Kids till my tongue fell off, but I couldn't do that either."

"You're very protective of her. It's clear you loved her, you're grateful to her. But you can still talk about her freely, here with me."

"What if I don't want to?"

"Fine. What does it feel like here, then? To be without your name, without all the things she gave you?"

"I still have a name. You probably know it. You can say it."

"It's important that we don't. You exist in this time, free to rebuild and reconstitute what makes you, without those things that have been put on you. Only one of them is a name."

"Honestly, those things that have been put on me are one reason I'm anxious to get out of here. I moved to help my grandmother, yet here I am."

Again, Dr. Sloane writes something in her book.

"What was it like, then, to see your grandmother as an adult?"

"Different," he says easily. "Like I said, I visited her one other time, when I was twelve or something, but otherwise our relationship was pretty limited. Even so, I always felt a connection with her. She and my mom were so alike they almost couldn't stand each other. I got the sense that it made my grandmother proud. Not sad. I dunno."

"Was it helpful, being with her again?"

Now Dr. Sloane looks like she's searching for something he won't give her.

"I came to help *her*."

"Have you?"

"Not yet."

Again, another note. Another glance.

"Honestly, I'm not sure I've done much at all. I actually tried . . . No, never mind."

"Go on."

"When I first got to LA, I tried to find a stuffed animal like the one she gave me years ago. I think that's why I thought of that trip just now. I hoped seeing it again might help her remember something, too. Maybe even me."

"And did it?"

He pictures his grandmother's alert but blank stare looking back at him. Hard plastic.

"What do you think?"

"I think it's interesting that you went there."

A moving mosaic of tiny heads, all different hair colors and textures, shuffled around the Disney Store, their hands tugging at shirts and pant legs, while the parents, nannies, and chaperones squinted at their phones. Everything about it struck Lucien as failure. Children, occupied with cute capitalism, while their parents wanted to be anywhere else. His mother understood; what children need is to be included, not a pyramid of rabid-looking plush fish. Giant eyes and smiles lined with white felt.

Dr. Sloane writes again in her notebook.

"Do you think about New York?" she asks without looking up.

"I try not to. I find it hard. After my mother—well, even the way the air was just starting to turn colder, the leaves of the maple on our old block turning red—I couldn't take it. How everything was proceeding just the same."

"And here?"

"Here at least nothing is the same."

Dr. Sloane licks her finger and swipes a few pages back in her notebook.

"Perhaps you weren't aware of how precise we can be, in your treatment. How we could have removed that last bit; kept your mother minus the guilt. That burden you carry. The how."

"I am aware."

"But you chose not to change a single thing. I think that says a lot."

"I guess I don't think we get to choose what happens to us," he says. "What we carry."

"And you'd be right—until recently. You see, we do get to choose."

"I think you're confusing my words," Lucien says. "I don't doubt that you have the ability. I don't think it's ours to choose."

"I understand. Then again, let's say Jane Doe is walking home from work one night. Jane Doe gets assaulted. Now Jane Doe can hardly sleep, let alone walk outside by herself. Does she really deserve a life of fear? Of constant trauma? Does she deserve to carry that forever?"

"No, of course not."

"And yet, such is her fate. Unless we help her forget."

"Sure, that seems—well, that only seems fair. To have the option."

"Exactly," she says. "The option."

"Right," he says. "I'm just saying, not for me."

Lucien feels like he is getting a hard sell for something already forgone. He made his decision. And he would do anything to avoid repeating that first night after his treatment. The emptiness he felt inside and beside himself.

"Why do you think you've had such a hard time letting go?"

"Excuse me?"

"Of your mother."

"What do you mean? She's my *mother*."

"*Was* your mother."

"Is it helpful to be cruel?"

"I'm sorry," Dr. Sloane says. "Is it cruel to ask you about yourself? To not make this about your mother, but about what *you* need now, to feel whole?"

"She will always be my mother. I'm not trying to let go of that."

"And I'm not taking her away. But I'd like to talk about you. So, without talking about her, why might *you* be having such a hard time letting go?"

Lucien no longer feels he is talking to someone human. How can he be expected to explain why he is sad? The sadness is enough, without opening it up to examine it. Is she doing this to push him? Toward what?

"I don't have to explain to you why that is hard."

"Of course it's normal to grieve the loss of a parent. But need I remind you that here we are, sitting in a rehabilitation center because you needed, so desperately, to escape yourself that you endangered your own life, and so the *question* I am asking you, is—why?"

"I have no idea."

"Try."

"I just—maybe I don't know who I am without her."

Dr. Sloane nods.

"Close your eyes, go there. Go inside."

Lucien closes his eyes and waits.

"Am I meant to be speaking?"

"Sure, whatever comes up," she says, her voice now noticeably different. Coaxing.

"I spent most of my life feeling both in awe of my mother and paralyzed by her. And I got so used to needing to take care of her. I had to."

"Why did you need to take care of her, your parent? Was she incapable of caring for you?"

Lucien opens his eyes.

"No, she always took care of me. But when my dad left, I felt like I was all she had. And I could make her so happy. And when she was happy she was *so* happy. It was . . . pretty amazing actually. I've never met someone who could be like that, so sad but then that much happier than anyone else. It's addictive, almost, making someone that happy. I think. Especially when you know the alternative is despair."

Lucien feels he is being led somewhere, but he keeps talking, keeps finding the words to figure it out.

"How did it feel, to be left by your father?"

"Well, not great. I guess I tried to be easy, for my mom."

"Did you ever feel unwanted?"

"God no," he says. "Look, I was a kid. It was hard for a little, but we got into a rhythm, and she was the best. She was talented and charismatic. Everybody loved her. Even strangers wanted to be around her. But you know, it's like—what's a kid with a parent like that supposed to do?"

Lucien notices Dr. Sloane wince as he talks about his mother, and he wonders if he is so pathetic to her that she cannot hide it. What must he look like from the outside?

"What do you mean by that?"

The more she pushes, the more he wants to crawl inside himself.

"Nothing."

"Go on, you've clearly thought about this."

"Well, either you hate them and resent them for attracting so much light that there's nothing left at all, or you're attached to them for life. You're a half-person. I became like this other piece of her. And then when she got sick, all that other fun stuff sort of went away. But I was still a piece of her and she was, you know . . . without. She needed me."

"And what about what you needed?"

"What did I need? I was just preparing for college when she first got sick. And then better again. Each time we just wanted to get through it, so we did. Whenever the cancer came back, there was nothing else I would have done instead. I was on pause."

"And now?"

Lucien looks around, his answer in the quiet between the walls, the thick glass keeping out everything but the light.

As Lucien walks back to the common area, he sees the same girl from yesterday standing alone by the fireplace, another mug in hand, tea string hanging over the rim. The room is scattered with only a few patients; others have gone to their rooms, or to afternoon meditation. But the common area is more open than the rest of the Center, with its walls of glass and infinite ocean. People seem to linger.

Lucien still cannot place her in his memory. More details come back, more memories solidify, but nothing explains this electric feeling around her. She does not seem to notice him approach. Even as he stands nearby, her eyes rest on the flickering flames. She looks so calm in this foreign, blank place that it frightens him.

"I could swear I know you," he whispers.

She turns, her eyes frantic for an instant.

"You can't."

"What—swear, or know you?"

He sits on the stone ledge and turns toward her. Something inside of him rises at the sight of her. Knowing her or not, it feels like hope.

"Either."

There it is again, recognition rippling through him at the sound of her voice, the movement of her hand. He touches his hair, pulling a curl between two fingers. Pulling at something he can't quite access. What moments were left out? he thinks, searching back to that room where the many pieces of him were put back in.

"That's why you're here, isn't it?" she says absently.

"I guess so."

She picks a petal from the dried arrangement beside the fireplace and flicks it into the flames. Then she blows on her tea. Lucien's eyes linger on the tea string delicately looped under her finger until he notices where one of the bandages on her arm is missing; tight, raised skin flickers across the inside of her wrist.

She must feel his eyes on the marks because she jerks her arm away.

The tea spills and she gasps at the burn. Lucien gets up to find napkins at the nearby coffee cart, but when he turns she is another beige figure disappearing down the hallway.

He wonders if she remembers him, if she knows she is not meant to. Or is her reticence just a symptom of this place, where no one is meant to share much of anything?

Alone in their isolation, together.

This feeling could be a false recognition, his body readjusting to stimulus, however sparse. Or simply remembering the feeling of someone new, the excitement of a pretty face. His mind searching for something to grasp on to, for some victory that might kick-start the recovery those at the Center keep promising.

He wanders over to the farthest glass wall, where a quiet mist blurs the beach into a tan cloud. The man in the wheelchair who'd first sat beside him in the circle is facing the ocean, his hands resting in his lap. His eyes appear focused. Unlike the others here, who often seem frantic, this man has a sense of calm that draws Lucien to him. If he is distracted, it is only by his own peace.

Lucien follows his gaze out to the water, past where the waves break, and watches. Just before he thinks to give up, a spray of white erupts from the glassy ocean. The man's face softens for a moment, and his lips stretch into a slight smile.

"They come in groups," he says without turning. "There'll be another."

"A whale?"

"Gray whale, or could be a humpback. Now, that'd be something."

As predicted, another spray appears a short distance from the first. Then the splash of a large dark mass.

"She's breaching!"

Lucien feels a purity of joy coming off the man's enthusiasm; he has not felt it in quite some time. The intrusion of nature on such a pristine, controlled environment. He thinks he sees a hand rise out of the corner of his eye, possibly to wipe away a tear, but now Lucien cannot move his eyes from that spot on the sea either. A wide, flat tail flips up and creates the biggest splash yet, disappearing again behind the froth.

"Fuck," says Lucien. "I could watch this all day."

The man looks over, as surprised by Lucien's enthusiasm as he is.

"I do."

The man holds out a hand and Lucien takes it, though neither of them do the thing that happens next, the courtesy of giving the other a name by which to call them.

What no one mentions is that a name is a place in your memory, nothing more. Like a label for the filing cabinet, it keeps things tidy. And it recognizes that there will be a folder. We say we are "committing someone's name to memory," but that isn't it. We're committing to the fact that they will have a place in our memory, and that place is marked by their name. Lucien always thought himself bad with names, even resented the embarrassments and unintentional insults forgetting them results in. But how he misses them now.

"Whole thing's a bit awkward," says the man.

"You said it."

"I tell you what, what I like to do is this. We shake, and we look at each other's eyes."

He takes Lucien's hand in his again, then places his other hand over it. His hands are warm. Then he stares into Lucien's eyes, deeper than Lucien feels comfortable, yet he lets him. There is a kindness here, in being seen.

"Now you remember something about me—and you name it."

Lucien opens his mouth, but the man interrupts.

"Don't say it," he says with a grin. "Save it, that's yours. That's me for you. I've got mine. I've got you now."

The man taps his temple, then looks back out to the ocean. Lucien watches with him for what must only be another few minutes, but he is not yet trained in this act of waiting that the man seems to have mastered. He will not tell him this, but Lucien committed not a name but a snapshot to memory. A visual label. The man's eyes, opening against his smile. A squinting kindness.

When Lucien starts to say goodbye, the man's eyes are closed, and Lucien thinks he sees one of his feet twitching from deep in sleep. He wonders how long he's been in there; at the Center but also in his chair. What memories circulate behind his eyes? Lucien thinks how, depending on the present, memory can be an escape—or torture.

Running, walking, jumping, when all you can do now is wait.

Chapter 7

BEFORE

Here are a few things Lucien knows. You can be someplace and gone at the same time. Sitting with his grandmother feels no closer than being across the country all these years. Holding her hand will not shock her back to clarity. And lineage is not a superpower.

Here's another thing. Los Angeles is lonely if you're alone.

New York should be, but it isn't. Lucien walked through and out of his loneliness countless times in New York. He always felt held by the city. Perhaps it was the height, though the same was true in Manhattan or Brooklyn, on a busy avenue or a low-lying cobblestone block. Even in his lowest moments—his mother sick, friends not getting it—Lucien appreciated the community of strangers. Everyone in Los Angeles seems to begrudge everyone else for being here at all. For contributing to the traffic. In New York the people were the place.

As he lies on the new mattress in this new apartment—the first place he's ever had to himself, paid for by loss—his mind is back in New York, staring at both past and present, imagining where else he could be in this same moment. What else could have been? His life and apartment here in Los Angeles feel like someone else's. None of its smells are yet his own.

The other day Liv from the juice store–slash–café below his apartment invited him to a Halloween party. God knows why she asked him, beaming with an energy that actually made him smile. If he was unsure of going to a stranger's house party, at the invitation of someone he barely knows, he is more unsure of who he will be at the end of another week spent alone in his apartment. Lucien is tired of waiting for his life to resume. He's tired of giving up, over and over again. Tired of finding himself in a place that feels entirely wrong, yet doing nothing to change.

From his car Lucien squints against the darkness descending on Beachwood Canyon as every turn takes him higher into the hills. The streets twist like coiled rope, getting narrower and more overgrown until even the curbs become nonexistent. Around one sharp curve, the backlit HOLLYWOOD sign reemerges from behind the landscape, freshly typed across the night sky. Houses appear up and down from each treacherous bend, with glowing pumpkins on doorsteps lighting the way. A few more turns and Lucien's navigation cuts out. He guesses the next, one after another, until he is suddenly descending, and the same fairy-tale stone gates he had passed moments earlier announce that he is leaving Historic Hollywoodland—the storied neighborhood where, true to its vintage, all cell phone reception seems to vanish.

A missed call from moments ago lights up his screen. Natasha, his dealer, again.

A car honks and speeds around him. Lucien creeps right onto Cheremoya Avenue, wondering where he went wrong. *One more try and then I give up*, he tells himself, soothed by the idea of bailing. He turns around, then heads back toward the stone gate. He taps to resume the navigation while he still has service, his car once more pitched to climb.

Lucien doesn't even like Halloween. The last time he really dressed up, he must've been five. He remembers standing on the sidewalk, his ears turning numb where they stuck out from his cowboy hat, as he kicked his boots through the piles of leaves filling the spaces between tightly parked cars. *Kissing*, as his mother liked to describe their bumpers. He remembers the sight of his parents that night, illuminated behind the giant stained-glass window on the first floor of their castle-like walk-up that looked so out of place in Prospect Heights, with its tiled roof and bright blue door among rows of uniform brownstones. Its stained glass like lace laid over thick amber. The beauty of that window was simple; it obscured people on the inside. The curve of its decorative lines detached heads from necks, warped familiar figures into funny shapes, even made it hard to discern laughter from tears, or struggle from embrace.

Even now, twenty-some years later and across the country, Lucien could trace that window's delicate lines in his memory. *This window*, his mother told him one day after his father left, *was left over from a princess who used to live here long ago, before there was even a city, or anything but this house. She stared out of it, too, wondering what was next. Back when it was ten times the size of what's left here now. This little piece that's ours to look after. Isn't it exciting, to have something to look after?*

Lucien still hears her voice in his head. He shakes her away. Passing home after home, lit up from inside, it occurs to him that if he returns to theirs in Brooklyn, he will see another family, their privacy now protected by its warm amber veil.

The thought of his childhood home, empty then filled with another family, hollows him. Could they have settled in enough by now to feel it their own? To forget that they are new to its history as they clear out all that it was? Before he loses himself entirely in that aching, the navigation sounds again, announcing the destination, and Liv's smile pops into his head. The way her pale blue eyes nearly disappear behind it; the golden fleck that dances behind them. The way seeing her makes him feel less like himself, and isn't that something?

Cars line the streets in all directions. The only other sign of a party is the roar of voices over music and what sounds like water splashing. Lucien barely makes out a door in the tall wooden gate that stretches an entire overgrown block. He checks the address again, then finds its skinny silver letters reflected in the glow of passing headlights. Hardly the backyard barbecue he was expecting. Lucien tucks the case of Red Stripe he brought under the passenger seat and smooths his hair.

Liv is the first person he sees once through the gate. She stands by the front door of the house with several people all in costume. The momentary relief of being in the right place quickly passes, as Lucien realizes she and her friends now have to watch him as he makes his way down the landscaped path toward the house. Is it too soon to wave? He smiles at his feet, convincing himself he's laughing at something funny that must have just happened.

"You came!" she says.

Liv leans in to give him a hug. She is wearing a blood-soaked prom dress, with handprints smearing the thick red paste across one of her cheeks and into her blond hair. The deep red color looks pretty, the same way red lipstick shocks a face into focus. Lucien scans the guys' faces to say hello, but neither looks his way.

"I know, Carrie—so cliché, right?" She fluffs her tulle skirt. "This is beet pulp though, so I like to think I made it my own."

Lucien smiles and nods, unsure of what else to say with the audience of strangers that refuse to look in his direction; unsure why he is still nodding. He now wishes he'd taken his own costume, a half-assed riff on a BuzzFeed meme, more seriously. He can't even look down at the dumb DIY T-shirt. At least the rest of it is still tucked in his back pocket. Maybe no one will ask.

"Hey, guys, look alive," Liv says pointedly. "This is Lucien, my new friend."

"Mark," says the shorter one dressed as Don Johnson, like he hadn't seen him before. He extends a pack of cigarettes in place of a handshake. "Fucking LA, man."

All right, here we go, Lucien thinks as he takes a cigarette.

"People don't even let you smoke on their decks anymore," continues Don Johnson, talking with the looseness and entitlement of someone with a few drinks in their blood. Unless that's just an LA thing. *Fucking LA, man.* "It's one thing inside the house, but half of this place is open-air. Like, smoke diffuses and shit."

Lucien takes a long drag, longing for that six-pack in his car.

"Now we're relegated to the front steps like fucking intruders or something." Don stamps out his cigarette. "I gotta get out of this place, man."

"Where are you from?" asks Lucien.

"Pacific Palisades."

Lucien laughs, then conceals it into a cough.

"But I live in Silver Lake."

Lucien turns to the other guy, dressed as the Dude from *The Big Lebowski*—bathrobe open over a white tee and loose pajama pants. It feels grossly intimate, for a first meeting.

"How about you?" Lucien asks.

"Silver Lake," says Lebowski under his breath.

"I'm not far from you guys, Echo Park."

Both of them start laughing. Don Johnson puffs on his cigarette, then watches the smoke curl from his mouth. "Dude, it's so over."

"It was over five years ago," says Lebowski. "But where do we even go?"

"Montecito Heights? Even Highland Park, man."

"Fuck that noise, Highland Park is too far. I don't want to drive twenty-five minutes on the 110 just to get decent Thai. There, I said it."

"Dude, I hadn't even thought about that."

"No way in hell Jitlada will cross the LA River. Daddy needs his khao yam."

"You know I dated that girl over there for like four months—the model, with the voice."

"Oh god, I remember her," Liv says.

"I mean, she had a sick place with a sweet yard and a dog. I still miss that dog. But she always wanted to spend the night over there, and there was nowhere to eat."

"Right, you've got like two options. Maybe three."

"I need the hills," Liv says.

"Hills!" echoes Lebowski. "Yes, okay, obviously Liv gets it. Hills are key. They keep out the riffraff."

Lucien is tempted to turn around and walk right back up the hill, fading into darkness, and he would do it, too, if not for the awkward amount of time it would take to fully disappear.

Liv slaps Lebowski's bathrobed arm.

"What?" he says. "I'm sorry, but they do. Have you been to Venice lately? Loaded with riffraff. Flat as hell."

"You're a terrible person, Mick," Liv says, laughing.

Lucien watches Liv, considering the weight that such an early interaction holds. She is, maybe, not a great person. She also might have bad taste in people. Look who she invited tonight. Lucien freshly resents having been included. *From what she's seen*, he thinks, *I'm the worst. I sulk, I don't appear to work. I'm not friendly.* He knows that's not true, not usually at least. Lately, yes. But not *usually.* Worse still, is that what she likes about him?

"Look, I don't mean the homeless." Lebowski is still talking. "The homeless are the last thing saving Venice from becoming a basic-ass promenade. I'm talking blogger bitches and their dirtbag CrossFit boyfriends. No one in the industry lives in Venice. Nothing good, or at least intellectual, happens west of Fairfax. Tell me I'm wrong! Bel-Air— whatever, if you've got the money you can bring the culture to you. Malibu? Sure, why not, but also, like—who wants to fuck with the PCH?"

"Echo Park shoulda been it, man," says Don Johnson. Lucien feels like reminding them that that's where this rant first started. "They've got hills and it's still kinda dirty enough to keep out the Insta-models."

"Almost."

"You guys sure like neighborhoods," Lucien says sharply.

Don and Lebowski look at him with a mix of hatred and respect.

"It's all the same to me, honestly," he adds. "I just moved here."

"From where?"

"New York."

"Ah, man, well then, yeah." Lebowski squeezes his shoulder. "How you hanging in, dude? I lived in New York for a couple years."

"Me too, I did my time," says Don.

"Cool cool," Lucien says, amazed at how much conversation can be spent on place.

Moving on, moving on, he thinks, though he is pleasantly surprised by the momentary escape from his own thoughts. To be so completely consumed with pity for these goobers.

"Dude, where were you in New York?" says Lebowski to Don, and Lucien feels the entire conversation about to repeat itself.

He glances at Liv and is relieved when she smiles back knowingly. She flicks her cigarette butt into a patch of succulents.

"Ay!" says Don.

"Relax—they're like ninety percent water." Liv holds out her hand and Lucien takes it, following her through the front door.

"I'm surprised you smoke," he says from behind, into her ear. "With all the juice."

"I don't!" She turns, and her hair brushes his cheek. It smells like coconut and palo santo. "Never. Only when I drink."

The house sprawls beyond what its low, midcentury exterior suggested, with an addition doubling what must have been its original footprint. The interior space features open-air sections connecting the various pieces puzzled into the steep landscape. A large living area in the center is oriented around a hanging metal fireplace and interior landscaping extending out to an expansive deck. The wall of sliding glass is retracted for the party—or all the time, Lucien thinks, remembering where they are.

Beyond the deck is a sheer drop down the hillside. The view stretches past the Hollywood Hills and to the ocean in the distance, recognizable only by the absence of lights. Lucien takes in the vastness of this city, understanding something of those two guys with their need to define themselves within it. With the stars twinkling above and the lights of the city below, it looks like two skies mirrored across the horizon.

Halloween is playing on a large flat-screen just inside the open-air living room, Jamie Lee Curtis screaming in terror at Jason and his bad hair. The outdoor walls have been set up with projectors, too, so *Psycho*, *The Hills Have Eyes*, and *Scream* are playing on every surface, the actors' faces twisting in pain and terror while people at the party cluster. Laughing, hugging, catching up. Occasionally the silhouette of a partygoer crosses a projector's path, unknowingly catching the *Scream* mask stretched across their torso, or knives covered in blood against their back.

Lucien follows Liv through the living room toward the kitchen. Every piece of furniture is something reclaimed—driftwood for the dining room table, old industrial gym lockers at the bar area, an antique secretary in the hallway. The party itself appears to have already entered postproduction, with any awkward guests, spilled drinks, or costume flops retouched out of the scene. Even the costumes strike Lucien as well-curated. He tries not to think about his own, which would have been a hit at the casual party he imagined he was on his way to tonight. The kind of party where trying too hard would have been embarrassing, not the other way around. Here, he gets the impression there were entire costume departments at their disposal.

Dead ringers for Cleopatra and Charlie Chaplin mingle in the crowd. There's a young Tom Cruise, an old Tom Cruise, a very committed 2005 Tom Cruise standing on a couch and laughing hysterically. Hot cheerleaders, dead cheerleaders, and even the token Frida Kahlo or two. No, make that five.

"So, this is the Boy Next Door?" says a doe in a brown unitard and tights. On her nose is a black dot, surrounded by white face paint down to her mouth and more around her eyes. She touches her antlers as though twirling hair.

"This is Rachel," Liv says apologetically. "One of my oldest and least mature friends."

"Lucien."

"So, what are you?" Rachel asks.

"I'm a photographer."

"Sorry?" Rachel says. "Oh, no. I mean, what *are* you?"

He looks down at his white T-shirt, BUZZFEED spelled in glossy red tape.

"Oh, I'm a meme." He reaches for the cat ears tucked in his back pocket, then slips them on. The plastic headband is sharp behind his ears. "A cat meme."

Liv bursts out laughing, then makes a face that looks remarkably similar to one's actual reaction to a cat meme. Adorable laughter, with just a touch of pity.

"So what are you doing here, then?" says Rachel, speaking close and directly into Lucien's face. He smells the vodka on her breath. "Liv thinks you're a convict on the run."

"I do not," she says, barely laughing. "I don't."

"Oh, no that's okay," says Lucien. "Flattering really."

"I was just joking. I told Rachel that you—"

"She said, there's a mysterious new tenant above my shop," Rachel interrupts, as though doing Liv a favor. "What did you call him? A handsome loner? No, that wasn't it. Lonely? I can't remember."

"Christ, Rachel. We haven't even gotten drinks yet."

Liv's face is bright red, and not just from the beet pulp. Rachel closes her eyes to take a sip of her drink, and Liv pulls him away before she sees. As they walk, she greets everyone they pass with a sort of cheerful indifference. She is different here than Lucien's initial impression of her, and he realizes now that he got her wrong. He wonders if they had met here tonight, would Liv have spoken to him at all? Would he have wanted her to?

Finally, they find a quiet pocket beside the marble island in the kitchen, where shiny brass pots dangle overhead.

"Sorry about that," Liv says. "Some of these people! We all grew up together. Lots of us left LA, then came back. Casey, whose house this is, he just moved back."

"I can tell," Lucien says, deadpan. "I wasn't going to say anything, but it feels very . . . unfinished."

"Casual, right?" She laughs. "He'll move again in a year. I think he's trying to get married."

"To who?"

Liv shrugs.

Behind her head, a magician in a tuxedo makes a card disappear in plain sight and then finds it in Grace Kelly's clutch. The small audience cheers. Rachel walks by, though not before kissing Liv on the cheek and shouting something unintelligible. The kiss is so wet it smudges the beet pulp. Liv looks so embarrassed that now he feels sorry for her.

"Hey, I'd hate to be judged based on my friends from high school."

He thinks of George and Reggie sneaking forties onto the rides at Coney Island. Though he'd be there in a second.

"They're not all as bad as they seem. Rachel especially, she's just trying to impress you."

"Well damn, I'd hate to see her when she's not."

There are worse things than misplaced loyalty, he thinks. Some worse things, at least. Look at him. The only place his mind goes lately is to the past, to childhood. What kind of man does that make him now?

"Most everyone here knows each other—so you throw fresh blood into the mix and people start peacocking, you know? To show where they stand."

"What about dates?" Lucien hears the word before realizing he said it. "I mean, there must be lots of new people, all the time."

"Honestly, everybody just dates each other."

Lucien looks around the party, wondering which of them Liv has been with. Maybe one of the guys outside. Lebowski.

"Actually, I guess the guys are always bringing new girls," she continues. "But no one expects anyone to talk to those girls."

"And you like that? Only the same people all the time?"

Liv reaches for a carrot stick from the island. The carrots have been sliced to resemble stubby fingers, with slivers of almonds pushed into the ends like fingernails.

"I invited *you*, didn't I?"

She dips the end with the fingernail into something green and crunches off a bite.

"But no, nobody really likes it," she adds. "You just get used to it."

Get used to something long enough, Lucien thinks, and you'll forget whether or not you liked it to begin with. Just then, one of the Spice Girls trips over her shiny platform heel and spills sangria all over Liv's dress. Some even splashes up her neck.

"Oh my god," says Posh, sleek bob and pinched lips. "You daft twat!" Their British accents are painfully bad, but Lucien admires the dedication.

He whispers as Liv wipes off her soaked dress. "A bit on the nose, don't you think?"

She wipes her nose.

"No, I mean—the Carrie thing."

They both laugh and she leans into Lucien. He catches the smell of her hair again, and lets himself relax into the absence of anything else in his head for the first time in weeks.

The Spice Girls return with napkins, and Sporty bends over to mop up the floor. She is the one wearing sneakers and track pants, after all.

"Get her more towels, for fuck's sake," says Ginger, her lips outlined in brown pencil and filled in with glossy pink that makes her red wig appear orange. Baby Spice stands to the side, guilty. Her baby tee is splashed with red, too, but no one is helping her. She pouts, true to form.

"That's really enough," Liv says as Ginger dabs her tulle skirt. "Now you're just mopping off my costume."

The Spice Girls step back and laugh. "Oh my god, right on. Carrie, that is so spot-on."

Lucien walks around the kitchen, looking for supplies. One of his best party tricks is that he actually makes a great cocktail. Years of tending his mother's parties at home, learning the preferences of her very particular guests and friends. One sculptor only took his martini with a "breath" of lemon, whatever that meant. Another liked his Negroni with a slice of orange and an olive, but only if it was Castelvetrano—not to worry, he brought his own. Another poet always asked for a gimlet, but she specified vodka instead of gin and tonic instead of lime juice. Oh, to be so respected that you go on thinking your vodka tonic is a gimlet without ever being corrected.

This fridge has it all. The fancy, deep-burgundy cocktail cherries; glass small-batch-soda bottles and fresh juice mixers; an array of artisanal bitters on the countertop.

"What's your specialty?" asks Liv.

"How about a martini?"

"Oh, that's the kind of night this is going to be?"

"I can make you anything."

"Martini, please."

He finds a jar of fancy imported olives that look promising. Then he scans the liquor lineup and laughs when he sees a bottle of Nolet Reserve next to an empty bottle of Tanqueray. He once photographed a party at the Rainbow Room that went through five bottles of this special Nolet, retailing for $700 each. He never got to try it, and he can't imagine it's right for a martini, but fuck, if this guy puts out a bottle like that—

"Lucien! You have to meet a dear, dear friend of mine," Liv says. "Sophie, this is Lucien. Sophie is my loveliest and most talented friend!"

Long, colorful peacock feathers are stuck into the back of Sophie's leotard. Her makeup is drawn well outside her eyes, sparkling and merging where her nose begins, creating the effect of a shimmering beak below. Some of the sparkles have fallen to her cheeks, dewy from the crowd. And her hair is pulled up high into a tight bun.

"Oh my gosh, stop it," Sophie says, blushing.

She holds out a hand, gracefully, as if moving through water. Lucien notices a tattoo across her knuckles.

"Lucien is making us martinis," Liv says. "Do you want one?"

His mind starts to do the math. Sixteen shots in a bottle. Three shots in a drink. That's $131 a martini. He laughs, turning it into a friendly nod.

"I would love nothing more," says Sophie. "But I think I'm done. Early rehearsal tomorrow." She holds up an empty cup, and her long, lean muscles show every movement through the leotard. "You know they have a cocktail bar set up outside, right? With, like, three bartenders. There's an entire spritz station."

Lucien feels a cold sweat on his neck, shot glass full of Nolet, two more in the shaker. Was this not for the party? Jesus Christ, could he pour this back in without anyone knowing?

"Then we'd have to go back outside," Liv says. "Besides, Casey told me—help yourself to the drinks in the kitchen. And I want to taste yours, Lucien."

Then she turns back to Sophie, genuinely horrified. "Wait so, you have rehearsals the day after Halloween?"

"Super early, too," she says. "Auguste is really on my back lately. I think that means he likes me now? But it also means he won't let up until my pinky toe falls off."

Lucien looks at the Martini & Rossi extra-dry vermouth, hesitating. He pours the slightest dash, adds a handful of ice cubes, and shakes. Then he slips an olive each onto two wooden toothpicks from a sterling dish and places them in two wide glasses.

"Sophie is the most brilliant dancer in LA," Liv is still saying, over Sophie's protests. "She is the lead in LABC's next show, La . . . Sulphide?"

"Sylphide," Sophie laughs. "La Sylphide. I am, the sylph."

"And we'll be in the front row," Liv says. She glances at Lucien, suddenly shy. "I mean, I can't wait."

"Congratulations," Lucien says as he pours. "That's amazing. What's a sylph?"

"It's like a woodland fairy, a sprite of sorts."

"No big deal," says Liv.

"No pressure either, I imagine," offers Lucien.

"Exactly."

Liv looks between them. She reaches out a hand to Sophie's arm and strokes it to get her attention. "God, I miss you so much! I never see you," she says. "You look gorgeous, but what else is new."

"I've been swamped lately, with Chateau and rehearsals. I don't even remember how to socialize for real, off the clock. I should've dressed as a zombie tonight."

Watching Sophie among this crowd of false confidence and lubricated bravado is like watching a crane walk through stormwater. She makes tucking a strand of hair behind her ear look as profound as anything.

"Oh, the life of a beautiful and talented ballerina," Liv coos, catching his attention again.

He hands her a finished drink. Seven-hundred-dollar gin, chilled, with an olive.

"To new friends and old," Liv says before taking a sip. "Damn, that's good."

Just then another magician or James Bond rushes into the kitchen and grabs a spoon.

"What's with all the magicians?" Lucien asks.

"Casey's dad owns the Magic Castle," Liv says. "Literally every party is like this. His last birthday dinner at Gjelina, a magician pulled a card from the cake."

Sophie nods, confirming. "Ace of spades."

Toward the bottom of Lucien's glass, he really starts relaxing. He remembers what it's like to feel comfortable enough to own a room. Sophie brushes a stray wisp of hair from her face with ease as though watching herself in a mirror and then fans herself with the same hand as she shifts in place from foot to foot, which Lucien now notices are neatly turned out. Even standing flat, they look full of intention.

Lucien catches the delicate letters tattooed across her knuckles again, but attempting to read them upside down makes him feel even drunker. Has he eaten anything since breakfast?

"So what do you do, Lucien?"

"He's a photographer," Liv says, proud of what she learned only moments earlier.

"Haven't really been doing it much lately," he says.

"Lucien is from New York."

Sophie laughs. "Are you his West Coast rep?"

"Believe me, you don't want that job." Lucien finishes his last sip and sets down the glass. "I was a professional photographer in New York, parties and things. But my own stuff, too. I do sort of collage-meets-photography for my own work. I stretch and I skew."

Lucien listens to the words coming freely and haphazardly out of him. He hates describing what he did working parties during those years to people who weren't there; nothing could explain it. He either sounds like he's glorifying something sad, or like he had a pathetic job, bottom of the totem pole, when in fact, he'd made the rankings. Although anything is better than talking about his own art.

"Professional photographer," Liv says. "Like, weddings?"

"Not really. Have you heard of Max Yorn?"

"Of course," Sophie says, then to Liv, "He comes into the Chateau all the time. Nice guy. Cocky as hell, but not a total creep."

"I know," Liv corrects her in a way that adds a competitive edge to their conversation. "We used to see him out all the time in LA. Back when we went out, you and I."

Lucien notices a subtle tension he hadn't before.

"So wait, Lucien, you did the party circuit?" Liv says. "Did you know I lived in New York for a year? Or six months I guess, after I left Trinity. Maybe we crossed paths! Wouldn't that be sweet? Us babies at the same party?"

"Sure. Parties, galas, openings, shows, street style, all that shit," Lucien says. Then, noticing her disappointment in his answer, he adds, "We couldn't have crossed paths though."

"Why's that?"

"I'd remember you."

Liv and Sophie exchange looks, and he cringes inside at how easy it is sometimes to give people exactly what they want.

"What brings you to LA, then?" Sophie says. "Besides this lovely gal."

"Oh, no," Liv says. "He and I just met."

"Family," says Lucien. "My grandmother is sick—or at least, she isn't doing well. Alzheimer's. I don't recommend it. But as of recently, I'm her executioner. Wait, god no that's not right. Executor? Exec-utor. God, what is that word? I'm next of kin." Lucien suddenly feels extremely drunk.

"I'm so sorry," says Liv. "That's terrible."

"It must be hard to see her that way," says Sophie. "My grandfather had dementia. I was just a kid, but it was so hard."

Lucien feels suddenly defensive of his own lack of grief. He weighs the need to qualify it.

"I don't really know her that well anyway, to be honest." Does that make him sound worse? "Not since I was a kid, at least."

"What about your parents?" says Liv.

"My dad isn't around. This is my mom's mom—and she passed away recently."

He feels their faces shift, and his whole body or the floor or the earth itself trembles. He wonders for a moment if there was a way around this, another path for this conversation that doesn't end up here, but that thinking doesn't work in real time. Not when the alcohol is slowing down the pace of everything so you're already two steps behind. Has he been silent for too long now? Have they?

"Lucien, I'm so sorry," says Liv. "How recently?"

"Uhh." He hears his voice wavering and fights it. "About a month."

He tries to get the words out as quickly and flatly as he can, thinking about other things. His growling stomach. The spinning floor. The plastic cat headband indenting behind his ears. The spinning floor. His car. How will he get it home? He would give anything for someone to speak.

Liv reaches a hand to his forearm. Her body beside him feels different than moments earlier, when the space between them was charged with attraction, not sympathy. Lucien has hardly been touched, not really, since his mother's service, when he was so squeezed and patted by everyone that his body stopped feeling like his own. A rag doll for their grief more than anything. Liv's fingers are light and cool, but whatever quickened in him beside her is now still.

Suddenly the living room empties, the kitchen momentarily full of passing bodies.

"What the hell," says Sophie. "Where are they all going?"

A guy dressed in what Lucien figures could be the original Cowardly Lion costume, tattered and outdated, stops briefly. "Hud has Mem, some Olympic ski jumper from Nagano, 1998. Fuck me up, dude!"

Before any of them respond, the Tin Man—or woman—rushes alongside him, naked but for underwear, her entire body painted silver. She grabs his hand and then they're gone. Sophie and Liv look suddenly uncomfortable or displeased or both.

"What was that about?" Lucien asks. His first thought is a video, though that seems oddly specific, and would anyone be so enthusiastic for, what, Olympic memorabilia?

"Mem," says Sophie. "Are they not doing that yet in New York?"

"Not that I know of," he says, considering everything that could be another name for; meth, Molly, oxy . . .

"Bane of my existence," says Sophie. "It's all over the Chateau."

"And it's what, oxy?" says Lucien.

"Bless him," Sophie says to Liv.

"It's a new drug that delivers memories, consciousness and all," says Liv. "Apparently it's the ultimate escape. But what it *looks* like is someone cracked out and twitching on the floor, totally gone. Pathetic, really."

Liv throws back the rest of her martini as Lucien feels the floor shift again under his feet. He puts his hand on the marble island.

"I wouldn't touch it," she adds. "Hud can hardly keep his shit together. He's like a totally different person. It messes with your head."

"I'm sorry, are you talking about Memoroxin?" Lucien's palm is clammy against the cool marble. "My grandmother takes that for her Alzheimer's."

"No way," Liv says. "I mean, it's totally different for—"

"Well look," offers Sophie. "I'm sure it helps some people. Medically."

"Right, of course," Liv says.

Lucien pulls off the plastic headband and turns toward the sink. He runs his hand under cold water, then through his hair, over his face. If the Cowardly Lion, all six feet of out-of-shape, is on his way to experience the Olympic height of a ski jumper midair, who's to say someone upstairs or across the sparkling expanse beyond those living room doors isn't coasting through Lucien's grandmother's memories right now? Reveling in the things she held so private. Moreover, what would he feel, then, if he took one of her pills? Who might he see?

"Okay, I'm going to find what promises to be an extremely chic bathroom," says Liv. "And then let's get out of here. I don't even like being in the same house as that stuff."

"I'll walk out with you guys," says Sophie. "I meant to leave an hour ago."

Sophie and Lucien stand next to each other in silence. His mind is all over the place, trying to make sense of what this means for his grandmother, her treatment. Or selfishly, for him.

"Liv is the best," Sophie says finally. "How'd you guys meet?"

"I just rented the apartment above the juice place where she works."

Sophie laughs abruptly. She has a certain detachment Lucien thinks creative people possess, some better at hiding it than others. He is immediately drawn to and intimidated by it all the same; such people usually make him feel like everything he says is slightly misunderstood, unreachable by their sheer originality. It's a quality his mother possessed and did little to contain.

"Sorry, but the thought of her *working* in some juice store is so great," she says. "She owns that place, opened it last year."

"Oh yeah? I didn't realize. Wait, why is it funny?"

"No, sorry," Sophie says. "It's not funny, I'm a waitress, clearly I don't think that's funny. It's just . . . because of her dad, you know."

"Her dad?"

"Bob Kohn . . . of Paramour Pictures. The LACMA Kohn Wing."

Lucien rethinks their conversations, his reaction to the excess at this party. He remembers the free juice she brought him when they first met. His sad, empty apartment she had seen inside. Does she own his building? Suddenly it all feels embarrassing. Though of all people, Lucien understands hiding from a parent's success, wanting to define yourself outside of it. At least occasionally. But was he supposed to know?

"I just assumed, because everyone . . . Shit, I hate this stuff, please forget I said that. Or whatever, what does it matter! Liv is really the best. I don't even know what I'm saying, see what I mean? Zombie. I should not be allowed out."

Lucien laughs because she seems nervous. But even her anxiety is enchanting. Then he hears a cheer from upstairs. Liv reappears beside Sophie.

As they walk toward the front door they'd entered hours earlier, the entire downstairs is noticeably quieter. Lucien glances up the open staircase. He sees the fingertips of a hand curl, then relax, from around the corner on the floor.

Lucien wakes later to Liv tiptoeing across his bedroom, navigating the mess of cardboard boxes with one arm over her bare chest, the other out for balance. He is relieved that every canvas scattering the apartment is turned to face the wall, their wood frames catching the moonlight rather than his failed attempts at progress.

He watches her naked silhouette until the light disappears behind the bathroom door. He looks at the clock, *4:00 a.m.* However crazy that party had gotten, they were at his place by eleven. He has not slept so deeply in weeks.

He lets his eyes close as he waits for the light to reappear. When he opens them, her shape in the shadows is now etched in jagged tulle. Lucien would like her to stay. To sleep here beside him. There's a cold pocket now where her body had just been warm. And he is ashamed if she feels the need to flee. Had he made her?

"Hey," he says, and Liv jumps at the sound of his voice.

"Oh god, I thought you were sleeping."

"You're welcome to stay."

"Thanks?"

"Sorry, it looked like you were . . ."

"Oh, I just can't sleep naked," she whispers, tiptoeing back to the bed. "I get all sweaty, it's a whole thing. Scoot over."

She lifts the covers and pushes her tulle skirt underneath as she lies back down.

"You're going to sleep in that?"

"I am," she says, and kisses him on the cheek.

Lucien realizes now that he probably should've offered her something earlier, and he wonders at all the other things he hasn't done. But asking at this point feels effortful, and the tulle prickling against his leg doesn't feel as bad as he expected, nor does the starched, beet-crusted fabric against his chest that smells vaguely like vinegar.

Liv's body relaxes into his, and the stomach muscles she must have been holding in beneath his arm loosen, until her whole body becomes heavier on top of his. This is the part he dreads; not the closeness of it. But what happens next, now, when her body drifts deeper into sleep, twitching as she falls, reminding him of how human and simultaneously mechanical we all are. That there are places we must go, alone.

In the morning, there is a note beside Lucien in bed. Even Liv's handwriting is happy, each letter rounded and perfectly uniform, slightly italicized so even her scribble has an air of sophistication.

Had to run down to the shop, didn't want to wake you. Signed with a heart.

Lucien takes his time in bed, noticing the difference even alone—how it feels immediately better to have your day share the context of another person's. A new face with endless unimaginable thoughts behind it. Someone who, for a moment, makes him forget himself. He thinks back to what her friend said last night, what he had so little time to consider within the pace of party conversation. Later on, when he asked Liv where her place is, she said *in the Canyon*, which he took to mean Beachwood, though now he supposes there could be other canyons. When he suggested they could have gone to hers then, apologetically, her response was *But it's fun to stay here.* Or had she said *funny*?

He doesn't care if she judges him in some way. If anything, Lucien was feeling self-conscious about renting this place by himself with money from his mother's estate—with no job, not even working on his own art with all this free time. The idea of Liv finding this lifestyle less-than is a relief to the alternative.

Downstairs the sun is already lighting up the interior landing. The birds sing in overlapping loops all at once, and frenzied. Lucien slips outside, past the entrance to Liv's shop. He wants fresh air and to feel a bit more space between her note and his showing up. What if she had just written it, and then there he is already? Outside the grass and palms and blue sky look overexposed in the sun's bleaching light. He squints, but it hardly helps. It's a brightness that feels like noise.

Lucien walks over to the jacaranda tree in the yard, its shade mirrored by indigo-blue flowers dusting the grass. He lights a cigarette, savoring the first breath. From there he sees into Astral Bodies through the large bay window. Liv is behind the marble counter talking to another girl. She looks elated, comfortable. He enjoys the bump of adrenaline at seeing her again. Whatever happens, it's worth sleeping with someone new just for the distraction.

The other girl turns to look at one of the shelves. Liv's friend from last night. The peacock. Liv appears to be preparing a smoothie of some sort, pulling down an assortment of glass jars one after another and scooping powders using a fancy gold spoon, while her friend rises to her toes then slides back and forth between each foot. She tilts her head, dark hair cascading down her back, as if Liv is coaxing her into something, then she tucks her face into her open palms.

Liv pushes the concoction toward her on the countertop—an offering—and her friend steps back, fanning her hands. Her ribs expand in her thin T-shirt and she lifts both arms into two arcs overhead, then turns her head to look over her shoulder. Lucien steps sideways, away from the window. When he looks again, she is on her toes, heels rising up and down as her body remains unmoved. She seems to float. Liv smiles, hands clasped at her heart.

The friend raises both heels and freezes, suspended in the air. Then one leg taps and lifts, and she spins so fast he can hardly make out her face. Her hair rises, all around her. He wonders for a moment if she sees him, caught in a glance as she turns.

Lucien finishes his cigarette and tosses it in the empty soup can he's left outside the door. He wonders if his landlord has noticed. Liv's face lights up when he walks into the shop.

"Good morning," he says, "and hello again."

He leans in to kiss Liv's cheek and catches her friend's eye. He wonders again if she might have seen him outside. Even in the daylight, away from the stress of a party, she makes him nervous, though not in a bad way.

"Long time," she says. "Sophie."

She smiles coyly at Liv just before her mouth and nose disappear into the glass jar full of her frothy blue drink. Clearly Liv told her about last night, after the party. Liv rolls her eyes, loving the attention. Enjoying the quiet awkwardness.

"I was just on my way out," he says. "But I wanted to say hey."

Liv leans into him now, her own *Hey* back, and stretches her arm around his neck. Her hair smells like coconut and sandalwood, and Lucien has a flash to last night, on top of her upstairs; her cheek, impossibly smooth against his neck, her breath in his ear. His own, quickening.

He catches his face in the mirror across the room, his cheeks ruddy like they get when he's excited, or embarrassed, and his hair is dangling into his eyes and in every direction.

"What're you up to today?" Liv says, swirling the metal straw in her drink.

"Just a bunch of different things," Lucien says. "I'll catch you later."

He palms down a few rogue curls, waving as he heads out like he has somewhere to go.

Chapter 8

TODAY

Lucien can't sleep. He slips through dreams like falling through floorboards, landing with a rattle on that same metal table in the blinding brightness. He wakes sitting up, over and over, then throws his body into the mattress to interrupt the loops. Alone in the dark, his mind twists itself back to places he wishes not to go.

He hears the faint scratch of paintbrush on canvas. First like a rhythm in the background, one sweep then another, a smaller tap, another sweep, and then it takes a rhythm of its own. When he opens his eyes, he's six, asleep underneath his mother's easel.

He lies there watching her eyes from below the wooden frame. They narrow and soften, staring at the canvas. Her head tilts. It's such an intense focus that he savors the moment, the feeling of having all her gaze. Seeing what she looks like to her work. She sighs and pushes her hands through her hair, fluffing it at the crown. Then she fans a hand, disregarding her last strokes. Lucien scoots back until he sees only her feet and her shins, and he stares up at the back of the canvas, sheer where light hits the places she hasn't yet touched.

Lucien was sick, vomiting all night, but now in daylight being home with his mother is enchanting. As if he, invisible, gets to witness her everyday routines without him. It feels like a superpower.

Suddenly her face appears beneath the easel, a wave of her hair sweeping the floor.

Come on, Luce, she says, *are you hungry?*

The thin sheet tangled at his legs makes him feel claustrophobic, and when he wakes up, Lucien suddenly feels like he needs to get out of that bed, that room, the Center. When he gets to the closed door, he is surprised to find it unlocked. He must not have checked before. He walks into the dim hallway, lit by moonlight from the atrium in the distance. As he approaches the common space, he finds a blood moon overhead. The fireplace burning from the top down. He walks toward the glass wall where he stood with the man in the wheelchair. He stares out at the now-dark sea. How different it looks at night. How much deeper, how endless.

In the daytime there are enough other people—even if blank, forever strangers—to distract him. But the pain sits back, rests, and waits for its time alone. His pain is nocturnal. He understands now why all their activities end at sunset; everything feels less threatening in the day. With his memory replacement, there is a freshness to Lucien's past. His mother's death is no longer buried where he imagines it was; now he has to dig it up and swallow it, jagged, all over again. In the daylight Lucien knows that pain is just the pills, the therapy working, and that his body will soon learn how to hide it, where to put her again. But what if he had not been able to before, and that is why he ended up here? Will he continue, over and over, to bury the thing that swallows him whole?

Lucien sits in one of the Wassily chairs facing the sea. The flat leather draped over the metal frame is not particularly comfortable, but familiar at least; they had one in their living room in Prospect Heights, where his mother benefitted from high-end discards from artist friends whose tastes predated the popularity. He lets his body relax into the suspension, his head falling back until his neck rests on cold metal, and blood fills his head.

Over the pulsing pressure—or inside it, he can't tell—Lucien hears a voice. Then another. He pulls himself upright, and a hush follows the waves as the throbbing subsides. Dizzy, he waits. He hears the first voice again. He presses his hands to his ears, but the whispers are not from inside. His first thought is of getting caught outside his room; going back on that cold bright table. He slips into the closest hallway off the common area, in the direction away from his room. A door is cracked open, and a plane of light stretches toward him. He's gone closer, not farther; then the murmurs turn to words and he cannot help but listen.

"I'm fully aware of the history, of the source of her disturbance."

The voice is Dr. Sloane's. He approaches the sliver of light, careful not to let his foot cross it. His back and hands slide against the wall.

"Don't you think it poses a risk to other patients," says another, "to have someone in her state roaming with the same freedoms—"

Lucien tries to recall all the female patients he has seen, but he only remembers the one. There could be others in private, locked rooms reserved for those who are a threat to themselves. Perhaps the girl's beauty is a Trojan horse, bearing a dangerous interior. He remembers the scars along the inside of her forearm.

"I don't think she's a risk to anyone but herself," Dr. Sloane says. "She's been cleared twice. She's clean."

"Then why are the fits—"

"Look, I don't know, we don't know. But she's clean. She just needs more time."

Lucien notices the tension in their conversation. The unspoken fear. He holds his breath, afraid to leave now in case moving makes a sound. He scans the upper corners for a camera. His heartbeat throbs in his ears.

". . . it's becoming a liability, the level of sedatives . . . we can't keep—"

"What would you have me do? Send her out? You're worried about other people. Well, we have control here; we have containment. She would be a press nightmare."

He hears an alert, or a buzzer, and then footsteps approaching the doorway until the sliver of light widens, and then he is leaping long and low around the corner into the common area and back to his own hallway. He slides into his bedroom and closes the door behind him. His heart beats so fast his ribs ache. Two sets of footsteps pass his door. Lucien opens it and watches as they hurry down the hallway and turn the corner.

He knows he should get back into bed, take another supplement and let that calm him into some lonely sleep. He tiptoes down the hallway anyway, telling himself he can always turn back. He can't close his eyes again, not yet. Not when his insides feel so blurry.

He turns the corner. From behind another door comes a shriek and Lucien hears a struggle. The rustling of bodies. He steps back to hide himself, then leans forward to see two men in white lifting someone parallel to the floor. Her. The girl is being held in the air, her legs writhing to get free, as a nurse and Dr. Sloane stand beside her.

His first thought is desperate. They're hurting her.

Dr. Sloane places her hand on the girl's restrained arm and says something to her, but the girl twists—a flash of ugly urgency in her face—and she manages to bite the male nurse's arm. In the chaos, Dr. Sloane looks up, right at Lucien at the end of the hallway. He jumps back behind the corner, and when he looks again, one of the men pulls a needle out of the girl's arm and her legs dangle limp.

Lucien waits a few beats, expecting to see Dr. Sloane walking toward him now, but when he looks he sees the four figures proceeding toward the staircase at the end of the hall, still holding the girl horizontally. Once they turn, Lucien follows. At the stairway, marked RESTRICTED, he stops. Rests his head against the cool glass. Then he pushes open the door.

At the bottom of the stairs is a corridor, with two rooms off either side. He follows the voices and peers through the window in the door. A metal table, just like the one he remembers, in the middle of the bright room, the same bright room. Lucien's breath feels short and acidic. Inside the nurse rubs gauze across the girl's skin and then places sticky pads along the trail. Two on her forehead, two across her chest, just below her clavicle. More on her arms and on her legs, where the nightgown has been hiked up. Her arms and legs sprawl, motionless, until one of the nurses fixes them.

The nurse who had been with Dr. Sloane before places an oxygen mask over the girl's face—her beautiful face that, moments earlier, was snarling, enraged—and strokes back her hair. Suddenly, the girl gasps and tries to rise, then shrieks because she can't. Dr. Sloane turns from across the room and calls something Lucien can't hear. Another shot in the girl's forearm. The same nurse holds her head while her body relaxes.

Lucien turns away. He considers going back to his room. He shouldn't be here, but he looks again. Now a small machine is positioned beside the metal table, beside her. There is something plastic in her mouth. Suddenly the girl's torso thrusts up several inches. Lucien braces for the screaming, the shrill cries, but instead there is only an eerie, heavy silence. Her body rises and falls. One leg, then another. Then her shoulders. The heavy, silent thud of her. Like a horizontal puppet triggered as they watch, unmoved.

Lucien wants to burst in. His hands are fists. He could pretend to be having an incident himself, an emergency. Anything to interrupt them. Just as he works up the nerve to scream, the door opens into him, and two familiar eyes appear through the glass.

Lucien sits inside the office where only moments earlier he had lurked outside the door. He faces Dr. Sloane at her desk, her dark hair shining almost white beside its lamp. She watches him for longer than feels natural. Then she sighs and shuffles a few papers. The persona from their sessions has been shed for someone entirely human—and exhausted. He should be on edge, more so now than when hiding earlier, but he's not. He even feels a stability returning to his consciousness. This is what he needed to reconstitute a self, someone else to worry about.

"I know what you think you saw," says Dr. Sloane.

"Do people know you're doing that here?"

Lucien feels self-righteous, and it feels good. He is a patient, but he is not powerless.

"Everything you saw tonight is part of that patient's treatment and has been agreed upon, by her, in prior discussions," says Dr. Sloane. "I get it, electroconvulsive therapy has a bad reputation from decades ago when it was administered without proper anesthesia and restraints. And without patient consent. Would you be more comfortable if I showed you her signature?"

No names, Lucien thinks at this empty offer.

"What about side effects?"

"Like what, memory loss? Confusion?" Dr. Sloane tilts her head. "I don't think you understand her situation. Any memory loss from ECT would be a *blessing*. That would be progress. We're shocking her back to life, doing whatever we can to let everything else fall away. We can replace any memories of hers that are affected in the process, that's the easy part."

"I don't understand, she seems—"

"Certainly it isn't lost on you that one might seem one way from the outside. She is struggling, that's all I'll say. Don't trouble yourself, we're doing everything we can for her."

"It just doesn't seem fair."

"Well, very little in life is fair, is it? Grief touches down like a tornado. It ravages one person while sparing others around them. I know it can be hard to reconcile, the seemingly random nature of suffering. But I don't have to tell you that, do I?"

"I guess not."

"I've seen you two. I've seen you watching her."

He hesitates to explain, or even suggest he might have known her before. What does he know for certain, anyway? He can't remember. Their meeting must have been mundane if it didn't show up in his memory for anyone to take notice. So why should he mention it—what if then they could no longer see one another, even in the common spaces? Blocked before he even gets a chance to remember.

Just then, a chirpy rhythm interrupts the silence of the room. The vibration on the table and the tinny sound of its tune trigger something familiar in Lucien. His hand twitches by his side, hungry for its own.

"Darling, are you home?" Dr. Sloane whispers into her phone. "I'm sorry, I had to come in. I left you dinner. Oh, all right."

Lucien considers a partner on the other end of the line, and Dr. Sloane's face comes into focus. The softness around her cheeks, and the crinkled skin around her eyes where laughter must have once passed.

"Sorry," she says, putting the phone down. "Children."

"Yours?"

"If you can imagine. Everyone here thinks they're my children. It's just the one, but she's a handful. She's supposed to be at college. God forbid anything go as planned."

"Supposed to?"

"She lost someone, a boyfriend," she says dismissively, then catches herself. "He took his own life, and apparently her future with it. I'm sorry, I shouldn't be telling you this. It's entirely inappropriate." She pauses. "And yet, it's related, is what it is. You need to take care of *yourself*. Look out for you, no one else will."

Lucien fidgets in his seat. The way she looks at him, the way she sees him.

"I know you," she adds. "Don't forget. I know you've been taking care of people—or a person—for a very long time. And now here you are, in the midst of recovery, already setting yourself up to start that again. All for a stranger."

Lucien wonders how she could have missed their connection. Or is this part of the game? Is she trying to get him to say it? Does she already know? She has seen everything he has inside of him, if she paid attention. And yet he resents the implication that her access gives her any say. He never asked to be told who he is or how to live his life. His life. His.

"I understand," he says, "but you're right, I don't even know her. We sit next to each other occasionally in the common area. As does everyone else."

"You're doing very well here, you know," says Dr. Sloane. "Though the complications from taking a relative's Memoroxin are considerably less severe, so you have genetics to thank. And good genes, I suppose. Still, you need to stay focused."

Lucien thinks of all the things he could focus on, if only he had a book, a notepad, his camera. Staying focused on being yourself feels like asking someone to focus on homeostasis, cellular respiration. To age. Attention only makes it seem impossible.

"Right, sure," he says.

Dr. Sloane picks up her cell phone again, checking for a message that isn't there.

"What's going to happen to her?"

"She'll be fine. My daughter is many things, but at least she's resilient."

"That's good," he says. "But I meant that girl."

"Like I said, you're lucky. Consciousness is a very fragile construction, and we are not in the business of magic. Rehabilitation takes time, especially when one's memories have been as tainted as hers. It only takes a moment to corrupt a consciousness, much longer to restore it."

"Maybe someone should be with her here, every night."

"You don't think that's why I was called in? With three other nurses on shift?"

Lucien shrugs; he senses a defensiveness in her voice.

"She gets more than enough attention here. What she needs is to find herself again, and no one can do that for her."

Chapter 9

TODAY

Sophie is under a cool cloud.

Sophie is on a metal table.

Sophie is drifting.

Sophie is eighteen, back in Minneapolis.

Sophie is leaving for Los Angeles tomorrow. For a spot in the corps de ballet at the famed Los Angeles Ballet Company. An ensemble member. Louise is taking her to a performance to celebrate her departure, this new beginning, and their goodbye. Louise is Sophie's friend and fellow dancer, the only one left from their years of hard work in middle school, then through high school. Louise will be going to Macalester in the fall, to study literature, and Sophie feels like she is jumping off a cliff, alone.

This performance is by a new dance group holding open studios in Minneapolis's burgeoning arts district. The large industrial space appears to be shared with a ceramics studio, with cloths draped over amorphous shapes on tables at the other side of the room. This group, Louise explains beforehand, practices something called Gaga, and when the lights come on and there is no music, only the dry-powdered sound of feet on wood, Sophie's stomach lurches with embarrassment for them. That thump, the drag and slide, the breath needed to propel a body through air, these are usually sounds of shame because your director has cut the music to correct you. Only as the dance continues does Sophie realize this is intentional; there is no music because music hides the struggle. They want to show the physicality. The work of a body.

Eventually there is music, too. Sophie longs for the silence. Watching them suddenly feels distant, like part of the performance has been taken away, no matter how much the music coaxes her further toward feeling. On a basic level, she misses the knowledge, how hearing the work itself invites the audience inside. Each dancer switches between perfection and seeming chaos. Impeccable posture contrasted immediately with a beastly hunch. What bravery, Sophie thinks, to move with such seeming abandon. What skill, to make the visceral appear beautiful. At one point during the performance, Louise leans her whole body into Sophie, as if to say, *See?*

Sophie is lost in every movement.

Louise wants to join the group. She thinks maybe she could commute from Saint Paul since they're not a traditional ballet company with such strict rules. Sophie feels like she is being left behind, even though she is the one moving away. They stay after to chat with the dancers, their bodies strange in street clothes just like Sophie's often feels after performing.

Sophie is defensive in the car on the way home; she gets angry and says something about the tiny crowd size, then immediately regrets it. Of course, she loved it, too. *It's an outlet,* Louise says, nibbling on a protein bar. *Maybe it's not always about restraint. They're all trained in ballet like us. It's not the training but what you do with it now that makes you an artist.*

Sophie has been told countless times that ballet is dying, if not already dead. Even an instructor in contemporary dance once said that when all the older people die, there will be no one left to care, let alone buy tickets to the ballet. People don't just grow into old-fashioned taste. Times have changed, but ballet has not. Sophie told herself it was just the instructor, bitter at teaching dance to high schoolers who will soon outgrow her. But every performance, she scans the crowd and cannot help but notice the mature faces staring back, and behind them the young aspiring ballerinas, awe in their eyes. A system sustaining itself.

Seeing this performance with Louise feels like confirmation. What if Sophie is committing to something that will no longer exist? What if she is jumping off a cliff, into nothing?

Louise pauses before getting out of the car in front of her parents' house. Then she turns to Sophie and says kindly, *It takes a lot of restraint to make something look that free.*

Chapter 10

BEFORE

Sophie stands with her arms extended high, her skin prickling in the cold air of their dance studio currently being taken over for costume fittings. Her hair is still damp at the roots from the morning's rehearsal. She watches herself in the wall of mirrors while one of the designers pins the costume in place, trying all different cuts and colors.

Sophie has never been such an integral part of the design, showing up only later for the finished costume to be taken in here, out there. This time, as the sylph, the star, all of the costumes will be designed around hers. Inspired by her portrayal, her movement, her—the culmination of Auguste's vision.

She hardly believes what's unfolding around her in this space that has seen so many days of relentless rehearsal. The same space where she has caught her breath and tapped her muscles to stay focused, to persist. Now nothing could look more right. A fog of baby's breath is tucked into her bun and behind her ears, hovering like a crown, and vibrant flowers wrap her arms intermittently, on the vine.

Just earlier today she and Antoine refined their pas de deux, attempting it for the first time in full before Auguste and the rest of the company, over and over, until he was satisfied. If he ever was. Toward the end, Antoine excused himself to vomit in the bathroom, a fact confirmed once he returned. Each time he stood behind her, Sophie felt his hot, putrid breath creeping over her shoulder and tried to shut off her nose. She took shallow breaths through her mouth, though her core ached for more. What no one sees from the stage is the vulgar intimacy that ballet entails; how, pressed in close, you share sweat, you breathe each other's air, you hear their quickened panting inside of your own. If ballet is to look effortless, it requires a certain distance.

The designer sisters who agreed to do the costumes are so focused they hardly speak, not only to Sophie but even between one another. They work with an unspoken rhythm and mutual taste. One sister sends their assistants back and forth to the samples, swapping out one pastel fabric for another to play with, while the other experiments with pops of color against the fabrics; a bright red flower tucked against the palest pink; a tangerine ribbon against the faintest mint green.

In Auguste's production of *La Sylphide*, there will be no stitched-on fairy wings for the sylph, but rather a cape that billows as she spins, floating only with her momentum, hovering in the air even as she finally falls. One after another, the colorful fabrics flutter in and out behind the assistants, all for Sophie. The taller sister holds a swatch up against Sophie's arm, her hair, her lips, and seems to like it, that faintest green. She motions to her assistant, waving her hand, which must translate to something knowable because when he returns he holds two ribbons in different shades of yellow. The taller sister lights up—*perfection!*—at the marigold velvet.

In place of a true crown or any jewelry, the other sister slips two golden shoulder pieces, sharp sunbursts, around the thinnest part of Sophie's biceps.

"Do you think you can dance in this?" she asks softly.

"We don't need her impaling herself, or her partner," says her sister, laughing. "But it's heaven. If you can," she adds, to Sophie.

The taller sister talks faster, more loosely than her partner. Even the most serious things she says are undercut with humor, while her sister speaks gently and thinks between each word.

"They suit you," she says, adjusting the baby's breath in Sophie's hair.

"It's divine. Reminds me of our Fall 2018 show, in the park. When it poured, ugh, that was such a disaster. But god, those pieces were my favorite ever."

Sophie glances back to the mirror, tilting her head to admire herself. She looks more like a religious icon than a fairy, but that's Auguste; he came to Los Angeles to break with tradition, not perpetuate it. To reimagine the future of ballet. Where better to start than with one of its classics? *La Sylphide* is traditionally performed with a forest backdrop of ornately painted screens à la Renaissance landscapes; his scene, he had told Sophie multiple times now, would be deconstructed birch trees with no tops, a kind of minimalist dreamscape. All over the floor and suspended from the ceiling, pastel ferns and floral arrangements would hang in the place of leaves of the forest canopy. It would be whimsical and magical and ethereal. It would be unlike any ballet Sophie had ever seen. Of course, the sisters are no strangers to the avant-garde; they dress Hollywood's cool girls, always with a retro-inspired, subversive touch of the feminine.

The shorter sister moves around to face Sophie directly, holding a large palette of bright smudges in a rainbow of hues. She dabs a finger in what appears to be pure shimmer and looks into Sophie's eyes.

"You don't mind do you?"

"No, not at all."

"Good, let's just play around a bit!"

First she dusts Sophie's eyebrows, brushing the hairs in the opposite direction, using a pale powder until they almost disappear. Then she taps a fingertip into the shimmer and sweeps it under Sophie's brow. It feels good to have someone take such care to her face, not only the touch but the attention, the gaze. The sister dabs the same finger, this time in a coral, and pushes it into the cavity below Sophie's brow bone, down to her inner eyelid.

Then she pushes her pinky into another pot and presses fuchsia into the center of Sophie's lips. She mimics pressing her own lips together, encouraging Sophie to do the same. When she sneaks her finger back to find another color, Sophie glances at the mirror. She looks otherworldly, this forest creature. With her eyebrows dusted away, the context of her face is suddenly foreign to her. For a moment, she doesn't even recognize herself, and it feels truly liberating.

"I think we got it," the taller sister says, pulling off the soft tulle in one movement. She tosses it over her shoulder, where it lands in a beautiful cloud, and then begins unpinning the structure of Sophie's costume.

The other sister tilts her head, locking Sophie's face to memory, before dusting shimmering lilac onto her opposite cheek.

"Ugh, it's going to be so good," she says, already turning to pack up just as Auguste approaches.

"Auguste, you brilliant creature, thank you again!" says the taller sister.

Sophie already misses the colorful fabrics; she has never felt so beautiful, so ethereal yet strong, as she does in the sisters' gaze. In their hands. Now with the fabric swatches removed and only her pale leotard underneath, the makeup on her face looks even more surreal.

One day soon she will wear the finished costume, fit perfectly to her body. Her body that will show through every movement, the clothing merely accentuating her form. For a moment it frightens her, to want something so badly. To have it so close she can feel it still on her skin.

Auguste and the sisters stand together going over their choices. "This makeup is too light, no?" Auguste says. "The audience will never see her."

"It's not just about the crowd," says the taller sister. "It's about the photos. It's about marketing. It's about the impact. A light touch is less stagey."

"But it is, after all, a performance," says Auguste.

"Yes—but there will be so many photos leading up to the show. Magazine spreads. I don't know how else to put this, but—we're involved. And you? It's a dream. People will already know what her face looks like; they'll have seen it everywhere. And people will remember her."

"We have it, Auggie. Don't worry!" assures the other sister. "Our vision is—Grecian nudity dusted with confection. You will see it and think it was all your idea. We promise."

"I'll send our notes later," follows the other. "Full recap, with sketches for everything."

"Do you hear this, Sophie?" calls Auguste. "Are you ready to be remembered?"

Meanwhile, Sophie leans toward the mirror, angling her face to admire the shimmering pigment in places not traditionally meant for color. The sisters continue describing to Auguste just what he wants to hear. That their production of the *ballet that built ballet* would make the audience catch their breath. It was not to be taken lightly, even if the dancers looked like they might just float away. No, their production would not be romantic. Rather it would make one reexamine the way they think about gender, possession, and love itself.

"I love that you say this," says Auguste. "Because when I first decided on *La Sylphide*, I chose it because I wanted to reimagine femininity itself . . . *comme une tragédie*."

At home, Sophie pours a glass of pét-nat and takes a sip while standing in the relief of her open fridge. Autumn heat waves have been one of the hardest things to adjust to in Los Angeles. The wineglass fogs and she presses its cool sweat against her cheek.

Sophie smooths the wrinkles in her dress and resists making it worse by sitting, though her legs still ache from rehearsal. The stiffness of the fabric makes her feel strong, armored even, like its vintage style might provide protection from today's dating scene. The more precarious the setup, the more Sophie leans into a vintage look, as if to say, this world we live in, with its transactional dating customs, they are not mine. As if to say, tread lightly. Despite the dress's structure, the flirty ruffles at each shoulder still make her feel feminine, each one just high enough for her to tilt her head behind, coyly.

This is how she imagines herself from the safety of home. In reality, Sophie knows she will press the ruffles down the moment she feels eyes on it. The moment she meets her date's gaze. She will fail to commit to the illusion she had so firmly believed in—her poppy lips behind the upturned frill, Marilyn Monroe on the air vent. How ironic that as a professional performer she still lacks the very drama—or courage—to act exactly how she would like to be seen offstage.

As much as she hates first dates—the painful, probing conversation at the start, the obvious motives in showing up at all—she does appreciate the anticipation. This excuse to feel anxious, something she so often feels without reason. The desire to sedate that anxiousness with alcohol, and the triumph one feels if both sides then agree on a second, or a third drink.

Sophie thinks back to the other morning with Liv and the new guy she's been dating, their tender awkwardness in that early stage. Liv seemed to revel in it, totally in control. Dating seems so easy for her, like a game she enjoys. Whereas Sophie so often feels trapped inside of herself, Liv articulates the things—and relationships—she wants then presents herself to get them. She makes it look simple, with an ease that makes Sophie desperately jealous of her friend, then ashamed.

Hadn't Liv only recently broken up with the last guy? Jackson. He was also from New York, though one of those people who said he *came from family* in Rhode Island, as if everyone should know what, or who, that implied. Sophie never liked him. He and Liv were only together for six months, but practically lived together for all of them, until it turned out Jackson had been mostly waiting for the appropriate time to ask for a meeting with Liv's father, his shitty screenplay finished and waiting. Liv was *devastated, betrayed*—but just like that, she had already found someone new. At least he doesn't seem to care about that.

Sophie cannot stand the overly groomed men of Los Angeles, with their trainers, dietitians, life coaches, hairstylists—they had all their masculinity manicured out of them. Lucien seems different, clumsy in a way that makes Sophie's chest ache. She feels guilty even acknowledging that, but it seems like a waste, him with Liv. Sophie imagines for a moment being the one to make him smile, the one he tucks under his arm as they walk. She imagines being shorter, like Liv, so that she fits perfectly. His sharp, green eyes looking at her. Sophie pours herself one more sip, or two, just for the taste, then realizes now she might be late.

Sophie was relieved when Keegan suggested a drink. He had texted two wineglass emojis that Sophie took to be decidedly more romantic than cheers-ing beers but slightly less suggestive than two martinis. So many of her recent dates have been sober—a hike in Solstice Canyon, a trip to LACMA, a picnic at Echo Park Lake. Sophie has so few daylight hours to herself when she is not rehearsing or training or working at

Chateau Marmont; she would rather not waste them making small talk that ruins a hike she could easily enjoy alone.

She could like Keegan so far—his confidence, his brevity. Though it's easy enough to project onto a text correspondence. She can't believe Mick has a friend she hasn't met yet; the fact of this makes her skeptical. But tonight, regardless of who shows up in person, regardless of what face would be put to Keegan's text bubble, and what soul she would sense within moments of meeting him, regardless of all that—she is going to have that second drink and maybe a third.

The harder rehearsals at the company have become, and the more perfection they demand, the more Sophie feels a deflected destructiveness building up inside her. Some people live in restraint without the need to match it with equal and opposite force, but Sophie lives in extremes. Yesterday on Third Street she bought an entire cake from the bakery she passes every day. The woman behind the case, tattoos covering her taut arms, insisted on decorating the three-layer red velvet with a message, and Sophie finally went with *Congratulations!*

She ate forkfuls of frosting from the top down, sitting in the front seat of her car, then feverishly took a few more bites of deep burgundy cake before shutting the cardboard lid and throwing it into the backseat. It was probably still sitting in the dumpster behind her building. This is not the first time since then that she has considered checking.

Somehow drinking feels safer. Anything requiring company feels safer. At least having company protects her from the boundless appetite she might succumb to at home. Drinking with a date also brings potential for ending the night with a warm body next to hers; not onstage, where she has to be perfect, and not someone she pays to massage her just to feel the touch. Sophie wants to be ravaged, not lifted. Fondled, not spun. For once, she wants to regret it in the morning, to roll into her pillow and exhale it all out in blissful shame.

She takes out her phone to call a Drivr so she can drink with abandon, but also in case she goes someplace else after. Then she runs back to the bathroom to add more eyeliner, crisping the whites of her eyes with a smoky pencil. Tonight she might as well play at being someone else.

The Drivr slows to a stop in front of the arched awning of the Dresden, its large white letters still suspended in a time before this neighborhood became all Blue Bottle Coffee and cactus stores. Though the entire curb is open, the car stops right beside a couple having a tense exchange. One of the young women covers her face, bare shoulders rising and falling.

We have arrived at your destination, the Dresden, the car speaker announces in automated self-satisfaction. The things this AI cannot understand—decency, for one—Sophie thinks as she steps out of the car, right in between the couple. The women freeze, newly united over this affront to their privacy, and Sophie feels compelled to shrug, nodding back toward the car, though it is already gone.

The Dresden was Keegan's choice, and once inside she picks him out by the look of satisfaction on his face. He is already sitting at the bar, an empty stool beside him. She will not tell him, but lots of guys suggest this as a first date, whether for its place in film history glorifying a certain type of "Hollywood dream" in *Swingers*, or simply because one rarely runs into someone you know here. Maybe it just makes a good conversation starter.

The Dresden might have once been elegant, with its exposed stone walls and leather banquettes curving along the mirrored interior. Now its preserved charm, indie fame, and menu of shrimp cocktail and prime rib attract those who want to drink ten-dollar Manhattans, pretending they were born in the wrong decade, while simultaneously swiping on their smartphones. The fact that the Dresden was named after one of the most notoriously bombed—and once elaborately lovely—cities is not lost on Sophie, though she suspects it is on Keegan, who smiles at her from behind his unwashed, dirty-blond hair that falls to his chin.

As she approaches, a flash of recognition moves between them. Then Keegan reaches back, twirling his hair into a tiny bun, and Sophie notices several string bracelets tied around his wrist. His strong, tan forearm. He stretches out a hand to shake hers, not standing from his stool, and his smile is mischievous, immediately sexual. She blushes, and suddenly the stiff, frilly dress she chose feels costume-like. She slouches, hoping to overcome its effect with her own casual ease.

"So, Mick has told me a lot about you."

"Is that right?" she says, pretending to look around. "I'm sorry—are you . . . Eric?"

Keegan looks at her for a moment, then breaks into a smile, rubs the cleft in his chin. Sophie feels proud, reminded that she is actually quite good at first dates. The ones that come after, not so much.

"Never trust Mick's opinions," she adds. "Unless of course they're all good things."

"I like this," he says, flicking one of her shoulder ruffles with his finger. She cannot tell whether he is being genuine. "Very ladylike."

Sophie catches the bartender's eye and orders a martini, dirty. She's wanted one ever since that Halloween party and has not been able to shake the craving. Plus it comes with a snack and she skipped dinner.

"Like, as many olives as you can fit," she adds to the bartender.

"I like your style," Keegan says.

He's holding an IPA, which Sophie adds to the rapidly growing profile in her mind.

"So, what do you do?" she says. "Mick has told me virtually nothing."

Keegan smirks, and she wonders briefly what that means.

"I'm a writer."

He proclaims this a bit too proudly to be a real one, she thinks.

"What kind of stuff?"

"I write VR for a start-up in Pasadena."

"What on earth does that mean?"

Keegan laughs, though she senses his annoyance. Joking about jobs is Sophie's favorite first-date test; how someone reacts says a lot about how seriously they take themselves.

"I write story for VR. As in, virtual reality. You know what that is, right? Fastest-growing subset of entertainment? We're putting movie theaters out of business, if you haven't heard."

"Whoa there," Sophie says. "I actually *like* movie theaters. Anyway, of course I know what VR is, but what does that mean—you write code?"

"No, I write situations. Scenarios. Like, you score the winning goal in World Cup soccer, in a stadium of ten million fans. Or you're sky-diving from a peak on Mount Kilimanjaro, a bird flying alongside you through the clouds. Things most regular people won't get to experience, except for maybe you."

Sophie senses a hint of derision. Condescension. But after a few big sips of the cloudy martini, its glass too thick and olives rock-hard, she feels her perception loosening. And her filter.

"So, what exactly are you writing, then? Ideas? You write ideas down?"

"What exactly do you *dance*?"

Maybe she won't have that second drink after all.

"All right, I guess Mick did tell you something about me."

He ignores her, keeping the conversation on him.

"I write people's fantasies," he starts again, overly confident in how enticing this makes him sound. "I design and then execute the scenes everyone wants to experience but never will. I give them lust, drama, excitement, happiness."

"I thought there was a drug for that now."

At this he perks up, the mischief back in his smile.

"You into Mem?"

"Are *you*?"

Sophie doesn't tell him how her brother has been in and out of re-habs, her parents' home practically transformed into a halfway house back in Minneapolis—not Mem, that's not gotten there yet, but just about everything else. She doesn't tell him how any interest she might've had in experimenting with drugs vanished when she saw the pain his addiction caused her parents; gone forever, when she held the shell of her bright, athletic brother consumed by his dependency.

"Where do you think I get my ideas?" Keegan says with a wink that obscures whether or not he is serious. He speaks with such certainty that Sophie wonders if he's ever lost anything, or cared about anyone enough to notice. "If you wanna slip tonight I've got a friend—"

"I've got enough ideas of my own, thanks."

"Oh, do you?"

Sophie is not sure what to make of the undertone in his voice. Maybe she's better off telling him now that there is zero chance she will be convinced to try a drug she spends multiple nights a week cleaning up after, while watching exceedingly talented people turn into passive sacks of jelly. Lest Keegan take her resistance as a challenge.

"So, tell me something I don't know, then." His voice resumes its light tone, and Sophie finds the hint of artifice intriguing, in the same way she used to watch *American Psycho* to fall asleep. "Who is Sophie Marden?" Now, that's a line.

"Well, I dance," Sophie says, finishing the last sip of her martini. Her jaw tightens from the brine. "But I guess you know that. We're just finishing rehearsals on *La Sylphide*. I'm dancing the—"

"Classic," he interrupts, looking past Sophie and clapping his hands.

A couple in their late seventies takes the stage, or the open space where a few dining tables have been cleared. Sophie remembers the other reason guys like to suggest this for first dates; everyone thinks it their original quirk to enjoy a kitschy jazz duo. If Elayne pulls out her flute, or Marty sings at falsetto, all the better. Keegan turns to her, suppressing a smug grin.

"Have you been here for Marty and Elayne?"

She nods. Holds up a finger to the bartender, then taps her empty glass. He smiles at her sympathetically.

"They've been doing this since 1982."

"Is that so."

The couple starts—Elayne wearing rouge and a gold blouse, Marty with black hair that defies his age—and they maintain eye contact as she walks the room. Their connection seems to transcend time or place.

Sophie takes out her phone, hoping for a missed call or text; maybe then she could excuse herself. The screen shines empty—the photo of her family dog, Basket, uninterrupted.

"Where do you live?" Sophie finally asks. After a few seconds of silence, she looks up to see Keegan also checking his phone. He glances at her. They both laugh. That's something.

"Highland Park," he says, putting his phone back in his pocket. "I work in Pasadena."

She raises her eyebrows, nods. This, then, is how a date dies.

"Shit, I already said that didn't I?"

Sophie shrugs. "What's the name of your VR company?"

"Altruistic Media."

She snorts, unable to control herself.

"What's so funny?"

"I just—virtual reality never struck me as something altruistic. Getting us more addicted to these things. These increasingly expensive things."

She waves her phone.

"Well, we started out doing therapies, mostly to build proof of concept. Touch aversion modules for children with autism, trauma therapy for burn victims."

"*Annnd* now I feel bad."

Keegan smiles, and there is that cleft again. She can almost feel his stubble in her fingertips, against her cheek, her neck, her chest.

"It's okay, I'm used to the VR opposition. That will fade once people become less ignorant, you know?"

"*Ignorant!*"

"Well, you just said, you didn't realize—"

"What happened to reading? Books? That's how I learned to escape my situation, my body, my mind. My *ignorance.*"

"Sure, that's a common concern. Reading. But look, that was already changing long before VR."

"Don't you worry about people who are tuning out the world? Everything looks better on these." She nods to her phone, then takes a long sip of the fresh martini.

Maybe it's been so long that her body is desperate for any friction, but the distaste she has for him now feels like heat. Keegan watches her, also charged, and she can't tell whether he wants to rip off her head or her dress.

"I have one in my car if you want to try it out."

"You drove?"

He smiles, and Sophie thinks, of course he would drink and drive. Irresponsible. She spins around on her stool. Only when Keegan motions for the bill does she realize she took that for granted, and she hedges—reaching for her wallet.

"I got it," he says in a way that makes her feel kept. She reaches in her purse and hands Keegan a twenty-dollar bill. He looks insulted but accepts.

She finishes the rest of her martini in one sip.

Keegan's boxy convertible is parked on a side street where bougainvillea petals cover the sidewalk. Inside the car, he reaches into the backseat, and even the waft of his musky deodorant stirs her longing for physical contact enough to cover the annoyance at everything else about him. He turns with a thin glass headpiece and powers it on, the blinking green indicator the only light in the darkness.

He slips it over her head, careful not to pull her hair, and she adjusts the lens until it aligns with her eyes. The glass blurs for a moment, and then her vision goes blank on the screen. Slowly, bubbles emerge in front of her, and the blackness fades to a murky depth—soon interrupted by a tiny white-and-orange-striped clown fish floating toward her. She holds out a hand to touch it. Wonder and genuine joy bubble up inside her and Sophie thinks for a moment that she misjudged both Keegan and VR. In the silence of the car, she feels Keegan watching her.

Then she hears him stirring beside her. She thinks she hears the roof opening, then feels the chill of the night air on her skin. The clown fish squirms away as a giant shark creeps into the background. Dread fills every inch of Sophie's body, and though she knows the image to be false, she feels him tracking her, stalking her as prey.

Just as she turns to Keegan, she feels his arm come down on the seat beside her, supporting himself. He pulls a lever and suddenly she lies flat, the shark still meters in front of her, lurking—displaced but entirely unmoved.

Now Keegan's stubble is on her neck, her chest, scratching across her breasts, but her arms are pinned down by his body so she cannot even remove the headset. Is this his game, luring women into his car to check out his "writing" and then—

His movements are clumsy and his knee hurts the muscle on top of her thigh; she winces and he apologizes, kissing his way down to her lap. Her body feels charged with fear and arousal, the second martini making her less sure of which. *This is what you wanted*, she reminds herself as she tries to keep up with what is happening. Does her consent change his intention?

"Is this okay?" he whispers.

The shark darts out of sight, just as a larger one emerges where the windshield of the car might be. Her breath quickens, pleasure heightened by the terror that its fin might slice right through her forehead. Keegan's hands slide under her dress onto her torso, wrapping her ribs, and for a moment Sophie can't move or breathe—she's underwater, sinking—and then Lucien flashes into her mind. The face she had thought of while getting ready, his hair dangling down to his eyebrow.

Sophie's body lights up. She gasps as Keegan pushes her dress up toward her face, but it doesn't matter because she still has the headset on and her entire body is pulsing now. She imagines Lucien's green eyes where the headset stops, his breath panting in her ear. She isn't sure whether it's the attraction she put off, or the guilt of it, or simply the feeling of slipping into someone else's life, but now she is pulling him closer and it still isn't close enough.

She imagines her body from his eyes—his eyes on her, his hands on her—and she enjoys Lucien's single audience, maybe even more than the touch itself, the turn-on no more his doing than her own.

Just as she feels close to something, some spreading pleasure radiating throughout her, he pulls away from her and sighs a long, satisfied *Fuuuuuck*. Sophie pulls the headset over her head, surprised by the fresh disappointment of this world. The awkwardness of Keegan's position, his butt on the dashboard, knees on either side of her, hunched despite the open rooftop.

Though he tries to touch her, to help her finish without him—swift, what modern-day romance!—Sophie pulls off his hand, repulsive now that it's attached to his face, his person.

"Careful!" he says when he notices the headset dangling in her hands.

Keegan takes it from her, reaching all the way over her toward the backseat, smothering her with his chest as he lays the headset gently in a case. Then he slides back to the driver's seat. The air outside is cool now. Even the stars overhead look dull compared to the definition of that created world. Keegan presses a button, and inch by inch, the roof closes until the air is still and Sophie feels further trapped in that car, her body.

She wills away the thoughts taking up space beside her. Doubts over Keegan's behavior, the lack of effort or tact he displayed to get her there; doubts over what just happened and what that says about what he must think of her; doubts at forgiving it all momentarily for the sake of her own pleasure, not to mention where she had gone inside herself. When she looks over at Keegan's smug face, she cannot escape feeling that, in trying to satisfy her own desires, she might have validated his.

The next morning she curls into herself at the memory. That open roof, the darkness of the street. Her nakedness. Regret is different in the morning than what she anticipated. Imagined, or on-screen, such abandon never includes the sweatiness, the smudged makeup, the alcohol on the breath. The laziness of the mind when pursuing its own satisfaction. But recklessness is always better in the foreground.

As soon as Sophie sits up in bed, she remembers her body. Even her face feels bloated. She cringes at the mess she remembers making in the kitchen last night. She remembers an entire jar of almond butter mixed with granola by the spoonful. Her dry mouth the proof. She almost choked swallowing it down, then immediately followed with more. Her jaw aches. What a waste, drunk-eating from such healthy provisions.

Sophie's phone buzzes from underneath her pillow. She knows immediately how she feels about Keegan by how much she hopes it is not him.

Fun times last night. What r u up to?

She throws her phone into the covers, but it lands faceup and the screen lights up again.

I'd like to take u out to dinner. Someplace nice ;)

Everything about Keegan now troubles her, his texts no exception. Does he think that what happened last night—the VR bait to get her in the car, his jumping on top of her while she wore the headset, the speed at which they went to him inside her—was somehow all within the bounds of a normal date? Making his first move while she was in-capacitated? Was this his idea of courtship? He had no way of knowing what Sophie hoped would happen last night, that she wanted someone to use right back. What if she had not been open to the idea of kissing, let alone sex? She had been literally blindsided by his mouth, and only later did he ask if it was okay, once he had her pinned.

Even his texts are different. He *tells* her last night was fun, no chance for her to weigh in. He asks what she is up to, without waiting for an answer.

She grabs her phone and lets her fingertips run, covering all the things she smiled off the night before, things she has smiled off for years. So much of Sophie's time is spent suppressing this growing rage—accommodating a rude customer at the Chateau Marmont, nodding as Auguste tells her she is not trying hard enough, or that she, sacrificing everything, is letting the company down—and for once, she wants to say the damn thing. Say it.

Honestly? I should have laughed in your entitled face the moment I saw you, but I gave you a chance. What you did in the car was awkward and demeaning, and just because I tried to get off instead of putting you in your place doesn't mean that it was okay—or even paid off. I would say I got about as close to coming last night as you will get to seeing me again, and I'm sure that doesn't break your heart, but I hope in some small way it breaks your ego. On behalf of the other women in LA . . . take a fucking pause.

She lets the words sit there, exorcised, with no plan on ever sending them. It is enough to have that expressed, in the most extreme terms, and she breathes easier with it outside of her. She taps to highlight the rant so she can delete it, but her hungover fingertip taps near the little arrow instead. Not exactly on it, though! That couldn't be enough to—and yet the arrow darkens, the text traveling up and into their conversa-tion. It fills the entire chat screen. The unspeakable, spoken.

Sophie laughs, then gasps.

Three typing dots pop up momentarily on Keegan's side, and then disappear.

She waits, but nothing. The typing dots do not return. She expects, for a moment, to feel worse. But then she doesn't. She stares at the now-silent, stable screen. Her apartment is peaceful, the morning light warm. What if we just said the things we want to all the time, she thinks. She pictures other women she knows, some younger, some older, all equally searching for something. All navigating so many needs alongside their own. Who cares if what she just said, or what they did, gets back to Mick? Maybe she hopes it does. Mick should know. It's not Sophie's fault his friend is an asshole. It's not her fault how he treated her.

Sophie spends so much energy trying not to offend, trying to make life easier and never harder for others. But what's the harm in standing up for yourself? In saying the thing, unapologetically speaking what someone deserves to hear? For once Sophie had, and look at that, the world didn't end.

Chapter 11

TODAY

Angelica Sloane sits at the breakfast table, staring at the newspaper spread across her lap. She takes a bite of dry toast and a sip of coffee to get it down her throat. The coffee has gone cold. She imagined the obituary would be printed today, yet she cannot quite accept that here it is, between her fingertips, in her home. *David Stein, 18, mourned by his loving mother and father, Diana and Jonathan Stein, and his classmates at Brentwood School.* She doesn't need to read further; all that would prove is how little anyone knew the young man. Especially his parents, or whoever writes something like this. Remy would have done better; she's a wonderful writer. Angelica chokes on the thought.

It's over now, at least. *Oh. What a terrible thing to say. To think.*

Angelica recalls the moment she realized David and Remy were together, or however they put it these days. How dire things had felt then, with the simple confusion of it all. The awkwardness. Now those problems seem charming. A better parent would have been familiar to David from the beginning, before he ever became her patient. How could her own daughter's boyfriend not know her, or at least *of* her? Even Remy's classmates at Brentwood School should probably know her mother, but Remy's boyfriend? The person Remy disappeared to see at every chance—the one she refused to let her mother meet.

David was a year younger than Remy, which allowed Angelica to imagine that's why they had never crossed paths; like otherwise Angelica might have bumped into him at a class bake sale, if they still had those.

What Angelica can't get out of her head, even still, is the look on David's face when he first realized it. The stupor, the disbelief. Not just that she was Remy's mother, but that she was *a mother*. He didn't have to say it; she could see.

Angelica has never considered herself overtly maternal, not by nature or appearance; it was only natural for David to assume she was all alone. She wears no ring, after all. People in Los Angeles think they are so progressive, but the subconscious is not. The subconscious is traditional, old-fashioned even. Angelica had published an article on the topic her first year at Johns Hopkins.

Her mind returns to the problem she cannot fix, there printed in the newspaper, collecting crumbs. If only she had combed David's memories more thoroughly at the start, maybe then she would have seen—but no, there was no precedent for such a thing. She believed it unethical, even, to explore a patient's memory without specific boundaries in place. David was a quiet young man. Exceptionally polite. Guarded, as teenage boys are. How deeply would she have had to peruse before stumbling into the sexual escapades of her underage patient, only to discover that his partner was—the horror—her child? Not a child, no. Remy certainly is not a child any longer. Angelica had long assumed leaving for college would mark an end to that, the child suddenly independent, but in truth it had not. What marked that change is this.

When she picked up Remy at LAX a few weeks ago, the girl was different. Gone. She will heal, and lord knows Angelica hopes she will thrive, but Remy will not return to the girl she sent off to Brown. Loss makes an adult. It doesn't even have to be death; any love lost will do. Angelica knows about that, too.

Angelica had always been so curious about her daughter's boyfriend, but as it turned out, she knew things about him even Remy did not. He had so much potential. How could Angelica ever explain to Remy that she felt protective of him, too, in her own way. She, too, felt the loss. She should have foreseen this. But there is still no filter for predicting self-harm. He never showed any signs of suicidal thoughts. Angelica's treatment for David's depression was a gentle exposure therapy to childhood memories, a targeted self-soothing mix to instill in

David what others naturally seem to have, an ability to build a future off the positive, nurturing experiences of the past. Perhaps it was too gentle. But David had a tendency to latch on to pain and spiral. He indulged revisionist narratives that made him stupid, unlikable, unlovable. When the reality was that everything in his life seemed to confirm otherwise, the least of which being her inscrutable daughter's discerning taste. David was Remy's favorite person, and Angelica lost him.

Angelica takes another bite of toast and puts the newspaper down just in time to see Remy plodding down the stairs with her terrible new blue hair, which seems to taint everything she touches, including the new white towels, the cashmere throw on the sofa. Two months at Brown and already home. Angelica had been so proud to see her go; her only child, a prodigy of her own making. College had been one of the few things they agreed on. A place for Angelica to put her enthusiasm that Remy actually accepted, even shared.

Remy is dressed for her job—a reclaimed one—working at some trendy coffee shop on the Eastside, where twenty-somethings with no jobs hoping to "break through" sit around looking like they already have. Remy, her daughter, froths their milk. Something she apparently needs to dress like Rosie the Riveter to do—work overalls, bandana around her hair.

Angelica finishes her last bite of toast. She dabs at a crumb with her finger.

"I really wish you wouldn't feel the need to work at that place; you don't need the money, not anymore."

Remy looks at her with a vacant stare that Angelica knows is meant to break her heart.

"You know that isn't what I meant," she says. "I just know you had that job before to save up for trips to see—look, I just don't want you worrying about money right now. We should find some time to talk; this is an important moment, and how you handle it will determine—"

"That's why I'm working there," says Remy. "It distracts me."

"Well, fine, I'm all for that. But wouldn't it be better to keep up with your schoolwork? Return to Brown in the spring with a few credits. Remember what I said about that patient of mine? She offered to put you in touch with the assistant dean at UCLA and said they'd be thrilled to have you take a few classes."

"Not interested," says Remy. "I don't want to go to UCLA. I actually like to press buttons and give people things they want. I like to see random faces all day long."

"It'd only be for the term, darling. Just until you go back to Brown."

Remy stares at the floor, like she does every time Angelica mentions returning to school. Like the whole premise of college and the rest of her life had suddenly been made irrelevant. Angelica is too afraid to push further, lest she cement this into something more permanent.

"You need time," Angelica says. "To grieve, I understand that. But if we don't talk—"

"I'm here now, aren't I?"

She ignores this, her daughter's poker-faced call. Inciting Angelica to talk now, fully charged, just to prove there is nothing to say. She has tried this too many times. Instead Angelica lights a cigarette—a doctor! who smokes!—and resumes reading the paper the old-fashioned way she insists on, its edges crisp and its long pages hiding her face. The cigarette dangles from two tightly pressed fingers, and she feels Remy staring. Her daughter coughs elaborately.

"Well, David's funeral is tomorrow," Remy says. "If you care."

Angelica lowers the paper and stares at her for a moment, wounded. She would go if she could. It just doesn't seem appropriate or respectful to his parents. What would people say—what could *she* possibly?

"I would, darling, but I have to be at the Center all day for sessions."

"Sure," Remy says, rolling her eyes. "Of course you do."

"I do," Angelica says.

"Haven't you ever loved anyone, ever?"

Remy's voice turns sharp, like it finds strength in its anger toward her.

"I love *you*," Angelica says. "You have such beautiful hair, darling. This new color doesn't do justice to your nature."

Remy slams the door and the house is suddenly quiet. The paper crinkles as Angelica sits up straighter, turns the page. She swallows her guilt. The hatred she feels radiating off her own child. That accusation. Angelica hears it echoing in the silence.

Haven't you ever loved anyone, ever?

Angelica carefully folds the newspaper and moves to her home office, attached to the house but with its own separate entrance and bathroom. The memory of that day comes back in full. David needed to come in on a weekend, and Angelica suggested he come to her home office, rather than both of them driving to Pacific Palisades. Some patients only saw her at the home office; she had been toying with the idea of letting her other space go altogether. She opened the door to find David standing there, headphones slightly askew, adjusting his backpack. He looked more nervous than usual, and like he didn't want to be seen.

The first thing he said was *I'm sorry.*

"David, for what? You're right on time."

"I didn't know her address, I only knew her house. Your house, I mean. I dropped her off so many times I just knew how to get here. I thought it was a coincidence, that you might be neighbors or something."

"It's okay, David. Come inside."

"Did you know?" His voice grew frantic, afraid.

"I still don't know what you're talking about," Angelica said, though she was certain by now. Her own distress was momentarily kept at bay by the performance of calm she knew her patient needed more. "Whatever it is, we'll figure it out."

He sat on the small couch facing her, his feet crossed, shoelaces untied, one sneaker bouncing as always to some inaudible beat. He had often mentioned his girlfriend before, and as he spoke, Angelica fought to keep her mind focused on him, rather than scouring her memory for details that should have tipped her off. Was her daughter so foreign to her that she couldn't recognize her? Should she be able to? Would another mother be able to?

By the end of the session, they decided that they would talk to David's parents first, and then Remy. She would be leaving soon for Brown, which would address at least the immediate complications. David had been struggling significantly more given his girlfriend's impending absence, all of which Angelica knew and his girlfriend, her daughter, did not. No one else could give David the kind of treatment Angelica was providing; outpatient Memoroxin therapy was still rare and exclusive. But Angelica felt immediately protective of Remy as well, despite her fondness for David. She didn't want her daughter to become his salvation. Tethered to someone who might hold her back, when she was just about to leave, when she had worked so hard.

She was so young. They were both so young.

In her small office bathroom, Angelica smooths her short hair, pinning it behind her ear with a bobby pin from the jar she keeps on her desk. She likes it this way, a sleek curtain she can hide behind. She licks her pointer finger to slick down the few stray wisps, dyed grays no doubt, and watches her face until the familiar voice inside begins questioning what she sees.

When patients ask whether Angelica has ever administered Memoroxin therapy on herself, her rehearsed answer is that, of course, for her clinical studies she was the subject of her own memories undergoing the therapy. She believed it an important step to understanding a patient's experience; and believes the treatment to be not only effective, but safe for anyone. What she doesn't tell them is that years ago, still in research for her PhD at Johns Hopkins, on one of the first teams developing the technology to transfer memories, she had not in fact volunteered for Memoroxin therapy as a patient; she had taken another researcher's batch.

Sahar, her girlfriend at the time, had been deeply invested in the project as it related to her research on PTSD in veterans. Ever more ambitious and adventurous than Angelica, Sahar was one of the first volunteers for initial extractions. Hers was one of the first examples of an effective memory capture and transfer. Even then, Angelica knew the risks of ingesting someone else's memory capture, but she couldn't help herself. She was desperate to step inside the mind of such a brilliant, fascinating, and beautiful person. And she trusted Sahar, with her life. Her love had been so strong it surpassed the value Angelica held for herself, her sanity. It violated it.

Angelica and Sahar had just begun living together, a year into their relationship. There was no part of Sahar that she did not want to see. And one night, when Sahar was distracted with her own research, Angelica administered a tiny dose of Sahar's Memoroxin to herself. Back then they weren't fancy pills, but a dull powder to be mixed with water, dropped into a petri dish, and pressed into a dissolving edible strip. There were no sedatives in the formulation at that point, so you were present for the entire trip, making it a deeply disorienting yet revelatory experience.

Angelica's first time in Sahar was intoxicating. To experience a jolt of the person you love more than yourself—well, it was impossible for Angelica to ever explain afterward. Words failed. One evening, sitting in their shared apartment in Butchers Hill, Angelica resorted to tapping keys on the piano in melancholy but sweet, lingering notes. Nothing could adequately convey the sense of Sahar. In that moment, Angelica felt she had stumbled upon the most potent gift one lover could give to another—their heart, their soul, their very consciousness—to be relished in tiny, exquisite doses.

Being inside of Sahar, or having Sahar's memories and feelings inside of her, was an intimacy stronger than any Angelica had physically experienced. But soon enough Angelica wanted more. When she was with Sahar, she felt the disconnect; she had gotten direct, unfiltered access, and now the shell of Sahar she lived with was unbearably false. But the more of Sahar's extraction she took, the more lucid the memories became. She felt her love deepening with every moment she experienced, as if instead of simply listening to her favorite song, she had finally learned to play it. No, she had become the notes themselves, both floating through the air and delighting her own ears.

Then one day, after a particularly potent dose, Angelica recognized herself in Sahar's memory. For a moment, she saw her own harsh beauty. Its sleek, groomed perfection. A rigid intensity. Angelica never considered herself that way, and the perspective was both flattering and embarrassing, to think that she came off so calculated, so severe. But the memories went on. Angelica saw—and felt—how Sahar saw her, and how that had already changed over time; how it hardened, too, and especially how it differed from Angelica's idea of herself. Even after she came out of Sahar's memories, she couldn't unhear the critical voice at her every move. *Angelica would be prettier if she frowned less, if she softened.* She felt how Sahar hated the way her forehead wrinkled when she smiled, the way she pushed her lips together right before kissing, the smell of her breath in the stupidly blissful moments in between. How she was always, always around. They were the worst kind of insults, felt too deeply to be voiced, so woven into the consciousness that they seemed mere truths.

Angelica tried to forget; she tried to understand. Sahar swore her love to her. She acted like it was true, too. Of course, we all think terrible, judgmental things without knowing. No one is meant to see themselves through another's eyes. Angelica couldn't tell Sahar what she had done, or how she knew there was more Sahar had left unsaid; if she did, they would be over. Not only their relationship, but Angelica's career and possibly Sahar's. Angelica would be admitted to testing, the violation of which made her feel physically ill. But the more Angelica tried to open herself to the love she still felt for Sahar, the more she hurt. This is what she tries to convey to her patients at the Center while healing them from misuse; that she understands their pain. That there is a way through it.

Angelica never considered herself particularly kind. All her life she felt different—cold when other women fawned, numb when they gushed. But after Sahar, Angelica understood that she was in fact kind, deeply so, and it was the world that was not. No matter how much others smiled and praised each other, deep down, they judged. They resented. And from then on, she felt no shame in forgoing the superficial pleasantries she had so often forced before. She let her face relax without forcing a smile when she said hello, she replied honestly whenever someone asked how she was, and she kept herself safely sequestered from the wound she had endured through Sahar's eyes, so that when it finally healed she would not open it again.

Then, eighteen and a half years ago, she made one crucial mistake in keeping that plan. Angelica adopted a baby girl, and her heart—tightly closed and always measured—exploded, laying open and vulnerable every day since. No matter how Remy treated her, Angelica felt herself splayed. Unwavering. Unrelenting. She was and always would be there for Remy, and she would do anything for that child. Even if she was no good at showing it.

With Remy gone for the day, Angelica might pour a glass of wine and get back into bed, regardless of the time. Then this Saturday might unfold like so many others. She might take out the carefully curated capsules she made herself a few years ago once she had the authority; she might sample from the array of moments where she could still enjoy the comfort of Sahar's smile, the invitation of her deep brown eyes, her bright lips. Her hair that smelled of gardenia. Memories of her own, where she could still see the love in her partner looking back.

Memories from the happiest years, before Angelica saw herself from the other side.

Chapter 12

TODAY

The circle clears for the day. The other patients return their chairs to their respective places and either go back to their rooms or take another supplement on the nearby couches to nap. Dr. Sloane walks back to her office. A meditation workshop is being held shortly in the quiet room. The girl sits in the chair closest to the fireplace, totally still.

She looks so peaceful. Still Lucien cannot stop seeing her, strained and frantic, just two nights ago. Just before, he had stood in this same room, seeking peace for himself. Looking for something he does not know. Following a feeling. He considers what Dr. Sloane said, about how appearances obscure what is underneath, but there is some deeper truth to this girl's appearance that he cannot let go of. The fact of her beauty, irreconcilable.

Who's to say the flutter he feels around her is no more than some phantom false recognition? Here, of all places, nothing would make more sense. Déjà vu could be a fancy scented candle burning in the common spaces, and Lucien would believe it. A trick of the synapses that feels like memory but shifts like fog.

And yet here they are, together, waiting for themselves. The most stubborn kind of waiting. Waiting for something that is already there.

The pieces of him that should feel most fresh, the most recent ones, elude him. Everything in the few weeks prior to coming here feels faint, or loosened; had his grief made him so detached that he barely remembered what happened around him?

Lucien returns his chair to its place by the long glass wall and then walks toward the fireplace. He sits down on its stone ledge, beside the girl still in her chair. The stones are warm from the fire. So much of this place is stark, cold. Lucien never wants to move.

"You seem well," the girl says. "Are you leaving, then?"

"I don't know how soon, but eventually," Lucien says. "That's the goal, right?"

"Any goal is the goal, I guess."

"Aren't you?" he asks.

"What?"

"Leaving, eventually?"

"I think I've already overstayed my welcome."

"Is there a time limit?"

"Everything has a limit," she says, pushing the grout between the stones nearest her chair. Her fingers remind him, L-O-O-K-U-P.

"I thought this place was a public service."

She scoffs aggressively, and he remembers her leg, stretched and flailing in the air. He reminds himself, *this is a person he does not know*, but all he really knows is what he still wants to be true.

"Public rehabilitation centers? What country do you think this is? Welcome to America, land of privatization. Welcome, we'll put you on the wait list and check your credit."

Lucien watches her, feeling out her anger, coaxing it like a puppy he might hook his arm under and pick up. Finally, their eyes connect. He senses her settle.

"So if this place is private, who's paying? I know I'm not."

She tilts her head, the whisker of her butterfly bandage puckering around her eyebrow as she smirks. On her cheek under where the earlier bandage was is a faint scratch, almost gone. The skin is glossy, and Lucien wants to run a finger over it, down to her full lip.

"It's the Big Pharma Spa. For the amount of money they're making, they can afford a few rehab centers like this for their new wonder drug. At the very least it's good PR, probably even cheaper than the old-fashioned kind."

"I thought this was—isn't the Center run by Dr. Sloane?"

"Sure it is, but she's not funding it herself."

"But they can't possibly treat everyone who's been using."

"They look like they're addressing it, that's all that matters. Get a few off the street, especially the problematic ones. You'll see some famous people come through here if you stay long enough."

"I haven't," Lucien says, looking around the room.

"Maybe you just don't recognize them," she says, and he cannot tell if that implies they look different, that he simply can't remember them, or both.

"How do you know so much? Are you—undercover, here for a story?" She laughs for real for the first time. He nods toward her bandages. "A bit over the top if you ask me."

They sit together, smiling, until they're not.

"My brother is an addict," she says. "Telling you that is probably wrong, or against the rules, but whatever, it's one of my few certainties these days. I've seen everything with him. Countless times. Never Mem, but—that's how I know. About these places."

"What for?" Lucien asks. "Your brother, I mean."

"Meth, most recently. But that's not how it started. He's still on some wait list for another rehab. My parents have been taking care of him for the past year by themselves, through withdrawal, everything. They don't even know that I'm here. I can't quite believe it."

"Do you remember what happened?"

"Not since a few days after I got out of the hospital, in an urgent psychiatric center."

"What was that like?"

Lucien lifts a hand, only realizing as he does that he expects to find a cigarette. He glances at his hand, almost impossibly sure of it. He brings his fingers to his lips anyway.

"It's the place they send you to when you're a danger to yourself or others," she says. "And no one else seems to want you. How do you think it is?"

"So how'd you get here?"

"They realized I was fucked up from Mem," she says. "Then I guess someone decided I mattered. The golden ticket."

She slips a foot out of her beige slide and holds it in both hands, pushing her thumbs into her sole with intention. She closes her eyes. The pleasure shows on her face.

"Is this your way of asking me to let you be?"

"All this pain, and somehow my feet are fine," she says. "Just sore, but that's nothing new. Anyway, you probably don't know what that means for me. I mean, of course you don't."

"Tell me."

"No."

"Okay, your name, then?"

She leans her face right up to his, so their eyelashes nearly touch. She bites her upper lip, flattening the bow. Her eyes flicker with the flames.

"No."

"Please."

"Why should I?"

"I'm Lucien."

He feels a rush at the release of it. The reinstatement of his name, his self. There was something to withholding after all; it makes the reinstatement feel like something sure. She pulls at the back of her neck. Then glances around the room. And speaks so softly it sounds like breath.

"Sophie."

"Sophie," he repeats, feeling a familiar haze around the name. Or is it just the relief—the rush—at having a place to put her in his mind. "Tell me everything."

"I don't know."

"Tell me anything."

They laugh in the silence. Their mutual uncertainty, the crippling fear of it all, of where they go next. Something rises from the pain inside him. Happy without reason. If he weren't next to her, confronted with her face, he'd think this was another trick of the treatment, phantom happiness projected onto the present. If her beauty, even bandaged, weren't sitting there, proof.

"Like, how are your feet sore here?"

"What do you mean?"

"We don't do anything," he says. "We don't walk. There's nowhere to go."

Sophie lets go of her foot and rises from the fireplace.

"Where are you going?"

"You asked me to tell you something about myself."

Sophie leads him to the hallway toward the bedrooms, then around the corner. He pretends not to know where they are going, the way to her room. With every couple doors they pass, Sophie turns to check that he's still following. Or to check for anyone following them.

Once inside her room, she shuts the door behind them. Lucien is suddenly worried; he feels a responsibility given what he has seen. What he heard without knowing. For the fact that he is here, with her, alone. Her room is nearly identical to his, though the window is in the opposite corner. Still, somehow, this feels like seeing her home—the way she makes her bed, the faint impression of her left in the sheets. Sophie.

He stays.

Without speaking, she shuffles down her baggy jumpsuit and peels the tape off the remaining bandage at her shoulder, wincing as she rolls it out. He looks away, but then glances back at her body, in a bralette and briefs. Slowly, she rises onto her toes, lifting her arms high overhead, her fingertips delicately arched; then she switches back and forth, ankle toe ankle toe, as if it were the most natural motion on earth. One by one she lifts each foot to her opposite knee, triangles forming and disappearing. Here, in this room with soft shadows and no sound but the sweeping heels across sanded wood, Lucien wishes he had a camera, as every angle of her body invites him to freeze it, to hold it forever.

A wave breaks outside, though they can't hear it, and then he sees a flash of her—the dancer, the peacock. She comes in bursts, emotions tugging him from this moment, with the rush of her smile, those long fingertips, her laugh, Liv's arms around her. Sophie starts to spin, his memory rushing in now, the dry martini, him in the purple shade, her arms two arcs. He pushes that away, wants only to stay in this moment with her, the two of them and the sound of her breath as her body forces air in and out. The whip of her figure through space. So often we watch the body move drenched in notes that tell us how to feel about it; to watch in silence is to know the breath at each movement, the chance of success against the gravity of failure.

Click. He places her in his memory, snapshot over her shoulder, arm raised, her eyes delicately facing downward. Click. The languid arch of her back as she creeps forward, losing the precision of before. Click. The arch of her feet that seem poised to snap or spring her straight through the ceiling.

Lucien always imagined eyes and sight and perspective worked just like the camera, recording things as they are, objectively. Here he wonders if we could truly see through another's eyes, would our color blue be the same as theirs? How about red? What if another person's blue was your red? How could we ever know? For that, he wishes he could remember whatever he had seen on Mem. How the world looked, even in the most basic sense. Something of what it felt like to see, as another. And now here is Sophie, staking out her space, filling it with movements through every inch of air. Making what was otherwise empty alive and beautiful. Showing him how she sees.

She rises light, then comes down hard. He feels the smooth wood against her feet, and the weight on her shoulders as she hunches only to once again float up to relevé. It's as if the gods would not have it, as if they could not help but pull her back up to the sky, and for a moment she looks entirely free, her toes hardly touching the ground, though they bear the entire weight of her.

"Sophie," he whispers, approaching her from behind.

The name now means something, attached to a memory entirely his own. Lucien matches his body to hers, only inches left between them, the hovering baby hairs outside her bun tickling his nose. Before he can tell her, before he can reintroduce himself, revisit those things that might help them both to remember, his hand grazes hers.

She jumps. In another breath she is across the room, backed into the frame of her bed.

"Sorry," he says, and takes a step toward her, but she shrieks so loudly that he reaches both hands to his ears. Her eyes look straight past him now, and she cringes at something he cannot decipher. He turns, but sees nothing.

"Sophie!" he says. "Listen to me, Sophie. It's okay."

No, no, no, no, she says, beating her head with the base of her wrists.

"I'm sorry." He waves his hands in front of him, helpless, and backs up across the room. "Look, I'm over here. I didn't mean to—I thought . . . What did I do? Talk to me?"

Two nurses push through the door, rushing straight to Sophie without seeing him, and Lucien slips into the doorway. One holds a syringe extended, and the other holds long gray bands that are quickly wrapped around Sophie. The latex stretches thin over her points of pressure, nearly white at her elbows. She screams, voice cracking, and something inside of Lucien feels like it is breaking.

Then the door is shut with him on the other side, and Sophie's screams become muffled like the waves outside the window, tightly sealed out, but crashing, continuously, relentless.

Chapter 13

BEFORE

Last week, a body was dredged up from the bottom of Echo Park Lake.

Police cars parked up and down Laguna Avenue. Lucien's neighbors introduced themselves for the first time to share their annoyance over the street parking, as if this inconvenience overshadowed the body, lifeless and waterlogged, the witnesses, the family to be called. But life is a string of selfish responses, Lucien thought as he nodded along, holding his groceries, a box of cereal and orange juice.

When Lucien first saw Echo Park Lake from his window, it struck him as a mirage, its glittering water broken only by swans languidly crossing its surface and couples in swan-themed paddleboats looping the lily pads. On weekends when large families cook out, the smell of carne asada and hot dogs drifts up to his window and fills him with hunger but little appetite. Children chase each other, shrieking, around and under picnic tables, and part of him feels sorry for them—the inevitable loss that waits as they play at being afraid. By evening, pink light fills his entire apartment, just before everything darkens. And drunken shouts ripple off the water.

He first met Liv outside the Victorian house, around the same time everyone was talking about the dead body, and the parking. She was picking up the pieces of some smashed Halloween pumpkins; one she'd carved with *Beet It* in fine cursive, another featured an intricate rendering of assorted vegetables. It was hard to be sure whether they had been smashed for the bad pun, or in protest of Michael Jackson. Even picking up the rotting pumpkin pieces, Liv seemed delighted. This fascinated Lucien; it still does, though the closer he gets to her, the more that fascination makes her feel further and further away. Now especially after sex, it's like they're floating in oppositely traveling ethers, her fingertips curling around his. Almost impossibly, holding on.

He sneaks by the window of Astral Bodies on his way out, the latticework casting shadows over Liv's curated selection of ceramic mugs and succulents alongside her juices. He wonders who it is that commutes from home to sit in another quieter home, in a city that stretches indefinitely with the same quiet, low energy. Lucien first went in looking for hand soap after moving in. He found it. Only, the soap was twenty-seven dollars, powdered, and alkaline, whatever that means. He thought at least he could get a black coffee instead, but that was eight dollars and came with your choice of ashwagandha, ghee, or coconut oil.

The past few weeks in Los Angeles seem at once like a long weekend and also like months and months could have already passed, with nothing anchoring Lucien to time; no balancing jobs and friends with his responsibilities to his mother, her doctor visits. No events or odd jobs; no work of his own. The days progress, untouched by season, and instead of being liberating, this feels like a trap—as if leaving Los Angeles might one day hit him like an astronaut returning from another galaxy, only to find that his world has grown old without him. It's no wonder his grandmother lost touch with reality. There isn't any to hold on to.

. . . *memory goes, not all at once, but like lace, a hole here, another there,* Lucien reads to his grandmother from the newspaper unfolded across his lap. One of the many things she saved over the years that he has scoured for ideas since being here, this *Financial Times* from 2012 had selected fiction around the holidays. She must have loved the story, to save it all these years. Or was she already fading then, all by herself. Maybe she read it over and over, surprised each time.

He pauses to study her eyes. They sparkle green, like his mother's, like his.

"You wrote that?"

"No I'm Lucien, your grandson."

Her eyes shift with confusion.

"You know me, I can't write shit." He laughs, inviting her to join him; at the very least, to tell him not to curse.

"Well, it's beautiful."

"This was a story you kept," he continues. "Written by Teju Cole." She nods and smiles, unclasping her tight grip on his hand. He watches her face for some recognition. She points back to the page. He reads a few more lines, until her eyes close, and then he folds the paper.

"Nice of you to visit," she says wistfully. "You're a wonderful writer." Lucien wants to shake her.

"Thank you," he says flatly instead, to her eyelids.

When he looks up, Mickey Mouse in the safari hat stares back at him from the cleared shelf across the room. Mocking him. He walks over to the stuffed animal and slaps it down, but the hard plastic nose makes contact with his fingernail and it stings. He sucks his finger and picks up the little plush body. Then he walks back to his grandmother's chair and sets Mickey down on the side table. He crouches to her level again, studying her now that her eyes are closed.

This might be what his mother would look like, older, in another universe where she had the time. He looks for the traces. The long, strong nose. The same smile lines, because if he remembers anything, it's that they laughed the same. His grandmother's brows look like his own, arched more over one eye. They give the illusion of her attention, even now.

Would his grandmother recognize him without the illness? An adult, no longer the goofy kid always happy to go along, fascinated by everything he saw. An adult, he thinks again, disparagingly. Her skin looks sallow against the thin polka-dotted cotton of the nightgown she seems to wear every day. Would it be weird to intervene in her clothing options? Why should the nurses listen to him? He wears the same striped sweater every day, or the faded green flannel, and the gray T-shirt he hopes they assume he has in bulk. But who bought this generic gown? He cannot believe she would have chosen it. Every photo he's found shows her in silk robes, feathers along the bottom. Even in his limited memory, he remembers her in color.

Next to her on the side table attached to her floor lamp is a small pill bottle like any other, with an official label that reads MEMOROXIN 780, 110 MCG. FLORENCE J. BENNETT. This is the first day they've had more than a passing moment alone. Lucien remembers the Halloween party the other night, everyone rushing upstairs. Desperate for whatever Florence has here in excess. The limp hand on the floor. Reaching.

He lifts the bottle and twists off the top. The pills sparkle, iridescent inside the orange plastic. He carefully taps a single pill into his palm and studies it. When it rolls along his palm, a trail of shimmer comes off, right along his lifeline. Shit. He pinches the pill, more coming off on his fingertips, and drops it in the front pocket of his shirt.

His heart beats fast against it.

He replaces the lid and returns the bottle to the table. He glances at Mickey, and Mickey looks back at him with bright, empty eyes. The past two weeks, it's never occurred to him that the pills she takes are something he could experience, or that he could follow her to where his mother was still alive—to live in that consciousness, in any but his own. The nurses won't notice one pill. There must be forty, fifty in there. And why shouldn't he, this is practically in his blood. Just a taste, anyway.

Maybe he won't even try it.

He wipes the pearly residue on the side of the recliner. His face feels flushed, his T-shirt damp though it's barely noon. Florence's house, with its generous shade and thatched roof, has no central air, not even a proper AC unit. He imagines she never needed it before. The only time Lucien visited Los Angeles, he must have been twelve. She kept all the windows open, a cool breeze following the speckled light from the courtyard. Everything about Los Angeles felt easy.

His mother had several meetings for an exhibition she was being featured in at LACMA titled *Women in Color*. The show highlighted female artists in the last century who didn't shy away from color. His mother scoffed at the title and its premise, especially the fact that it was a show of all white artists. One night she came home, when Lucien and Florence were eating pasta in the backyard, and exclaimed, *Any show at a major museum is always twenty years too late, and thirty years behind.*

Lucien spent their entire stay playing with an old Polaroid camera his grandmother gave him, photographing plants and lizards in her small overgrown yard, and walking around her neighborhood, exotic and strange. The air felt brighter, and so did the people. His mother was busy with meetings all weekend, and when she wasn't she was painting in the courtyard, frantic and inspired. Unreachable, as he photographed the fallen bougainvillea petals clustered around her feet and slowly watched them turn to color.

At one point his mother proclaimed that they were moving to Los Angeles, that she had no idea why she had ever left the California light, but then two days later she and Lucien were on their way back to LAX and never visited again. His grandmother called regularly after that for a while; she liked to ask him about photography, for him to describe any interesting images he'd captured. Then either she stopped or his mother stopped answering. He could never tell if his mother was embarrassed of Florence, or if they simply had different energies, forever pushing and pulling in opposite directions, better off loving one another from afar. Lucien saw so much of each of them in the other. And yet the only thing either of them agreed on, it seemed, was him.

The French doors to the courtyard are shut with the blinds down. Lucien stands to open them and let some of the fresh air inside or, at the very least, unsettle the scent of sanitizer and gauze that has taken over. The courtyard is once again cluttered with bougainvillea petals in fuchsia, coral, and faded brown, rustling as the doors swing open. Lucien remembers how the petals floated in the breeze, that image of his mother's feet, overlaid on this new reality. He wonders if his grandmother still has that photograph, something he could take. He closes his eyes, trying to remember the honeysuckle from the neighbor's yard, but he cannot get past all that sanitizer.

No wonder she doesn't remember a thing stuck in here. His mother would never have let this happen had she known, had she been out here to see what this treatment entails. Or maybe she had, maybe she did. He considers, for a moment, that this was all her doing, her instruction. Then he lets himself settle into resenting her, if only briefly.

Mostly, the fresh air makes him want a cigarette. But so does everything. All this sunshine makes him want a cigarette. The way the nights here have a chill and the light turns tangerine over the skyline makes him want a cigarette. And the way his nerves tighten every time he gets into the car to go someplace makes him want a cigarette. The way he wants more than ever to focus on his body, on the air he breathes, makes him want a—

"What do you say we give your grandmother a rest?"

A young nurse stands in the doorway. She waves up a hand in apology.

"I'm sorry," she chuckles. "Oh my lord, your face."

Decades younger than the other nurses and with a bright smile, she is a relief in that stuffy room. Lucien sidesteps his grandmother's recliner, suddenly feeling himself looming beside the nurse's petite frame and the low ceilings.

"I don't think we've met. I'm—"

"Lucien. The grandson, of course. I've spent a lot of time with your photographs, with Florence. You're a cutie."

Lucien's cheeks burn like a wine stain spreading.

"*Were* a cutie—as a boy. Oh god," she laughs. "I'm Trina, nice to meet you."

"Really nice to meet you, Trina."

"I switched off with Gloria a while ago, but I heard you back here and, you know, wanted to give you some time. She loves the company. And the reading. Don't you, Florence?"

Florence's eyes remain closed, a slight smile to her mouth. As nice as Trina seems, Lucien recognizes the practiced optimism, implying his presence means a damn thing. He faced the same prescribed kindness, the soft eyes and gentle nods, from the nurses caring for his mother over the last few years in New York. During the bad days, their optimism had felt like ridicule. And his mother's recovery after each episode had only validated their pretension. Maybe this is just something nurses are specifically trained in, between administering intravenous medications and taking vitals. Such treatment from an older nurse was one thing—from someone his own age it feels like a betrayal.

Trina walks closer, humming as her cotton uniform swooshes, clinging to her curves. Her dark shiny hair is pulled up in a tight ponytail, the arc of which just touches the back of her neck. The room feels different with her there, more alive. She is so much better at being here than he is. As she leans down next to his grandmother beside him, he smells her fruity shampoo.

"Time for some memories, pretty lady," says Trina as she takes her wrist for a pulse. She nods once, satisfied, and his grandmother gazes at her now with calm, happy eyes. "Doesn't she look lovely today?"

Trina turns to Lucien, and he realizes he has no idea how to talk to his own grandmother. Not in this state. Not compared to the ease at which Trina moves around her, lightening the absence that lurks behind Florence's eyes, inside her entire body. For a moment, he resents her.

"Isabel," his grandmother whispers, looking up at Trina.

A deep, sharp pang at her name. In this room where his mother spent so much of her life, she is both remembered and forgotten all at once. In some ways, she is still alive. Trina smiles—not correcting her—and brushes a white wisp of hair out from his grandmother's eyes, tucking it behind her ear.

"That's real good, Florence. Must be your guest. Sparking all kinds of memories."

Florence leans farther into her touch. He admires the generosity of her comfort. He also wonders just how much of his grandmother's misplaced memories Trina has heard. Trina reaches for the same pill bottle, and Lucien holds his breath. A tiny pill sparkles under the lamplight as she places it on his grandmother's waiting tongue.

Lucien steps closer. Florence's entire body relaxes, and her muscles seem to unfold. The tiniest wrinkles in her face soften, as though the years are dissolving away from the inside out. To anyone else these changes might be imperceptible, but Lucien has been watching her closely, attentive to even the slightest spark that might hint at some internal progress. He wonders where she goes, remembering the pill in his pocket, and suddenly he's desperate for it. Maybe his mother is there.

Just then, Florence's eyes open wide for a moment, sparkling green. He leans in closer, forgetting Trina, forgetting the stripped-away shell of this once home, forgetting everything but what he might find in her eyes. But those same eyes that once opened wider at the sight of him quickly become crowded by an opalescence that could make even the hollowest of objects appear full, their emptiness obscured by an impenetrable sheen.

"Where are you in there?"

"All over the place probably," Trina responds.

He sits back on his heels, and takes his grandmother's thin, wrinkled hand into his.

"For Alzheimer's treatment like your grandmother's, they don't choose certain memories to put in each pill. They pull a wide assortment from her whole life to run by her, flooding her brain with them, really. Sometimes not even a full memory makes it intact among the shuffle. Sometimes it does. You never know what will trigger the synapses that are still there, or what's left uncovered by plaque that we can stimulate. Think of it like heating them up using her memories, melting the plaque away. Running them like an engine, turning it over until it catches."

"Ah, a car metaphor," says Lucien. "Now I get it."

"Sorry."

"No, I'm just joking," he says. "I appreciate it, really. But is it unpleasant? Flooding someone with memories?"

"Oh no, it's not unpleasant at all. And just to be sure, there's a mild sedative in each pill to make sure she stays relaxed and doesn't come out of it prematurely. She's cruising in there. Who knows, she might even be with *you*."

Lucien likes the thought of his younger self keeping her company, helping even if he can't. A better self, at that.

"Would she recognize me?"

"Of course," says Trina. "It's not like playing old family videos or showing her photographs. The memories in her Memoroxin carry her consciousness—all her thoughts and feelings from the moments themselves, and like I said, there's a little something to suppress whatever's going on now, too, so she doesn't get confused."

Florence mumbles softly, the corners of her mouth turning up. Lucien squeezes her hand, encouraged by the idea that it might be him making her smile. She murmurs something again, and reopens her eyes.

She looks at him startled, then angry. She pulls back her hand.

"No," she says, her voice hard. "Not you! I don't want to *see* you!"

"It's me, it's Lucien."

"After what you've done?" she says, her voice stretched thin and tight, on the brink of cracking. "You ruined everything!"

"It's Lucien," he repeats, but she doesn't hear him. His mind races. She must know then, he thinks. What he did. What he didn't do. He feels it in the way she studies him, his eyes, his face. Finally, the blame he deserves.

"Florence," Trina interrupts calmly. "This is your grandson. All the way from New York to visit you."

"Never," his grandmother continues, certain. "And you'll never see my daughter, do you understand me, Conrad? Never."

Lucien gets up, knocking the stool over, and he stumbles to fix it. Meanwhile Trina steps in front of him, beside his grandmother.

"Calm breaths, Florence," she says, stroking her hair. "This is my friend, you don't know him, okay? He wanted to meet you. Look at those handsome green eyes."

Florence looks ready to protest, but her eyelids begin to blink, opening more slowly each time, until they don't.

"That's right, let it happen. Good girl."

Lucien's hands are shaking, and he shoves them into his pockets. Conrad? So she wasn't really seeing him, or talking to him. But how does she know about his mother, her daughter? Why would she say that, if not to him? When he looks over at Trina, she's typing into the tablet at the nursing console. His grandmother's eyes are closed. Only a flicker under her eyelashes.

"Sorry," Trina says as she places down the tablet. "Just wanted to get that down. We keep a transcript of the names and things your grandmother says, both awake—which are a bit more limited—and under Memoroxin. In the off chance something surfaces. It's standard to keep track of them to measure progress, to see if any memories are resonating, or if she recalls them later."

"Can I take a look?"

"We aren't allowed to share it with family; it can be overwhelming, I guess. But your mother gave us a list of names, places, and terms to look out for. So if Florence hits on any we'll let you know."

The word *mother* strikes him before he even realizes it; how he longs for her to be as alive as the word is without her. He cringes at Trina's assumption that she is.

"If—that means there's been nothing yet? How about Conrad?"

"Not yet," says Trina. "Conrad does come up a lot, but he isn't in here."

"How many names did my mother give?" says Lucien.

"Eighty-nine," Trina says. "And that's a good number, right within our ideal range, so we've got lots to go off. Lucien, it's not that she doesn't say things, she says plenty of things. We just need to make sure they're coherent. She might call me Isabel, but that doesn't mean—"

"I get it."

"Your mother was very thorough," Trina says.

His mother wasn't thorough. Maybe that is the thing prickling under his skin. Her mind was so often elsewhere, constructing canvases and cross-referencing poets and sculptor friends she would later send letters to, and all this had made her endlessly special, sure, but no one would ever say she was thorough. She forgot birthdays. She lost her keys once a week.

"I should get going," he says, his hands still shaking.

He thinks to kiss his grandmother's forehead, as he often does before leaving, but decides against it. With a nod to Trina, he grabs his backpack and walks toward the living room. His grandmother's house has the same stale smell as yesterday, the wall-to-wall carpeting once fresh now fetid. The sage-green paint on the walls, nearly faded to white from the sunlight, holds the shadow of what once hung in its original hue. The entire house has been stripped of most of her things—probably to keep it clean, he thinks, to simplify things for the nurses. Somehow the dust remains.

The front room had been pristine and eclectic, with velvet couches, and shells in all shapes and sizes scattering the shelves. Stepping inside it was a like entering a tiny boutique museum. Now it looks vacated in a hurry. He looks hard, as though searching for inspiration in this place where he remembers wanting to capture everything. Until recently, capturing a moment before it was over, from his particular perspective and experience and position, was the driving force to his days. The desire to explore subjectivity, how by showing one perspective you could reveal the others missing. The sense of his limitations, the beauty of a certain angle.

Now he sees only a deserted home, dated and decaying from too much sun. Lucien sees nothing but moments passing. He lets them slip through his fingers and feels no regret. No impulse to catch them. He remembers the Polaroid camera and walks to the built-in shelf along the far wall to check its drawers. But when he opens one, and then another, he finds them empty.

A large painting is leaned backward against the bookshelf, its bare canvas with a few scribbles exposed on the other side. He pulls it back expecting to see one of his mother's paintings. Preparing himself for her long horizons of surprising colors and grids.

His chest tightens.

A turquoise and mustard-yellow de Kooning faces him upside down. The broad swatches of intense color make him dizzy as he releases the thin, maple frame. It balances for a moment on its side, in the carpet. He wipes his hands on his pants, then lifts it gently again using the back edge of its frame and carries the painting away from the open, northern exposure. He feels the stickiness of the stale air on its thick paint.

"You shouldn't worry about that," Trina says from across the room.

Lucien points to the de Kooning.

"What is it doing like this, on the floor? On the *carpet*?"

"I meant your grandmother," Trina says. "Her reaction wasn't about you; the Memoroxin destabilizes her sense of reality as she falls into her dose. She could've been thinking of anyone. Just last week, she accused me of stealing her mail. Her checks. There was no reasoning with her. Then moments later, I was nobody again. Back to blank."

Lucien shakes his head; he doesn't want to get into all the ways he feels guilty for what just happened in there. Either his grandmother was entirely lucid and rightly blames him for his mother's death—or she is more far gone than he thought, confusing him entirely with someone else. Assured in her dementia. Which was the comfort?

"This can't be stored like this," he says. "Do you even realize—"

"You're right," she says, moving closer and reaching out a hand.

"Don't touch it."

"I'm sorry," she says. "I wasn't here when this came down. Is it one of your mother's?"

"An old friend of hers."

"You should take it, then," says Trina. "No one will notice."

"Shouldn't there be a process? Beyond some random pillaging? Who's to stop anyone from coming in here and taking what they want?"

"No one's taking anything," Trina says. "But if it's valuable to you, you should take it."

Lucien faces the canvas again, its frantic sweeps of color. He never could really see this one, despite his MFA, despite his mother's love for it. He just couldn't see it. But he recognized its value. The work should be in climate-controlled storage, on the walls of MoMA, the Whitney, LACMA. De Kooning was a mentor to his mother, through their network of artists in Southampton. The old Hamptons as they were slipping away. His mother always said the de Koonings were a lesson in how to be. It would kill her—again—to see the painting, a gift she gave away, like this.

"I shouldn't have it either," he says.

"Just to be clear, the majority of your grandmother's things are all in storage. No one has pillaged anything. Maybe this one was going to be moved there, too, and got left behind."

"We're trying to make her remember, right? Wouldn't that be easier if she could actually see her life around?"

"I thought the same thing when I started, but part of the therapy relies on a certain purity of the present, as they say. A blank, negative space means the memories she's given might be more likely to trigger something clean. She's all mixed-up in the present. None of this is any use to her. I do show her photos, sometimes. I recognized you, didn't I?"

Lucien nods, unconvinced.

"For most Memoroxin therapy, patients go into centers, into treatment rooms; this Alzheimer's outpatient therapy is just a test. But your being here, it's incredibly generous of you. Your grandmother is a lucky woman, to be so loved."

He could tell Trina how little he'd thought of his grandmother until he was left with nothing, no one. How only through his own selfishness did he even consider her. All those years, he never once visited again. Sure, Lucien's mother was partly to blame, but at some point he became an adult. He could have afforded a flight out here; he could have afforded a phone call. And now he is here not because it is the right thing to do, but to right the greatest wrong. One he can no longer bear alone.

"I have to say, your mother was very smart to sign Florence up for this. Florence has a full-time nursing staff; all her needs are being met."

He places his hand on the painting.

"Will she be coming, too, your mother?"

The hole Lucien has been tiptoeing around widens before him, its edges crumpling in. A single rock loosens, then plummets, spiraling into the darkness. Vertigo, right there in the empty living room.

"She passed away recently," he says as flatly as he can.

Before he looks up to face Trina, she smushes herself into his chest.

"I'm so sorry, I knew she'd been sick, but—I thought she was doing better."

"She was."

"Here I go making it about me," Trina says. "Making you rehash it."

"It was the end of a long battle," he says. "That's what they say, isn't it?"

"It's all bullshit," she says. "Cancer is bullshit."

"Total shit," he says, grateful for that. "Florence is the only family I have. I thought at least I could help her—for my mother."

"Look, I'm being one hundred percent straight with you when I say this treatment has the potential to bring her back."

For a moment, Lucien thinks she means his mother.

Los Feliz Boulevard is lined with all sorts of trees. Palm trees, of course, but also oaks, pines, and even cedar, all spilling down from Griffith Park. Driving after dusk Lucien has seen coyote eyes lit up red in the head-lights. *It is a bad sign when they start descending into neighborhoods*, he heard a young mother say at Dinosaur Coffee the other day, hugging her baby a little tighter against her chest. *It means the drought is pervasive, their food supply waning. There's nothing more dangerous than desperation.*

The de Kooning sits sturdily wedged against the console of his mother's sedan. A couple loose T-shirts Lucien found in the trunk are draped over it, should he get pulled over for grand theft before making it home. Not that anyone would know what to make of it, apparently.

Each time Lucien leaves his grandmother's he changes his route home. Crisscrossing the city feels closer to walking, a series of turns where he could happen upon something new. He needs to happen upon something soon, anything that might spark a new idea. That was the point, after all. Come to Los Angeles and work while being here to help his grandmother. And yet he feels blind here, in all the ways that matter.

When would he not see everything in terms of his mother, of his loss? Will there ever be a time when her death is no longer the frame? Lucien hardly remembers what gave him direction before. If not avoiding this pain, what was he doing? What was the point? And what does it mean if the thought of moving past this actually scares him more? Finally letting go, finding some other purpose, some other frame. As if he deserves it. As if he could ever, again.

The only thing Lucien is certain his mother would want is for him to create, to never stop. To use this pain and work with it, turn it into something. And yet—only in her death is he truly able to disappoint her. Had she shown disappointment in him during her life, he would be more equipped to deal with his fear of it now.

If only there were more tasks left that he could mindlessly finish and check off a list, like closing her estate, selling the house, or planning the funeral, but she had taken care of most everything else in advance, especially in the days before. She even spared him from having to pack up the house, her things, having organized that—a single phone call—two days before. She lived a full two days in the aftermath of her planned departure. But what he cannot stop thinking is, what if she was just waiting for him to prove her wrong? So that when someone showed up to take her things, she would wave them away from the front stoop.

But maybe after all those years, she finally felt like a burden. Maybe he let her. Had he not left her alone those last days, maybe she would not have done what she did; if he had only been there, in plain sight, she never could have done it so discreetly. She could not have convinced herself that this would be better for him, too. She would have seen how her choice would hurt him, more than any slow death.

He remembers the phone ringing. Tanner, high as shit, grabbing his phone, saying, *Oh fuck off* without looking at who was calling. Those words will stay with him forever. The way they lingered in the air, that smoke-filled emptiness of the afternoon, even then. Lucien knew, without looking, who it was. He had no idea what had happened on the other end, but now he can imagine. He will spend the rest of his life imagining. Maybe he did, finally, make her feel like a burden. Like something he would like to shed. One feels sorry for people gathered in hospital rooms, hands clasped in prayer, but they should not be the ones we pity; they have the opportunity to say goodbye and to begin letting go. Lucien and his mother were fighting her cancer so long that he forgot losing her was even an option. Her illness had become their life.

Back at his apartment, Lucien sprawls across his bed, his feet hanging off the end as they always do. He kicks off his shoes. He turns facedown on his pillow and lies that way for a moment, finding it hard to breathe and holding that sensation. Just before he can't bear it any longer, he feels something poking his chest, and remembers—the pill.

He flips back over and pulls it from his pocket. The oval pill is even smaller than he remembers and shimmers in the late afternoon light stretching across his apartment. He holds it, his grandmother's life between two fingers. He is sad for Florence, so trapped inside her body. Her life lost while still alive. But he is also jealous. She disappears into moments where his mother still lives, and where he exists, before all this. What could be the harm, in seeing what she sees? What damage would it do her to share?

He needs to see her again. Just once would be enough.

He lets the pill rest on his tongue and closes his mouth. Careful not to swallow, he sucks it like a hard candy, slowly dissolving into her.

Yellow paint inside a sunny room.

The unmistakable sense of his grandmother washes over him, and the many moments of her life unfold so fast at first that Lucien hardly catches anything more than their raw emotions. Waves of warmth and fear, pride and dignity. Some waves he's never ridden. Love. This must be what Trina meant by flooding his grandmother with memories, he thinks, amazed at his ability to remember himself with her consciousness wafting in and out.

Trying to distinguish between the incoming memories is like focusing on a single card in the deck while someone shuffles; as soon as Lucien thinks he sees something familiar, it is replaced by the next. He sucks the pill harder. The memories come in clearer, more fully formed, and Lucien finds himself adapting to Florence's consciousness, his mind working faster, his eyes becoming sharper. The more memories that pass through him, the more of her he understands for the next, and the next, until soon Lucien recognizes those he has never met before, understanding their relationships and his grandmother's feelings for them at that time, implicitly, for within her consciousness is laced a lifetime. *Fleur*, they call her when she's younger, and it feels right. Fleur.

Then Lucien's heart skips, and there she is—his mother. Isabel.

She is three years old when she first appears, and he recognizes her instantly by the smile. He feels his grandmother's overwhelming love—a mother's pride and worry—that he never truly understood, that no words from his own mother could ever explain, in leaving. Indescribable love. But she disappears again, and like the breath has been punched from him, Lucien looks for her in the cascading moments and faces that pass. Gasping. The next time she surfaces, she is *sixteen and yelling, face smeared in bright-pink lipstick and blush* that Lucien never once saw her wear, *mascara running from the mean, teenaged tears. Her mouth is stretched, spewing words too fast* for him to hear, but he feels them as sharply as his grandmother does, hot with hurt. What surprises him is how, underneath this personal slight or anger, is a baseline love that makes Lucien miss his own mother all the more for the daughter she had been and the life she had before he was ever a part of it. The sedative in the pill is beginning to dull Lucien's mind, but he sucks harder.

The next memories come out of sequence, but more vivid than ever—*Isabel in an inflatable kiddie pool, naked except for a duck beak stretched with elastic over her mouth, flapping her arms and giggling un-*

controllably in the same way she did at twenty, smoking a cigarette, lean and cool, and then again at thirty-five, when Lucien sees himself standing next to her. He shudders despite the surge of Fleur's fondness for him; he scans for the preteen flaws he knew he had then, finding none in his grandmother's memory. *He smiles earnestly back* at her, at himself; he's not wearing his signature preteen scowl, not seething with the insecurity he remembers at the time. Who was mistaken, or were they both and neither at the same time?

His mother, Isabel, again as *a baby, lying on a blanket in the grass; dressed up in a long, adult dress and high heels that her feet only fill halfway, pretending to smoke a cigarette with one hand and flicking a platinum blond wig with the other; behind the wheel, her long teen legs she hasn't grown into, stretched toward the pedal; shielding her eyes as she reads on the lawn; stroking his hair in the street outside their old apartment—*

Lucien can't stand it any longer—he swallows.

He imagines his tongue coated in luster from his grandmother's Memoroxin as the pill travels down his throat and enters his bloodstream, filling him with the sense of her. Only now he is fading as she comes on stronger, the sedative working faster, until he disappears completely.

* * *

The Vista's marquee announces the film on both sides in big, black letters. So final, so finished. The bright, round bulbs blur into a straight line in Fleur's unflinching eyes as others pass her to buy their tickets.

Alone again, sleep to sleep, sun to moon.

Her emerald dress hangs loose around the waist, its delicate pleats folding concave as she slides into one of the plush seats toward the back of the grand theater. The cushion prickles where her skin shows behind her arms and legs, and she wiggles herself against the fabric until it feels smooth. Her hands rest clasped in the emptiness of her lap that only days ago had life, heartbeat, company. The tiny body with tiny fingers and toes she had felt inside her all those months, Fleur touched only for a moment once out and knew she could never let go.

The screen comes alive with animated candies in their dementedly cheerful advertising jig, and Fleur's thumbs dance back and forth to the tune while the theater fills with couples. As two of them shuffle into the row behind her, giggling, she feels their purses and rear ends brush the auburn curls pinned low against her neck.

When at last the theater turns dark, she sinks deeper into her chair. Her green eyes widen. The opening credits appear like magic, text like fireworks—*An American Cowboy*—and she pushes her eyes closed, imagining the rest of the names she cannot bear to see. The theater grows quiet. When she opens her eyes, she is in the Wild West, sunset in the distance, the High Noon Saloon in the foreground.

She tastes the desert. She feels the sting of sunlight on her shoulders. And when the silhouette of the wide-brimmed cowboy hat turns to reveal a familiar face, she smiles.

And then it is all dust.

Chapter 14

TODAY

Angelica arranges a vase of pink dahlias in Remy's room. She is usually not one for pink, but there is something about the range of its shade in the dahlias, a deep hue that radiates into near white at their ends. It's a supple, human pink. Through the bedroom window, she can see her daughter lying in the backyard. Their California craftsman has needed so much work over the years, but Angelica loves the nooks, the way every piece of the house feels tucked in. Remy's room with its vaulted ceiling and exposed beams has always been her favorite.

Remy could be five years old again out there, her little girl who grew up on her own. Do all parents feel like they missed it? The moment their child no longer needs them, or even likes them? Or did Angelica, in fact, *miss* it? One of her newer patients at the Center has invalidated her own many excuses for herself; his mother was also a single parent, also unapologetically dedicated to her work. And yet, he will not speak a single unkind word. He blames her for nothing. Was Angelica too accommodating of her daughter's resentment? Maybe if she had doubled down, Remy would have grown up in awe of her, too? Then again, it is easy for children to hate their parents, living. Angelica has seen it before, how regret turns back into love after death. What a thing to hope for.

She can't pinpoint the moment her daughter stopped liking her, though she's gone over it countless times. There were years when she was her daughter's favorite person; Remy got homesick when away, always wanting more time with her mom. Only Angelica knew how to do things the way she liked, rubbing her back when she was sick, tucking her in at night, even though she never felt good at those things. She was still her mother, which made her home. Some time ago, long before David, that changed. And home—or simply Angelica—became a propulsive force Remy couldn't get away from fast enough. Before David's death, Angelica told herself Remy was like all daughters, pushing away in order to grow up. Claiming her independence. Even now, after such intense loss, Angelica knows her daughter loves her. She's angry with the world for losing David. And what is any parent but their child's world?

Angelica remembers the loose floorboard where Remy used to hide weed and gummies, starting in ninth grade. Angelica never let on that she knew or said anything about the weed. She wanted to keep the line open. At least Angelica knew where to look. She hasn't checked it in years; as long as Remy kept her grades up, Angelica figured, what was the harm. Her heart races as she kneels down beside Remy's bed and pulls back the wooden panel. But there's nothing. Dust. A spiderweb.

When Remy first found out about David, it was in between mid-term exams at Brown and with such spotty cell phone service there the news came in a wave through social media all at once. Former classmates at Brentwood School that she hardly kept in touch with posted their condolences. She called Angelica. Remy told her all of this, like a confidante, like her mother, before she could calculate that Angelica was to blame. Her daughter, finally sharing and looking for comfort the way a daughter should with her mother. Angelica was so taken aback that she momentarily forgot her own involvement. Her own mourning. Then she sensed the shift, even as they spoke, as Remy's choking tears subsided and she talked through what had happened. If only Angelica had been there to give her a hug, to hold her. By the end of the call, Remy was cold.

She pushes herself back up, smooths her hair, and glances out the window again. Remy is still lying in the grass, thank god. Her daughter walking in on Angelica in her bedroom is the last thing their relationship needs, even if Angelica is simply doing something nice. The flowers are yet another peace offering. Angelica loves dahlias, how from afar they look like simple rounds of color, but up close each petal is like a curved slipper, part of a larger conical beehive. The form is an engineering marvel, well beyond most human understanding. All of Angelica's favorite flowers hold this tell, the hint at the complexity of nature, disguised in beauty. Humans would struggle to create anything as perfectly intricate as the dahlia. Of course, they try in other ways. Angelica remembers the hideous neon-dyed daisies—shockingly, a relative of the dahlia—she used to see outside the bodega near her apartment in Baltimore. Is there anything humans won't ruin?

Angelica steps back to admire the vase on Remy's dresser. The flowers look too stiffly bunched and inert. She slides the stems around until they have just the right amount of lean. Then she lifts the vase to wipe off any water. Just as she holds it in one hand, the screen door slams downstairs, startling her. She loses her grip and the vase tips, spilling water everywhere. A single dahlia falls, bud first, to the floor.

She quickly wipes the top of the dresser, then opens the drawers to see how far the water dripped. She is blindly wiping out the inside of Remy's underwear drawer when she hears a rattle among the fabric. She feels around. In high school, Remy was always taking her bottles of ibuprofen, so they were missing whenever Angelica had a headache. She feels a bittersweet reminder that those things she thought she'd said goodbye to forever, in this house, with her child, continue now. But when she pulls the pill bottle out from behind a lace thong, she recognizes the amber plastic for another reason. First, her name. Next, David's.

Angelica's brain stalls.

Why does her daughter have these? Her daughter? Angelica knows, abstractly, the statistics on people abusing Memoroxin. She sees it in person every day at the Center. But her own daughter? She opens the bottle, as if that will clarify anything—it is nearly empty.

But. Oh god. How could she?

Angelica pulls out the tiny paper curled along the interior. She recognizes her handwriting—the key she had made for David, listing which pills to take when. The "up" pills contained pleasant memories to lift him out of a depressive episode; by how many of those remain, her first thought is that all the difficult, painful memories have been taken. Those were exposures they were going to work on together for integration, only to be taken sparingly. Angelica thinks of Remy, how they might have affected her if she took them, but then she realizes something far worse and suddenly obvious. David took all of them.

David. Her kind, adorable patient. She remembers writing this note for his first batch of pills; he must've held on to it and moved it from bottle to bottle. So careful. Oh god, David. She never thought of losing him. In all her years, she's never lost a patient. It makes sense now, why he would do it. The only way his own pills could be dangerous.

She hasn't heard Remy since the screen door opened downstairs. *Remy?* she calls. Angelica feels shaky with rage. How can she bring it up without showing she was snooping? She wasn't, not when she found them. Does it even matter? Her own daughter. How dare she. *Remy!* she calls, now running down the stairs. She hears the screen door again. Remy is nowhere in the kitchen. How typical of her daughter, freshly absent from every room Angelica enters. Only a half-empty yogurt container sits on the counter. *The apparition has to eat*, Angelica scoffs, channeling all her emotions into anger.

She pulls out the trash can.

Outside there is a screeching sound and then a terrible silence.

Angelica opens the door, the curious, annoyed neighbor, but she steps outside a mother. She runs, a mother. Remy's sneakers, the black high-tops she bought her years ago, the same tattered pair Angelica has tried countless times to replace, lay unmoving in the street. The driver has not yet gotten out of his car. Angelica cannot believe what she sees, the more it becomes clear. Remy, who she just saw lying in the grass. The same legs, arms, face. She cannot look, but she cannot look away, either.

Now the driver is panicking, talking endlessly, cluelessly.

How did this happen? How did this happen? A neighbor who rarely says hello appears beside her and holds Angelica's hand between her own. For a moment this feels awkward, as if awkwardness matters, as if anything matters. How did anything ever matter before this? Angelica realizes then that she is still clutching the bottle of pills in her palm, the woman cupping hers around it.

And then there are sirens, and an ambulance, and Angelica cannot stop looking at her daughter the entire time the paramedics speak, as they ask her questions and she answers, as she rides beside Remy, the entire way to the hospital.

Chapter 15

BEFORE

Lucien stops at Dinosaur Coffee to write the email he has been putting off for weeks, hoping to be buoyed by all the other people writing their own difficult emails. The sweet Novocain of working in public. Today he almost doesn't need the coffee. For the first time in months, he slept well. His body feels rested, relaxed as if forgiven. Last night he saw his mother, unclouded with any memory of his own. He still feels the warmth inside Fleur's memories, the freedom of her perspective not his own. Before taking the pill, Lucien would've said with certainty that he would give anything to go back to a time before, when there were other emotions that didn't all lead to loss.

He'd just never have expected to find that chance, sitting in a bottle beside his grandmother. Or that the time itself would not be his own.

As usual, Dinosaur Coffee is full of other seemingly dislocated New Yorkers who clutter the Eastside wearing layers in an overcast seventy-five degrees and sitting with their laptops open, idle, phones pressed to their chins, talking with an impatience that seems to insist they are from elsewhere. Lucien has never seen such a performative disruption in New York, his city that deals in disturbances, but maybe having one's feet so firmly planted in anxiety carries a certain weight in Los Angeles, where everyone else seems at risk of floating away.

He orders from the cashier he recognizes by her overalls and inkyblue hair.

"Lucien, right?" she says.

"Right," he says after too long considering. Not only did he for a moment feel a sense of Florence still lingering, but the recognition alone in a city where he still feels so out of place—he didn't see it coming. "Thanks."

"Hard to forget, I love the name."

"My mother's favorite painter," he reminds himself. "Lucian Freud."

"Never heard of him."

"Right, why would you? He painted portraits, extremely unflattering and sinister. Not sure what my mother was getting at there."

"A curse from your mother that she deems a blessing. Classic."

Lucien laughs; it feels good to talk about his mother like she's still alive, like he can still joke about resenting her for things that don't matter. After last night, she is, and he can.

"Well, Lucian Freud, I'll have to look you up."

Beyond the blue hair, Lucien recognizes the look in her eyes, like his own pain staring back. Even in the movement of her fingers at the iPad, he senses the sadness. Even as she smiles at him. He knows the way loss can change your face, how it drags the light from your eyes.

He pulls out a cigarette and heads out the retracted garage door to the sidewalk. Somehow even a black coffee now takes ten minutes, no matter how simple the order, but any wait time is more tolerable when put into cigarettes. Coffee, one cigarette. Waiting for the J/M train at Lorimer, two. Maybe three if it's cold. Here people pass him on the sidewalk, confused. One guy motions for a hit before realizing it's an actual cigarette, not weed. Not a Juul, not a vape, not a joint dipped in cocaine, just an actual fucking cigarette. Lucien couldn't get into the e-cigs, even before all the safety warnings. He spends enough time with electronic devices. He likes the way a cigarette starts and ends, the way smoking one feels like finishing something and destroying it at the same time.

Finally, he hears his name. He looks for a spot and is struck by the number of people—guys especially—formatting their screenplays while bobbing their heads to the chaotic music. The more of them he sees, the more unlikely success seems, and he feels sorry for them, despite their impenetrable self-satisfaction. They happily mimic the thing as if the act is all it takes. He has seen the same phenomenon with photographers who carry cameras around, approaching beautiful women to ask if they *wanna shoot*. Lucien could never, even with a solo show to his name and a stack of pay stubs that all say *I'm a photographer*. Mostly those guys seem to like talking about it, being the thing instead of doing the work. Lucien likes photography for the removal, the seclusion of the darkroom; that it depends on the finished product and not the performance.

He finds a spot at a low table. Next to him, two young women talk over cappuccinos, both their voices intensely mellow. One smacks a sugar packet against her palm while the other takes a photo of her frothy heart before lifting it to her perfect, matte lips. When she smiles, her nose scrunches around a tiny diamond. He's unsure of whether he has seen her on a billboard, or if she simply looks familiar for her manufactured flawlessness, the way one might recognize a mannequin in a storefront. The one beside him tosses her long hair over her shoulder, tickling his arm. He hates how good it feels, lately, to be touched.

Liv is pretty in this same way, though she's too careful to be so sunkissed. There's something buoyant about her, appealing for now, even if sometimes when she's talking Lucien finds himself wondering whether he'd be friends with her. Other girls he's dated have been friends first. If he's honest, Lucien cannot see himself being friends with Liv, not in his previous life at least. A bad sign for them both.

Lucien knows he has nothing to give. He is no better than his grandmother, his appearance only hinting at something behind the surface. Maybe his disheveled state translates to an affect of talent here; his haphazard curls and tall, lanky posture mark him as different and even masculine among the petite, the perfect, the pedicured. Even with the men scattering this space, he gets the sense that their stubble might wipe right off with a wet napkin; their round lenses might be full of clear glass; their tattered shirts brand-new.

He opens his laptop. He needs to write something, anything, to Natasha. Then she might stop calling. He just needs to buy himself more time. He feels so much better today, after just one pill, that he can only imagine how he'll feel tomorrow, and the next day, if he can get a few more. Enough to take his mind off everything, to get out of his own head. Maybe even to inspire him once again.

But what is there to say? Put simply, he has nothing to show. He needs time, though how much, and for what, he doesn't know. He doesn't know what's next. He feels stuck, desperate for a new approach, or a new subject. The overlay collage and blurring in his last series had become avoidance, a means of survival. He sees that now; that's about all he can see. But he can't send all that, knowing it's the last thing his art dealer wants to read.

Dear Natasha,

I'm so sorry I've been missing your calls—I think I need some time

He deletes it.

Hey! Can't believe I keep missing your calls—

Again.

I'm sorry. I think I need to reevaluate—

"Lucien—fucking—Bennett!"

Timothy Barber, a classmate from NYU, stands beside his table. Lucien doesn't understand how he missed him earlier, though he certainly blends in. Timothy motions to an open laptop a few spots down, screenplay aglow. Sophomore year, Timothy had a short story published in the *Paris Review* that went viral. The story got him an agent and a major book deal pitched on an idea, though as far as Lucien knows, eight years later there's still no novel.

"You're the last person I expected to get the LA bug, man," Timothy says.

"Yeah, well," Lucien starts, then realizes he has nothing. "You live out here?"

"A few years now. I've got this pilot with Hulu, off the story, and an overall coming up at HBO—crazy times, man. I'm stretched so thin, but I love it, you know? How about you, what brings you west? Don't tell me you've got a show opening! I saw that one in Chelsea, I mean, I didn't make it, obviously, but I saw the photos, major."

"Here because of my grandmother, actually." Lucien hears how strange it sounds, the way he fumbles finding the words, even now. "Just helping out for a bit."

"Wow, right on. Better man than I," Timothy says. "Hey, I was so sorry to hear about your mom, dude. Damn."

"Thank you," says Lucien, back in a conversation he knows well.

"I saw the article in the *Times*," Timothy says, pausing to allow Lucien the chance to elaborate, but he doesn't. "Did Schnabel really come to the funeral?"

"He did."

"In the silk pajamas?"

"They were good friends."

Lucien forgets how to leave a conversation, or at least how to steer it. Maybe it's the pill, still wearing off. Him too content from the wash of it. He wants to counter with his own question. *So, when is that novel finally coming out?* It's a voice Lucien never listens to, but others subject him to all the time. The voice that knows trigger points and pushes on anyway.

Timothy puts his earbuds in and holds up a finger.

"Hey, I got this call," he whispers. "Great seeing you, man, we should get drinks!"

Before Lucien can respond, Timothy is already on the call, rushing to face his laptop screen, talking loudly. Both girls look over at the sound, and Lucien actually thinks they look impressed. He turns back to his computer, the cursor left blinking—*I think I need*—but he can't finish it. Especially now. What he didn't tell Timothy is that one of the reasons he chose Los Angeles was because he had not expected to be seen.

The first time Lucien went to Dinosaur, he parked at a CVS a quarter mile away and decided to walk rather than driving, and parking, again. On his phone it looked close. But during the walk along Sunset Boulevard, the sidewalk disappeared, and he was honked at the entire way. For good reason, no one was walking. Trash whipped at him from the road. Only a few weeks in Los Angeles, and he will now drive from Gelson's to CVS, even though they share the same large lot.

Lucien can't remember the last time he felt out of place. His first year at Stuyvesant, sure, he remembers the rush to make new friends, meeting their families. He never felt like his home was different, until seeing theirs. But that was still New York. His life was oriented around the safety of that big anonymous place. Even the two years in New

Haven for his MFA never felt like being away from the city, not truly. You could still say *the city* and everyone knew which one you meant. For undergrad, Lucien chose NYU last-minute over Brown to be close to his mother; he even lived with her at home instead of the dorms when she got worse. By the time he got into Yale, he'd earned a little time away. His mother was doing well then, too; one term she even taught a studio class for the painting MFA—when they would have lunch, the two of them, at the little oyster bar just off campus once a week. Smiling at their luck.

Lucien went in the opposite direction of his MFA classmates and took a job afterward, working with Max Yorn, one of those photographers whose name had practically become a brand, who had launched his own fashion magazine, and who was recognizable enough to engage any room he entered. Lucien worked either alongside him at parties or, in the last two years, covering entire events for him. Those years held a duality; daytime Lucien was a dutiful son—the nightlife job freed his days for helping his mother with whatever she needed. The perks were not lost on him, either. Lucien knew everyone and no one at all. Models would call his name as he walked through Nolita, grabbing a bagel on his way to his mother at the hospital. Only he knew the disconnect between his reality and his gig. He decided what and who would be remembered at those parties. People wanted him around because he made them feel seen. And with the camera in front of his face, he disappeared.

Caring for his mother became an identity that stood in for his own; it even informed his work. Lucien built a practice from his despair. His first solo show was in a tiny gallery on the Lower East Side. It was a night of worlds colliding; friends from high school, NYU, and Yale all came. There were the requisites: an open bar, someone to document the Who's Who Wearing Who, the type of job Lucien had done countless times. Even Max Yorn came, kind of him though Lucien knew it made the guy look better. His protégé, an artist in his own right. It was the type of opening where people were looking around more than at the art. It was a success.

The show was a collection of his own photographs stretched and obscured and painted over, of his mother in varying degrees of illness and recovery. In most of them, he offset the images with a wash of color and thick, effusive white clouds. But the standout piece was a blown-up black-and-white, taken in the moment between sleep and wake. His mother looked regal yet ethereal. Lucien painted over it with bright colors and metallics to re-create the look of a relic, the Virgin Mary, grace herself. The piece sold immediately and covered a year of rent. The entire night was a mix of elation and humiliation; deep down Lucien knew the reason for the show was his mother's name and—most important—her illness.

His success cemented in his mother's pain.

The show got him representation. Natasha, a buzzy art dealer with a gallery off the High Line. That was a year ago. Lucien has yet to show her new work. At least before if he was stuck, or too busy to work on his own art, he was still shooting for his job. Still behind the camera. His camera was like an appendage, another set of eyes to make sense of the world. Now it feels awkward in his hands, and anything he looks at dries up in front of him. He's dealt with his own creative pressure before—the difficulty in reconciling what you imagined and what you made. Since his mother's death every photo he's developed looks dull, incomplete. The thing died the second it was born.

Art is an act of hope, whatever shape it takes. The impulse to make the thing, the faith that lets you listen to it. To try and create something that might speak to those you may never meet. That was all blind hope. His pieces featuring his mother were aggressions of hope, an attempt to make her permanent in the face of his fear. Now, across the country and cut off from everything and everyone he knows, Lucien sees like he has lost his vision, forgotten his eye. Moments pass him before they register. And he is all out of hope.

When Lucien arrives at his grandmother's, no one is in the front room to greet him. She must be awake, he thinks, but when he gets to the den, he sees otherwise. She lies fully reclined in a medical bed, with two machines humming next to her.

"Lucien," Trina says. "We tried to call you last night."

"Sorry, my phone must've been off." He thinks of it, buried somewhere between his sheets, while he slipped back and forth through time. "What's going on? What is all this?"

"Florence started having trouble chewing, swallowing," Trina says carefully. "It's a new development, obviously, but not one that's entirely unexpected."

"I don't understand, she was fine yesterday."

"It's her muscle memory failing now," Trina says. "It's all faster than we'd have hoped, for sure, but these things progress quickly, seemingly out of nowhere. This is when we really need the treatment to start taking, or she might need to be hospitalized, for more assistance than we can offer. We have every reason to think the treatment may still work; it takes up to six months for patients her age to show progress, and she's only at about three."

"And what—those signs of progress would be coming off the tubes, but she still might not remember anything, or be herself?"

"If she starts to regain her motor skills, it's a good indication that her memory will come back, too; we forget how much of the physical body is built on memory. It'll be a sign the treatment is working. And then it's just time."

Lucien looks down at his grandmother, the papery skin on her neck crinkled. He strokes her hair, trying to adjust her to be more comfortable, but she stays sleeping. Beside her, he feels her memories resurfacing—the faces he had known, surrounded by the feelings they stir in her.

"Fleur," he says softly.

"Fleur?" repeats Trina, as if hearing it for the first time. Lucien feels a shock of recognition at the name, and then fear. "How beautiful. I like that."

"It's what her friends called her."

"Well, she's on a heavier dose today," Trina says. "She probably won't be awake for several hours, if you want to come back later."

"I'll stay anyway."

He feels guilty. His unspeakable violation, all that he now knows without permission. But then there's his mother—available to him, alive again at any moment, in all ages. He cannot bear that those moments are being wasted on someone who doesn't even remember her daughter enough to miss her in the present. That those moments, the last trace of his mother left alive, should disappear in the faulty memory of another.

"Since you're here, I'm going to grab my book," Trina says. "I'll be back in a minute!"

He nods, listening for Trina's footsteps to fade before opening the bottle and shaking a few more pills from its abundant glow. His mother feels so close, her presence so tangible. Here it is, an alternate reality, preserved before everything went wrong. He would feel more guilt if he had any choice.

Lucien parks one street over from Laguna Avenue so Liv won't see his car. He is too good at this for someone who has never been deceptive in his life. He had too much freedom to sneak around; even as a teenager in the city, his mother only asked for details, to tell her a good story. Well, wouldn't this be one?

Back in his apartment, Lucien scatters the pills across the kitchen counter. He sets one full pill aside and then cuts the rest in half to stretch his supply. When they break, their pearlescent dust coats the laminate. Suddenly—footsteps on the stairs—Lucien crouches to the floor, waiting. He holds his breath until the footsteps turn toward the apartment across the hall.

What is he doing, hiding in his own apartment? Stealing from his grandmother? This, this is him helping? He grabs a bag of coffee from the cupboard and slides the shimmering halves over the edge of the countertop into the bag. When he looks inside, her pills seem to sparkle even in the dark. The nutty, caramel smell of the grounds rises up and into the back of his throat.

Lucien pinches the single remaining pill left on the counter and lets it roll along the lines of his palm. Which one speaks to fate, which to family? Why read palms, when the answers are distilled so neatly here? Seeing his mother, in all the ages he never knew, feels like extra time with her. Not just memories, but a little more life. He pushes the pill between his lips and sucks water from the kitchen sink.

He walks over to his bed and flops down, waiting for the sedative to set in. He is more desperate than ever to leave his own guilt. As he feels the sense of Florence return, he is finally no longer alone. Maybe Los Angeles isn't so bad when you have someone, he thinks. Even if they wait, captive, inside a bag of coffee grounds.

Lucien laughs, then can't remember why, and then his laugh is Fleur's—

and everyone else is laughing, too.

Chapter 16

TODAY

Dr. Sloane's absence hangs over the Center, a space already defined by what it lacks. Lucien has heard murmurs of a family emergency. He thinks of the daughter, the voice he knows only from the expression on Dr. Sloane's face. Concern displacing her careful insistence of calm. For a moment she opened up to him. She, who stares as if looking for his seams, had pulled at her own strings and almost come undone.

This morning's group exercise involves scented sachets, distributed during the circle. Another doctor, no name, mimics Dr. Sloane's even tone. Each sachet smells different, she explains, specifically designed to activate a patient's essential memories, so they are advised to hold theirs close. Not to share. These are scents found outside. Baby steps, to their return. Each patient takes turns describing what their sachet evokes. No specifics, only general scenes. When they get to the teen, eyes closed, he keeps saying, *Coookies! Coookies!*

At first it's funny, then haunting.

Had Lucien seen this place and its many hollowed faces, would he have taken his grandmother's pills? He can't remember the choice, but he must have been desperate. He will never know what he looked like at his low, or what got him there, though he imagines it from what he's seen—eyes glazed, maybe drool, that terrifying laughter at nothing. The parts of him that curled into themselves, idle on the floor, his smile enjoying every second as someone else.

Doesn't the body remember, even after the mind has been wiped clean?

Lucien saw plenty of people on drugs growing up. The painter Phillip Ash, always on cocaine, always excited about everything and nothing, frantic with energy and enthusiasm to the point of undermining the thing itself. The best antidrug platform is not showing the temptation and telling someone to say no, but rather showing what happens when you like it. Too much. Where saying yes, over and over, will take you.

After the group session, Lucien and Sophie sit together at the cluster of couches facing the fireplace that grounds all their public conversations. He likes the illusion of a shared purpose, and the ability to watch the flames, even as they speak. Lucien still holds his linen sachet, which looks like something one might place in a drawer of clothing; like something that might smell of lavender or cedar. Sophie holds hers, too.

Her feet are tucked neatly under her, her posture light and perfect. The same feet that, two nights ago, had crawled across her floor, desperate.

He has not stopped thinking about the moment Sophie switched so quickly from being there with him in her room, to someplace else. He knows nothing about where she goes, or what she bears inside. He wants to see her no less, to help her just the same. He wants to tell her that it doesn't matter to him, how she suffers or what she's seen.

At least he has finally placed her. Sophie. Though it hardly explains the draw he's felt here. Theirs was only a casual passing before; Sophie, as he knew her then, was flat. Undefined. He didn't yet know the curve of her eyebrows, or the way she closes her eyes just before she smiles. The anger she tries to hide. He remembers liking her fine then, too, and maybe he even thought more of Liv for being friends with her, but it's hard to imagine ever standing beside Sophie without feeling like he could never leave. Like he wanted to stay beside her forever. How did he do it, then? Was it just too inconvenient to see?

Lucien wonders how long it will be until Sophie remembers and if it would be better to tell her first. Unless she already knows. Maybe neither of them wants to say, to make it true. Lucien doesn't want to hurt Liv, but he also puts her out of his mind, no problem. Could Sophie do the same? As much as he grows tired of waiting here, he dreads leaving the Center, if leaving could mean losing her. At least here there are no names. No Liv. Lucien holds his sachet up to his face and breathes in deeply. *Car exhaust, cigarette smoke, alcohol in her perfume covering the clothes in her closet; sour chemicals from the darkroom; the sterilized sanitizer of hospitals, pen in hand as he does homework in the corner, his neck sore from hunching without a desk.*

He puts the sachet back in his pocket, wondering why his memories are all chemical. The sensation it evoked lingers, layers unfolding inside of him.

Sophie sniffs her sachet cautiously and closes her eyes. Lucien watches her, wondering where she is. She opens her eyes and smiles as if covering.

"Cut grass." She shrugs. "So basic."

Then she wipes away a tear.

Woven baskets scatter the common room. They look like they might hold fruit or seashells, but are full of blackout glasses, disposable like the flimsy ones one might have gotten at a 3D movie years ago. Smaller baskets are full of foam earplugs. Some patients fully tune out, glasses on, earbuds in, for the total experience if they want to go deeper; though most clearly don't need it. They sit capable of seeing nothing even with their eyes wide open.

Lucien hasn't been taking his supplements. He doesn't like the sensation of feeling himself at different ages, in all the anxiety of those times. If only his mother were more present in some of them, not in the background as she always is, then he might take them more often. If only he could feel her hand on his back, see her smile. Though of course she isn't; if she were, he would disappear into them and never want to come out. He might never leave. They would find him back in that bright room, on the cold table, OD'd from the liquid drip of his life. What a way to go, he thinks. Is it joint suicide if one of you is already dead?

"You're quiet today," says Sophie.

"Sorry," he says. "Just thinking."

"Are you scared of me now, then?"

"Not at all," he says, feeling guilty for not making that clearer. For not apologizing sooner. He looks her in the eyes, careful not to shy away. "I wasn't thinking about that. If anything *I* feel bad about that. I never should have—"

"Please don't feel bad."

"Okay," he says. "I'm good at that."

She looks amused, relieved.

"I'm sorry . . . you're going through this."

Saying it feels empty, and he regrets it immediately. Sophie doesn't respond, and he considers apologizing, again, for that. She closes her eyes, and sniffs her sachet.

"*Touch has a memory. O say, love, say, What can I do to kill it and be free?*"

Lucien watches, waiting for more.

"That's nice," he says when she doesn't go on.

"Keats," she says. "One of my favorite poems. I thought I understood it before, in high school. But I had no idea. No idea. It's funny, the things that come back clearer than before. I could recite the entire thing. You'd be impressed, wouldn't you, if we weren't—in here?"

She holds the sachet under her nose, hiding a smile.

"I'm still impressed," he offers. "It's about a broken heart?"

"I thought so, but no. I think it's about not understanding freedom until it's gone. Whether in love, or lust, or trauma, you're free until you're not. Then that thing, that state—it owns you. You can't see freedom until you want it back."

They sit in silence.

"If there's anything I can do to help," Lucien says, "because honestly, you do that for me. I don't know how, but your being here, it helps. And I'm not sure if there's even a question in there, or what I have to offer, but if you ever want to talk about—"

One of the nurses walks over and stands in front of the fireplace, between them. She picks up two logs and stacks them in the flames. She stands there for a few moments, holding her hands to the warmth. Neither of them speaks until she is gone.

"Come to my room again tonight?"

At the Center, so little feels personal or physical. One could go through the entire program without ever being touched. Skin to skin. The drug at the root of their addiction is so clinical—so precise—that the treatment matches it. Lucien thinks about Sophie all the time. Her graceful neck, the way it would feel to lay his mouth along its nape. Maybe because of the last time he touched her—and knowing now that he can't—he wants to that much more.

When he arrives at Sophie's room, Lucien lingers in the doorway, watching her rising and falling on her toes, wearing a white nightgown they must leave for female patients, not that he's seen any others. The thin fabric is nothing special, and the cut is loose—one size fits all—but on Sophie it is transcendent. Through the gauze, he sees the curves of her as one arm crests overhead, her gaze following, until she appears more arc than human.

Lucien has never seen someone so matched by their purpose in that moment. Maybe his mother when he caught her examining a canvas—elbow to her hip, paintbrush in hand, totally unaware of being watched—but he never understood that, not in the moment. Sophie turns at the sound of his footsteps, and as their eyes meet, he thinks, how is it possible to have missed someone you did not know before?

They sit on the hardwood floor, shoulders almost touching, in the near darkness of her room. Lucien wonders if others are doing this, visiting one another at night, or if they are being awarded some special privilege. Lucien doesn't know and he doesn't want to find out; he doesn't want anything to stop what he imagines could become a new ritual. Sophie leans back and Lucien follows her. They lie side by side, just close enough for Lucien to feel her nightgown fanned out against his forearm. The fabric feels special—charged.

Even in the silence, he feels something like bliss. Sure, there is an underlying, constant shame for not feeling a sense of urgency to get back to his grandmother, with no one to visit her but him. But each time he thinks of Florence, a heaviness takes over his stomach—guilt, he imagines—so perhaps it is better not to, not until it is finally time to leave. After all, it's not entirely up to him. He must drift off because when he wakes, Sophie is staring at him.

"Jesus, how long have I been out?"

"Long enough," she says. "You've had a nice life."

"Is that so?"

"I can tell just by watching you," she says. "I think our dreams are different here. I think they show us. You disagree?"

"About my life? I think it depends on when you'd asked me that."

"I'm asking you now."

"Right now?" he says. "I'd have to agree."

Sophie smiles, shy.

"Everything looks enchanted once you're far enough away," she says a bit wistfully.

"I'm not sure I agree with that."

"Then it hasn't been long enough." Sophie slips her hand into his, and scoots closer so that their thighs press together. Lucien feels wide awake. He waits for her to react, to fall apart. But she is still there.

"Want to play a game?"

"Sure."

"Okay, what do you see?"

Sophie reaches her hand over his eyes.

"Uh, nothing."

"Not yet!"

Sophie's other hand leaves his, though the one over his eyes remains. He sees darkness, the backs of his eyelids, prickles of color from the total lack. And then—he gets a wave of it. *The leaves in autumn once there are more on the ground than the branches. The figure of his parents in the window; his father's hand articulating something, furious or hilarious. His mother's face.* Lucien pulls Sophie's hand away and sees she's been holding her sachet under his nose.

"You're not supposed to do that," he says, sitting up onto his elbows.

"Fuck it," she says, and rolls onto her side. "So, what'd you get?"

"I got . . . I dunno, grassy perfume. Something a teacher wore." He lies and he's not sure why. "Okay, close your eyes," he says, reaching out his hand.

Sophie slaps it away.

"No, I don't want yours. I can't."

"Fuck it," he mimics.

"I don't want to!"

"Okay," he says. "I didn't even bring mine. Just trust me."

Lucien hovers his hand over her eyes, feeling her lashes flutter against the inside of his palm.

"Salt crusted on your jaw, in your hairline, on your tongue; water beading over your shoulder, facedown on a terry-cloth towel." He pauses to see it himself. "Eyelids heavy, thin seaweed plastered across your butt cheek."

Sophie smiles and he feels her breath on his hand.

"The ocean dripping down your back, off your hair," she adds.

"My hair?"

"Shut up."

"Overhead lighting, AC on blast," he starts again, then waits.

"CVS in the summer," adds Sophie. "Crisp magazines, everything plastic. Looking for nail polish. Seafoam and baby blues."

"Here's one," Lucien says. "Shadows faceting the spiraled structure like something carved out of clay." He speaks like he's reading a story to her, showing off maybe, and watches her mouth purse in thought, then curve into a smile. "Streams of people following its curves. Quiet, even when it's humming. Crowds like a symphony tuning, raucous harmony, until you enter the flow."

Sophie pulls his hand down. Her face now feels incredibly close, looking back at him.

"The Guggenheim?"

Lucien looks at her in performed shock at the naming.

"Stop it," she says. "What? I can see it, so clearly."

"It wasn't a riddle," he says. "I thought that was the point."

"Well, I've only been there once. I was just a girl."

"That's not how we play."

"I was in New York for a dance trip. A prize, really. And one day, we ended there for a holiday concert. All of us sat in chairs arranged in the center on the lower level, while waiters handed out drinks—hot cider for us—and trays of colorful cookies. I took two because they were so beautiful, but I kept them in my pocket until they crumbled."

"Crumbled cookies in your pocket," Lucien jokes, going on. "Sprinkles everywhere."

"The chorus descended single-file down the ramp," she continues, ignoring him. "My god, it was beautiful. Otherworldly. Or, out of my world at least."

"We used to go to that, too," Lucien says before realizing.

Suddenly it feels different to put himself in the scene, to bring up his family. He hasn't mentioned anything about his past. Not even where he was from.

"You and your family?"

"I miss that feeling here, in LA," Lucien says, avoiding. "How something as personal as a museum could feel intimate. Your own in some way, just like it's everyone else's, too."

"Los Angeles doesn't owe you anything," says Sophie.

Lucien can't tell how she means that.

"It's like you said earlier, missing a feeling once it's gone," he says. "Recognizing it once it's gone. I feel that way about New York all the time. I feel that way about a lot of things."

"Me too."

They lie still, looking up at the ceiling. White, though it looks blue in the dark.

They spend the next three nights together, describing the world outside from the dark, describing the things they are afraid to take for granted. Lucien pulls from his own memories, from his favorite photographs or feelings and tastes. Often when leading the prompt, he sees a still image, unsure of whether from his own life or a photograph so firmly rooted in his memory that he mistakes it for his own. Together in the dark, he feels they are building a world where they can go after this, made up of their offerings to one another.

When no one interrupts them, Lucien thinks he was wrong about the cameras in every corner. Had he presumed his own prison, when in fact they are largely free? What does it say when freedom feels like the scarier option?

"I want to tell you something," Sophie says one night. She sits up and faces him with her legs crossed. "I still remember things."

She says it like a confession, like it terrifies her.

"What do you mean?" he says, sitting up to match her.

"Things I'm not supposed to."

"How?"

"I don't know," she says, and then she starts to cry. Not the terrifying cries he witnessed twice before, but helpless, quiet tears.

Lucien considers what to say, remembering the phone call he first overheard, the worry Dr. Sloane could not hide from her voice; the sight of Sophie not so long ago, in the same room.

"How much do you remember?"

"Little things, really. Most of it is gone. I remember driving and feeling totally out of control. Like every passing thought might come to fruition. I remember it scared me."

"In your own memory?"

"Yes, in my own memory," she says. "But it wasn't really me, not after the Mem."

"Have you told Dr. Sloane?"

"She knows. I've had my initial treatment five times now. They don't know why it's still happening. Those should all be gone."

Lucien thinks of the cold metal table, how much he hated that feeling of blankness. How it haunted him for days, in dreams, until it didn't. He cannot imagine going through that again. And again.

"What kind of thoughts?"

"Have you ever stopped at a traffic light and watched someone crossing the street in front of your car, this big monstrous machine, and thought how delicate it all is? That fragile body in front of so much power? And how if you sneezed and jerked the gas, how easily all this could be over, for anyone? Who knows, maybe there has always been something wrong with me, somewhere."

That's not so bad, he thinks to himself, having expected much worse.

"I would be walking and see a small child, looking so vulnerable," she says, "and part of me would think how trusting they are, and how beautiful that is, obviously, but also—how easy it would be to change that. To rip them from their comfort."

Now Lucien wants her to stop, stop before he knows any more.

"I had all these thoughts, terrible violent thoughts." Sophie breathes deeply and wipes her tears. Then she shakes her head. "They aren't my own. But I'd be out walking, and I would see those same innocent children and start doing things, like touching their hair as I walked by, tugging at their clothes, not because I wanted to but because I could. It was like I was testing myself, like there was some trigger inside of me that made it happen to spite me, and then all of a sudden they weren't even my thoughts being acted on, they were tainted until they became things I never would have thought of, ever, and then I started to lose the ability to differentiate what was mine and what was *his*, and what I could stop and what I couldn't, and when I realized that, I had to . . ."

"You had to what?"

"When I realized that, I had to stop myself."

Chapter 17

BEFORE

Y ou Are Liberated.
    You Are Balanced.
    You Are Loved.

The affirmations are everywhere. They curl in painted script across the colorful tiles that scatter Café Gratitude's walls; they lay hidden on the inside of mugs and in the center of every plate, patiently waiting to be announced. They are so ever-present, in fact, that they lose all meaning inside the vegan restaurant's tinted-glass walls. Even the menu items are named in bold mantras, as if ordering a blue spirulina lemonade makes anyone Gracious. As if it could, ever.

Today in rehearsal Sophie felt inadequate, with all the doubt she pushes down daily creeping into her head every time she looked at the other dancers. Their form, their extension, their bodies. By the time practice ended she had convinced herself that she, the lead, was the worst of all. Moreover, that Auguste had made a mistake in casting her and everyone knew it. When he called her over on her way out, she braced herself for the blow. But all he said was to get her head on straight. *I need you here, every moment. You were distracted today. Don't second guess yourself, mon chou.* Of course, her own insecurity would be the thing she most has to fear. When he squeezed her shoulders, touched his forehead to hers, she almost cried.

Auguste is right, Sophie needs to get her head on straight. Find something inside of herself and hold it tight, no matter what attention comes later, good or bad. She feels a bit pathetic, for coming to this place in search of that. How cliché. She scans the rest of the vegan fare, scouring for more soft spots in herself. Who would create an entire menu of trigger points, then force customers to read them aloud? Claim the thing you most fear?

You Are Loved.

What does love have to do with romaine, wakame, and sesame seed gomasio? Why should failed relationships keep anyone from a delicious cashew kale Caesar?

"Would you like to hear the question of the day?"

Sophie looks up to find her waiter staring past her, toward a table of girls her age wearing crop tops and floral skirts in different patterns. One of them wears a crown that says QUEEN FOR A DAY.

"Sorry, one sec," he says, and heads in the other direction.

Their server sets down a massive slice of vegan pumpkin pie with a candle in it. This is the land of fake foods, where nothing counts. The girls take photos, though not one of them picks up a fork. Just then, the other servers surround the table and begin singing.

Annnnd a happy happy birthday, a happy birthing day, it's a happy happy birthday, and that is why we say—it's a happy happy person, who can truly say, live a happy grateful lifetime, with love and laughter—hey! Have a . . .

The birthday girl covers her face with her hands despite clearly loving the attention. Sophie turns back to find her waiter, waiting.

"Did you want to hear the question of the day?"

He must have fled so he didn't have to sing.

"I'm okay," she says. "Do they do that a lot?"

"The singing? Every day."

"Yikes. Hmm so, I'll have the . . . sorry, the kelp noodles? And could I get that with extra cashew cheese? And a side of kimchi."

"You are Connected," he says back, and Sophie can't help but feel a sting. "Extra cheese, side of 'chi."

Despite the intense brand of holistic-living sourced-positivity that Café Gratitude promotes—not to mention its alleged cult affiliations—Sophie finds herself frequenting the macrobiotic mini chain regularly on her way home from rehearsals. Tonight, she drove home first to shower, put on her most comfortable layers, and took a Drivr to the restaurant. The thought of pressing her foot on the gas pedal was too much after rehearsal. And there is something addictive about a bowl that promises to nourish your soul and body, especially when Sophie's feel so depleted. *Indulge. Nourish yourself. Fill yourself.* The seat hurts her sit bones; for once she wishes for the padding she works away every day. The waiter, Jamie, reappears with her food almost impossibly quickly. She smiles even harder against his energy, and his eyes do not soften but widen as he smiles back, hinting at an underlying rage.

"You Are Connected," he says setting down the bowl. "Kale pesto kelp noodles. Extra cashew cheese and a side of kimchi." The repetition of her modifications feels more like reprimanding.

Meanwhile, a waiter the next table over announces the question of the day—"What *challenges* you?"—lingering for a moment, ostensibly for them to consider and discuss among themselves. Instead, once their waiter is gone, a twenty-something wearing an ironic, oversized Hawaiian shirt, leans in and asks, *Have you guys taken a photo in the bathroom? It's SO good.*

Sophie looks back to her bowl. the kelp noodles twirled into an infinite loop flickered with green. As she twists some around her fork, the insides of her cheeks tingle in anticipation. She takes out her book and pulls the small candle closer. She has carried *Blood Memory*, the autobiography of Martha Graham, with her everywhere for the past year. She believes it gives her luck—rising to principal from the ensemble against the odds, getting the lead in *La Sylphide*.

Now she turns to it when she cannot sleep at night or when she wakes up at four in the morning too anxious to fall back asleep. Not only does Martha Graham describe her work with Baryshnikov, and Louise Brooks, and in the Greenwich Village Follies, but her words on dance read like poetry to Sophie, articulating the power and the struggle with an agility Sophie has never seen captured in language. She loves imagining what life must have been like for Graham, surrounded by talented friends like Isamu Noguchi and Charlie Chaplin; friends to collaborate with, or simply inhabit the same room. The very thought of that room calms Sophie.

People have asked me why I chose to be a dancer. I did not choose. I was chosen to be a dancer, and with that, you live all your life, Martha Graham writes.

Sophie has a photograph of Graham with Alexander Calder, Marianne Moore, Herbert Matter, and Marc Chagall, all laughing together in front of one of Calder's mobiles; it sits tucked into the frame of her mirror at home, a reminder of something. Something bigger. Bigger than delivering Chateau truffle fries to a table before they get soggy, bigger than the next starlet, producer, or director treated like royalty. Bigger even than her upcoming performance. The idea of that room and those friendships hints at some worldly rightness, some intangible hope that Sophie has to believe in. A collective heart that beats as hers, if only nurtured and surrounded by people like her. Or different from her—but open. Connected.

Reading about Martha Graham's financial struggles and the fight it took to keep her company alive does not comfort Sophie as much as it settles something in her—some fear, some inadequacy. To think that even her heroes still dealt with things like bills, budgets, and rejections feels like company in this lonely place.

Just then a pair of tight black jeans stops beside her table. Sophie senses who it is by the musky cologne, the orangey hand tapping the tabletop. Her back tightens. When she looks up, the effort it takes to smile exhausts her.

"Well, well," he says in the same rehearsed annoyance he likes to show her. An ingratitude for being pretty, in his eyes. Her nerve. So many "playboys" seem to hate women. She watches it over and over at the Chateau. This deep resentment for the pretty ones they pursue; an insurmountable jealousy at how easy they imagine life must be, never understanding the paradox of how hard they make it.

Sophie nods so as not to be unfriendly, then turns back to her book.

"Mind if I sit?" says Ray Delaney, already halfway down. He leans over the table so far that the string of his age-inappropriate hoodie dangles near her kimchi. "You vegan?"

"Nope," Sophie says. "I just come here from time to time."

"I'm vegan five years now. Never felt better."

How could it take such dedication to look so absolutely sleazy? Sophie wonders what would happen if he stopped. Would he drip into a puddle of slime and slither away?

"I've got a guy here," he says, leaning in closer. "Hooks me up with colostrum."

"Colostrum?"

"Mother's milk, that truly precious bit that comes out first. Very hard to find."

Sophie stares at him. "You mean human?"

"Technically it's illegal, but they do it all under the table here. Let me tell you, if there's a fountain of youth somewhere, it's spewing that stuff."

Ew, Sophie thinks. "And you, what, drink it?" She can hardly look at the man; the cloak of obligation she wears at the Chateau no longer covers her bubbling disgust.

"Yep, nothing like it," he says. "Only thing I break vegan for."

Rather than respond, Sophie smiles and looks back to her book.

"I'll get you some next time," says Ray Delaney as though closing a deal.

Sophie imagines what her family in Minneapolis might say, witnessing a grown man drinking mother's milk. An Impossible burger is one thing, but this oedipal, vanity-driven veganism with creepy exceptions—she cannot imagine them in the same room together.

"You've got such an amazing figure, you must be doing something right."

"Honestly, I prefer regular milk."

"Do you model?"

"I'm a dancer."

A different waiter, not hers, passes the table and Ray Delaney reaches out his arm, almost hitting the guy in the stomach. "Adam, how are ya! Gimme a kombucha with a shot of ginger. And tell Andre I'm here."

"Will do, good to see you, Ray!" His smile disappears as soon as he passes him.

"I know the whole gang here."

Sophie forks the kelp noodles, though her appetite is gone. Something about Ray Delaney's presence makes her eating feel performative, pornographic even. She twirls the noodles and lets them fall back into the bowl.

"What kind of dance?"

"Ballet."

"Ballet?" He laughs. "Well, that explains it then!"

"Explains what?"

"The posture, the composure. And here I thought you were just uptight."

Sophie holds up an arm for the waiter, any waiter. Still, smiling. Baring her teeth.

"Oh relax, princess! I'm just messing with you," he says, pulling her arm down. She hates the feeling of his hand on her skin. "That's just how I am, babe, ask anyone. You gotta learn to lighten up. Stick with me, it'll be good for ya!"

"I can take a joke, but I don't really see anything funny. You're insulting me."

She looks back down to her book. Even the sight of Martha Graham's name is a reassurance. *This is your world*, she thinks to herself, holding the page between her trembling fingers. *This is the world.*

"All right, you wanna read. I'll leave you to it. But we'll hang soon, finally. Right?"

"Sure."

"You're a real fuckin' pill, you know that?"

He smiles smugly. Sophie can't decide whether this man is delusional or just trying to save face, acting like this is some elaborate long game they're playing. How could one of the most successful producers in Hollywood be this oblivious? Or is that precisely why he is, given he is used to getting exactly what he wants?

Once Ray Delaney is safely outside, Sophie takes another bite of her kelp noodles, but the cashew cheese has congealed with the pesto, making it inedible. What a waste; twenty dollars is something she saves for, between meals of steamed frozen vegetables, brown rice, hard-boiled eggs, and Japanese sweet potatoes she cooks ahead for the week. She walks to the counter to pay, again noticing every muscle, but this time enjoying the accomplishment—sore because she is being overworked, sore because she is the lead.

She orders a turmeric latte for the ride home, hoping it might prime her for a good night's sleep so at least the meal would not have been a total loss.

"You Are Glowing," the barista says, handing her the compostable to-go cup. She says thank you, forgetting for a moment that he is talking about the drink.

The creaminess of the steamed almond milk mixed with the tartness of the fresh turmeric calms her, and she remembers again why she puts up with the names and the mantras and the moony smiles. She takes another sip, just as the thought of Ray Delaney's "mother's milk" pops into her head, and nearly gags. She checks her fuzzy white sweater for any drips of turmeric, and steps into the shadows of the parking lot.

The days are getting shorter now, surprising her with darkness each time she steps outside. Before she finds her phone in her backpack to order a Drivr, a red Tesla pulls in front of her. The window rolls down. For god's sake, it's Ray Delaney.

"Need a ride?"

"No thanks," she says, waving him off. "I'm fine."

"Come on," he says. "Now you're gonna hurt my feelings."

"I'm fine, really."

"Let me drive you home. I interrupted your dinner, it's the least I can do."

"I just ordered a Drivr."

"Cancel it," he says. The car lurches forward, in her way. "What, you don't even think I'm capable of driving you home? I wasn't going to mention tonight to Willow, but honestly. You can be a real bitch."

The car now completely blocks Sophie's path from the curb, giving her the option of walking back into the restaurant, sliding over its pristine hood, or obliging him. The first two options seem unbearably awkward, given that she will, in fact, likely see him at work again tomorrow night. Willow has fired people for less than offending Ray Delaney. And Willow knows everyone; she could easily blacklist Sophie from jobs across Los Angeles if Ray Delaney applied the right pressure. People like

Sophie disappear; the Ray Delaneys do not. Besides, Sophie is so close; if she saves enough from another month at the Chateau, she could stop working there altogether. Never see him again. She could focus solely on dance, finally. She's too close, has put up with too much, to let Ray Delaney threaten that now.

She opens the door.

"I'm not a bitch."

"Okay, princess."

Inside, she is struck by the smell of cologne so strong it makes the back of her throat sting. Here she is, in his car, against her better judgment. This must be the secret to his success. She pictures studio executives signing checks and contracts under the sheer social pressure behind his offers.

"I'm assuming you live east of here," he says. The car moves forward so silently that Sophie had not realized it was even on. "I have to make one quick stop first, but it'll give us a chance to hang."

"Sorry, but you said you'd just take me home."

"I know some people associated with the ballet here, you know," he says. "Financiers, mostly. But they have a say in things, if you know what I mean."

Not LABC. Could he know Auguste, too? Not him, too.

"I have to be up early."

"Relax. You'll age yourself. This'll be quick. You said we'd hang soon, and here it is, sooner than we thought."

Ray Delaney drives fast and carelessly, accelerating around the few cars on the road obeying the speed limit, and Sophie's stomach rises and falls with the gas pedal as they drive farther from her place. *Pull us over*, she thinks as they pass a parked police car along Beverly. *Please, please, pull us over.* As they approach the intersection of Melrose and La Brea, the light glows yellow, but Ray Delaney accelerates instead, clearly intending to pass the car to their side as those around them slow to a stop. But when the yellow turns to red before they reach it, he slams on the brakes and Sophie feels her seat belt catch.

She looks at her cup, making sure nothing has spilled, when suddenly Ray Delaney sneaks a hand around her knee, where her jeans are torn and her skin shows through. Sophie jerks away, spilling the golden drink all over herself, and his light interior.

"What the hell is that?" he says, waving his hand to get the hot liquid off. At first, Sophie thinks he might hit her. "Grab some paper towels, they're in the back. Ah, shit."

This is the first time Sophie has seen him lose his cool, and she takes some pleasure in that, though her favorite sweater is ruined. She twists in her seat, looking for the paper towels, but all she sees are different jackets in varying shades of leather, and two amber pill bottles, seemingly empty. She turns back around and looks at her legs, the saturated yellow turning permanent across her light denim thigh. At least his hand is gone.

The lights are barely dimmed in the near-empty club, the Woods. At first Sophie does not even recognize the spot she frequented years ago at the end of a night, back when your only hope of skipping the line around the block was to know someone, which she always did.

The Woods' palm frond wallpaper that had seemed so delightfully kitsch only a few years ago now peels in the corners and shows stains from countless popped bottles of champagne, the acidity yellowing the already antique paper. Sophie has never been to one of these places in the early evening hours, and it strikes her as sad. Even in its prime, the Woods was never a place you met for a cocktail after work, or for a post-dinner drink. This was the place you left at three a.m. and hardly remembered the next day. And yet, through the smoky haze, more fog machine than cigarette, she recognizes a few familiar faces. Sophie never considered that many of these people they used to party with would still be doing the same things now. That for them, the party was never over. They never got out long enough, sobered up long enough, to realize it had ended years ago.

Sophie lifts a hand to wave to a DJ she briefly dated immediately after moving to Los Angeles, though she quickly realizes he does not see her. He has an empty, flat look in his eyes, and his head twitches side to side, reacting to something not there. Sophie remembers herself in the car outside of the Dresden, the shark stalking its prey. But he isn't wearing any glasses.

"You want some, princess?" says Ray Delaney, suddenly beside her.

She follows his gaze to a velvet settee, where a beautiful, if surgically enhanced, woman lies reclined. Her legs tilt inward, with one arm stretched the full length of the chair, as though reaching for something not there.

"Margot Berry," he says. "She's a friend."

Sophie looks again. Of course, Margot Berry was one of the original supermodels, who now spends her time codesigning her own "celebrity" line of convertible furniture and pushing collagen powders on late night television. And, apparently, doing Mem at eight p.m. on a Tuesday.

"Come on, a little taste?"

"No thanks," says Sophie.

She wonders if Margot is using her own, some paid-off doctor in her pocket so she could relive her past glory, or if she's escaping into the memories of others. Sophie is struck by how laid bare and pathetic the users look. At the Chateau, under the twinkling lights of the courtyard, or up in a hotel room, the privilege of its privacy and the thrill of escape seemed part of the appeal. There, it looked like luxury. At the Woods, in this off-hour, Sophie sees more the meth houses in Minneapolis that had consumed an entire neighborhood by the time she left, that swallowed her brother and multiple classmates she had grown up with, that despite the bleakness were the only places they wanted to be.

"You can do it here," he says. "Look around, nobody cares."

He looks so pleased with himself, as though the rest of the world is outside wishing to be here. Nothing could appeal to Sophie less than lying down beside these people with so little left in their lives that they need to escape into strangers.

"I'm good," she says.

"You are so fucking spoiled."

"Excuse me?"

"Like I've said, I know a lot of people. And that can go one of two ways. You ought to think about that."

"I'm sorry," she says, a last-ditch effort. "I'm just so tired."

"Poor princess. Have one drink and I'll drive you home," he says, softening. "Besides, you'll never get a Drivr over here at rush hour."

Ray Delaney's hand moves to Sophie's waist, holding her in place. She knows her best defense is moderate appeasement.

"One drink, then you take me home."

At the bar, Ray Delaney is quickly flanked by two underage-looking girls. Whatever they've done to their faces it looks uncomfortable. Sophie feels a hand on the curve of her back and arches away from it. She turns to see two guys with different interpretations of the same undercut in varying degrees of height on top. This one is wearing a hoodie under a blazer and smells like tequila.

"You here with Delaney?"

"Captive," Sophie says. "I was getting a ride."

The guys nod to each other, confirming some joke between them.

"Classic Delaney," says one of them.

"You look like his type. Let me guess, actress?"

"No," she says. "And I'm not his type, we just ran into each other." She suddenly feels remarkably vulnerable. The way they look at her.

"You been here before?" the other one asks.

"Yeah, a few years ago."

"Aren't we too cool?"

Ray Delaney reappears with two champagne flutes and the two girls, who put their hands on the shoulders of one guy each and trade kisses. "What's good, brothers?" says Ray Delaney, so unnaturally that Sophie actually pities him for a moment.

He hands her a flute. When she takes a sip, it fizzes all the way down her throat. The champagne burns. Its bubbles feel sharp, different. When she turns, Ray Delaney is in her face, smiling.

"Good shit, right? Only the best for the princess."

Despite everything, he is still trying to impress her; to show her up, or off. The other men laugh at something she's unaware of, and now Ray Delaney's hands are extended into the center of the group, one tiny pill for each of them, glimmering under the hanging chandeliers, and Sophie feels the whole room wobble, the stained wallpaper pattern blurring into motion.

She grips Ray Delaney's arm, but he seems unaware, or unsurprised. Sophie's head suddenly feels heavy with the beat of the music, and only then does she taste the bitter chalkiness, the iridescent particles attached to each rising bubble in her glass. The room gets darker and the beat fades, time slowing and running out all at once. She spreads her arms, bending low in search of the nearest seat. Then suddenly, she cannot see a thing around her, and before she can call for help she feels her head

fall

back.

The knife enters slow,
  pushing, until with a pluck
it sinks, thick on either side of the blade.
   With a twist, the small body feels hollow, its insides soft.
   When it slides out, easy, the blade looks near black, dripping
dark drops that burst bright red against the white linoleum. The
knife goes in again,
  sweet delight,
   tough then easy, just as before, and the wetness spreads, covering
everything in a glorious gloss—hands, chest, shirt—splattering with
each push
  further, faster,
   until there is only a deep darkness covering everything.
   All these bodies keep hidden, stolen inside, waiting to be spilled;
that they should be so lucky to see all that they hold, what so many
never have the chance to know.
   Oh, that I would spill the beauty from them all.

Sophie wakes up in her own bed, feeling gutted for what she has seen—what she has done. The life he took, she felt. Complicit in the actions of this stranger latched on inside of her. What she joined in, whether or not already done, feels marked inside her all the same. In the moments continuously flashing behind her eyes even now, and in her fingertips, she wanted it as badly as him. The experience feels no less real than if it were her own.

 She still feels her hands pushing inside of the body. Even here, under her soft comforter, she feels the blade going deeper, unbelievably deep, and deeper still. She feels another person's life in her hands and then taking it. The quiver of it. The horrifying satisfaction that lingers inside of her, like some postcoital exhaustion, haunting her skin like pleasure.

That they should be so lucky. That I would spill the beauty from them all.

PART TWO

SHAPIRO: All right, thanks for hanging in there. This is Ari Shapiro and you're listening to *All Things Considered*. We're back with Dr. Angelica Sloane of the Center in Malibu. Before the break you mentioned a certain *second sense* that occasionally remains, even after treatment at the Center. Can you tell us more about that, this second sense?

DR. SLOANE: This is what we call the *phantom presence*—it does not show up on our screenings, in our tests, the lab work. And yet somehow, it remains in some patients. Such patients test as clean, or neutralized, but they are still feeling the lingering effects without understanding *why*. Naturally it is incredibly difficult to treat what you cannot detect. What for all intents and purposes has been removed. This is without a doubt our biggest challenge.

SHAPIRO: So what is the recourse, for such patients?

DR. SLOANE: Like any rehabilitation center, in many cases it becomes about lifelong management rather than a magic cure. Extraction and reimplementation, followed by continuous exposure to one's own memories is the only treatment we have found successful. Truly, it is the only option. And then we wait. We must starve the lingering consciousness of fuel, or anything to latch on to, until eventually the last remnants of its grip fade away.

I tend to overuse metaphors when talking about our work, but let's imagine a drop of ink added to a bathtub of clean water. You can scoop it out quickly, sure, but trace particles may remain. Now, depending on the consistency of that ink—of that particular consciousness—it may be more or less viscous; it may have dissipated too quickly for you to catch, and may no longer be visible to the eye. As such, it appears impossible to remove. The best way to ensure a clean tub, then, is to open the drain and run the water. For as long as it takes.

At the Center, we have very clean water.

Chapter 18

BEFORE

Another heat wave.

A wave doesn't so much describe the weather as its pattern of arrival. The illusion of concrete rippling, the air above it hazy like undulating rock. Concrete covers so much of this city that Lucien wonders how far it would stretch if you took all the freeways and driveways and parking lots and laid them flat side by side. Would they cover Manhattan? Maybe all five boroughs. If you stacked them up lengthwise, could they touch the moon?

Wildfires have been hopping freeways again in Ventura toward Santa Barbara, and the Santa Ana winds responsible for them have been pushing smoke to Los Angeles, casting a silk screen behind the nearest buildings and making everything in the distance a gray blur. The news has been covering the fires nonstop. Videos of what looks like volcanic hellfire approaching gridlocked traffic break first on social media, then on the major channels. The images are so surreal that Lucien half expects to see Universal Studios branding in the lower corner.

Wealthy celebrities pop in and out of the coverage praying for their properties. One even brings up his private vineyard, now in the path of the flames. His priceless film memorabilia. Entire counties watch their homes turn to scorched earth from the safety of their extended families' homes or local evacuation centers. Single objects remain standing in charred houses—a safe, a toilet. One photo showed a bedroom without its house, exposed like a dollhouse: paintings still on the walls, a quilted throw neatly folded across the soot-covered bed. The earth in the background, still smoking. The contrast is what unsettles Lucien most.

Civilians save cute animals along the fire-licked freeway; a bunny hops into the arms of a young man wearing a hoodie. The man nuzzles it until his face is bearded with soot, and the bunny's fluff persists in patches. In Los Angeles some residents have been leaving out buckets of water for displaced animals. A few nights ago, a coyote wandered down to the ocean in Malibu, taking a few cautious laps before he ran, eyes aglow, south toward Santa Monica. A bobcat was spotted in West Hollywood.

One news story on the radio highlights a luxury hotel in the Santa Barbara area opening its rooms to firefighters, evacuated residents, and those who have lost their homes. Lucien wipes away a tear as he drives, his eyes irritated from all the particles in the air, or maybe because he thinks he has never heard such kindness. Lately he wonders if he is okay, or if he is losing some great binding thing that previously kept him from falling apart. Then again, what is wrong with everyone else? How do they continue life as normal in Los Angeles with the smell of burning in the air? How do they reconcile their privilege of being so blissfully unaware? Still honking at fellow drivers along their commutes, asking for dressing on the side at restaurants, fussing over a spill. Meanwhile, entire neighborhoods burn. Schools. Libraries. The air is laden with the smell of loss.

Lucien drives along Los Feliz Boulevard in the direction of Beachwood Canyon. He's been avoiding Liv around his apartment and the café, savoring his time alone. His escape. But there's a time to come up for air. He needs to pace himself. He knows where this could go. His eyes are still irritated from all the smoke and ash, yet he notices a man running along the side of the road wearing the small white face mask they keep recommending on the news. Any suggestion of a blizzard coming to New York, let alone a hurricane, and every D'Agostino gets cleaned out, not a battery or bottle of water left in the greater metro area. Lucien grew up expecting advance warning—claps of thunder, charcoal skies. Even in a summer thunderstorm, there was that breath beforehand where the temperature drops, the light retreats. Here in clear blue skies, the Santa Ana winds whip through with a fury and leave just as fast. Lucien has never been someplace where the weather could hide such violence.

A woman in a tank top and jean shorts, with a giant scarf wrapped around her neck to cover her mouth, walks her Chihuahua near his grandmother's house. As he passes his grandmother's driveway and sees the thatched roof in the corner of his eye, he feels guilty for how happy he is not to be turning there. Though part of him is tempted to run in and make sure all the windows are closed, that the air filter he bought her is on. And, if he's honest, snag a few more pills.

The sun is just beginning to set as he turns toward Liv's house, low palms obscuring any remaining light into pink rays that blush whatever they touch. The particles in the air hold the color longer than normal and Lucien is surrounded for a moment by a startling beauty even as it ushers in darkness.

Liv uses tongs to toss the noodles in what appears to be some sort of curry. Coconut curry pho, she informs him as he comes up behind her, the steam making her hair stick to his face. He wraps his arms around her waist, lets his nose settle into her braid.

"Smells amazing," he says. "The food, too."

The soup smells like a sweaty subway stop as whatever brussels sprouts or cauliflower involved fills the air. Liv smiles and turns back to the stove, wiggling her hips into him.

"It's vegan," she says. "Sorry!"

Lucien feels a familiar performance between them, like Liv wants him to complain about that because that would fit his part in the dynamic she has decided for them. He doesn't tell her what he eats alone most nights—cereal, also vegan. Maybe a hard-boiled egg or two. Quesadillas with shredded cheese that expires a full year from its purchase, and bacon until he runs out of it. He isn't picky. He likes disappearing into Liv's routine, the smell of her and her home. She is assured enough for both of them, and there is something indulgent about spending time with her, a guilty pleasure that soothes him superficially. Even if Liv has defined herself against it in many ways, she is the most Los Angeles being Lucien can think of. And right now, embracing her feels like staying.

After dinner, Lucien turns his phone volume up before they go to sleep in case any alerts come in, and he asks Liv to do the same. Night seems to bring the worst of the wildfires; it's the winds, apparently. Liv laughs, implying this precaution is adorable. Lucien doesn't understand. With such proximity to devastation, how does anyone feel so untouchable? His attention to the fires seems endearing to her, but when he catches her mocking his concern, she is suddenly unattractive, shape-shifting before his eyes. Later the winds howl through the canyon, and he and Liv curl close to one another in bed.

Lucien has a dream in which his mother comes back. She visits Los Angeles to see his grandmother and is furious that the house has been emptied, that his grandmother sits in the same drab chair all day. That this no longer feels like their family. At the end of the dream, Lucien brings his mother water where she lies, crying in bed, but as soon as he puts the glass down she rolls away from him, and he cannot wake her, cannot even find her face from either side of the bed. When he finally pulls her toward him, he sees the face of his grandmother, her eyes rolled back in her head, iridescent pills spilling out of her mouth.

A long beam of light from the living room creeps over Liv's Moroccan rug and across the hardwood threshold into the bedroom. Soon the light will stretch across them, up to Liv's eyes, and Lucien will no longer have this time to think. But for now he watches morning unfold, the subtlety in its light and shadows, as if seeing again. Even after a few trips on his grandmother's Memoroxin, Lucien has noticed his eye returning. Or wholly new. His grandmother's optimism lingers in his blood. And seeing his mother again has temporarily filled the void that otherwise sucked everything into it. He sees in frames again. Moments he wants to hold on to—at least until the next time he can disappear.

Through the window, leaves and limbs are downed all around Liv's precariously perched bungalow, more fallout from the Santa Ana winds. The way people in Los Angeles test the hills, the canyons, the crumbling landscape. In the distance, a large mushroom cloud looms to the north, where he imagines tens of thousands wait, evacuated from their homes, and others flee hot terror as the smoke shifts, languid, and spreads toward the city that refuses to acknowledge its fear.

Liv rolls over to face him and gently tugs at her eyebrow, like she always does when waking up, coaxing her lids open. She groans.

"I just remembered—I have a Friendsgiving in Venice today," she says.

"Isn't it only just November?"

"People book up." She hovers her hand over her mouth as she talks, like she always does until she's brushed her teeth. "There are only so many weekends until Thanksgiving, and I have like three different ones before then."

"Brutal," Lucien says, stroking her hair.

"I'd rather a friend just have theirs on the actual day. Anything to keep me from the horror that is my family. Or better, if my mother could disappear for the entire holiday season, then I might actually be thankful."

Lucien stops stroking her hair and stares up at the ceiling.

"I'm sorry, I didn't think," she says after a moment.

He's never met someone who could be so well-intentioned yet so infuriatingly naive.

"You always do this," she says. "I'm sorry if I said the wrong thing, but you can't just freeze me out."

"I'm just thinking."

"You know, I'd be more sensitive if you ever talked about her."

"About who?"

"Your mother. Or anyone else in your family."

Lucien was finally starting to forget his guilt. Call it denial, but whatever is in those pills makes it easier for him to breathe. He could use one now. Even a cigarette. Anything to take the edge off. Is it an edge because it's sharp, or because you're looking over it, into the void?

"You're doing it again!"

"I talk about my grandmother all the time! But she's not exactly giving me new material. You know about my mother, and my dad's not around."

"I'm sure you still think about her," says Liv. "Your mother, I mean. I know you don't have many people out here to talk to. If you ever want to talk about her . . ."

"Got it."

Lucien feels himself hardening. He focuses on the speckled paint on the ceiling, though he feels Liv's eyes on the side of his face.

"It might be helpful, for us . . ."

"How does my mother have anything to do with us?"

"Clearly it upsets you. I mean, it's hard for you. You must miss her."

"And that involves you how?"

"Okay, Lucien, you don't have to be mean."

"I'm not being mean, I'm genuinely curious what it has to do with you."

"I wish you would let me in, that's all."

"Look, what do you want to hear? How I wasn't there when my mother died? Is that *helpful for us*? I spent her last living moments with my roommates getting high. Do you feel closer to me now?"

"Lucien."

"How I enjoyed ignoring her call? It was one of countless calls, and for once it felt good to not answer. I actually laughed when my roommate grabbed the phone and told her to *fuck off*. He didn't know who it was. But I knew. Is that enough honesty for you? You think it's helpful for me to go around *sharing* that? How she did everything for me and I let her—"

Lucien takes a break, to let the quiver in his voice steady.

"You want to analyze me or talk about me with your friends like some project? Go ahead. There it is."

Liv doesn't speak at first, and Lucien finally glances over at her. She is still watching him, unwavering. The golden fleck in her eye looks bigger under a tear. He looks back up at the ceiling before she can hold eye contact.

"I wouldn't tell anyone that," she says. "Lucien, I care about you. I want you to know that you can tell me anything."

Lucien doesn't say that his mother took enough pills to kill a horse. That she chose when she left him and how. Her choice, which holds his every burden, grips his insides like a clenched fist. Maybe he doesn't want to tarnish the version of his mother that he grew up with, the woman who would never do something like that. Though no one would do something like that, until they do. And even if he wanted to tell Liv now, there is only a small window for revelations like this and it's passed.

Most days he doesn't remember the facts as they are, anyway. His memory excuses her, having been so sick for so long. Having almost died, over and over. His mother was a kind, compassionate woman, but stubborn as hell. No doubt she thought she was right, that taking her life would be the solution to some problem. That she could answer some question. Take back some agency. If he searches long enough, thinks hard enough, Lucien will come up with the question her suicide answered. Him. How much more could she put him through? What he keeps coming back to is another question. What if he had just answered the phone?

She left, for him. To spare him. And this thing that seems to trap him from all sides was meant to be his freedom. Her final gift to him, goodbye.

"It's not your fault," Liv starts, but he laughs—to interrupt her, and it feels good. He hates the way people try to fix what they can't. As if they could pardon him. Lucien stares at the smoke detector in the ceiling. What he would give for it to go off right now. Running outside with nothing but a sheet, he would feel less exposed.

It isn't Liv's fault that Lucien has had this conversation enough times in his head to know where it leads. And it isn't her fault that his happiness bears the limit of his own memory. His mind returns to the moment again and again; Tanner's dumb voice, *Fuck off*; his mother finally having the answer she wants. But it was wrong, his mother was wrong. What was best for him was her. Fighting. With Lucien by her side.

"It was my fault, you don't understand."

"But she'd forgive you," Liv says. "I'm sure she—"

"Which is it, then? Was it not my fault or would she forgive me? In all the deep knowledge you have of my mother. Please, tell me more."

Liv keeps talking, but Lucien is no longer listening. Having this conversation only makes others around him feel worse, and him no better. No one knows what to say. The traditional condolences don't work. *At least she didn't suffer.* She did, he was there. *She was such a fighter.* The cancer was relentless, its sheer determination the least human aspect of it. Five years of doctor appointments, treatments, tubes, side effects. He lost count of how many times his mother threw up into something he held, how many sponges they went through in that first year, or—god help them—in the third. How normal sponges weren't made to absorb the kind of goo that comes up after one of those treatments. He had been there then.

When Lucien goes over those years in his mind, trying to remember how they got to that one afternoon, the guilt clouds his memory, covering every time he did show up. His mother had gotten better so many times. The cancer always came back. Lucien thought his heart couldn't take it anymore. But then it did. He wished he could stop feeling anything—the hope, the disappointment, the fear. And then that last week, the last day, in his apartment in Bushwick, six feet on the table, smoking weed with his roommates, he finally did. Their smoke fogged the room, dimming it like an old, poorly developed photograph in his memory.

"I'm sure you had your reasons," Liv says, finally piercing his familiar spiral. "You're a good person, Lucien."

"I don't see what one has to do with the other. Good people do bad things all the time. Look at me, I even treat my grandmother like shit. I can't help her. I wait to visit someone who doesn't even recognize me, or want me there."

"That's not true," Liv interrupts. "You do not *treat her like shit*, Lucien. Just your being here means something."

"That's what they tell every family who has to watch a loved one die." Liv grabs his hand under the covers.

"Think of all the times you were there, it's not your fault that the one time—"

"But I begrudged her," Lucien says, vomiting the words—and then there it is. "That one time, I actually begrudged her. My roommates could just sit there, lazy and high. I watched them ignore calls from their parents all the time, they laughed and groaned each time their phones rang. They blacked out and woke up places they didn't know. They'd gone through college either drunk or hungover or high. All those years I lived at home, I treated my cell phone like a fucking pager. I wanted her to stop interrupting my life."

Lucien cannot stop talking now; each new emotion expressed—confessed—demands another. He watches Liv's face as he speaks, waiting for the disgust, the horror, to show. He is almost baiting her now, what more could it take?

"I hate myself for saying this, but it felt good ignoring her. Hearing my friend yell at her like that. I remember feeling so satisfied. I'm an adult, I deserved to have some independence. To have something for myself. She was my mother and I loved her, but apparently I never fucking forgave her for being so sick."

"You're human," Liv says. "You're allowed to be angry. None of it is fair."

Now all Lucien feels is grateful, for the pace at which Liv keeps talking so he can breathe; grateful for the even, unfazed tone of her voice; grateful for the fact that when he looks at her, blurred through tears that he won't let run, she is looking straight back at him.

"She was my favorite person. Now she's gone and I've got nothing but free time. I've got nothing. That was all I wanted, right?"

"The more you talk about her, the way you miss her, maybe then it's like she's still alive."

"Maybe," Lucien says, and all he can think about are the pills.

Both of them lie in silence, staring at the ceiling. Then Liv presses her hand into Lucien's chest. He must've fallen back asleep. He almost can't believe he said all that. He rubs his face. Salt from a dried tear sticks to the outer corner of his eye.

"What're you doing today?"

"I was going to see my grandmother this morning."

"Why don't we go to the beach?" Liv says. "Your grandmother will be there tomorrow, and you deserve to have some fun. Plus the air will be clearer over there."

Lucien rolls over to think. He appreciates the attempt at diversion, Liv finally understanding. He still wants a cigarette. Or better, one of the pills in his apartment. He didn't mention those in his plans for the day. Now just the thought of that promised escape, the moment before he leaves his body, energizes him and takes him out of his despair enough that here, beside Liv, he can think of another way, too. Before she starts talking again, he leans into her, his face against her bare shoulder. Her skin is cool, even under the covers. The smell of her skin, coconut and citrus, makes him forget. He traces a freckle on her bicep with the tip of his tongue. Liv giggles and blushes as he moves toward her collarbone. He gets up on his knees, straddling her, then wraps an arm under her waist and pulls her down off the pillow so she lies flat, hair sprawled like a halo above her head.

Liv drives Lucien back to Echo Park for a quick stop on the way. She needs to drop off a fresh case of collagen bone broth at Astral Bodies. Going south on Sunset, Lucien feels a subtle effervescence under his skin as they pass the Vista.

"Another superhero movie?" Liv says. "They never show anything good anymore."

Lucien isn't listening; he's too focused on getting up to his apartment to grab a pill from his coffee grounds while she is distracted downstairs. To prolong the remaining pills, Lucien has begun grinding them into a powder and pinching a bit into a water bottle, to keep a subtle wash over everything he does. Just enough to keep him out of his own head. Just enough to crest without the obligation of understanding all that comes up. Only the escape. Only the forgetting. Enough to fill the emptiness inside of him with Florence's lingering wholeness. Her calming, optimistic synesthesia. With her he feels yellow. He feels sweet.

Lucien finishes the water bottle before they even reach the Westside. He's never enjoyed a car ride more in his entire life, though from the way Liv keeps smiling at him, she clearly thinks this chilled-out state is thanks to their conversation earlier.

When at last the ocean appears at the end of every street, Liv parks the car and leads Lucien toward the long wooden ramp to the beach. The tall palms lining the street level of Santa Monica above bend as though they, too, are stretching toward the breeze. Together they weave past beach cruisers in candy colors, fast and silent automated scooters, and the stream of tourists holding tightly to their children's hands as they look in all directions, the dazed attention of vacation making them harder to navigate around. Liv turns onto the sand, and they walk on the seemingly endless stretch of beach to the ocean, in the direction of Venice, where the pathway gets sandier and gradually there is more spray paint, skate parks, and weed wafting in the air. Lucien looks back to see the Ferris wheel fading behind them, Malibu all but hidden behind the haze.

Just then Lucien's phone starts ringing; it's Natasha.

"Natasha."

"The prodigal son, he lives! How are you? Don't tell me, you've gone LA on me. Am I catching you during yoga on the beach? No really, don't tell me, I'll kill myself. It snowed four inches today."

Lucien laughs good-naturedly, his palms already starting to sweat with the reality setting in. He cannot believe he picked up. He hasn't listened to any of her voicemails because in some way, he knows. He owes her new work, a new show—or nothing. They have nothing to talk about without that.

And he doesn't mention that he is, in fact, at the beach.

"Snow sounds nice. Have you seen the news?"

"Fires look awful. What is this world?" she continues. "Anyway, Lucien. You're a hard guy to track down."

"I'm sorry, things have been—"

"I've been calling because I have something too good to share in an email. We've got a show with Gagosian at the Frieze—and get this, darling, they want to show one of your pieces. Now do you love me?"

"What?" Lucien hardly believes it, news like this without any new work. "Which piece, how'd this come about?"

"I want to hear you say it first."

"I love you, Natasha."

Lucien feels Liv's side glance. If she could see Natasha, late forties, just five feet tall, glinting silver hair.

"It's a retrospective honoring your mother."

Lucien's heart drops. Any lingering high evaporates.

"No one could do that without your work, of course; that entire series was so good. Just brilliant, and such a hit. They're thinking of the one in the kitchen, silk pajamas. Now that the house is sold, and after the *Times* article, it has a certain cachet. But the one on the respirator with the clouds overlaid was also getting a lot of buzz if I remember. God, here I go. Sorry, I'm calling for *your* input. Though we might need to be flexible. Lucien?"

"Sorry, yeah. Right. No, any of those, whatever they think."

Lucien's mother was with Gagosian; of course they were interested in this series.

"Okay, so here's the rub," Natasha says. "I want to pitch some new stuff, too; a sort of while-you're-here run at another show, right? It's amazing that the excitement is still there for that work, really, but we need to leverage that before it's old news, or before you become too locked into one style, you know? Lucien, this is Gagosian. You won't get their eyes again soon."

Lucien feels dizzy at the thought of those pieces—his mother's face to scale, no makeup, overlaid with the cloudy ether he'd spread with a palette knife. They feel almost prescient now that she's gone, unbearable. *Before it's old news.* Lucien had dispersed his mother among the clouds when they were still together, sent bits of her up to the heavens for her to see. Those were pieces he could only do while he could still hear her in the next room. How could he look at them now?

"Lucien?"

"Sure, yeah, that makes sense."

"So you've got some new work?"

"I do, yeah."

He lies. Whether to spare Natasha or himself—what's the alternative, though? *Actually I haven't done anything worth showing in months and I may never again.*

"Fantastic. I'll set up a call in the next week or two to video chat; or we'll fly you back. Can the new stuff travel? What's the scale? We can always print here first, if they're large. Before you start to play."

You should leave me, too, he thinks. *Last one standing, just finish me off.*

"Lucien, have I lost you?"

"Let's do a call first," he says.

"I truly cannot wait. Hope you're inspired out there."

Lucien glances back at Liv, staring out to the ocean.

"Hope everything's good with you, Natasha. I'll talk to you soon."

Lucien cannot imagine going back; not to the city, or to the shows. Those pieces, bigger than him, so much bigger than her. But he also can't stand the thought of staying away, or missing it. Natasha hardly even presented it as a choice, did she? There was no question there. How could he miss an opportunity like that? His mother wouldn't want him to. And yet—a retrospective, already? How could he bear that either? She hardly felt gone. Fuck the shows; fuck the memory. That's what his mother would have said. You have to take care of you. That's what she'd have done, too. Through the work.

The air around him disappears, his breath shortening, the panic returning. How did he even get here? Liv stands beside him, waiting at arm's length. He hands her his phone and begins to peel off his shirt, unbuckling his pants down to his boxers and leaving them as he runs, sand sprinkling the backs of his shins, chest-first into the low tide. First is a shock to his chest, the grunt-searching for breath, and then— submerged—no hope of anything touching him. Not here, where the physical sensations of his body overpower everything, even his ability to breathe, bobbing in the waves.

The Santa Monica Mountains are silhouetted in varying depths of purple in the distance. Beyond those, a dull gray has settled from the smoke in the distance. Surfers in the water look focused in an untroubled way that feels so far from Lucien's reach. Once he's out of the ocean, Liv leads them back to the pedestrian path on the Venice Boardwalk, with its mix of tattoo parlors and Australian cafés; people eating breakfast burritos next to a shirtless man yelling at the seagulls that *Jesus Saves!*

A blueness hangs in the air, the sun just starting to go down and further silhouetting the mountains, shades that would look surreal if painted as they appear, in purple and cobalt. Sharp shadows cross the sand, peaked from the breeze. Maybe he will come back here with his camera, and another water bottle that seems to be giving him new eyes; or is that just the pressure from Natasha, finally manifesting?

No, this is more. His eyes, finally working.

Families on the beach pack up their things; many of them under tents with coolers undoubtedly drove hours to get here for the day. The little children running past him will be zonked out in the car within ten minutes of being back on the road. The thought of them in the backseat while their parents talk and drive is nice, but now Liv is saying something about how *tech bros* dominate the real estate here, making it inaccessible *and impossible to find a place for under two million*. They are also ruining the once cool restaurants with *SF vibes*, she says, but Lucien can't stop looking at all the families.

"Since we're over here," Liv says, sounding nervous for a moment, "maybe you can come with me to this Friendsgiving? It's right nearby."

"Liv, I dunno."

"Please please please. We'll stay five minutes, eat some food, and head back east. Come on, I'm starving."

Lucien feels manipulated, and now trapped. But he is starving, too.

They turn into alley after alley—Lucien now understands that half of Venice is alleys—until a grid of canals unfolds before them. Here the light is still stretching. Charming houses reflect themselves like Narcissus. A swan floats by, rippling their mirror. Elaborate patios are set right along the walkway, with barbecues so close passing voyeurs could grab a hot dog.

They stop on the arch of a wooden footbridge and look out across the canal at a tiny log cabin, a beach cottage, the modern glass cube boldly lacking an exterior wall or two, another tiny Swiss chalet. Liv holds her phone out over the edge to take a photograph, and when Lucien looks down, for a moment he doesn't recognize himself. Then a family of ducks floats under the bridge, breaking their reflection into ripples moving in separate directions.

Voices come from behind a row of hedges framing a trellised archway. Inside the gate, a manicured lawn with succulents, flowering cacti, and a trickling water fountain leads to a modified cottage with high peaked ceilings and a front of all glass. Inside is bohemian chic, with whitewashed wood and mismatched art on the walls. Bright pops of color, a leopard pillow or two. This is the kind of beach house you might see on a network sitcom, likely far beyond the means of any characters, but unassuming in its charm.

Liv points to the hostess, who she describes as a celebrity stylist, in the kitchen. The kitchen is open format, with brass details and a large pink marble island. Most people seem to be congregated here, which is promising. No party oriented around food can be that bad. The crowd cheers in the kitchen as the hostess, Amelie, flips a burger into the air and onto a potato bun, with cheese, smashing it together until it oozes. Lucien is relieved there appears to be no turkey, no stuffing. Another table holds dessert after dessert, brought by guests based on the mismatched plates and containers. There is something surprisingly chic to serving the most casual food executed to perfection. The lack of pretense in the kitchen; the lack of inhibitions in how many one might eat, as the smash burgers pile up, ready to go back around the room. An actress Lucien recognizes from a CW billboard he drives by every day walks past him as she takes a bite of her burger. She takes so long to chew that by the time she swallows she has already put the plate down and is engrossed in another conversation.

A few guests sitting on couches in the living room look familiar to Lucien, likely from his time photographing events in New York. He looks away when one of them seems to be watching him back; maybe they recognize him, too, though they'd never figure out why. The party reeks of the type who lives between New York and Los Angeles, never sticking around long enough to really get either one. What is New York without the struggle? Los Angeles without the boredom? To live in both places is to belong nowhere, but people claim it with pride. Lucien watches in amazement as, one by one, people walk over and start new conversations. The group is unusually welcoming, as most rooms are where everyone is someone—because the assumption is that you are, too.

"Lucien is an amazing artist," Liv says, and Lucien must have zoned out because another guy, early thirties, wearing an ill-fitted denim jacket, stands with them. He takes a bite of smash burger and opens his eyes wide, nodding as he chews.

Harry, a talent manager, tells Lucien what he does like he expects him to already know who he represents. But now all Lucien can think about is how Liv knows his art, and what she might have dug up online. Or does she just want him to be talented and so proclaimed it? He isn't sure which is worse. He wonders if she has seen the series of his mother. The rawness that made the collection a success also sent him running and now here he is, thinking about it again.

"He had a show at Wes Neilson. And his dealer just told him today that they want him to come to the Frieze this year. With Gagosian."

Lucien cannot believe her; he only told her about that because it made him anxious, the idea of resuming his work around his mother. He told her because he wasn't sure if he was ready.

"Liv," he says. "That's not definitely happening."

"Well, they want you," she says proudly. "The question is if they'll get you."

Again, he sees this other side to Liv. She prides herself on being grounded and detached from all the things most people clutch, yet here she is, parading him around despite knowing how he feels. If this is what she wants from him, she'll be disappointed.

"So what kind of art?" Harry says loudly, as if repeating himself. "I mean, that's probably gauche. What's your medium? Isn't that what they say?"

You can tell a lot about a person by the way they react to art in conversation. One doesn't have to be an expert, or in the art world at all, to be curious. Open. Unafraid. But some people react with such aversion. Defensive before they can be embarrassed.

"He's a photographer," Liv says. "He makes these incredible collages with fractured faces—exploring perspective and race and privilege. I'm sorry, am I embarrassing you? You don't look well."

Liv holds a hand up to Lucien's face and he takes it in his hand instead, giving her a squeeze. She needs him to be this, for some reason he doesn't quite see yet. Maybe there's an ex here, wandering about. Maybe standing right in front of them. Whatever it is, he won't be taken care of by her, or patronized.

"I'm fine," he says. "But I'm actually not sure which work you're talking about?"

"Oh," she says, embarrassed. "The one with lots of faces, or parts of a whole person, sort of pieced together."

Lucien contains a laugh. For one of his final projects in art school, he asked everyone in his MFA to take a photo of their favorite body part, which he then cut together to form some master compilation. The truth was, he'd been turned onto Kenneth Josephson's and David Hockney's photo collages earlier that year, and he hoped his mash-up would reveal some supremely modern image, crossing ethnicity, age, and gender. What it actually showed was just how homogenous their class was, the collective image looking a lot like this girl named Megan from Wisconsin.

Lucien wants to say a million things about how that piece doesn't represent him at all, how it was a momentary trying on of other artists' styles, but he cannot bring himself to embarrass Liv like that. Instead he stands in silence.

"What's it like in photography these days?" Harry says. "Gotta be brutal, eh?"

"Harry!" Liv says.

"No, I'm really curious—I think about this often. You know, I collect, so I try to stay informed. It just seems like that market has got to be hard. Everyone thinks they're a photographer now, with their iPhones and Instagram filters. How do you survive, man?"

Lucien is used to this question; in fact, he remembers now it's one of the reasons he avoids cocktail parties with those not in the arts but who like to feel hip. Allies of the arts, which usually means through money not heart.

"Lucien's work is incredibly distinct and reworked," Liv says shamelessly. "It's nothing like what you could do on some app."

"I don't know about that," Lucien says. "I think there's an app for everything these days."

"Ha, I like this guy."

"Honestly, I think it's great," Lucien says. "Technology has introduced so many people to photography and made art lovers out of amateurs. I think that's never a bad thing; and also I don't have a choice, right? There's no going back."

"But I mean, it's gotta be frustrating," says Harry. "To see people think they can do this thing just because—look, you must've spent a lot of hours in the darkroom, just to . . ."

"Hey, everyone can buy paint and fill in lines they trace on a canvas, right? You don't see painters out there trying to keep people from art stores. Do you think Rothko sales suffer because you could copy his work and hang it in your home?"

"I think it's different with a physical object," Harry says. "A painting is singular."

"Photography can be singular. If an image is manipulated during or after developing, it truly is. And if I were worried about someone taking the same photograph as me, I wouldn't be much of an artist."

"I just have to think, with these cameras today, even our *phones*."

"I don't work for *National Geographic*. A better camera doesn't make a better artist," Lucien says. "It's an extension of the eye. A way of seeing. The film and photograph are tactile, like oils and canvas for the painter, or steel and clay for a sculptor. Everything is in play. Calder for example constructed mobiles, but the goal was to paint in shadows, to take painting off of the canvas."

"Ah, I love Calder," says Harry, as he would.

"Do you like Baldessari?" Lucien feels powerful for the first time in a long time and wants to crush Harry's misplaced confidence. "If you did you'd know one can be an artist simply by repositioning past works of art to create something new based on their own structure, scale, and context. Photography has always been more than a finger on the shutter."

Liv puts her hand on Lucien's chest and he feels it again, her claim. She is so far from the person who lay beside him in bed that morning. Her grip now makes him want to run. He wants to keep talking, but stops himself. He has never felt the need to show off or put someone in their place quite like this; in fact, the role he just stepped into frightens him.

Harry looks just as energized as Lucien, like all he really wanted was exactly this. A heated exchange. "I told you," he says, "I'm no art person. I just know what I like."

"Lucien's mother was Isabel Bennett," Liv blurts out, as if under the pretense of excusing his attitude, but suddenly Lucien gets it. The parading, the awkward insertions. He imagines his face looking back at her, hollowed. *Was*. Isn't she still his mother, even if she's gone?

"Huh, nice," Harry says, pushing his chin out a little.

Was it worth it, for that? Lucien's mother used for a fucking chin-push. A check mark next to his name. Any comfort he felt with Liv earlier turns rotten inside him.

"I'm gonna get some air," he says to no one in particular, and catches Liv shrugging at Harry as he pushes past them to the door.

Which side of Liv is the real one, he wonders. At some point, does it even matter? Outside, the same actress Lucien recognized earlier is smoking alone beside a sky-high cactus. She stands turned away from the party, and her knee-high suede boots and short crochet dress look silly away from the crowd.

Her hand trembles as she takes a long pull, eyes closed, then holds the smoke. When she opens her eyes and sees Lucien, she shakes her head and apologizes, revealing an Australian accent. She extends her thin arm with the hand-rolled joint in hand.

"Thanks," he says, then inhales. "Lucien."

"Ruby."

"Party not your speed?" he asks, letting out as little breath as possible.

Ruby tilts her head, poised to answer, but glances past him. Or maybe those are just her eyes, distant-looking. Then hands squeeze Lucien's shoulders from behind. He coughs, startled, and passes back the joint as he turns.

"I'm such an idiot," Liv says. "I completely forgot I was supposed to go to this thing with Sophie tonight back on the other side of town. Thank god for calendar alerts, right? Our friend is hosting a sound bath. Do you know the band Envoys? Anyway, he's taking a break from touring to do these transcendental music experiences."

"I love that band," says Ruby. "Envoys."

Liv ignores her. She slides her hands farther down Lucien's chest, letting her head dangle over his shoulder. Something she's never done before. Lucien looks at Ruby apologetically. She smiles back.

"What time are you supposed to meet?" Lucien asks.

Ruby extends the joint in Liv's direction, but Liv shakes her head. Lucien peels off one of Liv's hands from his shoulder and leans in to take another hit. The smoke dulls something he is feeling. The earthy musk calms him. He finally feels like staying.

"Forget it, I'll barely make it with the traffic leaving the beach, plus I have to go up to Echo Park first to drop you," Liv says. "Maybe I should wait until traffic calms down and be a little late. Sophie's always late."

The idea of traffic dictating plans or how to live is something Lucien cannot get used to. Talking extensively about traffic is even worse, and he resents it for interrupting his buzz.

"I'll just find a ride to mine from wherever you're going."

"You're a lifesaver," Liv says, leaning into him. "Thanks, babe."

Ruby looks away.

Liv has never called him babe; here she is, trying it on for size. Again Lucien finds himself doing the things he knows Liv wants and then resenting how happy they make her. He wants to insist that really it's nothing, he just doesn't want her going out of her way for him. Downtown is clearly on his way home. And what's the alternative, staying at this party on the Westside alone?

"Okay, well let's just go in and say our goodbyes, then."

"You go," he says, waving a hand; he smells like smoke. "I'll wait here."

"Suit yourself."

Within moments Liv is hugging everyone in the kitchen, playfully slapping their shoulders when they obviously start talking about him, even gesturing toward the glass. Liv looks ecstatic and it makes Lucien feel—nothing. Even annoyance would feel better than nothing. *Whatever*, he thinks as his mind follows the smoke up into the air.

He looks to the actress again, hoping for one last hit, but she is reclined on a deck chair, passed out. In her open hand and across her thigh is the shimmer off a mermaid, and Lucien thinks how good this weed must be.

The sound bath is being held in an art deco office building on what might otherwise be a deserted block downtown. There's a small encampment directly across the street, and two young men with sharp cheekbones pace back and forth at the intersection, shouting at everyone passing by. Car horns blare until, one by one, each driver sees the cause of their holdup.

A steady stream of people hurry past. These people all look exactly as Lucien would have imagined, trying to be so different that they end up the same. Perfectly curated bohemians who all arrive separately in their own cars and fade into one discerning yet completely indistinguishable pack. Los Angeles, a city of extras.

Lucien stops, letting people pass them.

"Are you okay?" Liv asks.

"It's like everyone has been perfectly cast," he says, amused. Or maybe he's just high. "Have you ever noticed that? I keep noticing that."

"What do you mean?"

"I dunno, look around—everyone looks . . . exactly right."

He laughs. Liv laughs, too.

"Isn't it great?"

Before he can respond, Liv pushes ahead, taking his hand.

The building's exterior hints at grandeur from another era in the soaring details of its higher stories, while its current ground-level storefront announces a closeout sale on bright boxy signs. Once through the revolving door, they stop beside the bronze-detailed elevator, and Liv clutches her phone again. Lucien wants to tell her that watching the screen won't make Sophie text any sooner, especially if she's driving. Though he's also grateful for the break in her attention, and the chance to admire the space even as everyone else rushes through.

What aspiration, he thinks, to cover ceilings with ornately carved tin; to suspend chandeliers of thinly carved marble and gold; to expect people to look up. Such high hopes the architects of the 1920s had for us. Not just for Los Angeles, but for humanity, and yes, he is definitely still a bit high. But those architects probably assumed people would appreciate such craftsmanship in the future, instead of being drawn to the square plastic shapes of our phones and computers, kitchens and lives. Instead of "smart" buildings, soon capable of outthinking us. How could they have foreseen the desire to become passive in our own lives? Or the shift from showcasing skill not in ornate details but in lack thereof. He thinks back to the coffee shop they stopped in on their way to the Westside, which looked like an Apple Store with its light, stripped-down appearance and hidden appliances. How unremarkable our lives now might look to the designers of the past, all glass and transparency, design slowly becoming valued for being invisible, less decorated than optimized. He remembers the nooks in their house in Prospect Heights, the details that made it home, and entirely unfashionable. He hopes they still remain, but maybe not. Even their old stove there had charm, its colorful orange enamel.

"Still nothing!" says Liv, waving her phone. "How the hell do you just not respond?"

Lucien looks past her to the golden olive branches carved in the elevator door. He follows the curved lines of the Grecian man with his sword thrust into a coiling snake. Everyone sounds exactly the same, their mouths moving all at once, as they fill the elevator car. No doubt this massive building would be empty if not for the ironic choice of their weekend sound bath. Though the floor directory on the wall reads like a tally of emerging fashion brands, maybe they found these studio and storage spaces because no one else wants them.

Lucien's mother lamented how Los Angeles is full of architectural treasures, but many are either buried underground in a Metro no one takes, or forgotten in similarly neglected downtown buildings. The rest, hidden in the exclusivity of wealth, are set in the hills. Treasured for being kept private. The city's relationship to architecture was like an inside joke, with some of the finest restaurants tucked into concrete strip malls, between ubiquitous donut shops and smoke stores. Or in brand-new, soulless shopping malls. Even the more instructive store-fronts become misleading, in this city where you might find a five-star French-Filipino restaurant in the converted A-frame of an abandoned pancake house. Layers upon layers of kitsch and self-reflection, all of which seem to be lost on much of the population. Perhaps a city so accustomed to sets, to facades, his mother would say, is simply indifferent to depth.

With each elevator car that fills and rises, Liv looks increasingly distraught. She is clearly tallying the remaining mat spots upstairs, fewer and fewer, and he cannot watch any longer. He doesn't want to be here for whatever confrontation might come when her friend does arrive.

"Hey, I'm gonna call a Drivr."

"What? Are you sure? You could stay for the sound bath, or at least to meet Leif!"

"Another time, I'm suddenly feeling a bit nauseous," he lies. "I probably shouldn't be out, in case it's something."

"Really? Well then, I can drive you back, I—"

"No, you should stay. I'm sure it's just from all the time in the car today. I'll be fine."

"Okay, well—I left some magnesium and a collagen probiotic in your kitchen. You should take them! They work wonders."

She kisses him on the forehead and squeezes his hand. Then looks back to her phone. Lucien cannot imagine when she could have left those, or whether they were for him or for her, the equivalent of a toothbrush in the medicine cabinet, but he tries not to let his mind go there. Not while he's standing beside her, about to get away.

Chapter 19

BEFORE

Sophie's alarm filters in slowly. Its relentless ringing is a pinhole of light piercing her consciousness. She must have finally fallen back asleep. She feels her body against the mattress, the comforter against her cheek. Her right arm tingles underneath her. She rolls onto her back and is relieved to see daylight through the blinds. For a moment, she wonders if it was just a dream. Then underneath the covers she sees the same jeans and sweater, stained with turmeric.

The consciousness returns like a shudder. Even in the quiet of her apartment, she is not alone. She turns away, but feels a stranger inside her. This doesn't feel like a drug, not like a substance, lingering, but rather something implanted. How much of whatever Ray Delaney slipped her could still be in her system? How long has she slept?

Sophie hardly remembers getting home. She remembers only a blur—Ray Delaney's smug expression as she bent to the floor. She is relieved to be still wearing her clothing; and yet, he still could have—why else would Ray Delaney have slipped her Mem? What pleasure did it bring him? She doesn't know what to feel, or what she might feel now if he *had*—done what is unspeakable even in her own mind. So many ways of not saying the same thing. *Had his way with her? Taken advantage of her?* He had done that either way. No, say it. Rape.

The word sends a fresh panic through her body, fear of the thing she cannot remember. Now done, would it change anything, to know?

What truth lingers in her body? Shouldn't the body remember? But even her own feels newly strange.

Her phone lights up on the bedside table. Notifications fill its screen. Just now, a missed call from Liv, along with texts from Jonathan, and then Willow. Oh god, did she miss work? How could she have slept for days? Where has she been? She closes her eyes and presses a hand to her forehead as another image—no, full sensation—runs through her. A body bloody and limp, distorted in her arms. Satisfaction mixed with horror.

That I would spill the beauty from them all.

Now she remembers drinking the remaining half bottle of wine from the refrigerator, and then all the mini bottles of liquor she keeps like souvenirs in case she has company. She hoped the alcohol might quiet the voice and its haunting visions enough for her to sleep, but all it seemed to do was relax her own inhibitions, bringing the stranger on stronger, until she found herself once more frozen, fading, falling.

When Sophie stands, rocks inside her head, she thinks she might vomit. She stumbles toward the bathroom. Then she remembers the pain pills. After the alcohol, she had blindly shaken bottles in her medicine cabinet, one hand to her head, coaxing this stranger's memories down with the coolness of a wet washcloth while she looked for anything to interrupt this seeming possession. Finding only supplements and vitamins and generic ibuprofen, she shook for the bottle she knew was there. The one stuffed full of large, unwieldy pills.

She was prescribed them when she broke a toe last year. Stress fracture. She had to keep dancing with it taped up, yet she never took a single pill. She kept them anyway, as if she knew; as if somewhere this present was already in her future, even then. The only time she took them before was in high school after having her wisdom teeth removed, and they made her too nauseous to even sit up. She hates the stuff. But not just for how they make her feel. She hates them for what they've done to her family. Her baby brother whose social anxiety had fallen in love at the first taste, who had been prescribed them for reasons not unlike her own. Pain, short-term now long-lived.

Last year Sophie considered selling the pills when she got the flu and had to miss a week's worth of work at Chateau Marmont. She knew people who would take them. She needed the money. Still, she couldn't bring herself to contribute to the cycle of abuse. Or maybe she just wanted to prove to herself that she wasn't like her brother; that she could keep them right there in her cabinet, untouched.

Last night Sophie shook out two pills. As her mind got fuzzier, she longed for therapies of decades past, electrodes shocking her brain back to function, frying off any foreign matter. But again she found herself fading as the stranger's thoughts raced back in, cockroaches streaming from the open sewer, until she could no longer tell what was hers or his, or theirs. Soon her entire form was made of motion, swarming insects contained by static—and Sophie, their collected shape. The infestation in human form.

A new text from Liv lights up the screen.

Are you coming?!?! Do not flake on me I just drove 75 minutes in beach traffic ;)

This would make it Saturday. She missed two rehearsals and a night of work. A Friday night. What could they be thinking? How could she ever explain?

Sophieeeeee. I'm already on Olympic. Don't make me text and drive.

For a moment she hates Liv. Deeply and fully, Sophie resents her privilege; not the same privilege Liv has had all along, which is occasionally hard to swallow but not entirely offensive. She hates her safety. That Liv even considers herself angry. She had not been taken by Ray Delaney, poisoned, tainted. She never would be.

All Sophie wants is to pretend like nothing is wrong. To meet Liv as planned, for an afternoon of complaining about bad dates, about rehearsals, or the incessant tourists plaguing Chateau Marmont; things that once seemed urgent and now feel like luxury. Even listening to Liv drone on about the challenges of her juice shop, unaware of how lucky her problems are. All of it now feels bittersweet. Sophie would love to have a shift tonight, a series of orders and cocktails and plates to organize the chaos of her mind.

A wave of the stranger curls inside her, sharp as a knife, and she shakes her head, pushing it back down. That twisted sense of his pleasure. What could she say to Willow anyway? *Persistent is the madness.* Moreover, to Auguste for missing rehearsals? *Fuck the bodies, let them burn.* Absences are unheard of. Two in a row, he must be livid. She would tell them she was sick and—incapacitated. *Inky liquid, first it trickles, then it flows.* Food poisoning. The flu. Maybe she had been hospitalized? What else could they possibly think? She would never skip rehearsal; and she never misses work. *Hide so they don't know your face; hide until the end, then they'll remember.* They have to believe her. *Then they'll never forget.*

Sophie looks down at her arms, her thighs. She scratches her fingernails against her skin, anything to feel her body as her own. Then she tears out a page from the book on her bedside table and holds it up to her forearm. She'd known a girl who did this. She holds her breath and swipes the paper edge across her forearm, feeling the sting. Herself. She does it again. With each gasp, each sharp pain, she feels grounded. She feels the one haunting her slip away. The lines turn red and then pill. She squeezes her arm, watching the blood. Her own.

She will come back to herself, she thinks. Whatever Mem Ray Delaney slipped her was like a bad dream, a trauma that never happened. Because it hadn't, not really. Not to her. He cannot control her. She has to be strong. To will herself right. What she saw was no more than a hyperrealistic movie; what she felt was no more than that of any spectator. She is but a startled audience, waiting for the credits to roll. Wishing the lights would come on.

Persistent is the madness. Fuck the bodies, let them burn.

She crumples the paper still in her hand. Then pushes at the places where she hurts.

Maybe what she needs is a taste of something else, of someone else, to get this out of her head? Hair of the dog. Dislodge whatever seems to be stuck. She has felt anxiety before, the spiraling focus that picks up momentum the more it lingers. Like a song one can't help but keep humming; yes, maybe all she needs is a new melody.

But where and how? Who would ask the fewest questions? Keegan has Mem, at least he hinted at it. But then she'd have to see him again, and after what she said to him? She imagines his smug smile, like somehow he'd known before she did that, of course she wanted what he had.

She begins a new text to Keegan, ignoring her previous one that still fills the screen.

Hey

She sends without caring, desperate without hiding it.

What's up?

No typing. No response.

Okay, so . . . I'm sorry.

What're you up to later?

Still no answer. Finally, one more. The real question.

Still have Mem?

Three dots appear. Sophie anxiously taps her fingers on her legs as the dots disappear and reappear multiple times until, finally, his message appears.

Nope.

And then another incoming text hovers over Keegan's. It's Liv.

Sophie srsly will I see you there or not

Sophie's fingers grip the steering wheel, its vinyl tacky under her hands as she twists her knuckles back and forth, trying to anchor herself to the moment, to the road. Atop her fingers are those familiar letters. Only a few days ago she last traced their outline, feeling an urgency as she did every time, like a promise she was making herself.

LOOK UP

It's a dangerous habit, watching her hands as she drives. That's why, following one fender bender shortly after arriving in Los Angeles, Sophie started writing the letters in permanent marker. Most mornings that meant retracing the faded marks from the day before; at times she's thought the repeated practice already made their outline permanent. Now the practice is like a meditation. The last time she went home for the holidays, her mother said she was poisoning herself with chemicals from those markers on her skin every day. After that, Sophie even considered getting it tattooed, but she chickened out at the last moment in the parking lot.

Most people already assume it is a real tattoo anyway, and she doesn't correct them. Her tables at Chateau Marmont find it amusing, commending her for the sharp commentary on people's self-preoccupation and total disregard for their *servers being people, too.* The irony.

Those two words—six letters, six knuckles—elicit different takes from everyone. People see what they want to in the phrase. Her Rorschach tattoo. She has heard everything from *God is with you always, up there!* from a cashier at Trader Joe's to *Right on, don't forget the big picture!* from a barista as she reached for a lid at Intelligentsia. For Sophie, however, it simply means LOOK UP, IDIOT. One knuckle too short, the rest is implied.

Now all of that feels far away. Such certainty of herself hits like nostalgia. How can she be so close to something yet already miss it? Will she ever feel the same? Even the risk, the fear of driving distracted, now makes her wistful—that *that* should be her fear.

Sophie had made these plans weeks ago, to meet Liv at their friend Leif's sound bath. Leif who was always into some new drug or experiential quest. If he has Mem it would be good stuff, not like what she'd been given. Leif's Mem would be beautiful. Artful. Leif who organizes retreats for his friends to Norway, foraging for wild mushrooms to trip under the stars during the northern lights. This darkness wouldn't be Leif's idea of escape, and maybe whatever he has, if it is clean, if it is beautiful, maybe then it would clear out what is tormenting her. Or at least it would loosen the hold.

A rush of optimism bubbles up inside her and it feels familiar. Sophie feels it then—herself. If this is just lingering chemicals from the drug, it would mean that once more time passes, maybe in another day or two, these visions will be gone. These feelings will leave her.

She'll get something from Leif, just in case. Even just to ride out the lingering effects in her system with something more bearable. Anything to tide her over until she returns to herself. Imagine wanting something so simple. For most of her life, she's wondered how she could change, how she could make herself more palatable to others. More popular, more at ease. Only now does she realize what she's had all along—she had been, always, herself.

When Sophie finally rushes through the revolving door, Liv's face looks vacant. She almost doesn't seem to see her at first, and when Liv does say hello she barely makes eye contact before rushing off to the bathroom.

Can she tell? Sophie wonders. *Can she see it in my eyes? Can she feel it, the rage under my skin?*

A girl arm-linked with her partner, lost in laughter, sways into Sophie on her way into the elevator. Sophie shoves her back, and the girl shrieks. She rubs her arm and looks to her partner, who didn't see, waiting for him to step in from their place now inside the elevator. Sophie stares at them both as the doors close. Then she finds a water fountain to splash her face.

Keep it together, she thinks, sputtering water from her mouth and down her neck. Her hair sticks to her forehead, and the water is lukewarm, hardly does the trick. A hand on her shoulder, and Sophie reels backward, bumping into the fountain, hitting her elbow. The jolt of pain brings her back.

"Sorry!" Liv says. "Are you okay? Sophie?"

"Sure, yeah. You startled me." Sophie tries to smile, but it comes out a grimace.

"You didn't have to come, you know," Liv says flatly. "I was only joking."

"I wanted to," Sophie says. "I've been looking forward to this. I just—I didn't sleep well, and then traffic was ridiculous. I'm a bit fried."

"I can tell. Have you eaten anything?"

"What?"

Liv is still talking, but Sophie feels dizzy, surrounded by bodies all moving freely past her and around, and part of her wants to stop them.

"Sophie?"

"What? Sorry."

"I was just *saying*, this will be great. You can just relax and drift off. The last time I did one of these I practically hallucinated; I was dreaming up crazy things with my eyes closed, but totally awake. I wish I'd written some of it down, like full-on fantasy stuff—but you always think you'll remember, right? I can only imagine what this'll be like, with Leif at the helm."

"Have you seen Leif yet?"

"Not yet, I'm sure he's upstairs setting up. Or knowing Leif, hiding."

Sophie thinks they might as well get upstairs then, but cannot tell if she actually said it, and now they're standing inside the elevator, the doors closing as Liv watches her. The overhead light is so harsh, Sophie realizes, as she's staring right at it.

Her eyes flare when she looks back down.

"Are you sure you're okay?"

"I'm fine, I just need to sit down I think."

"Anyway, I thought I'd see you there," Liv continues, in the middle of a conversation with herself. "Of course with that crowd, Harry was there, too, but god, Sophie—it felt so fucking good to not be there alone. Like finally, some good karma. You know?"

"Sorry, where was this?"

"At Amelie and Luca's party in Venice! I was just saying, I took Lucien . . . You should've seen the look on Harry's face when Lucien brought up his mother's art. Absolutely priceless."

Sophie picks at a cuticle until she feels a sharp pain, then looks down at the drop of blood pilling, preparing to roll. She holds her finger to her mouth, and tastes salt. Her blood, hers.

"Jesus, Sophie, could you at least feign interest?"

"What? Sorry?"

"How many times have I listened to you talk about some new crush at the Chateau? Or celebrated another of your accomplishments with the LABC? It seems like every other week we're celebrating something of yours."

The other people in the elevator stare. Sophie tucks her finger into her palm and squeezes, grounding herself to the pain, and pushing the rising sense of darkness down until finally the elevator opens at the twentieth floor.

"I thought you'd be happy for me," Liv says. "I found someone I really like."

"I am happy for you," Sophie says as they file out of the elevator. "Really."

The space stretches forever. The entire floor is open, save for the columns that repeat in all directions, following lines where walls might once have been. Overhead is a tin ceiling with a few exposed pipes, and everything else is white-painted brick, giving the space a cool temperature. Yoga mats are arranged like a starburst fanning out from an open core. Silk pillows are placed next to each mat. Most of the spots are already taken, and Sophie senses Liv's frustration as they walk farther and farther across the floor.

Sophie scans the room for any sign of Leif, her mind desperate for his potential stash. As they walk, a red light begins to emanate from the center of the space, and suddenly the coolness of the room is charged, changed by the color radiating outward, where it fades into a golden hue. Sophie cannot tell if it's the red or her own exhaustion, but she feels once again unsettled.

The two mats they find together are in the orange middle ground, and when they sit Sophie puts her head in her hands and breathes deeply.

"I think it's starting," Liv whispers.

"Really? But we haven't seen Leif."

"I caught a glimpse of him, over there," Liv says, pointing toward a black curtain across the room. She laughs. "Classic Leif. I'm sure we'll find him after."

"Are these lights on the whole time?" Sophie rubs her face. "I didn't realize it'd be so . . ."

"Depths of hell?"

"Exactly."

"You can just close your eyes once it starts."

An actress Sophie recognizes from a sitcom she watched as a child, when the actress was also a child, sits down on the open mat in front of them. Her face looks off—similar to when she was young, but stretched and skewed so as to look almost grotesque.

"Do I know you?" she says.

Sophie turns away, but watches from the side of her eye as the actress slides a tin out from her purse, places a tiny gummy on her tongue, then slips the tin back in her purse. Everything is so casual, so contained. She licks her fingers and bobs her head to the ambient noise, letting her hair fall in front of her eyes.

Hide so they don't know your face; hide until the end, then they'll remember.

"There he is!" says Liv, hitting Sophie's shoulder.

Leif's face hovers bodiless, peering out from behind the curtain. Liv laughs loudly and waves, until he blushes and waves back before disappearing again.

"I'm going to go say hi," Sophie says, standing.

Liv grabs her hand and pulls her back down.

"Sit! It's starting!"

The lights dim to darkness and the voices begin to soften until it is entirely, terrifyingly, quiet. Sounds trickle in, natural at first, then defying logic or instrument.

Leif's music undulates like movement set to tone. Every time Sophie shuts her eyes, she races through thoughts, more flashes of moments she wants to forget. They surface with hallucinatory clarity until—just like that—the music shifts and the visions blur. When at last Sophie opens her eyes, the steam holding the red pulsing light appears charged with sound, as if chords could be painted. The space circulates with sound. She sees it. She feels it. The sound moves Sophie from one thought to the next, the red music a fever ready to erupt. *The bodies, covered in red.*

Sophie missed her opportunity to talk to Leif, and now she's stuck here. Captive in the hazy humming atmosphere filling the room.

How erotic when something familiar turns unknowable, uncanny, dismembered. You have to feel it. You have to feel it.

Sophie keeps her eyes open, but the thoughts persist as the music builds. *You have to feel it. The things we know best are the most surprising, once opened up.* Sophie knows such things now, too. About the ways a body bends until it snaps. About the weight of a life when a car hits it. How that, too, is a sound. How the body hits back hard.

This is not her. But where is she disappearing to, if not inside? What's worse is what builds now as the music rises. Her thirst for it—for life. To be the one to snuff it out. Sophie tugs at her hair, the prickling pain pulling her back.

Everyone around her is just lying there. So trusting with their eyes closed, throats exposed. Thirsty for ritual. Like waiting for some mass sacrifice. *I'll give them ritual. What they're waiting for is me.* Red steam, the hollowness of this space. *I will show them sacrifice. I will spill the beauty from them all. Cattle marching to death. Follow me.*

Stop it, Sophie says, and she knows this comes out loud because she feels Liv's elbow in her side, *that fucking bitch*. Sophie pinches her legs, trying to stay present. The music builds, soft staccato laced with a deep throbbing bass that feels like fate. This isn't real. This isn't real.

She presses her face into the thick rubber mat, in case losing her breath might cut off the voice. How much more could be left in her? The visions and desires latch on, defining her as they populate her own thoughts, suddenly tied to things that once existed, harmless, inside of her. What if this is just her now, forever changed?

"Sophie?"

She wants to slit her fucking throat. She jumps to her feet, slaps her own face, and Liv looks up at her with an expression that sends a shiver of shame through Sophie, while also tantalizing something deep.

"Sit down," Liv whispers through her teeth, like a parent scolding their fucking child.

Sophie shakes her head; she can't even look at her, she can't let Liv see whatever is behind her eyes, lest she see what she is thinking, lest she see through the redness and the haze. She doesn't trust herself. Not surrounded by such immersive, pulsing red. She turns toward the yellow edges by the windows, but feels trapped.

So many bodies laid up, and ready. For what?

She runs, jumping mats and stepping on a hand here and there, rustling the crowd until she notices a security guard on the other side of the room slowly walking toward her path. *Fucking ready*, says the voice inside her head, but she moves faster, faster toward the elevator, willing her body forward in spite of her insides, in spite of the redness pulsing everywhere, wrapping itself around her thoughts until, like her, they are gasping for air.

The cool air outside feels like safety. Sterilizing. When Sophie reaches her car, she doesn't immediately recognize the face reflected back in the window. She smooths her unwashed hair, pushing it down and back, and stares until her features are familiar. Then she smiles, watching her face unfold. Tears run down her cheeks. If she could only get back to herself, to her routine; to the things that sustain her, and define her. If only she could get through the night.

Sophie drives west along Beverly Boulevard, her mind too fuzzy for the freeway. A red light stops her at an intersection just entering Hancock Park, where the yards are wider and the trees taller. She pushes the cool heels of her hands into her eyelids, cupping her forehead. When she opens her eyes, a coyote stands at the curb.

At first Sophie wonders if she is hallucinating. She often sees coyotes in Griffith Park when hiking early in the morning, or later as dusk settles and the trails empty out, but she has never heard of them coming this far into town. The coyote looks stoic beside the road, as if in mourning. Humans are not the only ones being displaced. Sophie always felt a magic when coming across coyotes in the wild, their presence marking the crossover between when people own the city versus when the animals take over. From dusk until dawn.

She checks the traffic light—still red—and when she turns back, the coyote is staring at her. For a moment Sophie thinks they make eye contact; they understand one another. But that is a projection. This isn't a coyote from a children's movie; it isn't Pixar's animated and misunderstood predator with a kind heart. This is a wild animal. A scavenger.

Still, the coyote does not look away. Does it recognize something in her?

Sophie speeds along Olympic Boulevard, feeling for a moment like she might actually escape this feeling if she goes fast enough. Years of living in Los Angeles, and she can count on one hand the number of times she's made it to the beach. On Main Street in Santa Monica, she keeps driving as the brick buildings and vintage streetlamps give way to peeling plaster and spray-painted murals. The jazz playing on public radio calms her. Out the window, a dilapidated giant clown sculpture looms above a freshly installed neon CVS sign. She looks westward at each intersection to catch a glimpse of the ocean, but the haze from the fires has settled here, too. Even the horizon line is indiscernible. At one point, she thinks she sees sailboats floating into the sky.

Tan, wiry-haired surfers walk in front of cars with ease, carrying boards twice as long as their bodies like briefcases, coming home from work. As the street curves and narrows, buildings alternate between homes and all-new glass compounds, gated for the start-ups that have claimed the area. Burned-out windows sit next to chic signs that hint at expensive new restaurants. A corner hardware shop with its original sign advertises a GENERAL STORE, though it likely sells artisanal chocolates and expensive vintage jeans. General needs have changed.

When she finally finds a parking spot, Sophie hurries down an alley toward the beach, hearing the crunch of glass on sandy pavement under each step. The light is fading fast. The Venice Boardwalk souvenir shops and food stands are closing up for the night, and it has become eerily still. Most of the tourists have left the beach for restaurants and bars. Sophie wanders farther away from the well-lit stretch of boardwalk as the last light disappears.

She knows people come here looking for Mem. Not the fancy kind, no Nagano ski-jumping memories, but she doesn't need anything special. She tries to say what she is looking for, to speak it into the darkness, but the words get stuck in her mouth. It feels wrong to assume, to ask for something no one should have. A young man with crusty blond hair skateboards by, and Sophie blurts out *Mem* just as he passes.

She feels like an idiot, but so desperate she doesn't care. The guy stops and steps off his board. His nose is pink and peeling, raw. He looks around, then points toward a spot down the block. She rushes forward, and he skates past, sticking his tongue out at her and laughing. She is relieved once he disappears into the darkness ahead, but then she is alone.

Once she reaches the spot he pointed to, she approaches a man standing near a lamppost. The only person she sees. "I've got thirty," Sophie whispers. Thirty would be enough, but not too much to get her in trouble. "How many pills does that get?" She can barely see his face, only his ponytail flecked with sand. "Okay," she tries. "How about three pills?" He pulls out a bag of multicolored glossy capsules, and the full range of pastels. He shakes the clouded plastic until the pills rattle.

Just then another man appears behind her. He tugs Sophie's arm, then nods in the other direction. She follows him, surprised and somewhat reassured by his older age, his gaunt cheeks and arched back. He ducks behind cardboard and fabric she didn't see before, against the side of a building. Then he waves out a hand for her to follow.

Chapter 20

TODAY

What does a mudslide sound like?

Movement. But what is silence, untethered? A forest holds a cracking thunder; a hillside neighborhood, its wealth in weight. What are the latent sounds of an area, in stillness, that might be released in motion? Closets of clothing, dressers packed full; giant televisions made to appear weightless, hovering on steel brackets; cabinets stocked with spices in glass jars; refrigerators full of produce and cold meats. We live in silence that could suffocate us. Crushed under all that we own.

The only sound then is its path of destruction. Cars and power lines, stacked like the forest is still. Twisting metal and splitting timber. The rush of land made liquid. Can one even hear so much motion? By then, is it too late?

At the Center, patients have been evacuated down to the beach, its sand tinted blue under the full moon. They look like a cult, all beige and uniformed, not a single possession or adornment. No jewelry glittering under the moonlight. No shoes to show their different styles or priorities. On either side of the Center, up and down the beach, other residents and families stand with their backs to the ocean, facing the hillside, watching for something they won't recognize until it's there, if it comes. Living beside someplace so private must be strange. To gaze into the glass but glean nothing at all. Are they afraid, too?

As Lucien understands, the wildfires left scorched earth where they tore through Malibu and Topanga after the valley. Now the rain everyone prayed for has unleashed mudslides, since the roots that usually hold the land together were damaged by burn or gone altogether.

Lucien scans the beach for Sophie. He stayed behind until the last room had been emptied; she must be outside already. Even though they stand within steps of the Center, everyone looks different outside its walls. The fresh air is a reminder that they existed before and outside this context; if Lucien looks farther down the beach, or inland across this country, and others, they would all have parents, friends, or even children. At the very least, everyone has parents, at some point. Their lives would expand infinitely just as his does, touching others in all directions. But who would they find for him if they looked now? A single old lady, sitting alone in her house, with a nurse? Trina. How sorry for him would Trina be, that he thought of her second? Something in the expansiveness of this revelation, in being outside again, makes Lucien bashful both to look and to be seen. They all appear suddenly vulnerable. Exposed. Like running into a teacher at the grocery store, outside the familiar surroundings that establish our roles.

Lucien keeps scrolling the sand, the shoreline. Where could Sophie be?

Word travels through the crowd, across blankets stretched over the cold sand, over the mutterings of some who are hardly there, who have not yet come back to themselves, as they say in the Center. The crowd says Dr. Sloane is making her way back. She has been absent from the Center for days, maybe a week. Without phones or computers or changing laundry, it's harder to keep track of time. Lucien can confidently say she has been gone for three days or two weeks and it makes little difference.

Roads are closed. The PCH has been rerouted at Sunset due to a rockslide near Will Rogers, taking out an entire lane. Those farther out in Malibu might be stuck indefinitely. On their own as they are, with only a few nurses and the handful of technicians, certain patients are understandably getting nervous. Making their dependencies known.

Lucien walks back toward the steep hillside, where his friend in the wheelchair sits on a piece of forgotten boardwalk or docking wood at the base of the Center's stilts. A blanket is draped across his legs, and his hands are tucked underneath. He is in conversation with the teen with the crusty blond hair.

"I just don't get it," his friend says. "The ones who stay behind, convinced they can save their homes just because they never had to leave before. Because they've always had the privilege of safety. As if the past proves the present."

The teen laughs in agreement. "Totally. My family's in Topanga," he says. "I bet they're still there. But they'll be fine."

"Yes," says his friend, rolling his eyes at Lucien. "Of course."

Lucien takes the cue.

"Not exactly what I pictured for a night on the beach in Malibu," he says, interrupting. He places a hand on his friend's shoulder, in part to check on his temperature. Even his posture looks cold. "You warm enough? I'm fucking freezing."

"I'm fine," the man says. "All this time I've wanted to get down here by the sand, up against the water, and now that we're here it's straight up dark. If that's not life. Can't see anything but my breath. My breath, in Los Angeles."

He pulls his blanket farther over his forearms, until his feet stick out underneath.

Lucien bends down to tuck them back under the blanket, when he sees Sophie curled up at the other side of the property. Her face peeks out from a blanket, and her hair looks fuzzy on the top like she had already been sleeping. He forgets for a moment what he's doing.

"She's been through it," his friend says, noticing. "Used to have the room next to mine until they moved her. Then there she was again the next morning, sitting by the fire. I'm surprised every day I see her, still fighting."

Lucien gently squeezes the man's feet with the blanket, feeling for circulation, then to impart some warmth, though by his face it's clear that his friend doesn't feel it.

"She's stronger than she looks," Lucien says, less defending Sophie than he is convincing himself.

"You're right about that. There's something inside holding that girl up. And I don't have much of it left, that's for sure."

"You strike me as someone who'll be just fine."

"Don't get the two mixed up, I'm still here. But I've seen how trauma lingers inside us. Even when we think we move on, it's there under the surface, hollowing us out."

"I know the feeling."

"We're all rotting from the inside."

Lucien walks across the sand, zigzagging around reclined bodies staring up at the stars, into the infinite space with no glass between them and the rest of their lives. Once Lucien approaches Sophie, she's staring back at him.

Next to her the air outside feels warmer, or he forgets that he's cold, or something of both, but she holds her blanket out toward him nonetheless. He slips it over his shoulder, keeping most of it on her. Now that he's found her, he can't think of anything to say.

"Hello."

"Hello."

Then another murmur travels across the sand. Lights flicker on inside the Center, where everything had been off in case of fallen lines, or broken gas mains. Soon enough the glass house goes dark once more, the main room reflecting back the moon. And two shadows make their way slowly down the spiral staircase to the beach.

Lucien looks at Sophie, bashful for all of them. For their excitement, for their fear. Sophie smiles. She looks pretty tonight. Healthy. Her skin glows under the moonlight. Her hair is curlier in the salty air, and frames her brow along the delicate line of her scar. Neither of them has said another word, but it's enough. To be beside her is enough. As the figures walk into the open air, Lucien can tell from the sleek, sharp haircut who it is.

The question is, who is it attached to Dr. Sloane's side, who limps under her arm, with the blank stare on her face that marks most patients when they first enter? This girl seems calmer than most. She wears a hospital gown, wrapped in a blanket. Her hair is a very faint shade of blue, unless that is just the moonlight, too.

Another breeze blows across the sand—straight from the hospital, evacuated from the mudslides, which brings them in the middle of the night. The girl is hardly a patient at all—say the voices rippling in like the sea. The girl is Dr. Sloane's daughter.

Chapter 21

TODAY

Later that night, once the coastline has been cleared of immediate threat, everyone finds their way back to their rooms and the silence of sleep settles again over the Center. Sophie sits at the foot of her twin bed with Lucien beside her. She pulls at the muscles around her shoulders, behind her neck. She cannot remember when she last felt so stiff. She had no idea *not* moving could make you sore.

Sophie has tried to keep her strength, dancing in her room once the nurses have done their rounds and everyone is lost in their re-centering "soft" doses. She can only do so much in that small rectangle of a bedroom, the edge of her bed frame being the closest thing she has to a barre. And her mind is only able to focus for so long before she needs to distract it again, prolonging the time before she, too, needs a pill and the nighttime to reset.

Lucien's visits, when they lie on the floor and talk, reimagining the world, are the only things she looks forward to, though they keep her from practicing. Even if she practiced all night, and walked a hundred laps a day from her room to the common area, up and down the stairs, it would hardly equal a single hour of normal rehearsals, let alone the routine she kept on her own time to stay in shape. The stretching, the weight lifting, the time alone at the barre.

From beside her, Sophie feels Lucien's hand hovering over her own, in that charged space before touching. He gently sets his palm down on her shoulder. She waits for the lurch, the flinch, but there is none. Tonight, his touch feels like sight.

She puts her hand over his. It feels so good to be touched, finally. He puts his other hand on her opposite shoulder. With his thumbs, Lucien pushes against what feels hard like an edge until her muscle shifts then rolls as the release runs through her body. She holds her breath. Careful not to spoil the moment.

Sophie considers this a small victory, to touch and be touched. She is making progress after all. No matter what comes next, she has this moment. Lucien's hands on her, her body unfolding inside. Relaxing. Lucien pinches the skin on either side of her neck, and a familiar pleasure returns; she remembers this one, and that doubles its relief. As he continues pricking her muscles back into memory, the facts of what her body was once capable of return to her. She has felt tainted for so long. Wishing only to get back to the sense of herself she never understood before. The stability she took for granted. The privilege of a singular, solid existence.

Sophie spent hours when she was younger wishing other eyes into her mind. First, when she started ballet and couldn't keep up with the older girls, couldn't understand what she was doing wrong, or why they looked effortless while she still felt clumsy. Then in high school, when she was told she didn't see her body, not really, not when her weight dipped below what was described to her as dangerous, despite feeling at the peak of performance, and despite her being cast in each lead.

She went to a therapist who used to ask what she saw in the mirror. In her curves, there was the opportunity to get stronger and lighter, as if she might one day shed her body and become movement itself. This was not disordered thinking; this was aspiration, determination. And yet she was told, from everyone outside of her eyes, that she was mistaken. There were no curves, there was no room for improvement. After those sessions, Sophie would look down at her legs, seeing the thickness she wished away, and then she would try to look as someone else. Sometimes she could do it, too, she could flip the world and see it from their side; to see herself as she might a stranger, fighting for their life. She understood. At least, she made herself understand. Her mother, the doctors, the audience. From then on, the ability to see herself—that flip of perspective—became a talent, something that gave her an edge as a performer.

All Sophie wants now is to lose the ability to leave herself. To forget what she knows about other eyes, and to see the world through hers alone. Since Lucien has been coming to her room, she feels more herself every day. Now her body feels awakened, not guarded.

Lucien traces a line with his finger from the base of her neck toward her lower back, grazing her thigh as he trails off. He goes farther each time he touches her, making sure she feels comfortable, waiting for her glance to say it's okay. He becomes intent, focused. His restraint turns her on. He treats her body like a professional, attentive and kind.

He strokes a tight tendon along her arm, hitting a spot that sends a current through her body, and she imagines what it would feel like to have him touch her in a different way. Using the same fingers to create another sort of shiver. With him sitting behind her, she feels the warmth of his body, its strength, the smell of him that survives despite their mutually laundered uniforms and the sterility of the space. The scent she never noticed until one night after he left and then—bliss. She smells it faintly on her sheets. *Pheromones*, she thinks, *fuck*.

A clang from the hallway. A curl of Lucien's tickles the back of her neck as he turns to see. She imagines her fingers through his hair. He is the only thing she thinks about in the future; the only daydreams that take her back into the world.

Sophie slowly leans into him, tilting her lower back until it presses against his lap; she touches her hand to his thigh, and he continues stroking her neck, then down her arm, and she has forgotten the way an urge of her own could overwhelm her. This one threatens to consume her, but she doesn't mind. Her heart pushes against her chest.

She relaxes into the thought of him in charge of her pleasure as well. Eager to match his attentiveness with her own. Lucien's breath on her neck quickens, and she turns to find his mouth with hers. Electricity. She shifts to face him on the bed, but Lucien slides away.

"Are you," he whispers, so sweetly unsure. "What if you're not ready for this?"

"What do you mean?" she whispers back. "I am. Finally, something I'm sure of."

She leans in, desperate for him. The more concerned he is for her, the more she wants him. But Lucien puts his hands up against her shoulders and holds her firmly at a distance.

"I just don't think we should do anything that—what if what happened that other night happens again and we're . . ." He trails off. "I care about your friendship too much to . . ."

Lucien is still talking, but Sophie's pulse fills her ears. She fights back tears. He does still think about that night, then. She's humiliated that he saw her like that. Does he pity her? She must be repulsive to him, writhing like some monster in this same room where they sit now. Look at the other people in this place; of course she's the one he talks to, and he doesn't even want to fuck her. *Friendship*, she thinks, in physical pain.

What if he sees the vileness oozing from her? The things she's felt and can't forget, wearing them now as if they're her own. Sophie once attracted people she couldn't lose, and now the one person she wants looks at her like the worst thing possible, a patient. A friend.

Lucien squeezes her hand, still resting on his leg.

"Hey."

"What?"

"It's not that I don't, I think you're—"

"Just get out of here, okay? I thought we could have some fun. Forget it."

Sophie tries to brush it off, but she wants him gone so she can cry. Worse still would be him comforting her.

"Sophie," he says, and her name sounds like a curse. "I care about you, I didn't mean—"

"Like *you're* so stable. You're a patient, too, right? I can't quite remember."

"Of course I am," Lucien says. "I don't know what you're implying. Look, I'm as messed up as anyone else in here."

Sophie covers her eyes. Then she stands up and turns away.

"I mean, not that you're—can you just calm down for a minute? Can you sit back down?"

"You think I'm messed up?"

"We all are! Sophie, you don't know what I'm thinking, what I've *been* thinking—"

"I don't care, okay? I don't care what you've been thinking. Both of us are going to leave here and go back to our lives. And we'll never see each other again and that's fine."

She feels like an idiot for thinking this was more than a distraction for him. For imagining a future outside of this place. She paces the room, unable to sit. Unable to be so close to him. She is less angry than humiliated, and she wishes she could go back to a moment earlier and linger there in its potential. Never leave.

"I know you," blurts Lucien. "I don't know if you remember. You haven't said anything, so I wasn't sure. I'm sure they don't know, here, or we probably wouldn't be allowed to even talk to each other, so I just didn't want to—look, Sophie, I didn't feel like we could, or like I could let you do anything without . . ."

Lucien keeps talking, unable to stop. How, where, what does he know her from? Sophie can't hear him anymore, or make sense of the words, until finally he says something that sticks.

". . . haven't talked to Liv, but she . . ."

Liv. Her long, perfect hair. Her laugh that makes Sophie feel good, warm, but also small. Like she could never have it that way. Be that way. Effortless. Confident. Seamless.

Sophie blinks as the memory moves through her. How did she not remember? Of course. The person she has feelings for is taken, by someone she'd never want to hurt. Her friend who has everything and now has this, too. Whenever she pictures Liv, she's smiling. Lit by sunshine, but somehow never squinting. Sophie turns again toward the gray-shadowed, once-white wall.

Lucien doesn't say anything, and Sophie hates that in the silence she now imagines him thinking about Liv. His loyalty, to Liv. She was even more wrong than she thought. All this time, in every moment spent with Sophie, he has been thinking about Liv. Missing her. Helping Sophie, for her. Wishing he could get out of here to be with her. In the moments Sophie most cherished, his mind was with someone else.

"Get out."

She turns to see him. Adorable. Ashamed. Cheeks flushed.

"If it's about Liv—"

She points to the door and suddenly there he is, in her memory. Halloween. His now perfect face neutral, his voice not yet attached to her heart. She mostly sees Liv, her happiness, her excitement. Her hand lingering beside his, her body close to him. Back when Lucien was a passing person who meant something to Sophie's friend, not her. A momentary jealousy, perhaps. An attraction, maybe. But not yet tied to her survival.

The memory is so clear, the red Solo cup in her hand, the smell of Casey's house. She knows it is progress to conjure a memory all on her own. But, of course, it's the one that might just break her heart.

Chapter 22

BEFORE

Sophie's first full night's sleep since the Woods comes courtesy of the pills she bought in Venice, plus two pot gummies from her regular rotation. She never usually takes more than a sliver of the gummies; never enough to necessitate chewing, just enough to sleep. Certainly never enough to clump along her back molars and sink slow down her throat. But this time she needed to loosen the part of her that was too afraid to see whatever these new pills held. She needed the courage, if that's what it was, to try again what almost ruined her once.

The memories were more pornographic than anything, a series of sexual encounters with various partners: one woman facedown on a hotel mattress, fingerprint bruises across her pale plump thighs; another, skin slick with spray off a hotel shower, her dark curly bangs dampened into her eyes, droplets running over her supple lips. However explicit, the memories were flecked with the mundane; a mini shampoo bottle falling then rolling toward the drain, a tiny square of soap following it. When he leaned down for them, the water stung his eyes. His butt rattled the glass shower door; the smell of bleach in the hot mist filled the bathroom. Sophie almost felt bad for him, even from inside. Until he grabbed the girl hard to stop his nerves.

At one point he lost his erection and the woman rolled her eyes when she must have thought he wasn't looking. He caught it in the bathroom mirror. Only the latent mortification under each encounter surprised Sophie; she never would have imagined or expected it when in bed, not as a man. It surprises her even more than the sensation from his side, her body learning how it feels to push, not just accept. Sophie came when he finally did and it felt almost transcendent, this two-sided understanding of pleasure. The man's gaze was misogynistic and cripplingly self-conscious, sure, but there was relief in losing herself entirely in someone else, in following the impulses of his body, shamelessly unconcerned with the other.

Sophie hears two girls laughing outside and recognizes them as the new neighbors from across the courtyard who spend every day sunning on the grass. One of them keeps shrieking. They have no idea why other people need and deserve peace. A little quiet. Their voices, even loud, sound scrunched and cute. *They would drop the baby talk if she made them scream.*

Just like that the stranger returns, his sickening pleasure rising at the thought of their harm. For the first time in her life, the mind feels circular, not linear, but desperate for patterns to fall into and return to, over and over. Sophie's anxiety only seems to reinforce these thoughts, revisiting them like a problem to be solved, more fully understood, until no thought is free from the stranger's consciousness.

His memories, hers. His hands covered in red, her own.

The pills she bought did nothing to dislodge him, then. All that for nothing. The lingering pleasure from last night's pill now feels far away. She needs more time. No, she needs to skip ahead, to a time when this is over, if it ever is.

Sophie grabs her car keys and runs out the door wearing a long-sleeved black leotard and a short transparent wrap that barely covers her thighs. She's late for rehearsal; it is already the afternoon. One leg warmer is rolled down to her ankle, the other above her knee. She passes the girls still sunbathing in the courtyard, averting her eyes from the one with a high ponytail that she'd like to use to whip her down to the floor. Sophie glances at the other girl, wearing cat-eye sunglasses she must think flatter her bitch face. Their laughter follows her to the street, and now Sophie is nearly running, a bomb ready to detonate.

She can't remember where on her block she parked. She follows the sound of her car beeping, clicking the key repeatedly, until she sees it parked across the street, next to a tree she's never noticed before. Once inside the car, she admires the trunk through the window. The smooth skin—bark—looks plump underneath, dimples just like flesh. Supple like it might give to the touch. Like it could bruise. She turns the air-conditioning to high and points it directly at her face. Finally, with her eyes stinging from the cold, she can see clearly enough to drive.

Sophie drives loops around the parking lot of the Los Angeles Ballet Company, looking for an open spot. When she finally approaches one, the space turns out to be blocked by another car parked at a hard angle. The carelessness sends another rage through her. The guy is still there, exiting his car. Dangling one foot out as he changes shoes. Taking his fucking time.

She wants to roll her car over his body, slowly, then rest on top of him until he stops breathing. Her foot waits, ready to push the gas pedal until her toe hits the floor.

Another car honks from behind.

Sophie turns to see a male dancer leaning over his wheel. As he passes, he waves in solidarity for the parking struggle. Sophie smiles back at him, muscle memory. When she turns back to her near-target, a familiar face is staring back at her.

It's Antoine. Antoine, her partner in *La Sylphide*. Antoine who gave her a ride home from rehearsals every morning for a week during Sophie's first month in the company, before she had her own car, even though he lived in Culver City. Antoine who makes his famous champagne punch for every closing night party, even though none of the dancers drink it. Antoine, who had just months earlier become a father to a beautiful girl, who they named Sophie, too.

He taps his watch, clenching his jaw for dramatic effect.

Sophie speeds off. Through the windshield, dirty from leaves and sprinkler water, Sophie sees figures already stretching behind the frosted studio glass. She wants to run inside and apologize for missing two rehearsals, but she is afraid to, should the darkness rise again. She still feels that prickle in her chest, waiting to spread. She pulls her keys out of the ignition and fingers through them while her eyes stare blankly out the windshield. Her fingers rest on the smooth, oblong shape of her tiny Swiss Army key chain, purely for decoration. She flips the last lever to expose a miniature blade, then rolls the fabric of her leotard up to her elbow. Scabs delicate as hairs crisscross her forearm. Sophie rubs a finger over the marks, hard from healing.

Then she closes her eyes and slides the blade across their tracks.

When she opens her eyes to the stinging, a thin trail of blood runs down her arm. The sight of blood used to make her stomach turn, but now it's the only thing that settles her. Her mind—her very soul—might be tainted, but this blood is hers.

Her friend Jacqueline runs over as soon as Sophie enters the studio. Two bobby pins dangle out of Jacqueline's mouth, her hair half coiled into a bun.

"Where the hell have you been?"

Jacqueline reaches to hug her, but Sophie steps away. Jacqueline tilts her head to meet Sophie's eyes.

"Are you okay? Oh my god," she whispers. "I thought you were dead."

"Is he mad?"

"Auguste? I mean—mad? I don't think he . . . It's unfathomable to him that you're not in the hospital or something. That you just haven't been here."

"So he doesn't hate me?"

"He was about to call your family."

Sophie feels panic at the thought of worrying her parents. Of them ever knowing what she'd done, what she'd seen. She winces.

"Did he?"

"I said about to—he's been concerned, but he's still Auguste."

"Where is he?"

All around the mirrored rehearsal studio, dancers wrap their toes and make small talk in groups on the floor, while others stand stretching at the barre. Sophie feels their eyes on her, in the mirrors looking past themselves, dissecting her every movement.

"I think he's in back with Nathalie," says Jacqueline. "She's been filling in."

"That cunt."

She notices Jacqueline's eyes, concerned, on her in the mirror.

"Sophie, are you sure you're okay?"

"I'm fine."

"You seem a little . . . off."

Sophie focuses on her feet as she wraps tape around the places that blister. The sunlight casts shadows across the matte studio floors. Three other dancers sit close, gossiping as they peel off their layers of sweats and thick socks. Sophie's mind wanders with a single piece of tape left dangling from her pointer finger. She studies one of the dancer's necks. So long, delicate. Jacqueline takes the tape from her and lays it across Sophie's big toe. Then she smooths it for her and rubs her calf to warm it up.

Sophie pulls her leg into herself to stop the torrent opening inside her. Unexpected touch incites a rage. But Jacqueline slides closer and starts pinning Sophie's bun where it sits lopsided.

"Is it a dude?" Jacqueline smooths the top of her hair, and Sophie flinches again. "Seriously, I don't get it. Where have you been?"

Sophie lifts her arm to push Jacqueline's away. "Can you give me a break? You don't know, okay?"

"Well, I'm asking."

Then Sophie is at the barre, swinging her leg up and down in a stretch. She rises *en pointe* with one leg high and her torso bowed low. Even if Sophie told her, Jacqueline wouldn't understand. She couldn't. And if she wanted to help, Sophie wouldn't let her. Jacqueline should stay away, protect herself. Sophie extends her leg into a standing split. She closes her eyes and finally feels her thoughts, all thoughts, slipping away.

She lowers her standing heel and rises again, but the tape on her toes begins pulling. Over and over she rises to relevé, warming up her calves. The pain along her pinky toe feels like fire, but she tries to separate herself from it, as she was taught from age ten when she first began her pointe work, when she learned to deal with the dead toenails, to disengage as though it were not her own pain to lessen. She rises high again, then drops her torso, finding another standing split.

The deep stretch feels good, and she closes her eyes and exhales while the blood rushes to her head, dangling upside down. She wraps both arms around her standing leg, pulling her chest into her thigh. The loose hair from her bun sweeps the dusty, scuffed floor. Her head fills with more pressure the longer she rests upside down, and its pulsing unlocks something she has been suppressing since leaving her car, since running from those girls in the courtyard, since drinking Ray Delaney's tainted potion.

She jerks upright again, both hands to her face.

The greasy red blade, wiped against his stomach, T-shirt stained, until he starts again.

Jacqueline is there beside her, a hand on her shoulder, but Sophie pushes her away. She can hardly see straight, let alone think straight. And then she hears the studio door open and close. The shuffling of feet to attention.

"Sophie," calls Auguste, his accent stronger when annoyed. "Well, *La Sylphide* was written in 1832, I guess it can wait a little longer for your busy schedule."

Sophie wraps her hand around her forearm and squeezes the fabric where she covered her fresh cut with a folded tissue. She squeezes until she sees clearly.

Then something surprising happens. Nothing. Auguste faces the rest of the dancers, his back turned to her. It's worse than being scolded. She, the favorite, no longer exists.

"We're rehearsing the final pas de deux today. The sylph will meet her lover one last time, he will give her his scarf, a gesture of love—to control her, to consume her—and in turn it will destroy her. Nathalie, mon chou, are you ready?"

Nathalie looks to Sophie, a too-late attempt at deference. She seems to hold her breath. Astrid, standing beside her, squeezes Nathalie's hand as if that movement isn't reflected ten times behind them in the mirrors.

"Okay, let's go!"

"Auguste?" Sophie says to his back. Her voice sounds small. "I remember the scene. Every step."

"Two rehearsals." He turns to face her. "Not a word?"

"I never would have missed them, if it hadn't been important."

"More important than this?"

"No, important is the wrong word. Inescapable. I swear to you—"

"I'll tell you what's inescapable. If you miss rehearsals as the principal, without a word, you will no longer *be* the principal. We have an entire company ready to dance. All held up, by you. I'm not sure what you're *doing* here?"

She remembers Ray Delaney's veiled threat, how vulnerable she felt. How everything she worked so hard for still didn't feel certain, or safe. She was afraid he knew Auguste. He didn't need to.

"I'm so sorry."

"You should have called," Auguste says. "I'd have told you to stay home."

"That's very generous, I wish I'd—"

"Today, I mean. You need not be here."

"But something happened." Even Sophie is alarmed by the desperation in her voice. "I was . . ."

"Kidnapped?"

The other dancers giggle. Sophie's blood simmers.

"Honestly. In a way."

The entire room is silent.

"I mean, I can't think of a better way to explain—"

"Stop it. Just stop. Whatever happened, it's done. We're moving on."

Auguste turns back to Nathalie and twirls his fingers. The other dancers hop up and take their spots. Antoine kicks his feet, preparing for their dance.

"Fuck, would you just let me explain!"

Auguste spins on his heel.

"We'll talk outside."

The music starts. Sophie watches the other dancers in the mirrors, extending into the room forever. An infinite number of eyes, all on her. Endless exits and only one way out. Once in the atrium of the lobby, Auguste stands close to her and talks hushed.

"Obviously you do not talk to me like that in front of the other dancers."

Sophie has never met someone who could use politeness to convey such anger. They stand alongside two large fronds, the wide leaves allowing them privacy. She doesn't quite remember walking there.

"I like you, Sophie, you know I do. I think you could be truly great. This is why I like you. But behavior like this can stop a career."

A glimmer of rage dances up Sophie's back; it pirouettes around her spine, then lands in her stomach. Her body isn't made to hold this much disappointment. The darkness waits, opening its arms to her, saying, *I know, I understand. I can help. We can make them understand. We can make our pain theirs.*

She barely has the energy to fight it anymore. Now there is a satisfaction in the pain. Now it feels like a piece of her, too. Sophie pushes her thumb into the tissue pressed under the arm of her leotard.

"Sophie? Are you even listening to me?"

"Yes, of course. I'm listening."

Sophie catches herself in the reflection behind Auguste. She sees her hair pinned with baby's breath, flowers and leaves wrapping their way up her body. The regal gold starbursts around each arm. She imagines another universe where things are still going as planned.

You hear that, Sophie? Auguste had said. *Are you ready to be remembered?*

Her face, in focus, looks drawn. Sullen. Hardly her.

"No, clearly you're not. You say you're sorry, but you have no remorse. You're dripping with disdain, and I don't know whether it's for me or for this company or—"

"I love this company, and you—I am so *grateful* . . ."

Sophie is weeping, overcome, and Auguste waves a hand in the air.

"I don't know who's gotten into your head," he says. "Made you think the rules no longer apply. Maybe you weren't ready. Maybe it's my fault. Being at the top means you have to work harder, you have to be even better. Look at you. Your posture. Truly, it's like you've forgotten your own body. Now, I have other dancers watching. Go home."

"I can't," she says softly. "This show is everything to me."

"It isn't about you. I can't set this *précédent*. Besides, the Sophie I cast wouldn't be putting me in this situation. She was ready to perform like Marie Taglioni herself, dancing at the Paris Opéra."

"Auguste?" his assistant calls from the studio.

"Anïa, j'arrive!" Then he turns to Sophie, pained. "Please, take care of yourself."

Now the darkness isn't something she's pushing away but running toward. She blinks and Auguste's throat is in her hands, his eyes wide. She can't tell whether it's the force of her grip or just his startled shock, but his eyes are enough to make her let go.

She takes three steps back and starts, "I'm—" without finishing, without even being able to articulate the sorry that she feels, not only to him but to herself swallowed whole, lost entirely, and finally without return.

Sophie glances into the rehearsal room and sees more faces staring back. Auguste's mouth is moving, but she cannot process the words. Bless him, he actually looks concerned for her. Bless him, he is stepping toward her, not away. Bless him, she wants to slit his throat.

She blinks and he is closer. Once more, maybe twice, and he might be close enough to touch again. She squeezes her arm and imagines the blood as she runs to the parking lot.

Sophie's hands tremble. She turns the key in the ignition. The same air runs hot, then cold, pointed directly at her face. Her eyes water. She is crying. Sobbing now. The radio plays yet another pop star covering a holiday song, and she slaps the button for silence. Moments ago she was in this same seat, but now everything is different.

She tries not to imagine Nathalie inside the studio, already lifted in Antoine's arms; the inevitable excitement she must feel. Nathalie is a soloist. She had been training for Sophie's role as an understudy. She would have hoped for this. Nathalie would now become a principal, too. Sophie's brain tortures her. It shows her the unreliable loyalties of her fellow dancers; even Jacqueline would forget her. It shows her Nathalie, *en pointe* for the final pas de deux on opening night. All eyes on her. Auguste's grateful praise.

Sophie pushes her fists into her eyes, anything to make it stop. To make this nightmare end. When she looks again, a few of the dancers are outside on a break and leaning against the front glass, laughing as they suck their e-cigs, stretching their legs back and forth. She considers driving her car through the studio walls.

She needs to get out of here, though there is nowhere to go. She can't go home, not with those girls taunting the growing rage inside her. Then one of the dancers nudges another, and they all look in Sophie's direction.

Sophie drives. The longing to hurt grows. She tries to focus on the road. The ink reminding her to LOOK UP still covers her knuckles, though she can hardly tell whether those are real traces of ink, or simply the memory of what once was.

Fast. Faster. Fastest. She isn't sure where she's going, but she has to get away from that studio, from all the people she wants to suffer. She looks in the rearview mirror and expects to see the stranger—shaved hair, tattoos across his pale forehead—the person responsible for this darkness now braided to her very being. Sophie keeps driving fast and north toward the hills. She needs to get someplace safe and open. Someplace she can breathe. Someplace she can think. When she finally hits Los Feliz Boulevard, no choice but to follow its curve, she chooses the first path up through Griffith Park, toward the Observatory.

Parked cars line the street all the way to where the wide lawn levels in front of the art deco building. Dozens of families have already staked out spots in the grass, with colorful blankets and picnics. Later they will set up their own telescopes. Sophie weaves through the patchwork picnic blankets, making her way toward the building that overlooks the park. When she first moved to Los Angeles, the Griffith Observatory was her favorite place to come think, her North Star in a city that felt lonely and disorienting in every direction.

A little girl with pigtails and big brown eyes smiles up at Sophie as she passes. Her family sits nearby on a blanket, but she's somersaulting through the grass toward a cluster of beach towels. She must be only three. She stops and grabs her feet with her hands as she rocks on her back, pushing her tiny legs into the air. Sophie thinks of herself at that age, mostly what she remembers through photos. An aspiring gymnast, before her first ballet lesson. For a moment, she forgets everything; why she's here, what she's fleeing, the loss she's feeling. Then the little girl's dress falls down toward the grass, her chubby legs still stretched overhead, pink underwear covering her bum. The stranger begins to stir. Itching. A woman—the mother—smooths the girl's dress down. Then she rubs her daughter's back, steering her toward their blanket, keeping an eye firmly on Sophie.

The woman's expression makes her stomach turn. Sophie holds up a hand and forces a smile as she hurries toward the Observatory. *She wanted to hurt the child.* The woman saw it, she knew. Sophie had wanted to take the little girl's legs and twist them until they snapped.

When she finally reaches the Observatory, half its white exterior is in shadow; the iron dome of the roof reflects the sun, and the harsh corners of the curving walls create an abstract, surreal backdrop for the park views. In the distance, the city sprawls infinitely, ending only where the ocean extends to the horizon.

Sophie walks the balcony that juts out over hiking trails, where happy couples approach the end of the main trail with proud smiles. *That they should be so lucky. That I would spill the beauty from them all.* Sophie shakes her head. She runs her hands through her hair up to where her loose bun takes shape, then she makes a fist around it and squeezes. She realizes how she must look, a girl in ballet clothes, erratic. If they only knew. She slaps her face, and then looks down to see a young boy staring at her, holding a plastic camera, frozen. She lunges at him, and then runs from herself.

Sophie hurries farther around the perimeter of the balcony. From afar, it looks like a porcelain egg, pure white decorated with little arches and scalloped edges, but up close the building is scratched all over with initials and promises and threats. *Remember me*, they say. The scratches look frantic all piled on top of each other, and Sophie's eyes revel in the frenzy, so many visitors scratching each other out just to make themselves known.

Around another corner, she comes upon more children—*these terrible, tortured bodies, waiting to be spilled*—sitting in a school group, drawing. Sophie looks all around, but there is no chaperone in sight. *One prick was all it took for that blood-red beauty.* She squats down next to a little girl, the smallest in the group, with mousy curls and a tiny upturned nose. Then all around the girl, Sophie sees blood pooling, seeping out from under her overalls—but no, no, she presses her palms against her eyes. The girl smiles up at her. Plain concrete shines white in the sun. *It's a deep, greasy red that these terrible tortured bodies keep hidden, waiting to be spilled.*

Oh god, fuck.

Who would care? Waste of skin. Organs. Bone. Better to spare them what they'll soon learn. They should be so lucky to see all that they hold. Sophie looks down to see the little girl's hand in hers. No, it's her hand around the girl's wrist. The other behind her neck.

"Get away from her!"

Sophie pushes the tiny head away and backs up until she hits the balcony ledge. *Sorry, sorry,* she tries to say, but nothing comes out. Another woman calls back the children who've crowded, curious, around her. Sophie feels for the ledge and hoists herself onto its rough surface. She looks down at the initials here, too; so many lives wanting to be seen, to leave a legacy, when all Sophie wants is to disappear. To finally stop the thoughts, end the cycle. She thinks—*remember this*—as she turns to face the ravine below. The city appears as a beautiful blur through her wet eyes. She closes her eyes and takes a deep breath.

That I would spill the beauty from them all.

The darkness rises faster now, a figure rushing the distance inside her, and before it can catch her again—Sophie rises to relevé and takes one step, then another.

Chapter 23

TODAY

"Trauma doesn't require truth," Angelica says. "It is capable without out proof, without reason. If you fear someone is going to harm you, are you any less terrified in that moment because you end up being right or wrong? You experience the panic, the terror all the same. Truth comes after. And truth speaks in outcomes, exists only in knowledge. Lived experience stays the same."

Angelica looks out at the circle. Faces that have been there weeks and others only recently arrived. The newest, her daughter. It hurts her to see Remy in this place coupled so closely with addiction, but she saw an opportunity and took it. Only with distance does Angelica even see the choice. When Remy was lying in the hospital bed, there was no way to know if her memories would come back naturally, on their own. Moreover, Angelica had no idea how many of David's pills she had taken or what the impact had been. The force of the car, then her head on the asphalt, had caused severe trauma to Remy's brain. In that moment, it seemed a miracle that she would ever wake.

Running it back in her mind, there is no solution where they don't end up here. Remy could have wasted months waiting, passively, for her memories to return. Angelica had no choice but to do everything she could. And now in just another week, her daughter will be home. And then, hopefully, she will leave. Happy. Again.

She turns the sound therapy up with the sleek metal remote. Another train rolls by. Angelica likes watching their faces light up differently with each cue. She likes to be the one who observes and dictates the change all at once.

Remy sits next to Lucien. He looks tired. Sophie is absent from the circle—a late night, one of the nurses said. To Lucien's other side sits Jeffrey, who will never leave his wheelchair, who she wants to help by freeing him from those moments he will never have again. Jeffrey who loved to walk, who chased his son and taught him to dribble a basketball. Who tossed him up and down, watching the sun fade in and out behind his small silhouette, and told his wife that this was the most beautiful sight. Who lost her, too. Angelica could help him find peace, if only he would let her. If there is peace, anyway, in forgetting.

Lucien prefers to keep the pain, his own. At times his love for his mother still feels spiteful, like more evidence of Angelica's inadequacies with Remy. Now the two of them sit side by side. Angelica has never been good at separating herself from the experiences of her patients; she measures herself, even as they share their pain. But this is another level.

She turns up the volume further. Another thunderstorm rolls in. Blue sky outside. Water smooth as the glass. Remy will be happier without David. She will be free.

"Close your eyes if you haven't already," Angelica says. "Let your mind wander."

None of the nurses know. Keeping David out of Remy's memory altogether was simply cleaner for everyone. The omission would leave serious holes, yes, but Angelica could act like this was the chance fault of her emergency procedure; like the accident had damaged too much for a complete retrieval. No one would know. She had been given an opportunity for something extraordinary. How could the accident, and its resulting amnesia, not feel like fate?

Remy would learn to rebuild. And maybe even find more space for Angelica in the gaps. The privacy she still afforded her daughter during the scan was selfish; in truth, Angelica was afraid to see what might be there. Even Lucien, who values his mother's life more than himself at times, has thought things no mother would want to hear. Angelica has always felt inadequate. Seeing herself through Remy presented the possibility of simply being too much to bear.

Of course, removing David from Remy's memory also meant Angelica would not have to face Remy's use of his pills. They would not need to have that conversation, and Angelica would not need to confront her own great hypocrisy. The entire thing feels like a gift. Especially with her upcoming NPR interview; she couldn't risk the story. The fact is, she understands Remy's choice. Hadn't Angelica done the same with Sahar? She still revisits her love only to feel its loss over and over again. Her daughter had merely repeated another of her mistakes.

She watches Remy sit with her eyes closed, wondering if there is a place for her behind them. Wondering where she will go when she leaves. Wondering what Angelica would see in those moments she kept, just in case, before they were removed from Remy's world. Wondering if she has done something irreversible.

The thunder cracks and rumbles.

Chapter 24

BEFORE

Lucien never liked tuna melts. He always gave his friend a hard time for ordering tuna fish, even on bagels, whenever they ate together around Stuyvesant, and in the years following when George came home from Williams and they met for lunch at Veselka. It always seemed to be tuna fish, even at Veselka. Lucien knows that can't be right, not every time, but the memory insists, which says more about the strength of his distaste than anything. What other menu item dictates what your company tastes, too? What could be more controlling?

He wants to see his mother. He begrudges every one of Florence's memories that is of something, or someone, else. How cruel, to wish someone's life away even once inside it. But there are only so many opportunities, and fewer and fewer pills.

And yet here he sits. Tuna melt between his buttery fingers. Savoring every bite of the toasted bread with its mountain of salty tuna under an orange blanket of cheese. At least he's alone at the counter. With empty red-patent stools on either side, Lucien can lose himself in his thoughts, and hers. He's been craving everything differently with so much of Fleur influencing how he thinks and feels, her memories mixing with his own and shifting something inside him. Perhaps he feels better simply being someone else.

He hadn't noticed at first, but he even finds his mannerisms changing; a hand ends up over his heart when he thinks; he tucks hair that isn't there behind his ears; he moves through a room differently.

When he enters, he senses the eyes on him now. He anticipates them. Lucien never considered himself looked at before, or thought much of it if he was, but now he feels it everywhere he goes—this new threat of being seen. Of being too direct, too serious. Of course, when he glances up, no one is ever looking back.

The 101 Coffee Shop is one of those retro diners that purposely serves things defiantly outdated to their young clientele, and then executes them in an over-the-top way. Their ice cream sodas tower. Their burger needs a steak knife stabbed handle-high just to keep it upright. He drove there on a hunch. A craving. He was right. Even the height of his tuna melt, arguably a modest sandwich, is comical. He debates using a knife and fork, but he wants to consume it too quickly for that. With each bite, something inside him settles. He takes a sip from the water bottle he brought, its cloudy iridescence hinting, he hopes, at some vitamin supplement or protein powder. This is Los Angeles. Call it *Spirit Dust*. No one will think twice; Liv sells a jar of that at Astral Bodies.

Each time Lucien wakes after a trip on his grandmother's Mem, he is ashamed. Ashamed for taking what belongs to her, and moreover for how the thought of not having these pills, of one day having to say goodbye to his mother again, for good, makes his hands shake and his throat tighten.

He takes a sip. Another bite. He feels pathetic, but insatiable.

Back to Dinosaur. Black coffee to go. Hair so blue it's velvet.

Can color be enough to beckon? Its tone tempts him like a siren's song; to dip his eyes under the waterline, to let go of whatever keeps him from being fully submerged. Another call from Liv vibrates in his pocket. No voicemail, one text. The low level of Florence makes him feel drunk, loose. He watches himself double tap to <3 it without losing a minute, without changing the screen. Easy.

He hasn't seen Liv since they spent the day together in Venice, but he is too numb to express his annoyance. Letting his feelings show would only lead to further conversation, when really there's nothing to discuss. He has nothing for her, and maybe he never did. He's so tired, of all of this. Every moment in his own body feels heavy. Every thought a waste.

Back to the same line of customers, impatiently wasting time on overpriced coffee. Back to the well-balanced pour over that burns his hand through the cardboard in a familiar way that takes away the pain. Can anything so routine feel fresh enough to hurt?

The blue barista hands him his coffee, the sadness in her eyes better than a smile. He takes a sip and is pulled back into his body, into the room.

"Lucien, the painter," she says.

"Close."

He takes another sip.

"Damn," she says.

"And you're . . ." He tries, but his mind is still yellow sunshine in an open room. "Sorry."

"Remy," she says. "Wait, don't tell me—that artist I meant to look up. Lucien . . ."

"Freud. Though he's Lucian with an *a*," he says, talking more than he realizes. "Painter, not a writer, my mother."

"Like the psych guy? Now we're getting dangerously close to *my* mother."

"Actually—grandson of the psych guy."

Another sip of coffee. Another taste of himself.

"I was totally joking," she says. "What a family. So your mother named you after a painter and you don't even paint?"

"My mother's the painter," he says. Bless contractions, for hiding the past. "She loved his portraits that were obscure and deformed, where nobody comes out looking very good. She loved his ability to see. That's why she named me after him, she wanted me to see."

Lucien laughs abruptly.

"So you can see, then?"

Lucien tips his cup toward the girl, then slides over to grab a lid so he can get back home. Back to the discrete memories that deliver him out of body. As he looks for the right size lid—how many sizes can there be?—fumbling with the stack, still yellow inside him, sunshine everywhere, he overhears a conversation.

Words blowing the cloud off his hot-coffee brain.

These shoes? I got them in India, they were like three dollars. I know, cute, right? But the airport in Mumbai is a total disaster, and the line for security—well, because none of the women travel alone, I think.

I wouldn't do another retreat there, the friend says. *Not if you paid me.*

Lucien nearly trips over a guy with a low ponytail squatting on a stool as he turns for the exit. He apologizes, still moving, but the conversation seems to follow him. Or maybe it's a new one. Same voices, different hosts.

What's the difference between migrant workers and refugees? Is there one?

He feels like a character trapped inside a campy horror movie, when other people's words slow and distort, with everyone around him in slow motion and Lucien unsure of why, exactly, their words are getting him so riled up. He surveys the rest of the room; how does everyone act like this is normal, can they not hear? Lucien misses those regular moments on the subway—the kindness one could catch between strangers, even amid chaos. A simple look, a nod. The humanity.

He feels himself unraveling, yet keeps pulling at the loose strand. Has spending time in his grandmother's memories made him less tolerant of his own generation? Are her eyes, inside him, influencing how he sees? Or is this him, breaking through her kindness?

Back to the side streets, stop signs every block. From his car, each view looks flat and colorful like a Hockney painting, with that impossibly blue sky. Back to his apartment, quiet on the stairs to make it up without alerting Liv. His apartment feels different lately, like it finally holds pieces of home. Or is it him, now, who holds the pieces?

Lucien goes straight to the kitchen, to his coffee bag of pills. He wants only his mother, only the ones that matter. And he wants them faster. His friend Tanner had a coke habit-slash-addiction, and at one point started dusting cocaine under his tongue, rather than snorting it. Something about the high concentration of blood vessels delivers it faster, stronger. Lucien cuts a pill and taps its dust under his tongue. Then he snorts what's left off his fingertip.

Back to his bed.

Back to his mother.

Back into Fleur.

Florence is at the Pasadena Playhouse waiting for friends by the bathroom during intermission. Helen and Daphne are girls from the editing room, where she recently transitioned from the switchboard. They are the only other two girls in the entire department. The courtyard is twinkling, with people gathered and discussing the play in a low, excited hum.

Home from Wellesley with her beau, Henry Willis III, a Harvard boy. Her father, Dr. Gabriele Benedetto, is practically levitating with excitement. Her mother keeps asking to see the ring, then clutching her chest. Once Florence hears the last door shut in the house, the last light out, she sneaks away in the middle of the night. Catches the first train. She asks the man next to her with a cap pulled down low where they're going. He says Los Angeles.

A tall man stands beside her at the Pasadena Playhouse, waiting for someone as well. The line is long and unmoving, the second act starting soon. He looks older, but has wavy, wild hair that seems to defy age. When he catches her looking past him to the courtyard, he leans forward and asks what she thinks of the play so far. Florence only realizes once talking that she has many thoughts, to say the least, on the female lead. The man loves the fervor with which she speaks of the characters, the story, the arc. Florence's friends come out of the ladies' room arm in arm and whisk her away, asking who the handsome man might be. His name is Conrad.

Florence on the switchboard, at Catapult Pictures. Her first job, thanks to Betty Parsons, who she sat next to on the train. God bless Betty Parsons, with her tight bleached-blond curls and red lipstick. She recently got them all an extra half hour for lunch. She even found Florence a room in the same building where she and the other girls live, on Franklin Avenue.

Florence never answers a single letter from Henry. One day she mails his grandmother's diamond ring back to his parents' home in Hartford without a note. She cannot explain herself; Hank is wonderful, but she is unwilling.

• • • •

Her switchboard lights up, demanding decisions in a fraction of a second. It's a rush and a buzz and she's good at it. She wants more. She wants that same rush from solving real problems, connecting the dots through storytelling. The editing room, everyone says, is where women go from here. Stitching film is a job women do well, given the handiwork.

• • • •

She runs into Conrad at Catapult and he asks to join her for lunch in the cafeteria. Everyone lights up around him; Florence assumes it must be his talent. A director, maybe, who's already made a name for himself.

• • • •

The editing room is storytelling, crafting narratives and character from existing materials. Florence befriends Avery Gregor, one of the more sympathetic men in the room. He is about her age and an aspiring writer. She helps him with his script, cutting entire sections and suggesting ways to make his characters more human. She adds to the female characters wherever she can. He squints as she delivers feedback, his script sitting between them on the cafeteria table, covered in marks. But soon he sits back in his chair. *Well, shit,* he says.

• • • •

For days, she is in her trailer in the desert with a fever; it must be the heat, the long days, the pressure of thinking five things at once while they shoot. Transferring her ideas to Avery without stepping out of line, without anyone else knowing. One day, during a shot in the High Noon Saloon, she faints. When the doctor comes to the set, he tells her, in no uncertain terms—she is three months pregnant.

• • • •

Florence sits across from Avery again, her own script now between them. She could hardly let it go when she gave it to him days earlier in this same spot. He's quiet, and she wants to run away or crawl under the table. When he finally speaks, he is in awe. He's already shown it to a friend in production, who showed it to his boss, who wants a meeting. Florence leaps up from her seat and throws her arms around his neck. But Avery has to take the meeting for her, he explains, if she has any shot of the script being taken seriously.

· · · ·

The set is in the strange landscape near Palm Springs, a Western facade with nothing else around it. Pioneertown, as it's called, is arid and dusty. The dust gets everywhere, in her eyes, in her hair, her scalp, under her fingernails. When she takes her socks off at the end of the day, it looks like she is wearing a lighter pair underneath. She showers and watches the dust fill the basin. Then she keels over, vomits.

· · · ·

Florence's script sells in the meeting, and Avery never returns to the editing room. Over lunch of tuna melts and floats at a diner in Beverly Hills, he promises her everything, everything but her name.

· · · ·

A week before they leave to shoot, she hears some people whispering by the production offices. Everyone else, it seems, knows about Conrad's wife but her.

· · · ·

An American Cowboy premieres. Florence goes alone, doubly emptied, while her mother watches the baby. The baby, no name yet. To leave the hospital, Florence wrote down Baby. The day after she sees the film, she tells her mother she is keeping it. Her baby. Isabel.

· · · ·

Florence shows Conrad the script she wrote, the one that sold. She confides in him that it is hers, not Avery's. An American Cowboy, written by a woman. He roars with laughter, the ice in his old-fashioned rattling, like this is the most fabulous story he's ever heard. Then he takes Florence's head in his hands and kisses her. Beautiful Fleur, and a talent. He loves her, he says. Beyond that, he loves her work.

· · · ·

Conrad insists she should be on set; it's only fair, he says, with both hands on her waist. He gets her put on as a writer's assistant, to discreetly oversee the shoot. Avery's assistant, on the film she wrote. She feels their eyes on her, the assumption that the reason she's there is for being Conrad's girl.

Florence watches everything disappear by the biology of her body; it doesn't matter if it was her fault or not. She has the proof growing inside of her, undeniable. The baby is in her, not Conrad. And it would be there whether she wants to deal with it or not. There's no running away from a baby; even if she does pick up in the middle of the night, the baby would go with her.

When the baby is born, Florence thinks, *A girl. A girl I'll teach not to flee but to run toward the things she wants.*

Florence tells Avery to stop every message from Conrad, to alert her if he comes to set. Her body shivers with shame, foolishness. She is trapped. In every scenario she runs through, her future is forever tainted by this relationship. She loves her job at Catapult, but now people will think she got it because of him. She got nothing from him. She throws her cone of paper filled with water at the mirror, then rolls out enough paper towels to clean the whole sink.

The crew takes care of her, bringing water and wet washcloths for her face. No one knows. And that night, as she has done before, Florence packs her things. Then she disappears.

· · · ·

A check comes from Avery, and she has no idea how he found her. She tears it up.

An American Cowboy wins three Academy Awards. Conrad is onstage in a tuxedo, his wild hair combed down. He stands, surrounded by the cast, accepting the award for Catapult Studios. He thanks everyone.

· · · ·

Must be nice to be a pretty girl in this town, Charlie in the mail room says to her.

Florence gathers her things from the room on Franklin. She says nothing to the other girls on her way out. Never sees them again. She thinks of the shoot finishing in Pioneertown without her, but Avery will do fine. He knows the script as well as she does by now, having had to pass it off as his own so many times.

With the advance Avery gave her, money she had planned to save, she buys a small cottage in Los Feliz.

Florence sees Avery's films, every last one in the decades that follow. She always has notes, even keeps a diary. She doesn't blame him; what he did was generous, in a way. He did what he thought to be in her best interest, regardless of how it benefitted him, too.

It's a guesthouse to a larger estate behind it, right off Los Feliz Boulevard, built around its own tiny courtyard. There, among the mansions and landscaped lawns and private gates, she feels safely unseen. The small house feels both isolated and part of something larger, which she likes. The older couple in the back doesn't ask questions. But the first morning she wakes up there, a tray of muffins sits outside her door.

Another check from Avery, but her belly is larger. She cashes it. And the next.

Florence will give her mother the baby. She calls, and her mother agrees; she surprises Florence with her capacity for love, forgiveness. Florence is twenty-four, no husband, no job. Her mother is only forty-three. No one would ask questions. She has the baby with her mother by her side. Her father doesn't make the trip.

Avery's final film is about a young man who finds a notebook that belongs to a beautiful woman who cannot speak. She is mute and lives with an older, married sister. The man publishes her novel as his own, and later they marry. *The Proposal* is nominated for an Academy Award.

* * * *

Florence wonders, every day, what might have been had she only taken that first meeting herself. Had she not gone through the network of faces that could pass her work off as something it wasn't—the product of men. Subject to men. Isabel will be the product of her alone.

* * * *

Lucien's apartment comes into focus, and he reaches for the water bottle beside his bed. Like a dream that is clear for a few moments and then disappears forever, he remembers everything—for now. All this time he has been using his grandmother to see his mother, to settle his own sadness, never realizing his grandmother had her own secret pain. And Lucien has felt like a stranger in this city, when in fact, his grandmother's work contributed to the industry it is built on. Her contribution to the canon, still on all the lists of classics, made Catapult Studios what it is today. And Catapult made film what it is. Lucien's mother was not an anomaly; she had been born from an artist, an award-winning screen-writer who never saw her name on-screen. And Lucien is not an addendum to his mother's legacy, but another in a longer line.

What if all this happened for a reason, to lead him here, to discover this for his grandmother, for his mother? Lucien isn't a horrible person; he hasn't just stolen from his ailing grandmother and begrudged her for what he wanted to find. No, none of that was true if what he found now has a purpose. Florence had been forgotten, and what if Lucien, and Lucien alone, could make it right?

He grabs paper and a pen from his backpack and writes as quickly as he can, connecting the dots as he goes. He takes another long sip from the cloudy, sparkling water and it burns his parched throat on the way down.

He'll get his grandmother the credit she deserves; he'll need to find confirmation beyond this proof he can never share, but he'll look wherever he has to. He'll talk to everyone. This is how it feels, then, purpose! First, he wants to look into her eyes and tell her he knows. That he's proud of her. So proud to have a piece of her in him.

No more Mem. Not even the pills he has left. Well, maybe just that. Just to wean himself off of them, but no more. No one will steal from her anymore.

Back to Fleur. Bougainvillea lining the driveway, fallen petals up to the door. Her living room is bright from the empty walls reflecting across the bare wood. But no one is there. No one is inside. He rushes back to the den, where the other nurse, Gloria, is on the phone looking through the window shade. Trina sits beside his grandmother's chair.

When Trina turns, she wipes wet tracks from her cheeks.

"Lucien, I'm so sorry. Your grandmother, she just—a few minutes ago."

Trina gets up and moves toward him, but Lucien steps toward his grandmother.

"What? No. No!" he insists, as if he could argue it untrue. "No one called me."

"It just happened, we were just about to—we had the paramedics on the way, but it's too late. It came out of nowhere. But it was peaceful."

He kneels down beside her, still reclined. Her eyes are open, empty. Finally so. He takes her hand and feels it now, just a body. He had thought so before, but how wrong he had been.

"This was something we were cautious of," Trina says, looking to Gloria for help, but she is still on the phone. "None of us anticipated— we thought she was fine on the machine."

Was was was. Say it enough times and it stops making sense.

"I know," he whispers to Florence. "I know."

He wants to squeeze her cold hand and tell her he knows what she kept all those years. How it must have been lonely, but she wasn't alone with it anymore. He wants to ask if his mother knew. He wants to hold on to her forever, but instead of squeezing, he lets her go.

"That's them," Gloria says, rushing back out to the front. Trina follows her.

Lucien's mind is still catching up. His grandmother is gone. Gone and he's still here. He's done it again. He missed it. He used her and now she's gone, too. He feels dizzy. The room is spinning. This, again.

What is he doing here, without her? What good is anything he learned, without her living? What do his promises mean to anyone?

Florence's eyes stare straight ahead. The bottle of Memoroxin sits in its usual place.

When Lucien gets back to his apartment, texts from Liv light up the phone in his pocket. He turns it off and tosses it to the floor. The paper he had so frantically written notes and names on taunts him from the kitchen. All of his stupid promises. He lights a burner and dips the corner of the page until it catches. Then he drops the handful of flames into the sink.

Lucien pours all of Florence's remaining pills onto the countertop, where her life had just lain in words on the page. The pills dance glimmering until they find their place on the laminate. He grabs a handful and swallows them, dry.

A hammer still lays on the trunk that Liv found for him at the Rose Bowl. As promised, she found things to clutter his apartment. So that he could finally empty the contents of his few boxes from New York— books, a cast-iron skillet, his winter clothing that felt like skin he had shed and would never fit into again. And all for what, so he could find himself here?

He grips the leather handle and raises the hammer above the rest of the pills. He hits them one after another, watching them crack then crumble into iridescent powder. He swipes his hand across the counter, forming anthills that he levels, one by one, with each nostril.

Lucien reels back, eyes watering, his entire body quaking. His arms pull in close, hands twitching. One leg jolts with the memory of motion, then another, the seizure of Fleur's life shocking his own. He hardly feels her in the frenzy of moments cut together into milliseconds. There is no more yellow, but every color all at once. And then he is flat on the floor.

Then he is vibration.

Then he is light.

Chapter 25

BEFORE

Sophie blinks fluorescent, eyes sore from the pain meds. She glances down at her arm. Two IVs enter at the crease of her elbow. Bandages cover her wrist. She hears a low, guttural moan before realizing it is her. She lifts her hand to her face and feels a dull, wet pain.

Each hurt makes itself known one by one. Her eyebrow stings under its bandage. Her face must be swollen; it is visible through the corner of her eye in a way it shouldn't be. Another bandage pulls at her shoulder when she tries to sit up farther. Her entire body feels taped together. She glances down at her legs, two sticks under the sheet. She panics. She taps her thighs, her knees, her body tingling with terror. When she finally focuses, she sees the bedsheet wiggle above her toes.

"Don't try too much," a nurse says from the doorway. "Those pain meds are doing their job; move too much now and you'll regret it later."

Sophie can't find the words. Her throat closes.

"You're lucky. You didn't break a single bone. God bless last year's rain, you landed in some thick undergrowth."

"Ah."

"Somebody up there likes you," she says. "Come on now, don't strain."

The thought that anyone *up there* is looking out for her makes her prickle; if the nurse only knew who—or what—they had saved. Why is she even grateful for her feet, her legs? Why does any of it matter now? She tried to escape, and instead she is immobilized, flooded with drugs.

The darkness merely sedated by opioids swirling in her blood. None of it would change what is still inside. None of it would fix her mind.

"I'd like to rest."

"Can we call someone for you?"

"Please don't."

"We need to—"

"I'm begging you."

"Well, I can talk to them, or I can talk to you."

Sophie turns her head, the bandages pulling at her hair. She hardly feels the pain, but her eyes water nonetheless. She hopes the meds have dulled everything else, too. Though she feels that anger—Auguste's throat in her hand—as the nurse steps closer. Sophie debates ripping out the IVs; maybe that would ground her more clearly, and cleanly, to her body. Maybe it's the pain she needs, not the meds. She wouldn't need to cut herself if she were torn up at the seams.

"The blood work we ran showed Memoroxin."

"Oh."

Sophie glances out the window to the hallway, for police.

"Yes, oh. Here's the thing. In California, we have something called deferment of entry for the first-time offense. Didn't see anything on your record, or any illegal substances in your belongings. Are you following me?"

"Yes, I think so."

"So, you can do the work—rehabilitation clinic or classes, temporary probation."

Sophie swallows, pain. How did she get here? She heard these listed for her brother before, never understanding them. Never understanding a world with these options.

"Okay. Thank you."

"At Cedars we have a partnership. Anyone admitted with illegal traces of the drug Memoroxin, and displaying signs of self-harm, is eligible for a voluntary extended rehabilitation. It's a lottery, I don't know that you'll get in—but it's something you should consider."

"For how long?" Sophie asks. "The program, I mean. How long is it?"

"Long as it takes."

She has nothing anyway. No upcoming performance, no job.

"Just like that? Is there a catch?"

"No catch. Once you're stable, medically, we'd send you on your way."

"Is it covered by health insurance?"

"It's no cost."

Someone is always paying the bill, Sophie thinks. Money reflects interests; whether or not that information is public changes nothing. And there is, almost always, a catch.

"You're wincing, let me give you a little more. It's about time anyway."

The nurse adjusts her drip. *There is always a catch*, Sophie thinks again as the room floats around her. But there are other questions to ask when you're falling.

Chapter 26

TODAY

Lucien sees Sophie every time he closes his eyes. He cannot forget how her delicate features turned sharp; how he is now the one who hurt her, not the one to help. He knows the best thing is for him to stay away. He can't risk her progress by upsetting her any more. But when he falls asleep, he is beside her again with the illusion of a second chance. He feels the anger off the back of her head, the side of her cheek. He tries to speak, but nothing comes out. No matter how hard he strains, only silence leaves his mouth.

Why hadn't he told Sophie he recognized her the first night in her bedroom? And when he finally did, why hadn't he told the truth? That all this time he hadn't mentioned Liv because he didn't want to lose any time with Sophie. He hadn't mentioned her friend because, honestly, he hardly thinks about Liv, and admitting that out loud makes him feel cruel. More cruel still, that even before coming here he hardly thought of Liv. Distraction requires no commitment, no loyalty. And once diverted, returning to it seems pointless, problematic even. Love had never crossed his mind.

He tries to conjure the earlier moments with Sophie when they were together, him touching her, and neither of them wanting to stop. But the memory disappears as soon as it comes, back to the reality of what happened next. Why can't he see all the times he caught her gaze in passing, the very sight of her giving his days at the Center meaning? The excitement of a new beginning. Why torture himself, with the end?

His mind wanders back to Sophie's face when she first turned to him, her body pressed into his. Her expression was flickering. He felt the potential even then, the photographer seeing the full array of looks. In one second, the human eye can process ten to twelve distinct images before the illusion of continuity connects them into a larger movement. Seconds become minutes and there are multitudes within a moment. Lucien knows the way a thought can skew this way or that; the power of an expression to do harm. And he knows how one second turns a moment.

He looks back at the chances he had to say the thing he meant, to change the conversation's course. What becomes the story. In the moment, he missed it. He simply couldn't see it. They were each having their own conversation, totally missing the other.

The irony is that being with Sophie finally made Lucien want to look closely again; with her he was collecting moments that he wanted to keep. And, he had felt like himself again.

Lucien heads to the common room early, to wait there before his session with Dr. Sloane. Sophie sits away from the fireplace, in a chair along the far glass wall. Lucien walks up behind her. He hasn't seen her since two nights ago, when she told him to leave. He catches her glance in the glass before she shifts away from him. He doesn't want to push, or cause another fit. But he does want to talk. He needs to explain.

He kneels, his head hovering at her level. Surveying the shoreline, the water. Then he turns to whisper in her ear, if she'll let him, and her hair brushes his nose as she turns away. He waits in the closeness, eyes closed. He even thinks she leans into him, almost imperceptibly. Just then, he hears his name. Sophie's lips are pressed tight. He hears it again, repeated from far away. Lucien looks up. He looks around.

The room is still quiet that early, but then—through the glass to reception, he sees someone. Standing at the desk. Looking right at him. Liv.

Sophie pulls away and curls her legs in. She hasn't seen. Lucien stands and walks toward the entry, toward reception at the other end of the room. Liv, if it is her, looks frozen. Shocked to see him there, though he's the one who should be. He squints and keeps walking. She shows no sign of recognition. Could she be a manifestation of his guilt? Halfway there, a nurse steps in front of him.

"Dr. Sloane is ready for your session," she says.

When the nurse moves, the figure is already halfway out the door.

Dr. Sloane sits in the private, jutting glass room with a folder in her lap. She looks pleased, though she has looked that way ever since her daughter arrived. She lets him sit on the couch first, then hands him the folder from her lap.

"Good news today," she says brightly. "The nurses and I all believe you're ready to begin the discharge process. You've proven that your memories have implanted, you don't display any signs of continued contamination, and we don't believe you're at an elevated risk of relapse."

Lucien is shocked. He had forgotten, for a moment, about leaving.

"What do you think?" she says with a rare smile. "Speechless?"

His mind goes to Sophie, still not talking to him.

"I am, truly."

"Well, with a case like yours, this can be a smooth process. Now that you're stable, there's very little we can offer. I thought you'd be thrilled. To get back to your life. I know you have things to do. Now, if I don't see you again, best of luck with everything."

He remembers his grandmother and feels guilty for needing the reminder. What is it in the waiting that makes the end feel sudden?

Back in his room, Lucien opens the folder. A single-page survey follows, with basic and leading questions. He considers sabotaging himself so he has to stay longer, so he has more time to fix things with Sophie before leaving. And yet, the idea of tricking a treatment center capable of extracting your memories seems somewhat flawed.

1. I do not feel that I am a danger to myself or others.

1 · 2 · 3 · 4 · 5 · 6 · 7 · 8 · 9 · <u>10</u>

2. I am excited to start another day as myself.

   1 - 2 - 3 - 4 - 5 - 6 - 7 - **8** - 9 - 10

3. I feel like I have much to live for.

   1 - 2 - 3 - 4 - 5 - 6 - 7 - **8** - 9 - 10

He lies on the third question. All of them actually, just enough to make it seem realistic. He assumes that is what they want anyway. This survey seems more for the Center's records, a disclaimer should something happen once a patient is discharged.

Dr. Sloane was right: things would move quickly.

The next day, Lucien looks for Sophie in all the common spaces, but she is nowhere. He just wants to say goodbye. In this place where they had shared something. Lucien already feels he has abandoned her; he can't bear the thought of leaving, too. Shut out, he worries how Sophie is doing. What she does alone in her room. But then, by her own words, maybe he is wasting both their time. Maybe she really is better off without him. He who hurts everyone he loves.

He spots his friend in the wheelchair sitting in his usual position by the window.

"I'm leaving today. No fanfare, can you believe it?" Lucien says. "Dr. Sloane didn't even mention it during the circle."

"She doesn't mention much, does she?" the man says, still staring out the window. "I thought you might be, soon."

"Well, keep an eye out for me, when you're out of here. Maybe we can go to the beach one day? Yell our names into the wind for even the whales to hear."

"I'd like that. But I'm not going anywhere."

"Sure you are."

"Look, I've got a view that changes every moment, and I've got my wife and son on the inside. Not much more for me than that."

He glances down at the man's legs, then regrets it. When he looks up, his friend holds out his hand. Lucien takes it in his, wrapping their fingers together for a moment. Here in this space, the simple contact feels more intimate than a hug. He stares into his eyes. The fog of resignation. Lucien never noticed it before.

They have spoken so little, and Lucien knows nothing about him, per the rules, but he will miss him deeply. Lucien squeezes his fingers one more time, to say goodbye.

Of all the things they never forbid, touching.

On his way to the reception desk, he passes Dr. Sloane's daughter. Her hair is dyed a darker shade of brown that looks simultaneously wet and fried. She looks lost even standing in the middle of the main room.

He remembers the phone call with Dr. Sloane in her office, how she had talked about her daughter, never imagining she might one day be there, too. Dr. Sloane mentioned her losing a boyfriend and how she was derailed, a feeling not unfamiliar to Lucien. The only consolation he felt after losing his mother was from people who reached out with their own loss. He didn't want to hear from those who loved his mother, too. He wanted to hear from more people who had lost theirs. And who, like him, didn't want to feel better yet.

"I'm sorry," he says. "It gets easier, though it never gets better."

She looks back at him with a blank stare, as if he had spoken in another language.

Lucien's clothing is stacked at the reception desk just past the glass. His dark flannel shirt, stiff jeans. He runs his hands down his jumpsuit and thinks that he might actually miss it. But then he's at the glass wall and a car that must be waiting for him sits just outside the door, its wheels visible past the fern in the window. He takes his stack of clothing, pressing it to his chest and smelling it. He signs the release form on the desk and turns toward the door.

A delivery hits the pavement outside, and the car drives away.

For Lucien, there is one more waiver to sign.

I understand that, prior to my release, I will dress in my clothes and undergo one final treatment, during which my memories of the Center will be removed, and after which I will leave through a separate side door, without passing the main building.

The form goes on to say this is for the purposes of protecting the patient's persistent, unaltered sense of self; for providing a clear, simple concept of memory, and to clear any doubts. Nobody wants to see behind the curtain. If Dorothy could forget the Wizard, wouldn't she? Lucien understands now why Dr. Sloane did not press on his relationship with Sophie, and did not worry about them together once it seemed inevitable. How cruel of her to let them continue building something she knew she would only take away.

They should tell them this from the start. Or had they? Had everyone already signed once, before the memory was taken as part of their initial treatment? Lucien wouldn't have thought much of it then. But it seems wrong, to operate in an ethical vacuum.

He thinks of the Sophie he knew before his time here. The only fleeting glimpses of her that will remain in his memory. He thinks of all that has come since. How can he go back? Why does he have to lose everything he loves? Even if he refuses, if he stays and gets Sophie to forgive him, keeps their time together in his memory long enough to make it up to her, none of it would matter. It would all be lost eventually. Eventually they would still have to leave.

Then he remembers his grandmother. He pictures her sitting at home. Waiting, if she ever was, for him. How could he consider staying longer when he owes her his time? He has lost weeks, months. He feels like crying. A loose urge, untied.

Lucien's throat tightens as he signs his name. How long has it been since he's claimed it like that? His name. *Losing one thing and regaining another*, he thinks as he gathers his clothing and follows the receptionist down another hallway, out of the light.

Chapter 27

TODAY

D r. Sloane shuts the isolation tank and lets out a sigh of relief when it clicks, her daughter inside. Wouldn't she love to keep Remy in there, safely living the experiences that she has approved for her. These immersion machines have shown so much promise. Already they have given so much comfort. She touches her hand to the glossy white exterior, feeling an intimacy she often finds hard with her daughter in person. Here in the tank, Remy is so small again, so helpless. So much easier to hold.

Angelica knows there is some unspeakable violation in what she's done in withholding David. But this is what medical advancements are for—fixing what isn't fair. Illnesses are unfair. They strike without concern for timing, or the promise of their victim's future. What is more unfair than losing your freedom? Freedom is what tragedy ultimately takes away. Freedom is where it hits the hardest. As much as one mourns the loss, or feels the trauma, at the heart of that is the inability to proceed unaffected. Remy might have *chosen* to keep David in her memory, despite the pain, but only without knowing how much better she would feel without him. How much better her life could be. One shouldn't be allowed to decide such things for themselves. Someone who loves you, who wants what's best for you, that's who should be burdened with the decision.

Angelica knows it's hypocritical taking such control over her daughter's life. Especially for something she herself has never submitted to.

Angelica has been hurt; she has felt unbearable pain. Yet she would never have chosen to remove it. Angelica could never see past the fact that she loved Sahar, loves her still; she could not see through the infatuation then, or the pleasureful pain of missing her. But the scientist in her wonders what life might have been like had they never crossed paths. Had she not chosen to be destroyed over and over.

This is uncharted territory; rules for practicing can't apply when the very questions have no precedent. In years Angelica is sure that she will look back and understand she made the right choice for Remy. Others would understand, should they ever find out. Remy will go back to Brown. She will make new friends; she will build a life that fulfills her, free from the pain, free from the guilt of being happy when the person she loved most had—well, why speak it. Remy will be lucky to be kept off social media for all the standard, explicable reasons. And common decency will keep most people from ever mentioning David to her, since she will never bring him up. They will marvel at her resiliency. If she does find out about him later, which inevitably she will, she will be in a place where such knowledge cannot touch her. The truth will be a distant story, incapable of hurting her more than a sad book she once read, or a movie she can turn off at the end. And she will thank me, Angelica thinks. She will thank her mother.

Angelica would like to forget David, too. But not everyone gets the blessing of forgetting; someone has to remember. Someone has to carry the burden for both of them. To protect her daughter, she must remember. She places her hand on the vessel again, feeling it warm, the inside aglow as the wash of Remy's reinstated memories diffuse, reinforcing themselves in her mind. Her bright, strong mind, streamlined and refined to best prepare her to move on. To be the person she was on her way to becoming. If Angelica came up short as a mother before, which she suspects she has, this is something she can offer that no one else could. No mother who volunteered for every field trip, who was there at every soccer game, who handmade their children's Halloween costumes, none of them could give their children what Angelica could give Remy now.

Back in her office, Angelica opens the desk drawer and takes out the small bottle of pills marked N/A. She asked for them to be separated and distilled, a record of what was kept out of her daughter's reintegration. Just in case. In her hand, all the places David's life touched her daughter's. An extraction of the pain he left, even in momentary joy. No one else knows what she sorted by, or what was removed. These pieces of her daughter, no longer hers. Like a past that never happened.

Angelica feels she can hold time in her hands, prevent the things that should not have been. If only within the safety of this place. But that was something. She shakes out a single pill, shimmering. That *is* something.

What makes it so hard for her to understand, to connect with her own child? Will it be the same, once Remy is healed and off on her own? Will she push Angelica away just the same? The pill shimmers and refracts, elusive as its owner. How could she hold a little piece of her daughter, inside out, and not take a look? Who would she be if she didn't?

Who will she be if she does?

She is my daughter, Angelica thinks, bringing the pill to her lips. She is my *daughter*. Each time it sounds different. Once, a call to action. Next, an admonishment. But by the third time, she swallows.

. . . .

David's face through a fish-eye, his nose pressing against hers. She smushes his face until he smiles, willing it until it comes. And then there is nothing else but their two smiles, the one kiss.

. . . .

"I promise you, she doesn't like me like that."

"How could you possibly know?"

"Because, Rem-by, no one likes me."

David sits with his back to her, shoulders hunched. She brushes off the grass stuck to his T-shirt. He lies back down beside her. Remy nudges him. He does this sometimes, looping her into insults aimed at himself, but she doesn't mind because it places them squarely together.

Then there is this, the shame in her pause before assuring him that he's wrong—that he's wonderful and everyone knows it. The shame in hoping she doesn't convince him too much.

Remy sits on her twin bed, her quilted duvet wrapped around her. Her new roommate is at a party. The phone is warm against Remy's cheek; it's been there for an hour.

"Tell me something else."

"You should go out, meet people."

"It's too cold to meet people."

"Already? It's September."

"Tell me what you ate for dinner."

"My mom made lasagna. I'm telling you, I've got nothing. Go have fun."

"You good? I've been talking about myself this whole time. How's your girrrrlfriend?"

"I'm talking to her."

"I mean Ca-lis-ta."

"Come on. She's fine, so is Alex, her boyfriend. She says hi, you know. Always."

"Bitch."

She can hear his smile break and imagines his nose scrunched up, the way his cheeks push up into his eyes. It's Remy's favorite thing. Her chest hurts.

"All right, you monster, I have to finish my AP Calc."

"Ohh, now you're talking dirty and you expect me to hang up? I don't think so!"

"I'm serious, Rem. I have an exam this week."

"Ohhh, David! Yes!"

"Good night!"

"Okay, but—you're good? Promise? My mother isn't playing any mind games—"

"Stop, Remy. I'm good."

• • • •

The arrivals loop at LAX, the Lexus smelling of cigarettes and leather. Her mother hugs her too tightly, holds her longer than she should. For a second it feels good, but then Remy remembers her failure. The cost. She pushes her off. How are there no tears in her mother's eyes? Not even one. Remy sits for a moment, hating her but wanting to be held again. If her mother tried, she would let her. She doesn't.

Before, Remy always at least thought her mother was an excellent doctor. She respected that about her. She turns up the radio and pushes her feet into the dashboard. Being her daughter feels like a constant punishment for something Remy never committed.

• • • •

Remy escapes David's mother under the pretense of finding the Brentwood Track sweatshirt she left in his bedroom. She agreed to come over before his service so they could go together. David is not really gone, not if Remy can still do him favors; not if he still owes her.

The floral wallpaper in the hallway makes her dizzy, and before she can even reach David's room, she ducks into the bathroom. She holds the cold toilet between her hands, waiting, but the rising panic never turns to vomit, never leaves.

• • • •

Remy opens the medicine cabinet. She doesn't want to move a single thing, his last movements preserved. But she can't help herself. So many bottles for someone who considered water a styling product. She runs her finger over each one, imagining him doing the same.

She moves a tube of spot treatment and sees the bottle marked Memoroxin. Her mother's name in the upper right corner. She clutches the amber plastic in her hand and shuts the cabinet. She wipes her forehead, swiping away blue strands of hair that still smell of peroxide.

• • • •

Remy scoots forward and places her hand on the thin, skirted leg of David's mother. The smallness of the gesture quickly feels worse than doing nothing at all, so Remy swivels around to sit next to her in the limo, sliding diagonally between his mother and his aunt, wrapping an arm around his mother's trembling frame.

Holding David's mother makes Remy feel stronger. Maybe there is selfishness in compassion. Maybe that's why her mother makes a good psychiatrist, if she ever was. The three years they dated, David insisted they avoid this woman, and now here is Remy, holding her close, feeling her breath. She isn't so bad, Remy thinks, in the lottery of mothers.

She's so human. Maybe that's just because she's broken. For a moment, though, she is jealous of David. Even on the way to his funeral.

• • • •

Remy pulls out one of the pills from her pocket and rests it in her palm. A blue dot shines in the middle of the tiny iridescent drop. She tries not to think about her mother as she snaps the pill in two and slips one half back into her pocket. The broken pill dusts her hand with a powder like loose eye shadow, and then she thinks only of her mother as she draws a line through it with her fingertip, imagining the streak of David's life, a shimmering expanse.

David lost his right to privacy, and so did Remy's mother, when she lost him. When she with all the answers somehow still failed. Maybe if Remy only takes half, she can deliver the eulogy as herself—with a little bit of David, too.

The minister speaks in a detached monotone to guests across the great hall. Her voice rises and falls at the end of each verse, making Remy seasick from its smooth undulation. The little pill is turning pasty in her hand, but she still cannot work up the courage to take it. When she looks through her fingertips clenched in prayer, more of the iridescent residue has transferred to her palm. A firefly held too tightly.

"David was a source of light," the minister continues, speaking directly to them now. She sounds more human, no longer hidden behind the detachment of verse.

The chairs creak under the family's shifting grief. Remy keeps her gaze forward. Each silence is filled by the sound of a tissue being used or the shortness of breath behind stalled tears. It's the kind of silence that urges one forward, to say anything to fill the space, but the minister takes her time.

• • • •

Remy glances across the row, at the bowed heads of David's family. The pressure wrapping her throat starts to crawl up her face. Her chin quivers. Her eyes fill. At the end of the row, David's mother motions toward the podium.

"This is how David lives on in all of us, in our love of God and our remembrance of his life, so that we may honor him back into life, every day, in our own pursuit of God. David is not gone if we let him live on inside of us."

David is not gone if we let him live on inside of us.

What better way to honor someone's memory than with a taste of it, Remy thinks. She lifts her hands to her face, as so many others do around her, but this time she licks the pill.

⋅ ⋅ ⋅ ⋅

She looks over her shoulder and sees David—his photo blown up large. She sees the last time she hugged him before she left for Brown. From his side. Her smile faltering. His heart breaking. She sees herself walking away. And then it is all too much, and she cannot tell whether she is seeing or being seen, looking or remembering.

⋅ ⋅ ⋅ ⋅

Remy wipes the steamer, muffling its urgent splatter. The whirring quiets her mind. She holds on to the feeling that when she leaves Dinosaur Coffee at the end of the day, she will go see David. Working here again, she is back in senior year, back at home, back in the part of her mind where David lives.

At Dinosaur, she is working toward something, and every latte, cappuccino, and chia pudding moves her closer to more time together. To linger in that phantom happiness before it disappears altogether, she would work there for free.

⋅ ⋅ ⋅ ⋅

Remy scrolls through the myriad goodbyes and condolences that now adorn this extension of David, on a social media platform he hated while alive. Dozens of new comments and photos have been added since the service. Once filled with sarcasm and dumb memes, his wall is covered with earnest quotes and emoji-filled epitaphs like flowers and stuffed animals littering a roadside telephone pole.

She resents how her former classmates suddenly find trite words to share publicly; how they can only show compassion facing their screens. And she misses David more in the midst of it. She fights the urge to post some goofy meme—a pissed-off cat or a dog walking on two legs carrying an umbrella. Anything to cut the pretense.

She hates him in waves. Why couldn't he just wait? He still had her. He was her family. He was all she had, too. Remy reaches into her pocket and pulls out the broken pill, holding it lightly between her pointer finger and her thumb. Even in the darkness of her bedroom, it seems to shimmer. She wonders what memories might be in this tiny capsule, what he might feel like swallowed full, not licked in powder off her skin. Good, bad, it doesn't matter.

Come back, she thinks, as she places the pill on her tongue.

"I'm sorry, what? Is this a joke?"

"Why would I joke about this?"

"You're talking about my mother? You've been seeing my—did she contact you? Ew. I cannot believe you. Her, whatever, but you? How could you?"

"She helps me."

"She's ice. She's numb. She doesn't even see me and I'm her own daughter. How the hell will she be able to help you? I mean, do you actually think she'll—she's doing this to get to me. She's just so—"

"Remy. She didn't know. I only just realized it. I told her. And she thought it'd be best for me to talk to you first, and maybe then the three of us—"

"So you're going to keep seeing her?"

"I can't just stop. Besides, it's not like she's your 'mom' when we're—"

"She's always my mom. No matter what she tells you, she is my mom. Believe me, I wish that weren't true."

"She's not so bad, Rem."

"You don't know her like I do."

Remy lifts her head from the prickling Bermuda grass of her mother's backyard. Her mother's backyard. When did this become her mother's house and not her own? Was it always? The house she grew up in. Her childhood home. So many ways of saying the same thing.

The place where Remy took her first steps, lost every last baby tooth, learned to read, left for school dances. Those memories feel like another lifetime. If anything, a new sense of unbelonging haunts her, where photographs of her younger self still hang. Home is now distilled and pill-sized, resting inside her golden locket. Home lurks inside of her, filtering the way she sees and thinks, tainting her ability to act like herself.

Her blue hair is fading more by the day, its vibrant dye turning the water blue like Windex in the tub. Her dark roots are just beginning to show at the part, and the once-inky ends have turned pastel. Only a few inches in the middle remain a true blue. There is catharsis in this slow progression, she thinks, each day representing another loss, long and drawn out.

The day after the funeral, Remy shook the pills out of the bottle. It seemed fitting. Seven pills. Seven days. One last week with David, her own sort of shiva. Since then, she has been slipping out to the backyard each morning when she doesn't have a shift at Dinosaur, telling her mother that the sunlight is good for her mental health, when in reality it's her time with David. Mornings are the only time when her mother will leave her alone.

She's come to depend on these hours in the grass. To live for them.

Just a month ago, Remy was starting something. She had made new friends who she now may never talk to again. Their lives will stretch away from hers until it will seem impossible that they had ever intersected. Each day that passes without David opens pockets of loneliness she hadn't known existed before. Whenever she runs into parents from Brentwood they insist on how well she is doing. This is meant to be a compliment, but it feels like shaming. As though Remy should not be handling it well, as though she should actually feel worse. Or at least let it show. At times she feels fine. But the loneliness bubbles up slowly, like shaking cake batter in a pan, exposing itself in bursts. Interrupting the smooth illusion of acceptance.

In the yard with David's pills, Remy disappears as he emerges, and afterward—she feels better, not worse. Any remnants of David are welcome company, not ghosts. She doesn't feel haunted; she feels enchanted.

She has at least three more days with David before this long goodbye will be their last. More if she starts splitting his pills into smaller doses. She has considered telling her mother. After the last pill, of course, so she couldn't take them away. Later, as a kind of plea. Her mother owes her. Isn't this the kindest solution? Letting Remy live with David, in some way. It's what her mother does, after all; why couldn't she make just a few more of his pills? Maybe if she shows her mother how much better she has been doing, with the pills, maybe then she will understand. What a life. She could take him anywhere.

The yogurt Remy brought out smells sour beside her in the grass. She can feel her skin burning. She should take a cold shower before her mother comes at her with the sunscreen; before she looks in her eyes and sees. Remy stands to head inside. She stumbles at first, her head spinning. She must have underestimated the amount still left in her.

Today's pill was David's earlier memories, mostly with his mother, tender and vulnerable in ways Remy never felt. As she opens the back door to the kitchen, Remy slips into another one—the outline of David's mother holding him with outstretched arms, looking up at him, at her, on horseback. The faint scratch of the horse's hair on her legs. Remy hears her mother's wretched voice from upstairs, calling to her through the fields and the birds chirping where she, David, is riding, faster and faster. She wants to stay here, with him and his mother.

Remy turns around and slams the screen door behind her, afraid her mother might find her. Her mother, always scrutinizing, would be able to tell. Remy runs toward the street, enjoying the drunken feeling of being on the edge between these two moments, feeling her own feet stumble as David's kick the horse to go faster, until they are both galloping and the world is flying by—spring flowers blurring below them, cars whizzing beside her.

Remy holds her arms out, leaning her head back as she runs along the sidewalk, feeling the flutter of David's excitement and fear as the horse goes faster, as his heart beats faster, and as the world blurs even more around them, until suddenly the memory switches. David is at baseball practice, swinging the giant bat, his hands choked up high. Remy's feet stumble on the uneven sidewalk, but she wants to stay in it, to see him swing, to feel him connect with the ball, and she stumbles again, her foot skipping a step below and then finding smoothness, but now she sees nothing but David's hands swinging and the crack of the bat, the ball flying up toward the bright, bright sun, and then—a screeching that feels as though her pupils are splitting in two—

Remy opens her eyes just in time to see the flash coming at her, and then the pavement askew off the side of her face. And then there are footsteps slamming, their vibrations entering her head before they can even become sounds, and then screams, and sirens and nothing but darkness.

Angelica wakes slumped in her chair. She feels heavy but tender. She brushes her hair behind her ear, surprised to find it wet, tears pooled in the curves of her cartilage. Her office, her entire world, appears dull.

What has she done?

She stole from her own daughter. The person she loved. Even if David's death wasn't Angelica's fault, she took him from Remy. She *removed* him.

She convinced herself that this was kind, better. But what she meant was that it was cleaner. Now she feels the violation, the depth of her transgression. She couldn't have known best—not for someone she barely knows.

She took her memories. She *took* her memories. How will she face her? Again, Angelica has robbed herself of the person she wants most to be close to. Violated the sacred space between them. Made them forever far. Only this time, unlike with Sahar, Angelica sides with Remy. She understands her daughter, at last.

Chapter 28

TODAY

The Center feels empty even with the same number of patients. The seats in the common area fill up as normal, bodies staring off at the ocean, into the fire, or at their hands. Patients leave and new ones come. This has happened multiple times since Sophie arrived. But this time it feels like less sunlight fills the space. How is it possible that the only person who has seen her, who maybe ever saw her, did so here? When it is hard to imagine anything left to see?

You can't love something so desperately in a moment like that and hope to keep it.

One of the new patients, the one who took Lucien's room, walks by Sophie, whispering in bursts. For days, this woman has been finding her, and maybe others, then muttering as she passes. Sometimes the words are so soft they enter Sophie's mind like thoughts, for her to realize only later, once she sees the woman passing. It's against the rules, this kind of confession, but Sophie senses the woman needs to say it. And needs it to be heard.

Was Lucien right? Sophie cannot stop wondering now that he's gone. Maybe he did the only kind thing in pulling away. Maybe it makes him all the more attractive, that he had not wanted to risk her progress. He could've done whatever he wanted and then left; he could have told her about Liv later on, or never at all. And if he wanted to protect Liv, too, doesn't that make him all the better person?

In the moment, his worrying about Liv was too painful to fully process. The mortification of realizing you've been thinking about someone while they thought of someone else was too much. If only Sophie had taken a breath. Taken a moment to think. She might've agreed with him. She doesn't want to hurt Liv either. Maybe this newfound understanding is simply Sophie willing away the pain, wishing back the feeling that knowing him had filled her with. That hazy sort of happiness.

Lucien did help her. Regardless of how it ended, or her unwillingness to say goodbye, Sophie knows that much. Maybe some people surface to lead you places. He reminded her of who she is, of what is out there. Sophie remembers now what it feels like to want something so badly you cannot bear it. A determination she lost, and one she will need in order to get out of here.

What was she expecting? It isn't enough to be loved. That won't fix her. She has to find the strength, and no one can do that for her. Even if Lucien could have saved her, Sophie doesn't want to be saved. She wants to be met.

We held each other tighter knowing we would lose.

She had gotten distracted. Love is not everything. It is something, but not in her control. Love cannot live inside this place. Sophie needs to leave, and for her to leave, she needs to focus. She needs to believe that maybe the next treatment will work, and if not that one, the one after. And the one after that. Until finally, finally, she is free.

I only saw his feet.

Sneakers. Those clumsy feet that took my whole life from me even as I held it, hot.

After days of disconnected phrases, Sophie starts to find a linear pattern. Her mind, desperate for a task, pieces together what happened to the woman by remembering and ordering the phrases in a sort of catalog. Sophie, who had to write down every order at the Chateau, lest she mix up every table. Amazing, she thinks, what the mind is capable of when deprived of stimuli.

Sophie first noticed her because almost all of the patients at the Center are male. Either women are too smart to binge on other people's lives, with too much to worry about in their own heads already, or plenty of women are using, too, they're just better at suffering in silence.

Hiding their pain at any cost. Sophie had sooner thrown herself off a ledge than ask for help. At least that's what she's been told, of course; she can't remember a thing from the weeks leading up to her admission, but the scratches match the story.

By the time she realizes the sum of this new patient's pain, Sophie believes the human capacity for loss is boundless. Just when you think you're at the edge, you learn that it moves.

We died in each other's arms. Holding on and hoping, which is not unlike how lived. And yes I say we, knowing I'm still here, but that was it for me and I knew it then. I felt the last of him beat beside me. The floor was sticky, like it was keeping us there. Part of me hoped the smallness of that—the inconvenience of the details, that stickiness on the floor—might keep us both safe. But more bullets came and more bodies crowded ours and we held each other tighter, knowing we would lose. You can't love something so desperately in a moment like that and hope to keep it. I felt the last of him beside me, then quiet. I only saw the feet. Sneakers. New ones, can you imagine? Those clumsy shuffling feet that thought to get new sneakers, before. That took my whole life from me even as I held it, hot.

One afternoon, just the two of them by the glass wall, the woman tells Sophie more. She was in trauma therapy for a bit, after the shooting. After four months she still couldn't stop the shaking. She'd had to leave her job. She couldn't drive herself to work, and it cost more than she made to take a Drivr from Pasadena to Culver City each day at rush hour. The Memoroxin therapy started as exposure treatments—reliving pieces of the "event" as they called it, focusing on the details. Facing it again, then letting it pass. Accepting what happened just as it had occurred. But the pills only made things worse; it felt like tearing her open each time she felt her husband's body in her arms again, each time he wasn't yet gone.

His breath, the smell of beer lingering from the concession stand. Such expensive beer, she said. He had more than usual. They were having fun. He had his hands on her waist as they swayed to the music. His body held the warmth they worked up dancing, even after. On the ground. She couldn't get up; she waited until the police had done two rounds before she said anything, before she made a noise, incapable of words. Waiting as if she still had the choice to follow him out of this world. As if they could've stayed together.

She went through every therapy for PTSD. There was discussion of removing the event altogether, but she objected. She couldn't lose a moment with him, even her last.

One day, a neighbor who'd walked their dog since they were first married found her on the floor of their bathroom, the empty bottle in the sink. Thirty pills in her system. The sedatives in them would've been enough to kill her if the neighbor hadn't come that day.

But what a way to go, awash in the highlights reel of your own life. Maybe that's all death is anyway, she says, maybe that's how it comes. All through the woman's story, Sophie thinks of Lucien. Selfish is the brain in pain.

That night Sophie is led into a new treatment room next to the one she has visited so many times before. A glossy white immersion tank is full of glowing water. This new technology increases the penetration of memories and insulates patients from any infiltrating stimuli, Sophie is told, before a nurse drops a pill into her hand and then leaves.

Privacy, as if she has anything left to herself.

She looks at tonight's pill, same as all the rest. From what Sophie now remembers from her life before, she always tried so hard. Always. And yet here she is, stripped down and shivering. Afraid to try yet another treatment, another promise to restore what was never hers. Before, she spent so much energy orienting herself so that she would never have to fail, so she would never face the shame of being disagreeable to or disliked by anyone.

In the memories she takes in her room at night, she is overwhelmed by a feeling she had gotten so used to then that it was like air. Sophie had always felt on the edge of something. Failure. Expectation. Perfectionism was a means of self-preservation. She found safety in it. But the more it worked, the more she succeeded and the better she became at pleasing others, the closer she felt to losing it. Constantly. And the more she had to lose.

Even her fear had felt necessary. One family only gets so many mistakes, and her brother had taken the allotted amount for theirs. And yet despite falling, she survived. At least, she *is* surviving, so far. She wasn't allowed to, but she did. When she takes her pills now, the latent insecurity in those memories feels far away, and the fear that held her back even as she reached with success in plain sight feels no longer her own. Maybe, of that, she is finally free.

Sophie shivers, still standing there naked. She is nervous at the thought of her claustrophobia in that narrow plastic coffin, but as soon as her skin touches the lukewarm water, and her ears submerge, she is overwhelmed with calm. A gentle mist fills the air above the water level. Her heart tingles. In the immersion tub, her body feels contained. With the water sloshing around her, she feels, finally, constant. Like everything inside her is warm enough to thaw.

Her mind drifts as the water laps up against her neck, as she splashes beside her brother in the lake, as she picks wild raspberries for her mother and sneaks a few dirty, as she spins and spins until she loses sight of the audience.

PART THREE

SHAPIRO: And what about those who might say, such dirty water may never be clean?

DR. SLOANE: To them I say, that is what medicine is for. That is what I've dedicated my life to—helping the hopeless. That is the foundation of every medical practice. Streptococcus seems incurable, deadly, brutal—until you discover penicillin.

Chapter 29

TODAY

Everything startles him.

The smell of the air freshener, a pirouetting pine tree just below the rearview mirror in the Drivr they ordered him from the Center— *New York rainstorms, a cab so muggy he draws on its windows, the city through his fingertips, raindrops glowing red in the stopped traffic.* The sound of another car radio blaring out of tune from the adjacent lane along the Pacific Coast Highway—*hazy pavement, barbecue smoke in his eyes.* Cherry Life Savers from the Drivr's backseat console—*running through the sprinkler in Prospect Park.* He sucks the flavor until the disk turns sharp.

Each new sensation jolts Lucien out of the car slowly heading south, as if pieces of his memory are being turned on from a control room previously unmanned for weeks. Two weeks. That's how long he was at the Center, they said, when he asked before leaving. Though attaching an amount to a gap of time does nothing to fill the void. Two weeks, when you can't remember it, sits restless inside you.

The salty breeze along the Pacific Coast Highway reminds Lucien of where he is. Alone in a driverless car heading back to the life he had, apparently, chosen to leave again and again. Alone for the first time in weeks, it seems, although now who's to say? He doesn't want to think about what might have happened in that glass sanctuary; what could be so bad, or proprietary, that it couldn't leave with him? Either way, this seems an appropriate return. No need to make small talk while you slowly reenter the world. Given the traffic, he will be desperate, not worried, by the time they reach Echo Park. At least stepping out of the car will feel less of a risk than a respite.

Around Santa Monica, they—the automated system and Lucien— turn inland for the 405, which soon takes them up past Bel Air, the Getty Museum hovering on the hillside. Imagining those inside, for whom the museum is the most necessary place to be today, makes Lucien desperately jealous. Even those stuck in traffic beside him on the 405 make him jealous. Even the miserable-looking ones. Their misery looks simple by comparison. At least they know it.

The car moves across the city, in real life and on the screen of his shattered phone, where it occasionally jumps forward then back, whether a glitch in the app or the kaleidoscopic effect of his fractured screen. He was given his phone wrapped in plastic to keep the glass intact, and though he can't remember breaking it, he's somewhat comforted that even through the plastic his touch still activates and commands the screen. Still human, after all.

By the time they drop down through the Hollywood Hills and along Franklin Avenue, where chic art deco apartment buildings conjure Joan Didion and Raymond Chandler, Lucien thinks only of his grandmother. He was also told before leaving the Center that it was her Mem he took. A simple discharge report, which listed that as his reason for admission ("Status: dissociated, signs of overdose") and nothing else. He didn't believe them. He can't imagine what might have driven him to do such an irresponsible thing, and hard as he searches, he comes up with only the emptiness that lingers inside of him. A sadness, still. His mother. But he would never have risked his grandmother's progress for his own selfishness.

He wouldn't have.

Would he?

He looks at his phone again and swipes away the double-digit messages and voicemails still loading. He calls his grandmother's number, but no one answers. He curses the nurses, so short-staffed. He imagines Trina, sitting beside Florence, willing the phone to stop, for now, so it doesn't wake her. He can hardly acknowledge his guilt over having left his grandmother for so long. But alongside that, he feels a pang of hope that she might've had a breakthrough while he was away. That's it. The nurses are not there to answer the phone. And when he comes over later, Florence will greet him at the door.

Though anxious to see her, he wants to go home first. To shower. To put on fresh clothes. He doesn't want to alarm her, after weeks away, showing up looking disheveled. At least not more than usual. When the car slows to stop across the street from the Victorian on Laguna Avenue, the house looks less polished than he remembers, and a bit less inviting. Or maybe he just imagines himself less welcome. He doesn't want to see Liv. How could he? He cannot remember the details, nothing at all once he was using, so he has no idea what he might have done, or how he might have treated her. He hardly even knows how he got to the Center; they mentioned a young woman, who had pulled every string to get him in, but of course he can't remember more. There was too much Mem in Lucien for those memories to belong to him now.

He feels plenty of shame, but no desire to salvage their relationship. Distance confirmed his feelings there. The thought of seeing her, of dealing with her, exhausts his already tired mind. As he approaches the side gate leading to the upstairs apartments, Lucien realizes that he doesn't have his key. He checks the back pocket of his jeans just to be sure.

He takes a deep breath as he turns toward Astral Bodies. At this late afternoon hour, the café is nearly empty, save a few people still working, or pretending to, with ceramic mugs and glass jars of juice lined up beside them. Only Liv looks up. Her cheeks flush before she remembers to smile. She can't hide that she's excited to see him, but Lucien sees the hurt he imagined immediately confirmed. It's unspoken in her reserve.

He approaches her anyway, leans in for a hug, and whispers in her ear while he's close.

"Thank you," he says. "I'm so sorry, thank you."

She's teary when their eyes meet again.

"You don't have to."

Lucien nods to say, *I do*.

"I'm really sorry, too," she says. "About your grandmother."

Lucien's mind plays catch-up, searching for knowledge of something that simply isn't there. It's been wiped from him, along with the rest. He feels light-headed, panicky. "My grandmother, because she's . . ."

"She—passed," Liv says, like there might be a better word but she can't think of it. "I'm so sorry, did they not tell you? You knew. Before. You told me, on the way."

He braces for the blow that doesn't come. Strangely, it doesn't hit like he expects, or at least it doesn't feel fresh. Should he be crying? Is he? Maybe one can only process grief once. And after that it feels far away. He tries to remember if this is why he used her Mem, and when. Would that make it any better, if she was already gone?

"Right, no, of course. I'm all back up-to-date."

The words hardly make sense as they leave his mouth; he's never been a good liar.

Lucien wonders what else has been left out, what other trauma pulled. Liv looks at him curiously, and he wonders what she's noticing. What he might be showing her without knowing. He feels a bit like an experiment. And he recognizes a familiar feeling of wanting to disappear.

"I stopped by her house while you were gone," Liv says, and he remembers the way she sometimes just speaks to fill the silence, a most generous act. "To see what they needed. To tell them you were away, at the very least. But it was dark."

"You didn't have to."

"I hadn't realized—is that why . . ."

She doesn't finish the thought, but Lucien can't, either.

"I honestly don't remember much," he says, because it sounds more normal than to say he's been cleared of it completely.

"Did you just get out?"

"Today. Is my apartment—"

"Yes, of course. It's all the same, as you left it. Tidied up a bit, maybe."

"I'm sorry, I must've missed rent."

"Don't worry about it."

This used to be a joke between them, once he realized she was his landlord. Trading sexual favors and so on. Eviction notices. Though when it came time for the rent he left a check in an envelope at the café when she wasn't looking. Now this formal, tender exchange is tinged with sadness, and he wonders if she's thinking the same.

"Do you think you'll move into your grandmother's, then?"

Lucien is struck by her assumption that he won't stay here. Moreover, at how cleanly she says it. As if the conversation he thinks they're having now was decided long ago.

"I guess, that probably makes sense. So long as it's even mine."

"Well, you're welcome upstairs as long as you need."

I'm sorry, he wants to say again. To wipe the look from her eyes, but he knows he can't. He doesn't entirely know what he's sorry for.

"By the way, your art dealer kept calling. It seemed urgent. If you speak with her—"

"You talked to Natasha?"

"I didn't tell her anything," Liv says. "Just that you were busy. You had gone really deep into your new work. You were taking some time to disconnect, to take it further, I guess."

She smiles briefly, conspiratorial delight bubbling up and then disappearing as quickly.

"You didn't have to," he says. "To lie for me, I mean."

"It was nothing."

"Hey," he says, and Liv leans closer. "Do you think you could let me in upstairs? I seem to have misplaced my key."

"Sure, but then I have to get back."

Lucien wants to ask her if they spoke, before the Center, and just what he did to get himself there. What he might've done to her, outside of himself. He imagines it cannot be as bad as his mind might make it, lacking evidence beyond the fact of his now proven stupidity.

Still it seems kinder not to ask.

It seems kinder because he knows, standing there with her on the threshold of his apartment, how tempting it is to go in close, to smell her hair, to feel her body against his own. It might calm him, make him feel seen again, even if she never really understood him to begin with. Just the performance of being together tempts him. He is relieved none of this seems like an option; that's clear from her crossed arms, the way she avoids his eyes. She has gotten over it, and over him. Maybe his using was enough to turn her off forever. The space of time that now doesn't exist for him was likely filled with worry for her. At best, distraction. Or worse, guilt. He wouldn't wish that on anyone. He understands that she remembers everything he's been made to forget. That forgetting is a luxury, and also a curse.

"How was it?" she says at last.

He isn't sure if she's asking about the Center or the Mem itself, but he can't remember either. Given that she brought him in, he assumes she means the Center. He hadn't even considered that she might feel guilty, or unsure of the decision to take him there.

"It's kind of hard to talk about," he says. "It was very—limited. Does that make sense?"

"Damn it, Lucien," Liv says. She looks newly enraged, betrayed. "I stopped by, to drop off your phone. I *saw* you."

"You did?"

"That's it?" she says. "Break my heart, but at least do it to my face."

"I'm sorry, honestly I don't remember," Lucien starts without any idea how to finish. "I don't remember anything, really. I know that's not what you deserve, that I owe you—"

"The truth? Forget it. I hope you're very happy," she says. And then, softening, "I hope you're better."

Lucien is ashamed of whatever Liv witnessed that he cannot remember. Of what he may have done in this very spot, what Liv still sees in this space even as he faces her, unaware. Had he said something when she saw him at the Center? But what? He would not have been unkind. At least, he believes that. How strange, to have faith in what you cannot remember; to have no choice but to trust some consistency of self.

"Liv, thank you," he tries again. "I know it probably means very little, but really. Thank you. I don't take it lightly that you got me to a place that got me out of the total shit mess I made. Or what I probably put you through. I'm sorry I don't remember it enough to—look, I wish you were the one who couldn't remember and I did instead. I deserve to live with that."

"I'll see you, Lucien."

Liv forces a smile and leaves without another word. Lucien wants to follow her, to make her forgive him, to make her happy again. He remembers her being so positive that it was frustrating. But now it's not his place.

He walks to his bed and flops down face-first, letting the smell of his sheets—a bit musty now—fill his chest. His things spark pieces of him. He picks up the camera. He's missed it. The way it fits in his hand, the way it feels to look through it. The way everything feels safer, and truer, behind the lens. Even what you don't want to see is often valuable once detached, with a little distance. Was that something he had read, or heard?

Painting and sculpture are so often bound by beauty, even if only by projection, but photography doesn't have to be beautiful. People already seek out beauty; they are trained to see it. They turn away from the awkward, the subtle. So much is lost in plain sight. It's oppressive, this idea of beauty all around us. Everyone captures it on their phones, with apps that make anything look perfected. But what is that saying? Maybe beauty is a trap. No more intimate than a postcard, it doesn't engage what's behind the camera, or what happens moments after.

Better still, who decides what's beautiful anyway? Lucien likes capturing that which was ugly any other moment, that which contradicted. To find dignity in the obscene. To show what one might miss when they look away.

The camera still fits his hand just right, but the hard shell looks weathered. He holds it up to his eye, surveying his apartment. Mostly what he wonders is how many boxes it might take to pack it all up again.

He turns around, letting the viewfinder scroll across his emptiness, white walls and wooden floor, a few scattered clothes, until the frame fills with color. Long stretches of thick paint. Movement. The de Kooning. There it sits, just as he left it. He wouldn't mind crying, not now, not after everything. But no tears come. He lowers the camera and fixes his eyes on it, letting the vibrant colors blur in his stare. Still no tears. Then as his focus softens, he sees something he had entirely missed. In what had appeared only a frantic mess of thick strokes, Lucien now sees an order. The coral sweep that had been so pleasantly distracting, its surrounding beige an unexpected foil, now feels pointed and intentional. Not diversion but a directive. And when Lucien crawls forward to get a better look, he notices the signature in the lower right corner for the first time.

E. de K.

All this time he assumed the "de Kooning" his mother admired so deeply was Willem's, but this one, this masterpiece, was by Elaine.

Another brilliant, if overlooked, artist. Willem's wife.

A wash of tenderness ripples through him, and he feels his mother for the first time in a long time. He understands now why she loved it so much. Why she had given it to her mother. He resents his own assumption. He will have the painting properly framed to protect it, he thinks, though he has no idea where to do such a thing. He doesn't even want to know what damage may have already been done transporting it here, or from the dust it must have accumulated since his grandmother stopped taking care of herself, let alone her things. Though all that might add something to its story—pulled from obscurity, almost lost. That always seems to help in the auctions, the diamond-in-the-rough factor. No, he would have trouble ever parting with it. The unexpected combination of colors, the hidden movement. His mother would be proud. He had in fact saved a little piece of her story, undoubtedly something she treasured, which his grandmother could keep no longer.

Lucien still misses her in waves. It feels cruel to hold his grandmother's death so lightly while still crushed under the weight of his mother's. But Florence had become so inaccessible, so cut off, that there's peace in imagining her returned to herself, maybe with his mother. He likes the thought of that. Even if his mother had been an adamant naturalist. Pleased to rejoin the soil that feeds the trees that shade the animals that make the world. He gets to imagine her wherever he wants; that is the only gift left to the living.

He walks over to the sink for a glass of water. When he turns the tap, a small cloud of charred paper puffs into the air, then falls back down wet.

Chapter 30

TODAY

January. A new year. Fireworks scatter the sky, doubled as they reflect across the ocean. All night Sophie's sliver of a window lights up in different colors, pink, yellow, blue, though she cannot even hear the booms.

It is, finally, a date.

And soon after, a beginning.

Sophie leaves the Center with a handful of pills, just enough to get her through the first week on her own. Her first night in her apartment, she takes a pill before bed and wakes up feeling remarkably normal in the morning. Whatever "normal" means now. She half expects to get dressed for rehearsal or drive to her shift at Chateau Marmont. But then she sees the pill bottle, the discharge paper folded beside it. She notices her house plants, brown and wilted, across the room.

Sophie gathers the mail that has piled up and starts to make her way through the endless catalogs and bills and credit card offers. For the first time in available memory, she has absolutely nothing to do. And for the moment, she relishes the total lack of structure. No control. She sits on the floor, resting her back against the metal bed frame. She has never felt this untethered, and it is not as bad as she feared. She has barely enough in her bank account to cover rent, and if any surprises come up, she will have to move. Home to Minneapolis, maybe. There is some relief in facing that potential defeat.

Hidden among the other envelopes with their plastic address windows is a single folded piece of paper. Thick, fancy stationery. Chateau room stationery.

> Sophie,
>   Haven't seen you around. Checking to see that you're good. That we're good. No hard feelings.
>   -RD

Is he serious? Of course Ray Delaney thinks this is about him. And on Chateau fucking stationery? Sophie crumples it and gets up to run a bath.

As the water fills the tub, Sophie holds her hand under the tap. She has no shower gel, but squeezes some shampoo into the water, just enough for it to bubble. She missed the smell of her things—the sweet almond of her shampoo, the fresh scent of detergent on her towels. She looks at herself in the vanity mirror, checking her now untamed eyebrows. She went so long without seeing herself that she almost forgot. Her finger rests on the scar that now interrupts one brow, just past the arch. The thin line—skin, also hers—is smooth, but different. Glossy. Fixed. She looks into her own eyes, for the first time in months.

How does Ray Delaney know where she lives?

She scans her memory for some trace of their last interaction, but all she comes up with are the many that end like before. Him disgusting, her disgusted, but with no conflict for him to check up on. Nothing he ever seemed to notice, anyway. Ray Delaney was too busy pushing Mem on the young starlets of this city to ever apologize for his behavior.

How does he know where she lives?

Her hands tremble. And as simple or as complicated as that, she knows. She is certain.

The body remembers.

She turns off the water and sits on the tile floor. Sophie had been wrung out over and over, a hostage in her own mind, terrorized in her skin, and for what? Because she had rejected him? Because he couldn't reach her, have her, control her?

Who would believe her? She can hardly breathe. She grabs the pill bottle. Anything to calm her down. To reset her. She shakes out a single pill. They said this might happen. Too much too soon.

Everything she worked for, taken by this man. Her life had value, purpose. And he had the audacity to think a note, slipped under her door, would be enough? As if this passing thought carried enough weight to undo its wrong. He didn't even apologize, but why would he, in writing? He has no idea the pain he caused her. The torment she survived.

All those times Sophie swallowed her words around him, covered her disgust with a smile, and for what? She has no job waiting at the Chateau Marmont, she has no lead in *La Sylphide*. How many lives has he casually ruined? He should feel the pain she felt.

Now she has no reason not to—to what?

To make him see.

She clutches the bottle. These pills are clean. Finally they show no trace of the consciousness he put inside her. The poison. Hers will not show him the curse he let into her blood. But there is another kind of punishment. The pills contain her recent memories, rehearsals and waiting tables; she had purposely asked for those reminders of a time when she felt direction; when she felt cohesive and with a singular dream. In those same pills, Ray Delaney would have to catch a glimpse of himself in the other waiters' shared aversion, their utter loathing. In how they banded together, rolling their eyes when he flagged her down. The revulsion when he touched her hand. The way he made Sophie feel unsafe in her own skin. He would feel her disgust, his own.

She looks at the pill still in her palm. A pill to make him understand.

Finally he would suffer at his own hand. Reconcile the man who he is so proudly, unabashedly, with the one she knows. Whose very gaze is like a curse. One moment behind her eyes would be enough to make him see. But she will give him more.

She rotates the tiny orb between her fingers, shining neon green into orange, then yellow and purple, and green again. How beautiful, she thinks, the way everything comes back around.

———

Sophie pulls into the staff parking area behind the Chateau Marmont. She waves to the attendant and smiles, just as she used to. He nods and lifts his hand to his brow, just as he used to. The buzz inside the lobby is unchanged; everything appears to be exactly the same without her. Conversations scatter the chic, worn furniture and overlapping vintage rugs. Ankles are tucked upon velvet settees, tea service trays rest on rattan ottomans. Copper mugs and martini glasses glimmer in the candlelight.

Sophie feels calm, purposeful. She walks past the hostess toward the twinkling courtyard. She is almost invisible, no one questioning her. No one acknowledging her. Everyone must assume she is in for work, though not yet in uniform. For how concerned Sophie had been over what her coworkers thought of her, no one seems to notice that she's been gone.

As soon as she steps outside, she sees Ray Delaney seated just beyond his regular table. She appreciates the blow that must have been to his ego. She only hopes it was intentional. She turns her head and hurries toward the bar, expecting to see Jonathan. Instead another handsome bartender with long hair in a low bun waves a cocktail shaker over his head and winks when he catches her staring.

"Is Jonathan here?" she asks.

"Jonathan?"

Jon did it, then. He left. She smiles without realizing until the new bartender smiles back.

"Get you something?"

"No, no I'm fine."

"Long time," says Eva, putting her tray down on the bar. "We thought you moved. Welcome back!"

"I didn't," says Sophie. "Move, I mean. But I'm not working tonight. I just forgot—or I remembered something I'd forgotten."

"All right, whatever. Good to see you. Take care of yourself!"

Eva sets off toward another table. Like that, their interactions are over. None of it had mattered, what Eva thought or didn't think of her. Not then, not now. How liberating. To feel so lucky simply to exist. To feel. A burst of laughter escapes Ray Delaney's table, and Sophie remembers why she's here.

"Actually," she says to the bartender, "I will take a drink."

She looks around at the familiar courtyard, at the hopeful glamour in its history, its charm. It looks smaller than she remembers.

When the bartender sets down an old-fashioned, Sophie pulls out the Stevia packet folded in her pocket, which she assembled at home. A handful of pills, just to be sure. She pretends to tear the top, then shakes it—iridescent in the candlelight—down along the square ice cube.

"Aw, come on now," he says. "You didn't even taste it first!"

"I like it sweet," she says, crumpling the empty packet. "Sickeningly."

She grabs a skinny black straw and stirs, shrugging for the bartender over her poor taste, then puts down a twenty. Sophie licks the plastic straw, feeling it just as she hoped—*an anxious, familiar wash of her*—then tosses the straw into a standing champagne bucket as she nears Ray Delaney's table. He sits with two men his own age, for once, and an array of papers fanned across the table. He's the only one drinking.

"Sophie! You look ravishing, have you done something different?"

"Same old me!"

The other two men sip their water and hardly look at Sophie. She appreciates that.

"A refresh," she says, holding out the old-fashioned with both hands, cupping it from below like a precious gift. She places it in front of him, ice still swirling from her second stir.

"Not so fast," Ray Delaney says, grabbing her by the wrist. Then he slips his hand into hers. It's sweaty, or is that hers? "I'm drinking Manhattans tonight."

He shakes his empty glass and lets out a chuckle. The other two men smile dismissively.

"Just kidding, princess, thanks for this. Glad we're all good."

He raises her drink—liquid empathy, punishment, just desserts—and takes a sip. He rubs the stubble on his neck as he sets it down, purses his lips, and then raises it again.

"Damn, this new bartender is on fire!"

"Enjoy every drop," she says. "You deserve it."

Sophie taps him on the shoulder, then takes the empty glass and walks back out toward the lobby, passing Ariel. She hands him the glass and wipes her hands on her jeans.

She feels, finally, free.

"Dude, Willow is going to flip," says Ariel. "Where have you *been*? We thought you were, like, dead. What happened at your eyebrow? It looks cool."

Sophie hears a thump, then turns to see Ray Delaney lying flat on the ground. Through the swarm of bodies, the two men bent over him, she notices his feet point then turn out, in an almost elegant display. Then she hears him cry.

Chapter 31

TODAY

Sophie spins and spins. Her hair is not smoothed up in a bun, but loose, cut blunt and curling just above her collarbone. Sometimes the strands cover her eyes entirely as she moves; sometimes pieces stay stuck across her face from sweat and sway. It's a reminder that she's there. She's no longer trying to disappear behind the perfection of the choreography, but rather feels herself a vessel capable of conjuring and conveying emotion through the lines of her body, the working muscle, the scars.

The effort is the beauty. And the catharsis when it comes together, hers.

She lets her torso fall as she twists, her ribs and nipples visible through the sheer nude leotard she and the other dancers wear, hunching her back and then rising to her toes, letting her arms hang loose and then snap erect overhead. When at last she finally stomps herself still and faces the audience under the soaring ceiling at Temple Israel of Hollywood, she recognizes a familiar face, though it takes her a moment to remember why.

There had been talk backstage of a famous director and another actress in the intimate crowd that night, but she has a sense this one is more personal.

In the garden patio during the wine reception afterward, with a store-bought cheese platter or two, the young man approaches her. He holds a camera in one hand and brushes his hair back with the other as he gets close.

"I think we've met before," he says. "You're Liv's friend, right? Sophie?"

"Wow, good memory."

"Full disclosure, I saw your name in the program. But I knew I recognized you."

He holds out his hand and she takes it.

"Lucien."

"Are you working the event?"

He looks at his camera.

"Oh, no, I've been getting into playing with movement. In dance, I mean. I find this style so compelling. Honestly I've been all over town to every studio I can get into and this was the performance everyone seemed to recommend."

"That's very nice to hear," she says. "It's my first show with them. I was a bit nervous."

"You wouldn't know it," he says.

His green eyes pierce her in a way that feels familiar. She hardly spoke to him, those few times with Liv. And yet.

"How's Liv?" she reminds herself. "I haven't seen her in a while."

"Doing well, I hope. Things didn't really work out with us."

"That's too bad."

"It's okay."

Had Sophie even been sure they were really dating? Maybe they just slept together and it never went anywhere? He hardly seems Liv's type. But then, what does Sophie know? She hasn't seen Liv, or any of those friends, since being back. She can't imagine that she will.

"Would you mind if I took some photos of you sometime?" Lucien says. "Super informally, just rehearsing even."

Sophie puts the back of her hand to her face to hide her blushing. She hopes it looks casual, pensive. Now she misses the heavy ballet makeup that nothing shows through.

"I mean, sure, I don't know. You might be disappointed."

"I don't think so."

Lucien turns his camera to show her one of the images in its preview.

"Even this—you look otherworldly."

Sophie cringes, though she loves the image.

She pulls the camera closer, her hand touching his. A current.

"I look at this and see my posture is, uck, problematic. I'm out of practice."

"Disagree," he says, smiling. "You're in the ballet, right? Impressed you can do both."

"Not so much anymore. I was injured and I'm not sure I'll make it back there. Time marches on, you know?"

"Sorry to hear that, what happened?"

"I couldn't tell you," she says, hoping he'll leave it there. "But dancers worry about injuring themselves every day. In practice, at a show, walking home. It can be the end of your career if you land wrong or, worse, break something. And here I—well, I hurt myself quite badly, and yet somehow it's all okay. My feet. My legs. My back. Minus this little thing."

She tilts her head and points to the sliver of a scar passing through her eyebrow. If anything, it adds something—a hiccup to her otherwise symmetrical face. She sees him notice the smaller scars flickering the inside of her forearm, which she quickly wraps her hand around.

"For what it's worth, I like this," says Lucien. "This style I mean."

"Me too," she says. "There's more room for me in it."

"Here, let me get your number or email, or whatever you feel is least invasive. If you're really up for it, that is, no problem if not. I don't want to be that guy."

"No, it's okay, I'll just put my number in."

"Sure! Cool."

A chill rolls into the garden under the lightbulbs strung overhead, and they let the comfortable silence sit between them, almost warm, as she types her number.

There are holes in Sophie still. Spaces she cannot fill, whether removed or there all along. She doesn't know his, not yet. She doesn't know the things or people he has lost, but she senses them there. Maybe he holds similar voids that propel him forward and backward all at once.

Sophie has prepared herself to be alone. To fill herself, without waiting for anyone else to do it for her. And yet with enough holes, she thinks, maybe they could fit together.

"It's so nice to see you again," he says.

Chapter 32

TODAY

Lucien gets a text from Sophie. A friend of hers is putting together a pop-up dance performance in Joshua Tree and though it's short notice, she thought Lucien might want to come along and shoot, given the landscape and his preference for the *otherworldly*. He cringes—had he really used that word? And yet, she remembered it. She adds, *At least then it's not all on me.*

They meet at Trader Joe's in Silver Lake, ostensibly to leave with food supplies, but they're halfway to the desert before they realize they forgot to go inside. By the time they pass the windmills off the highway to Palm Springs, Coachella, and Joshua Tree, signs for date shakes start popping up on billboards and Lucien's stomach churns.

It's almost three p.m.

"Hey, so were you planning to spend the night?" asks Lucien.

"I don't know, I thought we could see. I guess it's kinda treacherous to drive back at night. The other dancers are all staying in some house, I'm sure we could—or you don't have to, I can always find another ride back."

"No, I'm down," Lucien says. "What time is the performance?"

"I think around six or seven."

"Good stuff," he says. "Are you hungry?"

"Starving," says Sophie. "I guess we should've brought some food."

They both laugh.

"Sorry, I'm sure this is my fault," says Sophie. "Being spontaneous isn't exactly my thing, in case you can't tell. But I'm trying it out."

"How's it going so far?"

"Decidedly well."

The landscape turns moonlike as they get closer to Joshua Tree. The ground stretches flat and dusty to the horizon, save the namesake stubby plants reaching up like outstretched arms interspersed among boulder formations so enormous and abrupt they look as though the gods left an unfinished game of Jenga.

Lucien is so hungry he wonders what they taste like. The trees, not the rocks.

Sophie's phone turns up two food establishments in Joshua Tree, both of which appear to be closed for the day, before she loses reception entirely. A tumbleweed rolls across the road. Lucien takes the next exit through the park back toward Palm Springs.

Ten miles in, Sophie squeals.

"Oh wait, turn off here!" she says, pointing to a sign for Pioneer-town. "Have you been to Pappy and Harriet's?"

"Pappy and Harriet's? Do they serve food?"

"Yes."

"I love that place."

"Ha. They have live bands and stuff. It's . . . okay food."

"I assure you I'm not picky," says Lucien. "Ten more miles and I might've looked at *you* differently."

By the time they arrive in Pioneertown, the sun is casting harsh shadows across the small desert town consisting of a single road. The horizon is dotted with the same gnarly Joshua trees and silhouettes of boulders in the distance. Two rows of buildings—facades—line the road. The High Noon Saloon. Pioneertown Bank. The post office. Preserved in dust.

"They shot a bunch of old Westerns here," says Sophie as she opens her car door.

The heat surprises Lucien after being in the car for hours, AC on blast. Everything appears to be covered in a thin layer of desert dust that immediately coats his car. It strikes him as Pompeii with a touch of Disney. The only other people here are posing. One girl wearing a cowboy hat and a long peasant dress shifts and pouts for her boyfriend with her hands on her hips, swaying them back and forth to get the most flattering angle, sticking her butt back, out of the shot. Depressing how a storied old film set now becomes an Instagram destination, he thinks, cringing at this place where they live.

"Oof it's hot," says Sophie, lifting her arms in the air. "I love it!"

She twirls, her loose T-shirt billowing where it comes untucked from her shorts, her hair wild and backlit from the sun. She kicks up dust as she spins. For a moment, Lucien thinks the dust shimmers as it falls.

"I'm guessing you don't want me to dance here. For the photos. It's a little cheesy, huh?"

She hops from one foot to the other, making it look graceful, making it look like a revelation. Watching her move, he almost feels guilty for having contained her in a car for that long. He lifts his camera. He feels like he knows her just from watching her dance, even that one time; like all the photos he's been taking in the past weeks have been searching for something, leading him here.

He can't look away. *Click click. Click.* He circles her, not the predator, because he feels himself capable of being devoured. For the first time in a long time, there is nowhere he'd rather be. No one he'd rather be nowhere with.

Someone calls out from behind one of the facades. The voice is followed by a creaking, back and forth. Lucien and Sophie exchange skeptical looks, but walk over anyway. As Lucien approaches, the High Noon Saloon's sign shading some of the sunlight from his eyes, he has the strangest sense that he's been here before. They push through the swinging door to see a full room built out. There's a mannequin of a woman, scantily clad and well-endowed, holding a tray with a beer mug full of what must be some sort of resin. Solid, bubbling beer.

"It's like Westworld, babe!" says the excited man-child to his girl-friend.

Lucien and Sophie turn to go back outside, into the cooler, fresher air, when something catches Lucien's eye. Above the swinging door is a plaque that reads: "Original Film Set of *An American Cowboy*, 1953." Lucien's body starts humming. Why? For this movie shot here ages ago, and one he doesn't even like that much? He hopes Sophie can't tell as his jaw tightens, his entire body trembles. Is this a panic attack? Heatstroke? Could that happen so quickly?

Then Sophie grabs his hand—hers cool against his—and leads him back through the squeaking door. Just the two of them stand outside now. Smoke from the grill at Pappy and Harriet's rises at the other side of the parking area, but Lucien has forgotten his hunger. He lifts his camera and watches Sophie take off across the abandoned road, twirling blindly but finding her way.

Acknowledgments

First things first. Thank you, reader, for doing just that. There are so many books to read and limited hours in a day. I don't take for granted that you chose mine. Unless you skipped straight to this page in the bookstore, in which case, *hello.*

It would be impossible to acknowledge every piece of writing, music, performance, and visual art that has inspired this story. I am beyond grateful to participate in the larger literary community that has sustained and captivated my heart and mind for so long.

To my agent, Christopher, your thoughtful notes and steadfast excitement nurtured this book at every stage, and none of this would have happened without that. Remember what we started with? I will be forever grateful that you took a chance and stuck around.

To Loan, will there ever be a day when seeing your name in my inbox doesn't make my heart skip a beat? I feel so lucky that you chose this book and am grateful for your brilliant eye. You saw it as it could be, before it was. Thank you. To Chelsea, for this surreal dream of a cover. To the entire Atria family, for everything.

To my New School community and its faculty, especially Helen, Jonathan, Tiphanie. To my wonderful writing cohort, Kara, Michelle, Elsa, Hilary, and Olga. Your support has been a lifeline. And to dear Olga for your later reads; I cherish you. To Taylor, for your generous feedback and encouragement. To Natalia, for our endless hours of conversation, and to many more.

And to my friends and family, who have been there throughout these many years, especially my parents and the best brother, Chris—thank you for a lifetime of love and for your support along the way. To my forever first reader, my mom. It's hard to be a writer without that safe place to send something as soon as you finish. To my dad, for your curiosity and compassion, which I hope to channel even a fraction of into my writing. To Teddy's entire family, I pinch myself to be among you and your warm creative spirit.

To Teddy, my heart. Your love and way of seeing inspire me every day. Thank you for being there at every stage of this book—for being a hand around its flickering flame, shielding it from the wind so that it could grow.

About the Author

Meredith Westgate grew up in Lancaster, Pennsylvania. She is a graduate of Dartmouth College and holds an MFA in fiction from the New School. *The Shimmering State* is her first novel.

CPSIA information can be obtained
at www.ICGtesting.com
Printed in the USA
LVHW030939030622
719933LV00004B/4